Gotham Tragic

Also by Kurt Wenzel

Lit Life

Gotham Tragic

A Novel

Kurt Wenzel

Little, Brown and Company
Boston   New York   London

First Edition

The characters and events in this book are fictitious. Any similarity to real
persons, living or dead, is coincidental and not intended by the author.

Library of Congress Cataloging-in-Publication Data

Wenzel, Kurt.
   Gotham tragic : a novel / Kurt Wenzel. — 1st ed.
      p. cm.
   Sequel to: Lit life.
   ISBN 0-316-09400-5
   1. Manhattan (New York, N.Y.) — Fiction. 2. Internet industry — Fiction. 3. Muslim
converts — Fiction. 4. Restaurateurs — Fiction. 5. Waitresses — Fiction. 6. Authors —
Fiction. 7. Fatwas — Fiction. I. Title.
   PS3573.E573G67 2004
   813'.6 — dc21

                                                                    2003054503

10 9 8 7 6 5 4 3 2 1
Q-MART
Text design by Meryl Sussman Levavi/Digitext
Printed in the United States of America

For my father, Clifford Wenzel.
And to my wife, Ty, and my son, Kyle.
(May he bear only a passing resemblance
to that other Kyle.)

Behind every fortune there is a crime.

—Honoré de Balzac

Gotham Tragic

The Great Kurban

All Muslims are mad, of course. Not mad in the sense of angry, though they are certainly that, but daffy mad, glazed-eyed-crazy-stare mad, ipso facto mad. . . .

Slunk down in the back of the cab, rain rapping its knuckles on the roof, Kyle Clayton heard these lines turning over in his head. This was the opening to the novel he was working on, and since he was prone to fits of anxiety over new work, he often found the words brimming at the surface of his subconscious.

Plus, he was fond of them. They had just the snap, crackle, and pop that he liked. The culture had turned into a bum's rush, he'd decided. You had to catch the reader early, kick 'em in the shins, or else they were gone, off to a new thrill. As the downpour beaded the window, he allowed himself a smile as he repeated the words once more, marveling at their reckless audacity, the sheer stupid nerve of them.

All Muslims are mad, of course.

Ridiculous, those words. Mere literary provocation.

Hurrying from the taxi to the shield of the restaurant's canopy, Kyle was greeted by a large man in a long gray coat, shoulders clad in royal epaulets. As Kyle hopped the sluicing moat that ran along the curb, the doorman lowered his umbrella and mutely clapped his gloved hands.

"Mr. Kurban," he bellowed, half surprised. "The Great Kurban!"

Syeed Salaam was the doorman's name, and he did not refer to Kyle Clayton as the Great Kurban because he thought the young man anything special — only Allah was truly great — but rather because there are few things in this world more glorious to a Muslim than the presence of a willing convert, and however unlikely, Kyle Clayton was now one such proselyte. This conversion was the cause of no little humor among his friends, since of everyone they knew, no one was quite so Western, so quintessentially American, as Kyle Clayton. *Kurban* (chosen primarily for alliterative purposes, they'd learned) translated roughly to mean "sacrifice." Funny, they thought, since the Kurban they knew had never engaged in sacrifice of any sort and, conversely, seemed wholly dedicated to the execution of extreme and reckless pleasure. In fact, Kyle Clayton was publicly notorious for being the very *opposite* of Kurban, and had achieved a modest fame by singularly embodying everything that sacrifice was *not*.

But Syeed Salaam, who was more popularly known as Rick, did not care for contemporary literary history and its various profligates. One of the regulars at the restaurant where he worked had embraced the Religion of Truth, and it was a thing to rejoice.

"Assalamu 'alaykum," Rick intoned, kissing Kyle on both cheeks and squeezing him with his powerful arms.

"Wa'alaykum assalam," Kyle answered without a hitch, thereby exhausting his entire catalog of Arabic. Although there was no way for Rick to know it, the conversion of Kurban was not everything he might have hoped for.

"You pray today, brother?"

"Twice this morning," Kyle remarked, hating himself for the fib.

To the left of the entrance was a shallow doorway used for deliveries. Rick reached in and removed the clean cardboard sheet he used as a prayer mat. In order to pray five times a day, as was his duty to Allah, he had to get in at least two prayers at work. During the lulls after the lunch and dinner rushes, Rick would run to the alley on the other side of street to fulfill this obligation.

Now, though, he held up the mat as an offering to Kurban.

Kyle shook him off, gesturing to the restaurant. "I'll catch up later. Business, you know."

"The business of living is Allah."

"Yes," said Kurban, smiling, "but I understand Allah has a rent-stabilized apartment. I'm not as lucky."

The ridges of Rick's brow contorted. "Mr. Kurban," he scolded, sternly shaking his head.

Please, Kyle thought, Allah was all-powerful but couldn't withstand a bit of ribbing? If Syeed and his Muslim brothers hadn't yet figured out that God didn't always take Himself so seriously, that He in fact had a roaring, knee-slapping sense of humor, what kind of real future could there be for Kyle and his new religion?

After a moment, perhaps remembering that the man was a paying customer, Rick switched his face back to the tepid grin he reserved for ordinary patrons and opened the thick entrance door. Inside boiled a cauldron of activity and appetites.

"Enjoy, brother," said Rick, throwing his arm out across the threshold. Kyle thought he detected a mocking tone to the gesture, as if nothing that lay behind that door should be of interest to the likes of the Great Kurban.

Kyle moved quickly past.

The unprecedented, overwhelming success of City had been a sort of accident, the kind of dumb luck that keeps New York restaurateurs up late at night, giggling to themselves at their extravagant good fortune. Somewhat inexplicably, the confluences of Wall Street, professional athletics, high-stakes publishing, and Hollywood's eastern contingent had all decided that City was the place, *the* restaurant of the century's end. The causes for such an occurrence might be easily cataloged: a high-profile billionaire owner who courted scandal and curiosity; a clubby masculine decor that went against the grain of effete feminine trends of interior restaurant design (therefore a place where the world's big shots could feel like big shots); a convenient Midtown location. But then one could mention twenty other restaurants with nearly the same virtues, nineteen of which, on this particular afternoon, were barely half-full. City, meanwhile, was bursting at the seams.

Kyle, who was tall and wore his dark hair thicker and wavier than was the current style, used his sinewy build to move through the crowded lobby, easily sidling his way up to the host stand. There he waited while a squat, pinstripe-suited man accosted the hostess in a shouting whisper that was apparently his idea of tact.

"Do you know who you've sat me next to in there?" He jabbed his stubby fingers toward the dining room of burnished rosewood and gold-inlay mirrors. "The CEO of DLJ! I don't want to hear his conversation any more than I want him to hear mine. Don't you understand anything about business?"

The hostess stood stoic in a black dress that fit her like a wet suit. This was her defense, her armor against the squat, pinstripe-suited men of this world.

You'd never have me, you ugly little monster. And you know it.

Ever polite, she asked if he would like to see another table.

"What? And have all my guests get up and move? I'd look like an asshole."

The hostess smiled an absolutely winning full-lipped grin that managed to be obsequious and mocking at the same time. As for looking like an asshole, her smile intimated, the matter had been settled long ago.

"What, sir, would you like me to do?" she asked.

"I'm trying to find out why this happened, since I come here at least four times a week and . . . Do you even know *who I am?*"

Kyle stood nearby, twitching nervously. He wondered if he should lend a hand. In the old days this would've been just his sort of gig. Like some debauched urban Robin Hood, he might have come over and stood above the little man for a moment, Kyle being comfortably over six feet, kindly urging him to put his dick away already and return quietly to his table. *Please, sir. Thank you.* Setting this in motion, he would then immediately parlay this good deed into an intimacy with the hostess (having already broken down the expansive barrier between customer and employee), and barring an engagement ring, or an anomalous sexual preference, be — more oftentimes than not — in like Flynn.

Instead, he decided to hold his tongue and admire the hostess from afar. Had marriage mellowed him? Certainly. Who escaped its mollifying effects? But even if he were making smarter choices now, the driving motivation for Kyle Clayton — what got his rocks off, literarily speaking — was the same as it had ever been: to be scorned. To be declared persona non grata. If possible, to be *despised*. In New York, be it in business or in the creative arts, it seemed essential. If you were not hated, then you had not challenged the competitive rhythms of the city. You had not inflamed the jealousies of the successful; you had not highlighted the failures of the left-behind. Here, in Manhattan, this could only mean one thing: you had accomplished nothing.

In being hated, Kyle was almost wholly successful.

He had also earned a grudging respect. If photos of him seemed to project an irritating self-satisfaction; if his work was inconsistent, and public interest in it had grown scattershot; if he had raised public hell, indulged in outlandish and not entirely benign mischief, seemingly in the name of nothing, well, then, he had also written what was arguably the novel of his generation, *Charmed Life*. Published in the late 1980s, the book was a watershed, a pop novel that was somehow more than pop. Even literary veterans setting out to destroy this obvious new threat found themselves under its spell, forced to agitated silence. It was success both high and low, and so Fame had come calling, followed quickly by its bullyboys Envy, Resentment, and Spite. Almost immediately the media had set about tearing up Kyle Clayton in a way he could have never anticipated; he was shocked and wounded as only great romantics can be and so finally came to a place where he'd found scorn both delicious and irresistible. For as long as anyone could remember (ten years as it turned out), Kyle Clayton had gorged himself on a particular type of New York contempt, had made a meal out of it, and was still, as of this late date, unsated.

He was America's last great Literary Fool, and not a little proud of it.

But to the surprise of almost everyone, he had suddenly got married, to a Turkish woman of enticing red hair, and now here came another flood of bile, another shower of laughter and scorn. *Page Six* had had a field day. A Muslim? Kyle *Clayton*? The sneers and taunts were even more cutting, more mean-spirited, than before, though underneath one detected a desperation. Were the dispensers of public ridicule worried that their whipping boy, their great fool, might be tempered by marriage, by faith? Were they getting in their last licks? Yes, Kyle *had* mellowed. He'd decided he owed his wife a semblance of calm — thought he might even do with a little himself — and so had been truly flying under the radar these days. Not that the conflicts would be completely abandoned, of course; they were too much his sustenance for that. It was just that now they would have to be chosen with greater discernment.

This rude, lumpy moneyman, for example, was something he'd have to overlook. Too easy a target. Utterly forgettable.

The hostess, on the other hand, Catwoman and her slinky walk, would be driven from his mind with somewhat greater difficulty.

She escorted him to his table, a banquette of plush cushions the color formerly known as beige, here called camel, the booths of rosewood halved so all the guests could face the dining room. Unfortunately, the table was also empty. Patience Birquet was late.

He checked his watch: 1:45. In fitting with the new Middle Eastern themes in his life, Kyle amused himself by re-imagining the brightly lit room as a splendorous feast in an ancient Pharaonic temple. The tableau was ripe for such comparisons, he thought. The male customers he cast as the royal court, silk-clad soldiers with tanned, regal foreheads, gazes still intense from the morning's battles. The few women in the room seemed to him like concubines, their often mummified complexions stretched like parchment paper, their necks adorned with gold-leaf collars, feet shod with gilt sandals. Then there were the enslaved servants, smaller, slightly hunched with toil, and, as always, darker. A Nigerian in a Nehru jacket strode by, cutting board held aloft, charred carcass gently smoldering on top: whole leg of lamb with cumin and curry. Kyle swooned as it passed.

And the pharaoh himself? That would be Lonny Tumin, audacious billionaire and owner of City. Word was that he'd bought the place as a lark. He could never find a restaurant to precisely satisfy all his appetites, so he built his own. You would often see him here striding through the dining room, the pockmarked arrogance of his face striking you cold. The Egyptians believed acne was the manifestation of the sins of past lives, though with Tumin it was assumed the sins were more recent — his ethical reputation being dubious, to say the least. Indeed, he carried about him the air of organized crime and had even played up this part of his personality, sporting it as a sort of glamour. He liked to intimidate his diners, Kyle had observed; meeting your gaze, he seemed to take your presence as an affront. *Who the hell are you?* demanded his eyes. *And just where do you get the* balls *to eat in my restaurant?* As if dining at City were a contact sport — though, on reflection, it often was.

Suddenly Patience arrived, wispy thin and not quite five feet tall in her padded shoes. The Puissant Pixie, as the agent had been christened in a famous profile, though others in the business had been known to speak her name with less laudatory adjectives.

Patience shuffled in like a blur, arms stuffed with galley proofs, muttering something about Algerian audio.

"No, I'm not kidding. Seventy-five hundred. Right, what the fuck? That's what I said."

Kyle assumed she was talking to him — naturally, since she was looking right at him — and though he'd never before heard of Algerian audio, doubted that such a thing even existed. He also didn't care (that being Algeria's problem) and so in his mind already had the seventy-five hundred deposited, withdrawn, and spent.

Then he noticed the microthin headset that jettisoned her cheek, and his heart dropped. Now he felt foolish as well as mercenary. It was what you saw everywhere now, on all the streets, especially in places like City — fervent, ambitious types muttering to themselves, barking orders into nearly invisible bars of compound graphite. *Madness,* Kyle thought suddenly. Madness because Algerian audio existed and was not his.

Patience plopped into the banquette, her pile of books knocking over an empty stem glass with a harmless *ping*. She removed the headset like a teenager unhooking a retainer.

"You get a load of that hostess?" she asked admiringly. "Boy, I'd like to spread her on a cracker . . . Oh, but that's right, you're married now. Blind to all temptation." The agent was just another of the throngs who saw the Clayton marriage, not to mention his new faith, as distinctly implausible. "So how goes the life of sacrifice, Kurban?"

"Successful, I'm afraid," Kyle answered. "I'm nearly broke."

"Unfortunate. There's not much I can do for you till the new book is finished."

"How about Algerian audio?"

"That's another client," Patience said, then giggled to herself. "Sorry, can't say who." She shook her tiny head in astonishment of herself. "Algeria," she said. "Am I something, or am I something?"

She was something, Kyle agreed, though what that something was it was too early to tell. He had just recently let Patience lure him away from Larry Wabzug, his kindly but ultimately feckless representative of old. It had been a heart-wrenching decision, but in the end Kyle felt that ol' Larry was just a little too out of touch with twenty-first-century publishing. When you got right down to it, Wabzug didn't know an e-book from a butt plug, and thought audio an abomination. Charmingly old school. Since his marriage, though, Kyle found that there were certain things he could no longer afford to be romantic about.

In Larry's place came Ms. Birquet.

To suffer Patience was not easy, especially if you lost sight of the money. She was Napoleonic in demeanor as well as in stature and trembled perceptibly, as if her slight frame could not quite accommodate such a forceful spirit. In a town famous for hard-asses, she was one of the most famous. This was not normally Kyle's style of comradeship, and so he attempted to read charm into her bullying approach. She was playing a riff on the stereotype, he told himself. The gruff agent. Look, there she goes again, he'd tell himself, watching her scream into her cell phone. Ha ha. Very self-referential, very funny. In this way, he'd deconstructed Patience so that he might tolerate her for his growing financial needs.

"Where's our waiter, by the way? I don't have all day." Already she had two fingers out, flicking them like a pointer at anyone who passed, not excluding customers — as if they might recognize her and leap to her aid.

By Kyle's estimation, she'd been in her seat a total of about twelve seconds.

"Oh, yoo-hoo," Patience called out to the space around them. "*Any*body."

Ha, Kyle thought, what a character!

"I'm *WAIT*-ING."

A few diners began to look over, and Kyle caught himself unconsciously sliding down the banquette, trying to conceal himself under
the table's crisp linens.

Blessedly, a waitress arrived.

"Pellegrino," Patience snapped. "Large one. And a Cobb salad
for me."

"Would you like to hear the specials?" the waitress asked.

"No, in fact . . ." Patience glanced at Kyle, who had yet to look
over his menu. "Cobb salad? Yes, make it two," she ordered, before
he could answer.

And then the waitress was gone.

Kyle sat stricken, reeling with an incredulous shock. City, New
York's greatest flesh emporium this side of Scores, and what does he
get? Some fall foliage and a glass of evaporating bubbles. Kurban
indeed.

"So, the Muslim thing," Patience announced, getting down to
business.

The "Muslim thing" was an excerpt from the novel-in-progress.
He'd thought the first twenty pages might work well as a short story
and had asked Patience to try and shop it as such. It was their first real
project together, a kind of test. She had sold the book based on just a
few rough chapters. Now was her chance to shine with the short stuff.

"Tough sell," she warned now.

Kyle tried not to look glum as the waitress poured out the bottled
water.

"Oh?"

"Let me show you something." She grabbed at the pile of galleys
she'd brought in and scooted along the banquette next to Kyle.
"Here's what's going on with some of my younger clients. This is the
direction you should be thinking about."

Kyle leaned over as the agent opened a galley to the middle, where
he saw a mélange of fonts, the text laid out spherically along the page
like a pinwheel. He took the book from her, trying to turn it in his
hands, but it proved floppy and cumbersome. He kept turning but
couldn't seem to keep his place in the text.

"How do you read this?"

"Publisher recommends a lazy Susan," Patience replied. "You spread
it out and spin it. I think there's a tie-in with Pier One. Three hundred

and fifty thousand," she added, meaning the advance. Then she reached for another book. "How about this one. This one's a beaut."

The book she handed him had no title, just a huge asterisk, *, though the author did deign to state his name underneath it. Opening the book, he discovered that this was a novel told entirely in foot-notes, each successive paragraph punctuated by this ubiquitous aster-isk. Patience muttered something about metatexts, about the ironies of the Information Age. About $500,000 advances.

She paused, glancing pensively at her watch.

"Is it me, or should our salads have been here by now?" She rose slightly in her seat, trying to peer between the heads at the table next to them and into the kitchen. "Jesus, how long does it take to make a salad? Throw some lettuce on a plate and bring me the fucking thing already."

Kyle barely heard her. He was looking off to his left at the server's gueridon. There, a baby pheasant was pouring off a captain's carving knife during a tableside vivisection. Perhaps it was the fat pooling under the succulent wedges, or the fragrance of burning hickory still emanating from the bird's lightly browned (and no doubt crunchy) skin, but some brute, atavistic urge began to boil inside him. What are my chances, Kyle wondered, against the captain and his carving knife? How many paces head start toward the front door would the element of surprise afford me?

Patience and Sacrifice, out to lunch.

Kyle forced himself to drag his eyes away from the bird as the agent pulled out a novel that came in a box, each chapter its own little booklet, some of the text readable only with a magnifying glass (included!), until Abu Hussein, the food runner, came over to the table with two Cobb salads.

"Mr. Kurban!" he exclaimed, placing the plates in front of them.

Abu patted Kyle warmly on the shoulder, and the writer half stood to embrace him.

"I'm sorry, Mr. Kurban, I see you before. Too busy to say hello. How are you?"

Abu was another of the restaurant's Muslim crew, or Bengali Mafia, as they were affectionately known, since they dominated the food-runner positions at New York restaurants just as the mob did jobs at the Sanitation Department. Abu had heard of Kyle's conversion through Rick the Doorman and was no less excited. Abu Hussein was a happy, round-faced man with a distinct paunch and a wife and two daughters in Astoria, Queens. Kyle had seen these children countless times, the faces flipped without a moment's notice from Abu's wallet, which he carried with him in the dining room. The writer was quite fond of him despite the fact that the last time he was here, Abu had dropped off the food for him and his guests and then suddenly removed from the table Kyle's glass of Châteauneuf du Pape — a quite expensive glass of superlative vintage, and from which Kyle had taken just a single, sublime sip.

Didn't Mr. Kurban know that alcohol is forbidden in Islam? Abu had wanted to know. A *haraam* of the first order? Kyle had been speechless as he watched the man walk off with his wine.

Now, again, Abu reached into his pocket for his wallet. "My friend, have I ever shown you my daughters?"

"Many times," said the writer. "Very beautiful."

Kyle looked down at Patience, thinking to introduce her, but the agent was already gesturing to her watch, chewing maniacally on her food. Either she wanted Kyle to start eating or was alerting Abu that the desserts she hadn't yet ordered had still not arrived.

"Well, enjoy your lunch," Abu said, getting the hint. "By the way, Mr. Kurban, I did you the favor of removing the pieces of bacon from your salad, along with the dressing — a red-wine vinaigrette. I also take off the chicken, since this is cooked on the same grill as the pork. Pork is veddy bad *haraam*, my friend. Veddy bad."

Kyle looked down at a plate of dry, spindly flora that reminded him of his wife's garden circa mid-February. Once again, he felt Abu pat his shoulder.

"Your Muslim brothers are looking out for you, Mr. Kurban. Enjoy!"

"What's the matter, Miss Erin?" asked Abu back at the coffee station.

Of the entire male staff at City restaurant, only Abu Hussein was not a little bit in love with the waitress, Erin Wyatt. He was married, after all, though the marriage had been arranged and was, secretly, not a very happy one. As for everyone else, this crush was a forgone conclusion. That nearly half of these admirers were men not ordinarily attracted to women did not in any way dispute the fact. On the contrary, if anything, the gay men of the staff seemed to have a leg up in the pursuit of Erin, since only they were allowed to stroke her hair during the preservice meeting, and only they were privy to the whispered confessions about which customers she found "hot" and which ones she didn't.

Erin was tall with auburn hair and a no-bullshit sexiness she managed to project even through the masculine uniform she wore as a City waitress. (Who else could make a Nehru jacket and boxy waiter's pants look so good?) But beauty was cheap in Manhattan, familiar enough to be almost generic, and so it was more her friendliness, her pleasant, easygoing manner that pierced their hearts. She was so nice, in fact, that most of her admirers at City were sure Erin felt the same way about *them,* so rare was her personality in the Metropolis of Mean.

But Abu felt that this pleasantness had been slipping. He was sure something had happened with Miss Erin recently. She had not been herself.

"These freaks on table fifteen," she said now, pouring herself a cup of coffee. "I'm ready to strangle them."

"You don't mean Mr. Kurban?"

Erin looked up at Abu skeptically, then watched him struggle to hold her gaze as she brushed away a piece of hair that had fallen on her brow — Abu, who was by no means in love with Erin Wyatt.

"No, I know that guy," she said, somewhat ruefully. "He's a writer, Kyle —"

"Kurban," Abu asserted with zealous fortitude. "He change his name. He's married to a Muslim woman. He's Kurban now!"

"*Muslim,*" Erin said, trying not to laugh. Obviously this was some sort of a put-on, she thought, not being a devotee of the *New York Post.* But Abu was nodding proudly.

Suddenly an angry call from the chef summoned Abu to the kitchen. This left Erin alone to her coffee and one of life's great questions: Was there anything more painful, was there a worse humiliation in the world, than having to wait on someone you'd slept with?

Not that she carried a torch. She hadn't given a thought to Kyle Clayton for years, except as a kind of benchmark for her own life. When she'd met him she was a single, struggling actress hurtling headlong toward thirty and hating herself a little for it, which was why she'd sought out someone like him in the first place. A kind of suicide mission. They'd hooked up at a party and then spent the next three weeks lying around her apartment having loathsome, drunken sex, stepping over bottles and empty cartons of takeout. It was all fun and games until she found herself getting a little attached, his moderate fame not inhibiting things in the least. Nearly simultaneous to this was Kyle's sudden, and completely thorough, disappearance.

Mission accomplished.

Of course, she'd sworn she'd have the last laugh, but then here she was, still taking orders, her acting career moving horizontally at best. Kyle, meantime, seemed more famous than ever. He had published two more books since then (was she counting?) and had even seemed to have smoothed over some of the rougher edges of his reputation. He was married (poor woman!) and probably rich too. Like everyone else, she hated him.

And where am I now? she wanted to know. What had changed for Erin Wyatt? Well, nothing, she had to admit, except that she'd gone right ahead and turned thirty.

It happened just last month. Naturally she hadn't told anybody, but people detected a change. She had turned *thirty* (or 100 in actress years) and was still a waitress and was fucking miserable about it. Recently, on those sullen uptown subway rides to work — starched white shirts in their sheathed plastic flung over her shoulder — she'd begun to get this feeling in her stomach. A dull, insistent nausea. The truth was that this acting dream she'd been chasing was pretty much over, just about done, and in her guts she knew it.

So Abu's instincts were correct. Not all was right with Miss Erin, and her veneer of good cheer was beginning to crack. Now, to top it off, she had to play servant to Kyle Clayton, who was not only an ex-lover but a walking rebuke to anyone who had come to New York with a creative fantasy and failed.

"Table fifteen wants the check," a waiter barked, cruising by to pick up a coffeepot for a refill. "And she sounds pissed."

"They just got their food," Erin complained, but he shrugged and hurried on.

Gritting her teeth, she printed up the total on the computer screen in front of her and headed out to table fifteen.

"Finally!" Patience exclaimed as she approached.

Erin looked down, deciding exactly how she was going to do it, whether to roll up the check and insert it in the woman's ear, say, or tear it up like confetti and rain it down on her shrunken little head. Perhaps a subtler approach was in order, like simply pointing out to her — calm but stern voice rising to crescendo — that she was still-Fucking-*Chewing*-HER-*FOOD!* But of course she wouldn't. Like all the other times, Erin would bite her tongue and remind herself that she would get her revenge when she became the famous actress she was going to be, that she would laugh about all this later in the *Vanity Fair* interview. It was a delusion that was getting harder and harder to believe.

Erin took Patience's credit card and noticed Kyle looking up at her. She surprised even herself then, for instead of sprinting out of there and avoiding her ex-lover, she decided to confront him head-on, to vent some of her exasperation his way.

"Well, if it isn't Kyle Clayton. They let you in these kinda places?"

Accustomed to antagonistic comments from strangers, Kyle looked up at her with the wincing incredulousness he reserved for such moments.

"Don't even recognize me, do you?" she asked.

Still a little glazed, Kyle shook his head. Nope, apparently it didn't ring a bell. But then, focusing suddenly, looking Erin up and down — and impressed, perhaps, by the way her hair fell around the collar of her Nehru jacket, the finely formed cheekbones — he suddenly sat up and started to look alive.

"Wait, yeah, sure. We met a little while ago . . . at that thing." He was snapping his fingers now. "When was it again?"

"Nice try," she retorted. "No, it was a few years ago actually. We screwed a couple of times."

Patience buried her eyes in the check, trying not to laugh. This was an old joke between them: Kyle had taken great pains to try to dispel his past to his new agent — mere myth and hearsay! he'd claimed — while every time they went out, the truth was reaffirmed.

"Is that right?" he asked the waitress.

"Yes, it is."

He waited, but Erin didn't budge. She stood there, staring down at him in denunciation.

"Well," he said, shifting a bit in his seat. He tugged at his jacket and looked up at the brunette with a wicked grin. "Memory seems to have failed me, but I'll have to assume it was good."

Among Erin's many talents as an actress was the ability to raise her eyebrows to both dramatic and comic effect. She did this now for Patience, turning to her and, with impeccable timing, sending a finely plucked brow arching skyward.

Then she quietly guffawed and was gone.

Tumin's Headache

At the Stonyhill Golf Club, Lonny Tumin sat in a high-backed leather chair looking out on the graying afternoon. The first-hole flag, usually visible from this vantage point, was almost completely shrouded in mist, and now the rain that had been promised began to fall in earnest. He had a headache. As a nondrinker and general health nut, headaches were an anomaly, a real event. But then it had not been the best of mornings.

It was a Wednesday in mid fall, and so the room, made up mostly of leather and polished oak, was empty. He sat alone, faux fireplace burning behind him. Although there was some staff on hand, none of them had appeared to offer him anything. Not lunch, which was long overdue, nor his iced tea, which he drank incessantly throughout the day. It was as if there were an invisible trench all around him that no server dared traverse. A de facto boycott.

What have I done to deserve this? he thought, crooked grin now appearing on his face.

Poor me. Poor Lonny Tumin.

Actually, it wasn't funny. The incident was serious. The only funny thing was how lucky the foursome had been until it happened. The prediction was for rain, but there weren't that many weeks left in the golf season and so they'd decided to risk it. A quick nine holes, then over to Tumin's house and the Sikorsky 913 helicopter, back at their desks by eleven. These were men accustomed to risk, after all, men who had got rich by challenging the common acumen, and so they were not at all surprised as they approached the first tee that the crisp morning breeze had stayed slight and the gray sky had not broken. The only sounds, in fact, were the crow squawks that echoed through the pines and the fiendish singsong of cell phones, which had been ringing insistently throughout the morning.

"Christ, turn 'em off!" Tumin had exclaimed. He had the kind of voice that made even the phrase "I love you" sound ferocious. "We might as well be back in the fuckin' office."

And so everyone but Tumin turned his off.

A few holes later, two golfers had come up behind them, the pair highly skilled and moving much more quickly than Lonny's foursome. By the third tee, the duo was right on their heels, looking on anxiously as Tumin's group dribbled ten-yard tee shots, hooked balls into the woods, and called endless mulligans, or do-overs, for which Tumin was notorious. Don Westly, who was part of Tumin's group and was considered Lonny's right-hand man, suggested they let the pair play through, citing common courtesy; Tumin wouldn't hear of it.

"Clinton," he announced, somewhat ambiguously. Tumin had played a round with the president a year ago and liked to remind everyone of this fact whenever possible. "Clinton I let play through; though let's face it, he'd probably be in my group. Anyhow," he added in his powerful voice, the pair of trailers clearly in earshot, *"these other schmucks can wait."* Well, by the seventh hole, the schmucks had had enough. One of them had called to the clubhouse to complain, and just as Tumin and his gang were approaching the tee, the course ranger had come putting along on his cart through the pines. On the passenger's side was one of the two men who had trailed them. He was nodding and pointing at Tumin.

Tumin didn't recall much of what happened next. When he lost his temper his mind seemed to shut down, almost like a blackout. He

left it up to his advisers to fill him in later, to tell him about the mess
he'd made and how much it was going to cost to clean it up.

In truth, Leonard "Lonny" Tumin was not quite a billionaire; his esti-
mated wealth was somewhere just over $900 million. But like a
slightly undersized linebacker, he preferred to list himself as bigger
than he was, something comparable to the big boys; for if you
weren't a billionaire in these turgid times, you were nothing at all. In
fact, by the year 1998, there were almost 10 million people in America who qualified as millionaires. That Lonny Tumin was in the top
1 percent of this spectrum did not mitigate his disappointment in the
least. Quite the opposite: Tumin was embarrassed and took it as a
personal insult to be, technically speaking, a mere millionaire. One in
10 million!

He'd begun to amass this now piddling fortune in the late 1980s
with a series of high-leverage buyouts, the purchases made with the
help of his old pal Michael Milken. In fact, Tumin had worked for
Milken for three years at Drexel Burnham Lambert, had been a star
there, and had charmed Michael with his irascible personality. By
1987, when he decided to break out to form his own company, called
Triad, Tumin managed to do so with not only Milken's blessing but
also some of his junk bonds. Using a loan from Drexel's copious sur-
plus, he managed to buy himself a doddering cola company. Once in
control there, Tumin began to exhibit what was to become his signa-
ture: buying second-rate companies and going at them with a blow-
torch until they turned a profit. "Turn and burn," he called it. He
fired the management, scared out unions, lopped salaries by 40 percent, eviscerated worker benefits — and had the company *back in
black* in under a year. Shortly after this, Tumin resold the cola company to a French conglomerate, parlaying his minuscule investment
into a cool $60 million profit. He was off and running.

Next, he leveraged himself into a cigarette vending machine corporation, then a coin-operated video games business. Though you
weren't supposed to know it, and though he denied any involvement,
he also owned a building company that was responsible for the
majority of strip malls in the greater Nassau, Putnam, and Westchester counties. (Suffolk had thus far proven more stubborn, with
local zoning laws and such, but he was working on it.)

Actually, there was a whole lot you weren't supposed to know about Lonny Tumin.

Such as where he lived. Few people knew exactly where any of the Tumin family residences were located. Kidnapping of the wealthy was always a worry, after all, not to mention serial suers and anticorporate assassins and Unabombers and every other goddamned thing. So all that was really known about Tumin's northeastern compound was that it had a spectacular view of Long Island Sound, that the two guys in suits wandering the grounds at all hours *were* in fact packing some spectacular hardware, and that the compound itself was a mere twenty-five-minute flight to Manhattan, helipad to helipad.

For all his success, though, Tumin was not satisfied. By 1993, he was number eighty-seven on the Forbes Four Hundred, but after a long, precipitous decline — set off primarily by the tech-market boom — he'd recently fallen off altogether. For Lonny, this was an event akin to finding out he had a brain tumor the size of the Chrysler Building. A disgrace. He barely deserved to go out in public, he thought, and he had kept a conspicuously low profile in the past few years. Then there was the matter of an interview he'd conducted with the *New York Times* just a few months ago, a piece he'd submitted to in which they'd promised him the cover of the *Business* section. Tumin had been excited. This was just the thing he needed. It would get his name back out on the Street, remind everyone he was still here and that they'd better watch out. He'd recently been imagining a great Tumin revival anyhow and had some new ideas on how to get back on top. The timing couldn't have been better.

Then the article appeared, and he discovered its theme was not the reemerging genius of Lonny Tumin. Rather it was a sort of "Where are they now?" piece about the famous financial wizards of the eighties and early nineties, comparing the almost quaint modesty of their wealth to more recent economic prodigies. The piece had made him look small-time, a has-been, and he was enraged to see his name aligned with the term *dinosaur* in a major newspaper. Instead of spearheading a comeback, he was humiliated, and after reading the piece at his desk, Tumin took the titanium golf driver he'd been given as a birthday gift and proceeded to practice his backswing to the tune of $10,000 in damages. Then he got on the phone, wanting to find out where the writer lived, what they could do to this bitch, how much they could get away with. It took Don Westly the better part of an afternoon to calm him down.

The problem with Tumin had been this one little thing, this tiny pimple on the ass called "tech." Though he prided himself on economic prescience — he had, in fact, predicted the crash of '87 within a few weeks, thus saving himself a bundle — Tumin had completely miscalculated the explosion of technology stocks. Why hadn't he ventured any capital in tech? people wondered. Why hadn't he turned and burned one of *those* companies instead of spinning his wheels for the past five years? Truth be told, Lonny Tumin was a college dropout who didn't feel comfortable in the world of the new technologies, who was almost irrationally averse to it. Indeed, when an employee of his had shown Tumin the Internet in 1993, had logged him on and told him to get on this right away, that the future was *here,* Tumin growled and told him that with opinions like these there wasn't much future for *him* in the company. (Incidentally, this same employee had recently entered the Forbes Four Hundred with his own Internet start-up, just as Tumin was exiting.)

But his nickname wasn't L. T. for nothing. Tumin had earned the moniker back when he was at Drexel, where Sunday afternoons were spent with his fellow brokers watching Lawrence Taylor and the New York Giants. L. T., as the great linebacker was known, had a fierceness and tenacity that reminded many at Drexel of Lonny himself. And now L. T. was back. Tumin had a new game plan, and with it everything was going to change. It didn't take a genius to figure out it was all going to level off, that things were wildly overvalued, but Lonny Tumin felt this was going to happen sooner rather than later. Not in ten years, as some economists were saying. Not in five years. But *now;* within months. Change was coming. He could feel it in his bones, and like his initialed namesake, L. T. would use these instincts to blitz his way back to the top.

In the clubhouse, Tumin turned to stare into the gas fireplace, the flames licking at a chemical-resistant log it could never hope to ignite. As the first-hole flag was swallowed by the mist, his cell phone began to ring, shaking him from his reverie.

"Where are you?" Tumin asked anxiously. "Did you get him?"

"Barnett got him," said Don Westly. "We got his number from the club."

"Is he gonna talk to us?"

"He'll talk."

Tumin's shoulders slackened in relief. "Thank God," he said.

"You're damned lucky," Don rejoined. "He was on his way to the police to file a complaint. Barnett got him on his cell. He was almost there, Lonny. He was like two blocks from the police station."

Christ, Tumin thought. That was his worst fear, that a complaint would be filed. Then the whole damned world would know. It could cost him everything.

"How is he? Is he mad? He's pissed, isn't he?"

"I don't know. I was told he sounded a little dazed. He's probably just very shaken up. I would be too. You humiliated him, Lonny."

"How much did you offer?"

"Nothing yet. Barnett just told him how sorry you were, how much we wanted to make it up to him. As instructed."

Tumin murmured something nasty under his breath. The thought of distributing large sums of money to a golf ranger was not a pleasant one.

"What did I do, Donny? I grabbed him a little bit, right? I squeezed his arm or something."

Tumin could hear his partner blow out a parcel of air. "You kidding me? You shook him; you shook him *hard*. You had the guy's collar twisted around your hands, and you were screaming. '*Do you know who I am?*'" Don yelled, imitating his boss, "'*Do you have any idea who the fuck I am?*'"

Tumin held the phone away from his ear. "All right, all right . . ."

"I mean, my God, Lonny."

The room was empty, so quiet you could hear the hiss of the gas fireplace, but Tumin lowered his voice anyway. "By the way, I never called that guy . . . What you said before. I don't know where you got that from. In fact, I resent that, Donny. I do; I resent it."

There was silence now on the other end of the line. Tumin cleared his throat.

"So, anyway."

"You said it, Lonny."

"No."

"You said it. 'Stupid fucking nigger.' You said it a few times, as a matter of fact. 'Stupid fucking — '"

"All right, all right. *Hey.*" Tumin covered the receiver and again looked around suspiciously, as if Don's words might be audible in the silence. "I don't want to hear that anymore, okay? We'll argue about it later."

The leather moaned as Tumin slid down a bit in his chair. He hadn't said it, and he didn't know why Don was insisting that he did. Perhaps it was to prepare him, he thought, since the golf ranger would lie and claim that he did. They would say he did because it was the last word anyone should hear coming out of the mouth of Lonny Tumin. These days, the most expensive word there was.

"They all call each other that anyway," Tumin added.

Don didn't reply.

"How much is this going to cost me?" Tumin asked. "He's gonna get someone, right? He's gonna go see someone."

In the receiver, Don Westly laughed without humor.

"Lonny, right now there's a black golf ranger on the phone with some sixty-grand-a-year moron lawyer, telling him that Lonny Tumin shook him by the collar this morning and called him a stupid fucking nigger. And you know what that lawyer is doing? He's got his hand over the mouthpiece, and he's jumping up and down, pumping his fist in the air, wondering how he's ever going to get that much shit off the bottom of his shoe."

Tumin took a deep breath, resigned now to his defeat. He asked himself what this could cost him, realistically speaking. Couple hundred thousand? It wasn't exactly the end of the world, he thought, but a pretty damned expensive round of golf. To think that he'd just paid for a man's retirement who didn't even *work* for him, who was probably a lazy son of a bitch in his own right, burned Tumin up to no end.

Gotta watch it, he thought. Next thing you know they'll have me paying *taxes.*

The next day, Tumin sat with Don Westly in his office on 44th Street, watching the NASDAQ climb 294 points with relative ease. It was the third day in a row over two hundred.

Tumin sat sipping his iced tea, seeming to have already forgotten about the golf ranger. He smiled, adjusting his glasses and squinting slightly, the better to see the sexy little Italian number on television standing on the paper-strewn trading floor, relaying what was nothing more than the bleeding obvious:

Market is going berserk!

Nothing like it in recent memory!

No end in sight!

"It's finished," Tumin said, just as the NASDAQ's gains broke three hundred. "It's like a blister ready to pop. Triad makes its mint with Monarch, a few months tops, then we cash the fuck out. I mean it's *over*."

And so Don Westly knew it was true.

Garbo Redux

Starting at the front door, moving through the foyer, it becomes immediately noticeable. The refuse. The clutter. The dust and disarray. To the right are the bookshelves, the wood cut in a Mediterranean style that was chic, maybe, in the early sixties, the boards sagging from decades of moldy novels and corroding humidity. Paper bags line the floor under the first tier, blanched and faded, the letters summoning the memory of stores that haven't existed for decades: May's, anyone? Gimbel's? How about White's for 200?

Inside these bags? Christmas gifts never given, books bought and ignored, underwear unopened, shaving kits, foreign newspapers, outdated perfumes, wide-brim hats still in their boxes. Everything and nothing.

At the end of the foyer, the apartment opens to what is, by New York standards, an enviously large living room. It is dark even in the afternoon light, and looking up for some source of illumination, one notices the bowed ceiling, the brown water stains diffused in spidery splotches, a grouping of electrical wires hanging unattended where a light fixture might have been. Panning down, it is clear that the walls are crumbling, the plaster giving way here and there, the old paintings, faux Rouault, hanging askew. The sofa too is a shambles, sinking back into the floor in its embarrassment, perhaps, the foam cushions bursting their fabric and covered over with old sheets and tablecloths. In fact, all the furniture follows this motif, pieces once desirable now missing their teeth, withered with arthritis. A dreary tableau of decaying garniture.

Along the floor, of course, are the newspapers. In this depot of refuse, newspapers are king. The *New York Times,* naturally, in mounds of various size: six inches, two feet, others stacked like truncated pillars in the corners. Are they holding up the drywall? one wonders. Overlaying a breach that might lead to the next apartment? Thousands and thousands of issues of the *Times,* ten, fifteen, *twenty* years old. The obsession. The floor is sloped from water damage, and one moves through the mounds of paper like a skier through moguls.

"Helena?" Erin called out. "Oh, hel-*lo.*"

Mercifully for Erin, lunch at City had broken up early, and she now had two hours to kill in between shifts. Foregoing a nap in one of the second-floor lounges, she'd decided to take the No. 6 train uptown, just over thirty blocks, en route to her eccentric, paranoid, infuriating, arguably unsound, and ever beloved Aunt Helena. There was work to be done.

"Hello?" she said again.

A muffled voice called from the back bedroom. "Coming."

Looking around at the sad diorama, Erin felt again the weight of melancholy. So many memories and so much work ahead of them. It really was hard to believe that after thirty-five years Aunt Helena was finally moving. Her husband had recently succumbed to a vicious and swiftly moving cancer, and now the apartment had become too much for her to bear. Though spry for her age, Helena was still seventy-five years old. She'd borne no children and had no real friends to speak of. Erin, her niece, was the only able-bodied person of any proximity, and so when Helena had decided last month to finally leave 72nd Street for a tidy one-bedroom on University Place, it had fallen on Erin's shoulders to get her out.

"*Hello, dear.*" Slowly, like a figure in a dream play, Helena emerged from the bedroom. No doubt the gloom of her apartment suggested an emaciated and disheveled figure, though Helena was anything but. This was one lithe and wholly alert septuagenarian. The building she lived in had been quite luxurious in its day, and on the roof there was an Olympic-size swimming pool that Helena had taken daily advantage of for the past three decades. She was also a great walker, though this habit was born more out of necessity — Helena was afraid of nearly all forms of mechanized transportation. Despite virtually unlimited resources, she had not taken a taxi in more than twenty years.

She was also a brilliant dresser. Helena had always sported an unusually au courant fashion sense and had recently taken to wearing dark oversized sunglasses and bright Hermès scarves, which only served to heighten her uncanny resemblance to Lee Radziwill.

"Thanks for coming, dear."

As they touched cheeks, Erin warned she had just an hour before returning to work for the dinner shift.

"Well," Helena said, looking at the mess with trepidation, "I guess every little bit counts."

What no one could understand was how her late husband had let this go on so long, for this was not the kind of disaster constructed in a day. This was, in fact, the Rome of apartment disasters, the result of decades of willful evasion and careful disregard. Then again, Dick had never been home much. Over the years he'd spent three weeks out of every month traveling the United States and Europe trying to solicit donations for the Project for a Stronger America, his Manhattan-based agency set up to influence public policy with its mostly conservative agenda on national security. His was the life of a diplomat, lived mostly in hotels, and so during the limited time he was home, the shabbiness could seem quaint.

As for his wife, her position had been made clear years ago: she could not be expected to maintain the house, she said, because she was a genius.

It was a conceit not unfamiliar to the Wyatt family. Their legacy had been one of grandiose dreams, featuring inventors, actors, writers, dancers, and musicians, the ambitions stretching back seventy-five years or more. And though there had been some legitimate highlights along the way — stints on Broadway and gadgets that had prompted real interest from investors — no one had really broken through with a sustained career or accomplishment. It sometimes seemed to Erin that *everyone* connected to the Wyatts had tried something heroic at one time or another. And with so little success to show for their efforts, the family began to suspect there might be some sort of a curse.

James Wyatt, Erin's grandfather, was an inventor, and the legend about him seemed to haunt the family forever. After years of struggling as a drone in a pear cannery, and later as an automobile mechanic, he had developed what the family referred to in shorthand as the "machine." This was a technology that peeled, cored, and canned pears, thus bypassing the costly and monotonous manual labor he had performed as a young man. A prototype was submitted to representatives from a major manufacturer. As it turned out, they were interested. There was cause for optimism. They could all be rich!

After much exchange of ideas, though, the "machine" was ultimately rejected. Unfortunately, James did not have a patent, and by the time he'd been persuaded to secure one, he'd found the manufacturer had suddenly developed a canning machine of its own — one nearly indistinguishable from his invention. James was devastated, and even if the story were an apocryphal legend, Erin certainly did remember her grandfather as a sorrowful, melancholy man.

But the machine debacle had not discouraged anyone. Not the Wyatts. In the generations to follow there was much creative ambition among the clan: the short Broadway runs, a few paintings sold, a novel nearly published. There was even another invention, this by James's son, Kenneth. Kenneth Wyatt had developed a soybean-based gasoline additive that would be immeasurably cheaper and cleaner than anything we were getting from the Middle East. But here too was another conspiracy keeping the Wyatts from their rightful glory. The big gas companies had too much to lose to suddenly switch direction with another fuel source. Despite the practicality of the additive, the companies decided it was not expedient to seek out change. They were already rich, what did they need with soybeans? For twenty-five years Kenneth's plan fell on deaf ears. He died at sixty-two of a long and painful stomach cancer.

But Helena didn't want to hear about it. She was going to break the spell with her book. Or, as it had begun to be known in the family, The Book.

The existence of The Book had been first spoken of in the middle 1960s. But no one had ever actually seen a manuscript. In fact, no one had ever seen Helena so much as type her name, though for two decades now she had been claiming to be closing in on a first draft. Or was it a second draft? The reports were ambiguous and inconsistent. May we read some of it? family members would ask. Oh, no, countered Helena, she never showed unfinished work, and besides, the contents of The Book were so earth-shattering, so unique and original, that no one could be entrusted with them — the temptation to steal, to claim them as your own, being too much for any mortal.

The only thing known about it specifically was its thesis. This Helena readily shared with anyone she met. What The Book posited was a conception of such majesty, of such overwhelming hubris, that it always struck Erin as odd how readily her aunt asserted it, and with so little embarrassment or humility.

The Book, so said Helena, this tome thirty years in the making, was nothing less than proof of the existence of God.

There was a locked space in the apartment, a second bedroom whose entrance lay at one corner of the enormous living room. It was only natural that this room prompted keen speculation and interest. *What the hell was in there?* everyone had wanted to know. After so many years of that locked door staring the family in the face, rumors had begun to abound. Dead bodies? they wondered. A kinky torture chamber? Reams of manuscript pages piled from floor to ceiling? The glorious infinity of the infamous Book?

Producing a key from an old coffee cup, Helena led Erin to the door.

"It's only fair that I show you what you're in for," she said ominously.

Erin's heart beat insistently as her aunt extended the key toward the knob. She wondered if there shouldn't be some pomp and circumstance to the unveiling, a drumroll, perhaps, or some of Bach's more sinister organ music. But then, before Erin could ready herself, the door was suddenly swung open — though it mysteriously stopped with a thud after just a few inches. The cause of this blockage, whatever it might be, had kicked up a billow of dust, some of which now wafted lazily out of the small opening. A dank odor emanated from the room, and this rank redolence only seemed to anticipate the extraordinariness of what lay within.

Helena seemed ready to venture a peek inside, stepping up cautiously to where the door stood ajar; she peered in with a hand on her brow to shield herself from the living room's light. Almost immediately though, she backed away, her mouth turned down in disgust. It was a reaction that only made Erin's anticipation that much more unbearable.

But what Erin found there not only disappointed her sense of imagination — not to mention her aunt's mythic and / or Gothic possibilities — but also enraged her, for what lay behind the door was not skeletons rotting in an old Iron Maiden, or even the cryptic folios of a redoubtable genius, but, simply . . .

"*Crap,*" Helena said ashamedly, a second before her niece could think of the word herself. "Nothing but crap."

What Erin saw was an ocean pile, a contiguous heap some six feet tall, all of it densely packed with *crap* and nothing more. And it wasn't even interesting crap. There were dresses and lamps and old mattresses and mounds of clothes and books and more shopping bags filled with God knows what. It was testimony to the madness of this accumulation that Erin could tell that her aunt had never really stopped putting things in there, that once the floor space had filled she had simply opened the door a few inches or so and tossed other items on top, as far back as she could. Old boots, a knit beret, a Lenox ashtray, a folding chair, a rusting iron — these items lay scattered atop the more organized piles of refuse that stood almost as tall as Erin. Literally, the cubic footage of the room was more than half-filled with crap.

This was no longer a move, Erin decided now; it was a *dig*.

"Sweet Jesus, Helena."

Sensing her niece's irritation, Helena attempted to marshal an excuse. "I'm sorry dear, I know it's insane. But it's the book, you see. It's just so *involving,* I don't have time for much else."

Well, of course, Erin thought, The Book. The excuse for everything. If there was ever a raison d'être, this was it. It occurred to her then with no little irony that if there wasn't a Book, her aunt would've had to invent one.

By four o'clock it was time for her to get back to work. On the corner of 72nd and Lex she passed a Wiz in whose front windows a bank of televisions was on display. A large crowd stood in front, their expressions in a state of what seemed like hypnosis. Taller than most, Erin craned her neck above the throng and saw what they were staring at — a televised stock market update, every set tuned to the same station. There was no sound, but in the lower right corner she could see the astonishing numbers.

She shook her head, amazed as anyone else. Then she shuddered slightly, remembering what this would mean for her evening at work. Right now, she knew, the reservationist at City was being inundated with demands for tables and private rooms, the sommelier holding bottles of wine with credit cards. On other, more private lines, there were the fleets of Town Cars being reserved, dealers of certain substances contacted, the escort services on full alert.

For the great orgy of indulgence, foreplay had begun.

The Idiot

"You know the only thing that's missing?" said Ayla Clayton that night at dinner, her accent Russo-Turkish, garnished with Bergen County, New Jersey. "The only thing that keeps you from being perfect?"

"What now?"

"Lack of spirituality."

Kyle put down his glass of wine and got up to lower the music. It was Liszt, or something like it, a CD he had picked up cheap at Tower Records Annex and that sounded good at dinner.

"*Spiritual,*" he said, returning to the table, "is a charged terminology."

"Oh, is it?"

"There are words, you realize, that no longer have meaning — in the age of superlatives."

"Like what?" asked his wife, stabbing at her plate. She was trying to spear a whole clam from its shell while at the same time wrapping her fork around some linguini *fini*. Lucky for Ayla, her husband —

intensely hedonistic but only modestly prosperous — had decided to become something of a cook.

But such good fortune is exacted at a price, of course, as she prepared herself for one of his wine-infused flights of pomposity.

"*Great,* for example," Kyle began. "What does that word mean now? Or *genius.* They're used up. We've been robbed of them by Hollywood and advertisers. Did you know that in my interviewing days, I never met one young actor who wasn't *spiritual*?"

Ayla rolled her eyes, murmuring, "Cue the overintellectualized deflections."

"How can you *over*intellectualize?" Kyle countered. "That's like saying *too smart.* What else is there to go on? Emotion? *Faith?*"

"You see? You say it like it was a dirty word."

"I'll take rational thought any day."

"But not, oddly enough, rational behavior. Now *there's* something you've clearly never been a fan of." She sipped her wine, smiling to let him know her jab was benign. "Anyway, you know that's not what I'm saying, Kyle. Who gives a damn how the rest of the world abuses language? If you follow your argument to its end, there's no sense in using words at all. Why bother talking? Why bother *writing?* I'm just saying I wish you were more spiritual, in the way that we both know I mean."

It was perhaps an archetypal New York marriage, in that each was a strong-minded individual who desired tyranny over the other. Not despotism, not cruelty — but *control.* A benevolent dictatorship. Ayla was way ahead of her husband on this front, having fought a long campaign against her parents' severe oppression for seventeen years. He didn't stand a chance.

It was also one of the results of being married to Ayla that Kyle often found himself on the losing end of arguments. He found this new wrinkle in his life quite unsettling and was sometimes tempted to remind her of the vows they had taken during their Islamic wedding: that the wife would *obey.* Not Kyle's word — *their* word, the Muslims. Obey! Here, finally, a religious edict the Great Kurban could endorse.

"We disagree on God," Kyle said. "What's the big deal?"

"I thought we wanted to have children."

"So?"

"So, what is Daddy going to tell them when they ask him if there is a God?"

She waited while Kyle swallowed a mouthful of pasta, a stalling tactic, she knew. "We tell them the truth. Daddy believes this, Mommy believes that."

"Great, they'll be schizophrenic."

"They'll learn that truth is subjective, that life is a contradiction. Get a jump on the rest of the little knuckleheads."

"Well, I'd prefer a consensus, if you don't mind. At least in our home. You have to be taught religion when you're very young, or you never get it."

"I see," remarked Kyle, obviously jumping on an angle. "Get 'em young, before they can think it through. Sounds like indoctrination to me."

"Yeah, well, given your lifestyle, mister, a little God might not have been such a bad idea. You're lucky I'd have anything to do with you." Again, the comment was a scold, but she made sure to temper it with a good-natured smirk. She both hated and adored his disgraceful past. "The things you've done."

"Dirty lies," he said.

Once again, she was right. He was damned lucky, and he knew it. She was Mongolian stock, via Istanbul — copper-red hair, eyes cut with a slant — so that even in New York, her beauty stood out as unique. She was thirty-one, had never married before Kyle, and had dated quite a number of men in her single years. Exactly how many, of course, remained elusive, and Kyle had by no means believed the number he was presented with back when they were dating. You take the number they tell you and multiply by two, he told himself; that was the rule. What he didn't know was that his fiancée was well aware of this dating math and had applied the trick known to modern Turkish women, which was to divide the number by at least *three*.

In this, as in everything, Ayla was one step ahead.

Not to mention the matter of talent. Kyle did exactly one thing well in this life (and even this was a matter of public debate), while his wife was extraordinary at any number of things. She'd left home at seventeen and thrust herself into the experimental life of New York with a vengeance. By the time she was twenty, she'd had bit parts in major films, had modeled professionally, and had started a punk band whose name some people still remembered. All this while Kyle was trying not to get thrown out of Bucknell and, in the summer, teaching kids at the Y how to tie-dye their undershirts.

In addition to English, Ayla spoke Turkish, some Russian, and a good bit of Arabic; had owned her own apartment (which they'd since sold for their summerhouse); and was, in fact, spiritual, in the most genuine sense. She believed in Allah and prayed to Him if not five times, then at least once a day. She also managed to help run a Web design firm that was not only cutting edge but also hugely profitable.

But she was difficult; Ayla herself admitted it. The battles she had waged with her family, particularly her father, and her years as a bartender on the Lower East Side, pre–Web design, had rendered a pugnacious streak in her. She was forever war-ready, even when there was no occasion for it. And then Kyle had seemed the most unlikely marriage material anyone could think of. It was no surprise that their first weeks as man and wife were a disaster. They fought. They threw things. Then they fought some more — the worst of it being that there seemed to be no common ground. Ayla had always lived alone; Kyle was notoriously self-indulgent. So compromise became like an exotic island too far and too expensive for them to ever visit.

No, she wouldn't stop smoking a pack and a half a day.

No, he wouldn't stop seeing his "insane" night-crawling friends just because he was married now.

No, she wouldn't stop redecorating the entire apartment to look like a woman's powder room from nineteenth-century St. Petersburg.

Yes, baseball *was* on every fucking night during the spring and summer, and the fall too, if his team made the play-offs.

Kyle called Ayla's sister one afternoon, wanting to know how you were supposed to put up with a first-class bitch like Ayla, just curious, because he obviously couldn't figure it out. Her sister laughed knowingly and reminded him that marriage was difficult in the beginning, that things would get better.

Ayla called Kyle's father just to tell him he'd raised a lout, a selfish monster. His father's reply was yes, he was sorry. He was surprised it had taken her this long.

I'll divorce her, Kyle told himself after the first two months. It's the only way. Poor thing, it'll break her heart. But better now than later.

Ayla, meanwhile, was already miles ahead. She had done all the calculations, factoring in her chances of getting the summerhouse in the settlement — a done deal, she concluded, given his dubious reputation. Then, no less than three men were put on immediate booty-call notice, divorce alert. Any day now, she promised them. And not a one of them a day over twenty-two!

But then, somewhat miraculously, things turned around. By the fourth month, the couple began to settle in, just as her sister had predicted. Love prevailed, or so they'd told each other. Only in their minds would they concede that attrition had played a role. Yes, there was love, but they'd also worn each other down. Compromise, though hard earned, had been the key: Ayla, tired of the relentless nagging, bought fewer packs of cigarettes and eased up on the feminine decor; Kyle, fatigued from conflict, went out a little less and stopped harping about the smoking, though baseball remained non-negotiable.

Almost by accident, they'd become a team, and now they were more attracted to each other than ever. Frankly, the sex had never left. It was what had drawn them together at the start and was the one place they'd still been able to go to during the bad times.

In the apartment, Kyle drained the last of his wine, then leaned over and told Ayla the things he was going to do to her after dinner.

"That's rather sordid," Ayla said. She looked up at him coyly, twirling her fork around some pasta she had no intention of eating. It was as if they were at a restaurant, on a date.

He leaned in again and told her more things, this time with that cold, tyrannical voice that made him seem like a stranger and absolutely destroyed her.

"That, I believe, is illegal," she said, somewhat hoarsely.

"Everywhere but New York," he countered. He ran a hand inside her skirt, stirring certain fragrances that did not correspond with their meal. "The Big Apple, I think they call it."

On their plates the plump clams receded, the linguini turned brittle. One of these nights they would make it through a whole dinner.

And through it all, the idiot harboring his stupid secret.

Having been married now for nearly two years, with a steady increase in happiness and ease, not to mention intimacy, support, and erotic excitement, it was now high time, Kyle told himself, that he find a mistress.

To track how this particular disaster would unfold, you had to go back to Kyle's childhood. His father had been an absent presence, his attentions concentrated on business. His mother, on the other hand, had been unconditionally adoring, reluctant to criticize even his most outrageous behavior — to which, even at an early age, her son seemed habitually devoted. And it was in this black hole of guidance that Kyle had turned to a series of surrogate fathers to counsel him, to give him a sense of direction and moral boundaries.

The fathers of Kyle Clayton, however, were a unique bunch. For whatever reason, at that impressionable age, Kyle had fallen for contemporary literature, was under its spell, and in the absence of faith, made it his religion. Thus his fathers could be counted as follows: Mailer, Roth, Bellow, Updike, and Cheever. A kind of holy five, at least to his mind. The novelists he held in admiration now, at the age of thirty-seven, might be very different from this list, but no matter his sudden ardor, these new writers could never affect Kyle in the same way as the holy five. These were the ones who had got to him first, had shaken him by his shirt collar and coaxed, charmed, and manipulated their way into his heart and mind at the age when such things sink in deeply, and forever. For general guidance, it was perhaps not an altogether terrible list. It boded well for creativity, for example, for imaginative thought. Some might even say for a moral vision.

But for advice on how to conduct oneself as a husband, for lessons in the art of marriage, one could probably get better exhortation from five men at your local penitentiary. If, for example, adultery had ever been decreed illegal in America, you might have wandered into a post office in the late 1970s and seen on the Most Wanted board the faces of Mailer, Roth, Bellow, Updike, and Cheever — in art, and / or in practice, the most notorious of American adulterers.

And, of course, selfishness played a role. Look around, he told himself. Wasn't everybody overreaching themselves a little? Wasn't everyone grabbing for a bit more than they deserved? He was nothing if not a man of his times, ready to gamble the portfolio, put the principle on the line. If monogamy was out, he wanted *in*.

So now Kyle was looking for a mistress, or mistress*es* if luck would have it. Hell yes, he thought, considering the plural, bring 'em on! Why not? It seemed his literary, if not inherent, right. The fathers had said so.

Thus far, the hunt had been disappointing. For one, his lifestyle had changed. He was no longer the man out eight nights a week, indefatigably trolling the bars for the various bottom-feeders and Vamparellas of the New York night. He was immersed in a calm, mostly quiet life of work and marriage. When he did go out, Ayla invariably came with him. Opportunity was problematic.

Second, the reception that Kyle Clayton received in his home base of Manhattan had hit an all-time low a few years back because of some unfortunate behavior, and had recovered only incrementally. People had been suspicious of him anyway (some might even say jealous, his success had come so fast), and then he'd clocked another writer with a champagne glass at a party. The episode had become infamous, part of the city's lore. That the other writer was both popular and gay, and that the face with which the glass had collided had been rather attractive, demonized Kyle Clayton all the more.

It was a reputation that had carried over into the more sensual arenas as well. Certain bars and restaurants actually refused to serve him for a time, his name forever associated with violence and flying glassware. And then he'd discovered that a small number of the opposite sex had taken up a sort of de facto boycott against him. It was not a coalition exactly, not organized in any definitive way, but then he had seen more revulsion in the eyes of women at the mention of his name than he cared to remember. They believed the newspaper version of Kyle Clayton, that he was a vicious and deranged young man, and this had certainly cost him any number of dates and ancillary lovers.

In the end, of course, he found plenty of bars to serve him, and most women had never heard of Kyle Clayton, or the unfortunate incident. Ayla, for example, had been living in Istanbul during the scandal and so refused to be scared away years later when friends heard she was dating Mephistopheles himself. But to this day, a residue remained. The city's antagonism toward Kyle was latent now, but persistent. This too dampened his possibilities for a mistress, diluted the pool, so to speak.

And strangely enough, he had discovered that the biggest stumbling block on the path to adultery was marriage itself. Who knew that a wedding band was not, as previously reported, a sort of sexual talisman, able to woo and hypnotize even the most reluctant of maidens to your nuptial bedroom? In fact, it turned out to be the very opposite! Young women seemed to view his little slip of gold with a hallowed respect, showing a regard toward the institution it represented bordering on the solemn and, despite all rumors to the contrary, appearing to take to heart the feelings and concerns of the wife in question.

All of which Kyle Clayton found deeply depressing.

So the odds seemed mounted against him and the mistresses of his imagination, but then Kyle had recently discovered what he regarded as a chink in the armor of this inhuman (and highly unliterary) monogamy. Erin Wyatt was her name — for though Kyle couldn't recall a thing about her this afternoon, he certainly remembered her now, and all her various attributes. This was another casualty from the years of drinking, he knew. This self-abuse had not dulled his memory so much as decelerated it, so that someone like Erin could be unrecognizable at noon and by four o'clock be remembered as a dear friend or old lover in acute detail. Her nakedness, for example, usually the most elusive of memories, had finally come strutting into view for him in all its brilliant minutiae: a wide-angle shot, lovely divot on her lower spine sharpening into focus as she tottered in high-heeled shoes along refinished flooring. *Clickity-clock, clickity-clock.*

"Er-in Wy-att," he said to himself. Bet your ass.

Certainly the best candidate to come along in quite some time, he'd decided. And he had no doubt as to how easy this whole thing would come off. Hadn't she sought *him* out, after all? Only a fool could fail to see what she was doing today, that faux-hostile repartee, so clearly a form of flirting. It was sort of shameless, actually. No doubt she'd requested his table when she'd noticed him, probably switched stations so that she might somehow make contact again.

Kyle Clayton, thought Kyle Clayton, was not a lover easily forgotten.

The Hordes

"Tonight's a-fish e-special," said Marco, the Portuguese captain, "is *a-gdddrrreeeled allibut.*"

"Gdddreeeeled allibut," imitated one of the Bengali Mafia. As if he too didn't carve up the English language like a Christmas goose. There was a smattering of laughter.

The staff was scattered throughout the dining room, a rainbow of colors and creeds, pens and dupe pads in hand. It was 5:15, time for the food specials and service reminders, for the cutups and dirty jokes.

"Excuse me," Marco said scoldingly, trying to locate the offender. He was older and somewhat doddering and did not, unfortunately, command much respect. "Can I get through deece? We're very beecey tonight." When silence fell again, the captain continued. "We also aff . . ."

Someone tittered, and so Marco looked up again, waiting to see who would crack. The Bengalis were silenced, and so he kept on.

"Poach-ed ocean-a strapped bath."

This time the laughter came in a great wave, and even Erin couldn't help herself.

Well, thank heavens for the humor, she thought. Without that we'd all just have to kill ourselves. And it *was* funny here at City. The amalgam of races and religions, of languages and sexual inclinations, made for a stew of nightly hilarity. She never forgot the night Bill, for example, the very straight waiter who ran the football pool, overheard that one of the new line cooks was gay.

"What?" Bill said, seemingly stunned. He put down the glass he was polishing with distaste. "Gay?"

Erin and a busser standing nearby both nodded, surprised he didn't know, or that he even cared.

"Well," Bill said, picking up the glass again, "that's the last time I let him suck *my* dick."

Stephen, the most laid-back and, therefore, most popular of the captains, sat with Erin along the banquette, massaging her neck as the meeting continued. This action couldn't have been more innocent, given Stephen's own sexual preference, but he nevertheless drew barbed looks from Abu, who was just now realizing how much he disliked the captain after all.

Then Raoul stood. Raoul was the temperamental sommelier and, coming from somewhere deep in France's Languedoc region, was the owner of a French accent richer than a double-crème Brie. How much you understood depended on how far removed you were from the origins of the English language. The waiters, mostly American, got about half; the busboys, decidedly Hispanic, took in about 20 percent; while the Bengali Mafia retained practically nothing, simply nodding at the jumble of sounds and continuing on with their business.

The phrase "fucking America" though, was always discernible.

There was an addition to the Wines by the Glass list, Raoul announced. To him this was an event commensurate with the introduction of a new European currency, and he expected everyone else to register the same excitement. He poured two-ounce tastes into the rows of glassware set before him on the gueridon. Then he passed these out for discussion, pouring a final splash into the silver tastevin he wore around his neck. The staff swirled and smelled, going through the motions of connoisseurship, though most of them could have cared less, being more interested in whether the tiny buzz this little gulp gave them would get them through their first rude table.

"Ooo-sane," Raoul said, addressing Hussein, one of the Mafia's senior members, "what do you dink of de swine, uhn?"

Hussein, who Raoul had suspected was Marco's imitator, looked up helplessly. He'd passed on the wine; all the Muslims on staff were excused from tasting for religious purposes. Even worse, he had not understood a single syllable of the sommelier's in the eighteen months he'd worked here. In fact, he never would have known he'd even been addressed except that everyone was looking directly at him.

"Come on, Raoul," Erin interjected.

He was being a prick, she knew, because tonight was so busy and his steward had called in sick. This meant Raoul himself would have to run up and down the stairs to the cellar for every bottle of wine that was ordered, an activity that he'd decided was beneath him.

"*Excusez-moi?*" asked the sommelier, lowering his Calvin Klein bifocals to address Erin. "What do we do if the customer axe about de swine, uhn?"

Erin offered a bright, ironic smile. "He'll say he doesn't know anything about it, since he's here to deliver the food, and then he'll call over our wonderful and ever charming sommelier."

There were some suppressed giggles. Stephen began to massage Erin's shoulders again, an action meant to dissuade her from getting too far into it with Raoul, who had a reputation for vindictiveness.

"And if the sommelier is bizey? Uhn? Bringing de swine up and down z stairs?"

"He'll get a waiter, or a captain — for God's sake, isn't that why we're tasting in the first place? You want food runners and busboys making major wine recommendations?"

This logic seemed to momentarily flabbergast the prickly sommelier. His back arched as he rolled his shoulders. Then, before Raoul could gather steam for a new retort, the diplomatic Stephen stood up to announce, my God, it really was almost 5:30 already, and they should all probably get the dining room lit for the first seating. The sommelier nodded a relent, and then everyone stood, gathering the dirty glassware as the chairs were straightened and the candles lit.

The music was turned on then, the lights brought down low. Through the paned glass of the foyer window the staff could see the first guests arriving, the backlog starting at the coat-check room. Necklaces and watches and earrings glimmered as the patrons removed their long coats and then, with a quick tug, righted their suit jackets or dresses made by the best designers. Except for a few murmurs, the staff had grown quiet. They felt it now, that anxious tremor that was the prelude to yet another busy night at City. The bird's-eye view of something remarkable, something unprecedented.

It was October of the year 1998. The country was richer than it had ever been, and the marshals of wealth were here to commemorate it, to give tangible evidence of the most hysterical accumulation the world had ever seen.

Upstairs, the lounges were full with private parties. Erin had drawn a bad card, being pulled from the dining room at the last minute to inherit a group of eight young stockbrokers, all jazzed up from a big money day. The young ones were always the worst, she'd discovered. They were new to the city and had no grace, no manners, not to mention *way* too much money. It hadn't seemed as bad years ago, when she'd first begun her illustrious waiting career. Back then they would begin modestly, forty, maybe fifty thousand dollars a year to start, an apartment in Hoboken or Jersey City, lessons from the veterans on how to dress, what to order in a restaurant. A beginner's humility. But now, with all the market lunacy, these jokers were pulling in five hundred grand six months out of the frat house and viewed Manhattan as a rite.

The room they had chosen was a cigar lounge turned into a private dining space — distressed leather club chairs and Indian rugs with a table set elaborately for eight. Erin held the door and tried to look happy as the group piled in like a band of Goths in a sacked village, flopping into the plush chairs and twirling their blazers around over their heads, whooping like cowboys. They'd hit the downstairs bar for at least an hour before they'd come up, and Erin was pretty sure there was some blow involved.

Over the shouting, she tried to recite the specials, needing two repeats until everyone shut up. The oldest of the bunch opened the wine list and ordered the Silvermark Cabernet, the broker's pick of the season and, not coincidentally, the very one Raoul had marked up to five times the wholesale price. Erin called downstairs on the phone, asking the sommelier to bring up at least a case. The wine was $250 a bottle, but one look at this group told her she wouldn't be able to pour it fast enough.

When she got back to the room, they were drumming on the table, glassware and cutlery ringing like glockenspiel. This, in Neolithic speak, meant they wanted to order.

"All right, *boys*. Take it easy." The motherly tone, Erin thought. It was not exactly fine-dining etiquette, but she knew she needed to take control right away, let them know she wasn't going to be their buddy, nor their date for the night, since a few of them were already beginning to leer. It was amazing how prone young brokers were to thinking women were impressed with them. Where, she wondered, had they heard that a band of conforming, unsophisticated heathens — who didn't even know how to dress despite their exalted incomes — dampened the panties of females everywhere? Had she missed a meeting?

Big surprise, they all wanted the same thing: Caesar salad and a Delmonico steak. Then someone added a lobster — and now they *all* wanted lobster.

"You got two-pounders?" one of them asked.

"I have three-and-a-half-pounders," Erin suggested. These were 125 bucks a pop, but what did money matter to high rollers like these? Plus, the tip was included, 20 percent on whatever they consumed; waiters at City were not in the habit of discouraging overindulgence.

For no discernible reason she could see, one of them suddenly let out a rebel yell, and then they all started drumming on the table again. Erin took this to mean they each wanted a Delmonico steak, a three-and-half-pound lobster, and a Caesar salad. Done.

She left the room.

The most exclusive of the second floor's private rooms was at the end of a long hall, past the display case of antique poker chips and corkscrews, past the men's room with the Charles Hoff boxing photographs, past the large cigar humidor with its individual lockers, their owners' names engraved on the front (and the cache of Cubans hidden in Dominican boxes on the bottom), away from every*one* and every*thing* else. A place of illicit business and ultimate privacy. The room itself was rectangular with a long conference table running nearly the length of the space, and along the back wall was an enormous mural of World War II fighter pilots on their way to battle in the Pacific. This had been dubbed the Airplane Room, and this was where Lonny Tumin sat alone nursing an iced tea, waiting on his team.

The day, which could not have started out much worse, had ended on a highly surreal note, one that had left the usually invulnerable Tumin in a high state of unease. After his conversation with Don Westly, he had called his pilot, telling him to put away the Sikorsky; he wasn't going to the office today. No way could he concentrate with this morning's golfing incident on his mind. Instead, as he arrived home, he had his driver take him directly to the airplane hangar that was the Tumin garage and, forgoing the fleet of sports cars and high-performance German automobiles, had the Saturn pulled around front. This was the car that his wife used occasionally for errands and for attending the local fund-raisers where she didn't want to seem pretentious. Her husband had found a use for it too, though for him it was, of course, strictly business.

There was a new lot Tumin was working on, twenty acres in northern Westchester County, cleared out, paved over, twelve units built on top. A strip mall, essentially, though he never let anyone on his team use that word — *rentals* being the preferred terminology. Lonny didn't like being associated with these efforts — it was strictly déclassé for someone of his wealth and stature. But the money was irresistible — quick and easy, and mostly cash — and so he had formed a covert building company, one bearing neither the Tumin nor the Triad name. Still, he never could resist the urge to show up at least once during the construction of a new site. Found it very helpful indeed. Just pulled up anonymously in the Saturn, a Curious George, a local schnook with nothing better to do. Then watch the foreman shit his pants as Lonny Tumin introduced himself.

No matter how much of the work was complete, he would feign shock at the progress, take a nip out of the foreman's rump. "Wow, we're a bit behind here, aren't we?" he'd announce, marching imperiously through the site. Amazing how the workers shifted into gear, Tumin observed, how they suddenly picked up the pace. It was a universal law, he believed, that no man worked up to his potential unless pushed.

Upon his departure, Tumin would engage the foreman's aptitude for paradox: you're never to mention me being here, Lonny would say, never to mention my name, but I'll be back next week. Get it? *I was never here, but I'll be back.* Though he never did come. You only had to show up once, he knew. The projects always finished in record time.

Back at the compound, Tumin had let everyone know there would be no bodyguards today — another unique occasion — and pulled out of the long driveway in the Saturn. Immediately he enjoyed the feel of the steering wheel, the kick of the gas pedal. He so rarely drove, after all, and getting behind the wheel was a great way to clear his head from the terrible morning. On the L.I.E. he turned up the radio, went a little too fast, zipped in and out of lanes. He rolled down the window to let the cool breeze blow through his hair, let fly a few *fuck you*s at discordant drivers. He was a young man again!

The charm of this quickly ended with standstill traffic near Kennedy Airport, a moronic, mind-numbing logjam. Construction, miles of it, and during rush hour! After five minutes of stasis, Tumin was nearly homicidal with rage. L. T. never waited for anything in his life, and with the Sikorsky, the closest he ever got to traffic these days was an aerial view.

On an enraged whim, he suddenly pulled the car into the restricted lane, plowing over two orange cones as if they weren't there. Immediately a hard hat approached the Saturn, a graying man in his fifties, steaming cup of coffee in his hand. Tumin knew his story in an instant: thirty years on the crew, recently made supervisor, he bought the doughnuts and occasionally deigned to wave a flag at slowed traffic. At $45 an hour, it was his job to tell Tumin to scram, his big task of the month. Lonny's window was already down by the time the man reached the car.

"Twenty-five fucking years I use this expressway, twenty-five fucking years of construction, and it's still the worst stretch of road in the country. The absolute worst. Why? Tell me right now."

The grizzled road man suddenly seemed tentative. He looked back to see if any of his crew was near, wondering if the driver might be dangerous.

And didn't he look just a little familiar?

"No, you know what, *I'll* tell you why," Lonny said. "Unions. You're a buncha lazy, freeloading motherfuckers, that's why. You make me sick." Tumin reached out and grabbed the man's coffee out of his hand, taking a sip. He grimaced, then handed it back to him. "What am I saying? You can't even make a decent cup of coffee for Chrisakes, I want you to fix a road? Fuckin' morons."

He rolled up the window and moved back into traffic.

Crosstown was worse. They should publicly execute whoever put up all those lights along Park Avenue South and be done with it, Tumin thought, and the Henry Hudson wasn't exactly moving at the speed of sound either. Here Lonny familiarized a whole new legion of drivers with the measurements of his middle finger, though this did little to help his cause. By the time he reached Tagert Falls, the site was already closed. Eight minutes to six, and everybody gone home!

That, you see, Tumin told himself, was why you had to check in.

He parked the car next to a dormant bulldozer and got out for a look around. Actually it wasn't bad, he thought. Pretty far along. Five hundred trees cleared out, the foundations already poured. On a nearby cement mixer there was some illiterate graffiti protesting the site. It was the first strip mall in the area's history. Precious deer country, they'd said, the last acres, and the whole town of Tagert was having a shit fit. Well, boo hoo, Tumin thought. Had to lose your cherry sometime. They'd threatened a boycott, but he was unfazed. *Go ahead,* he told them, *do what you gotta do.* He'd been through all of it before. Sure, a few stayed away at first. There might even be some pickets out front, an article in the local paper. They really got worked up in the beginning.

But when all was said and done, they'd give in. Six months and the place would be packed — the tanning salon, the Chinese takeout, the Wawa — the locals wondering how they'd lived without it for so long. Even the hard cores eventually became regular customers, Tumin had observed. Sometimes people didn't know what they needed until you gave it to them.

Dusk now, the crows exhorting the sun for another half-hour, *Pretty please?* The woods around the perimeter were thick, and Tumin thought he heard a rustling there. What, he wondered, was this? A pack of stray dogs? Gang of doped-up teens? No bodyguards today, Tumin reminded himself. It seemed wise to head back to the car.

Again he heard the rustling, and his stride quickened as he approached the Saturn. Inside, he locked the doors. Starting the engine, he looked around . . . There seemed to be nothing. He put the car in gear, and then, as he neared the end of the dirt path that led to the throughway, he stopped, startled by what he saw.

There, standing twenty feet to his left, was a ten-point buck.

The deer stood arched and powerful. Tumin decided that he'd never seen anything quite so magnificent in his life. And yet there was something disturbing in the scene. The streetlamps were on now, bathing the buck in a bluish, acetylene light. Tumin watched the animal move its head back and forth searchingly, as if looking for someplace to go. Just beyond them, the occasional car whooshed past. A common enough sound, but for some reason Tumin found this unsettling as well.

He lowered the power window, the electrical drone drawing the deer's attention.

"Go back," he called out. He put out his arm and waved it toward the darkness of the remaining woodlands. "Go back, you big dummy."

The buck remained immobile, locking its eyes on Tumin. The mogul had never seen a deer this close that wasn't hanging on a wall, and its expression wasn't nearly as vacant as he had supposed. The eyes were gentle, but also sorrowful. Perhaps, he wondered, even a touch accusatory?

"What?" he found himself asking out loud. Then he chided himself: I'm really doing this? he thought. Am I talking to a fucking *deer?* But the buck didn't budge. It seemed to neigh at Tumin a bit, then bowed its head to the macadam.

He had no idea why exactly, but Tumin was overcome with an emotion that couldn't have been more foreign to him — a kind of shame.

"Big dummy," he said again, though without conviction. The buck raised its head to look at him once more, still bathed in the garish electric light. Not being able to stand another second, Tumin hit the gas and headed back to New York.

"Where the hell's my wine?" Erin yelled into the second-floor phone. Fifteen minutes later, she still hadn't gotten the Silvermark. In her room, the hordes were clamoring.

"Eh, I am very biz-ey, you know," came Raoul's reply. "Lot of kesht-ons in the dining room about de swine."

Bullshit, Erin thought. He was down in the cellar flipping through the *Village Voice* personals even as they spoke, sipping from a bottle of rare Burgundy that he would later tell the owner was corked and had to be put out of its misery.

"Don't fuck with me, Raoul. I got eight guys in my room ready to pounce if I don't produce some vastly overpriced red wine in about three minutes."

"Eh, maybe you like diz pounce, uhn? Deez ate guyz? I doan know."

Erin held the receiver at her thigh. He was punishing her for stepping on his toes at the staff meeting, of course. Any other time she would to tell him to go fuck himself eight ways to Sunday, but she needed that damned wine.

"That's too bad," Erin said, "because while I've been waiting they've already drunk three bottles of the house red, which are like, what, thirty bucks each? That's already three Silvermark that won't make the check. How unfortunate."

"Uhn? *Three bottles?*" Raoul suddenly perked up. He worked partly on commission, and basically she had just told him he'd missed out on more than a thousand dollars in sales. She could tell the vastness of the situation had struck him when he shouted, "Fucking America!" Then the line went dead, and Erin knew her wine would be dispatched shortly.

She was approached then by Stephen, the upstairs captain, with an urgent, though apologetic, look on his face.

"What?" Erin asked, but then her heart immediately dropped. She knew what was up.

It was Lonny Tumin.

"No," she said.

"Party of four."

"Shit. No, c'mon, Steve. I'm on a double."

The captain shrugged. It was no use. When he came to the restaurant, Tumin wanted Erin as his waitress. He didn't even want to look at anyone else. If she was downstairs or on another lounge party, she was pulled. If she wasn't working, they'd try to call her in. And it was not the kind of flattery she could take any great pleasure in. Tips were pooled anyway, so it didn't pay to be Lonny's pet waitress. More skill meant more work, more pressure. Why couldn't she just be mediocre like everyone else? she'd wondered. Waiting on Tumin could be damned nerve-racking.

She had tact, that's what he liked about her. If he and Steve Wynn were going to scream at each other for three hours, as they had recently, Tumin could be sure a transcript wasn't going to end up in the *Daily News* the next day. If he came in with one of his mistresses, Erin played girlie-girl with her, pretending she hadn't met the fifty others. In this business, she knew, you left your scruples at the door.

Plus, let's face it, Tumin liked the way she looked. Sometimes when Erin came in the room to serve him, he would give her that look, *the* look, with those deep, penetrating eyes. And, well, you never felt so naked in your life. Absolutely voracious, that look. He ate you alive without laying a hand on you.

Finally, Raoul arrived with the wine. He dropped a full case outside her room, his corkscrew brandished quick as a gunslinger.

"Here, here," he snapped at Erin, furiously opening a bottle, "bring diz in the fucking room. Go, go. Hurry."

"*I'll* do it," Stephen said, stepping forward to take the bottle. Then he turned to Erin and jutted his chin toward the hall that led to the Airplane Room. "He's waiting."

Erin frowned and then, like a woman on her way to the gallows, headed down to Tumin's room.

Dinosaurs

In the Airplane Room, Tumin welcomed his crew.

Here they came, one by one: Don Westly, his main confidant and advisor; Rob Barnett, his highly touted protégé; and, tonight, his lawyer, the titanic Ivic Rennert, big as a house and even more unscrupulous, it was said, than Lonny Tumin. Rennert had been briefed immediately following this morning's events and was here to offer advice, perhaps even to make a prediction on what they could expect.

"All right," Tumin said when they were all inside. "What do you think?"

"Hello, Lanny," replied Rennert in his heavy accent; he ambled his girth industriously around the table, his greeting a pique to Tumin's lack of manners. Ivic Rennert was from Louisiana and believed wholeheartedly in the social formalities, believed in them as the very fabric of our Democratic freedoms. Along with being one of the best lawyers in the country, he was also a legendary eater and had recently become so large that colleagues feared for his life. Everything seemed to exhaust him, even the modest task of speaking. His breaks in between words were frequent, the intake of oxygen sounding like a hushed snore. "Well, I tell you what . . . ," Ivic said, searching for his chair, "I know this guy . . . this lawyer this golf ranger's got . . . Name's . . . *Wallace*. Dana Wallace."

Tumin did not rise as the three men approached their seats. Ivic found his chair, the one with the thicker legs and the extrawide seat. Still, the chair's foundation mewled underneath him as he sat. "So, what do you think?" Tumin asked the lawyer again.

"This guy's . . . *not* bad." Ivic wiped the sweat from his brow, still worn out from the one-flight walk upstairs and now from the Herculean task of pulling his chair up to the table. "Good . . . *amb*ulance chaser."

"No, no. What do you *think?*" the mogul repeated, sifting his fingers together for emphasis. Tumin figured the lawyer understood exactly what he meant, but he also knew that where Ivic came from you didn't discuss money until after dinner. Lonny didn't give a shit. "How much are they going to go for, Ivic? Don't jerk me around tonight."

The lawyer smiled at his boss's characteristic bluntness. "Money?" he said. "Well . . . *who* knows for sure. What I do know, Lanny, is this Wallace character . . . In two weeks I'll . . . *get* this call." With his wheezing voice he now slipped into his version of an effeminate accent: "'Thir, I hate to thstart talking about money, but I thup*pose* it's only fair to tell you . . .' This Wallace guy's a big fag from what I understand."

"I don't care if he fucks coconuts," Tumin replied hotly, and not at all truthfully. "What are we going to have to pay the son of a bitch?"

Just then the door opened, and Erin entered the room. Don Westly, ever polite, offered a muted hello, but Tumin looked tense, and the subsequent silence told her that she had interrupted something important. Of course, this wouldn't stop them all from indulging in a quick fantasy as she came around the conference table. Erin had discovered that no matter the proximity of their wives, no matter the importance of the business at hand, men could always get in a quick daydream fuck as she approached a table.

"Drinks, gentlemen?"

Without looking up, Tumin told her to have Raoul pick out some wine. Lonny himself rarely drank, but Don always enjoyed a glass or two with dinner, and Ivic would have a heart attack if wine wasn't offered, perhaps quite literally. Ivic, whose cholesterol level nearly doubled his lofty IQ, had been through a dozen coronary specialists, all urging severe diets — until he'd found himself a French doctor from New Orleans who recommended a bottle of red wine a day. A cure to match the man.

"Don't worry, you can talk in front of her," Tumin reminded everyone as Erin closed the door behind her. "She's my little monkey. Hear no evil, see no evil."

Barnett and the lawyer smiled, while Don winced imperceptibly.

"Now, Ivic," Tumin began again, "cut the southern comfort shit and give me the digits. Just the digits, man. Let's go."

Ivic sat up, dragging his body back up along his special chair. He wiped his brow once more with his silk handkerchief. "Well, all right, let's see now . . . I wouldn't ask . . . and I wouldn't expect this Wallace to ask . . . for . . . anything under . . . let us say . . ."

"Oh, fuck me in the ass."

"A million."

Silence fell like a granite column. Though Tumin's face was impassive, this in itself portended a colossal rage.

"We'll have to *pay* that much, or that's what he'll *ask* for?" Barnett inquired reprovingly, as if it were all Ivic's fault now. Rob Barnett was Lonny's boy, poached just a few years ago from Goldman Sachs. He was a piercingly handsome research analyst, known for hundred-hour workweeks and his feel for the big picture, the broad strokes of fiscal information. He'd been lured with the promise of eventually being made partner, the third link in Triad, a position that, somewhat strangely, had never been filled.

Once ensconced, Barnett had started off hot, but recently his golden-boy image had begun to fade. Don wondered if it wasn't Tumin's fault. Working for Lonny was no picnic, and he seemed to ride Barnett especially hard. When Barnett was hired, Tumin had a Murphy bed installed in the young man's office, along with a rather large refrigerator. The message was clear: *You want to make partner, pal? I want it all; you leave your entrails on my carpet.* But Barnett was not thriving under the pressure. Every morning, he came in looking less and less confident, and more and more exhausted.

But Barnett was also a survivor, Don had observed. Just as his fiduciary skills were falling off, the young man had begun exhibiting a singular talent for ingratiating himself to Tumin. Utilizing his facility for surveying data, he had learned to anticipate his boss's moods and opinions, to forecast where Tumin was likely to stand on market fluctuation, political issues, etc. At opportune moments — and obviously sensing his own plummeting stock within the company — Barnett liked to blurt out these conceptions as if they were his own, thus convincing Tumin of his prescient genius and annoying everyone else in the room. Especially Don.

"It's what he'll ask for . . . ," Ivic said, breathing in, "if he's smart, and . . . *it's* around what he'll get. Considering . . . *the* facts."

Barnett cursed under his breath, attempting to foreshadow Tumin's anger, but his boss didn't move. The rest of the men in the room sat there, watching Tumin warily from the corner of their eyes. Was it their imagination, or had their boss not blinked since the declaration of the figure *$1 million*?

Don Westly, meanwhile, had been quietly nodding to himself. It was what he'd been guessing all along. Of course, he thought to himself, what else had they expected? If this guy Wallace had any sense at all, he'd know that when this went public and Lonny Tumin was exposed as a heinous racist, few would ever do business with him again. In fact, Don wondered if $1 million might even be a little conservative.

Tumin rose from his seat, moving silently down the length of the table. The anxiety this initiated was palpable, for ever since the "dinosaur" incident in the *Times,* there had been a change in Lonny Tumin. Beyond the obvious embarrassment, there had also come an enormous sense of frustration. It was as if he understood now for the first time that there were things out of his control, and this realization had left him feeling vulnerable — and subsequently more volatile. His eruptions had begun to escalate. What would he do now? they wondered. Reach for a wineglass and crush it in his bare hands, as they'd seen him do just a few weeks ago? Pick up a chair and suddenly hurl it toward the gilt mirror? He'd tried that, too, recently, though he had miraculously missed. The golf club, thank heavens, was tucked away somewhere at the office.

Another minute. Still Tumin didn't speak. He had reached the other end of the long table now and was standing there, back to his colleagues, three fingers poised on a chair for support. The only sound was Ivic's gasping breath. He seemed to be slurping at the air, taking it in with a spoon. It only made things worse.

What the fuck was Tumin doing?

Don figured it was his turn to try to break the ice. "We have friends at all the major newspapers," he said placatingly. "If we do decide to go to court — and I'm not convinced that we should — they could turn this around for us, make it seem as if the golf ranger's playing the race card. Modest wage-earner looking for the big chance, trying to exploit a billionaire."

"I'll bet you he drinks," Ivic added, wheels already spinning. "Black guy . . . *work*ing at a golf course all day? C'mon. He's into . . . *booze.*"

"How about a deadbeat dad?" said Barnett, picking up the theme. "You're telling me this guy doesn't have a kid somewhere?"

"There you go," remarked the lawyer, admiring his colleague's pluck. "We get him on the . . . *stand,* I'll have him in tears." He called hesitantly down to Tumin, "What do you think, Lanny?"

There was another stretch of silence. Finally, their boss turned to them. His face showed concern, but the rage they'd expected was not apparent. He was surprisingly calm. He even offered a minuscule smile.

"How about we kill him?" Tumin said.

Barnett laughed, sensing a joke, but Ivic kicked his chair, just in case. They all looked up at Tumin, hoping for a punch line. Their boss's face was inert, absolutely deadpan.

It was clear now: Tumin had asked a straight, honest question. A simple business query.

"Jeez, Lanny, I don't know," Ivic said, rocking back nervously in his chair. "I'm not sure you . . . *need* that."

"Why not? I've been sued how many fucking times this year? I'm sick of it."

"Too high a risk paradigm," offered Barnett with gratuitous complexity; he'd intuited that Tumin would come to this conclusion anyhow — he couldn't be that crazy! — and wanted to be credited with first arrival.

His boss cut him with his eyes. "What risk paradigm?" Tumin asked. "People die every day."

"Well, that *is* true," Barnett replied. "I was going to say . . ." Then both he and Ivic turned to Don Westly for support, for stability and reason. Don, though, looked too appalled to speak.

Ivic held up his hand. "Wait, wait, wasn't there . . . *some*one else?" he wheezed. "Another golfer? Some sort of . . . *wit*ness, am I right?" Ivic looked over at Don Westly. "Do I have my facts correct on this, Don?"

"So, get rid of him too," Tumin said. For theater he picked something off his end of the table, a piece of napkin, a pesky crumb, flicking it away. "Lose the both of these fuckers; I don't give a shit."

The door opened, and here came Erin again. Moving toward the table, she waited for the once-over, but now nobody even blinked. The tension in the room made her limbs stiff; her legs moved as if trudging through a heavy surf. When she looked to Don Westly for a nod or a friendly smile, he gave her nothing, and so she quickly put down the menus and headed for the door.

As soon as she was gone, Tumin looked up again at his crew.

His eyes panned slowly across each face, to Barnett, then to Ivic, though when he got to Don, Tumin stopped, staring even harder. It was as if he was trying to glean something, trying to make some sort of decision right then and there.

"I'm just kidding, you dumb fucks," Tumin declared with a grin.

There was a relieved, forced laughter that Don Westly decided not to join.

Ivic called down to his boss, "Hey, you really . . . *had* us there, Lanny," trying to laugh it up now. He rapped the back of his knobby hand against Rob Barnett's thigh. "This guy's a . . . *sick* fuck, huh?"

Tumin pointed at Ivic. "No, *you're* the sick fuck, the both of you," he said, pointing to include Barnett now. "I make a joke about offing some guy, and you two are practically tossing the idea around like a football."

"You asked . . . What're we supposed to . . . *do,* Lanny?"

"I don't know. You're my lawyer, how about *advising* me. Grab me by my collar and tell me I'm outa my fuckin' mind . . . *Risk paradigm.*"

Tumin looked at Don and shook his head, as if conspiring to scold the others. But Don wasn't convinced. What was actually going on here? he wanted to know. Was Tumin really trying to see if there was decency and reason among his compatriots, or was he appraising loyalties, trying to determine who was ready to follow him over the ramparts and who was not?

And then, Don had a more outlandish notion: Was it at all possible that their boss had thrown out the idea of homicide simply to see if there would be any support? Ordinarily, of course, the very idea of this would have been absurd; L. T. was a billionaire (or nearly so), not a mob boss. But there had been a touch of desperation surrounding the company's operations lately, and certainly around Tumin himself. He seemed obsessed with making a comeback, with making the *Times* eat its words. Don knew that when Tumin really wanted something, he would simply bulldoze anything in his way.

Westly hoped at least that big-mouth Barnett might have learned a little something. By not speaking, by not showing his hand, Don had kept Tumin slightly off balance, leaving his boss unsure of where he stood. If Tumin *was* considering something reckless, he would have to think twice now. It's what Don had been trying to get Barnett to understand all along, what he tried to teach to all the young hotshots at Triad. The power of discretion.

Deathly bored outside the Airplane Room, Erin decided to head down the hall to see how Stephen was making out with the brokers. When she arrived at the lounge, though, the captain was nowhere in sight, and she noticed the blinds had all been drawn from the inside. Well, well, well, she thought, what do we have here? Naturally, she had her guesses, but whatever it was, she was pretty sure it included a pile of white powder the size of Mount Vesuvius. While nearly everyone had given up cocaine ten years ago, it still had a following among young traders.

She decided to peek in, just to make sure they weren't burning the place down. When she cracked open the door though, thus unlocking a cacophony of cackles and maniacal laughter, somebody cut in front to block her view — but it didn't matter, she'd seen it all. At the far corner of the room, one of the young brokers was bent at the waist over a club chair, held down by two of his colleagues. His pants were around his ankles while another man, standing over him on the chair, was pulling at the band of his underwear, tearing at it so that the fabric made a strident ripping sound as it ran up the crack of his buttocks. At the same time, another was paddling the young man's backside with the wine list. "Break in the new guy!" somebody yelled. It was, apparently, some kind of initiation.

Erin backed out of the room as fast as she could.

Disgusted and, for some reason, a little shaken up, she saw Stephen returning from the men's room. She shook her head, gesturing to the muffled sounds of hilarity that emanated from the room.

"Have they got their entrées yet?" she asked. There was rarely ever dessert at these sorts of parties, they both knew. After the main course and a round or two of brandy, guys like these usually hit the road, off to the bar at the W Hotel, or Asia de Cuba, looking for women.

But before Stephen could answer, an attractive, nervous young woman came ambling up the stairs.

"Phone's around to your right," the captain urged, anticipating the usual question. But the woman shyly shook her head.

"I'm looking for the lounge party," she said quietly.

Her voice betrayed her. Despite the sexy clothes, which were not at all appropriate for dining at City, she wasn't as old as she looked. Around twenty, Erin guessed. Perhaps younger. A girl, really.

Stephen seemed to hesitate for a moment, then nodded and stepped forward to escort her. "This way," he said.

As she stepped through the door, the young woman looked back at Erin, smiling with embarrassment and a sort of forced bravery, and the waitress felt her heart fall through her body. As the girl disappeared, a new round of cheers escaped from the room, and the captain closed the door behind her. Much as she tried, Erin could not prevent a certain phrase from repeating itself in her head: *Dessert is served.*

"What're we going to do?" she asked as the captain returned from the room.

"About what?"

"This," she said, pointing to the lounge. "I mean, we can't just let this *happen.*"

Stephen shrugged. He'd been doing this work longer than Erin

had and so was inured to certain realities. He knew that the brokerage firm in that room brought City $250,000 of business a year.
What, realistically, could he do? Alert the police, thereby forfeiting his
job, not to mention getting the young woman arrested? If Erin
wanted to butt in, then fine, he thought, knock yourself out. You're
not a career waitress — not yet.

You handled this, he knew, the same way you handled the customer's rudeness, the drugs, the chronic alcoholism — you acted as if
you didn't see it. You pretended it was no big deal, that you weren't
contributing to something awful, that they'd just get it somewhere
else. Then you went out after work and drank a few yourself and tried
to forget the whole thing.

"Ah, shit," she said, slapping her hand on the service bar in frustration. "What the hell am I going to do?"

"It's her life, Erin."

"No, I mean *my* life." She meant her domain on the second floor,
City itself, the whole food industry in which she had toiled for so
long. "I can't deal with stuff like this anymore; I really can't. I gotta
get out."

He drew her in as her head dropped against his shoulder. "You
will, sweetie," he replied. "You will."

Although Stephen was probably her best friend on the staff, he
had never mentioned to Erin that he had once been an actor himself.
Somehow, through all the banter, all the erotic confessions and pick-
me-ups, he'd never said a thing. Stephen was in his early forties now
and made a good salary. The restaurant paid for his health insurance,
and he made enough to own his own apartment. Life wasn't so bad.
But as he stroked her hair now to comfort her, he thought about why
he had never told Erin of his great, faded dream, how he hadn't
wanted to discourage her, and how, slowly but surely, this feeling of
not being able to take it anymore would pass.

Mr. Nightcap

Feeling the itch, the nightly tickle, Kyle moved from the leather chair where he sat reading and headed toward the kitchen. He ambled in his socks, hoping his wife wouldn't hear him from the bedroom, where she lay navigating a particularly obtuse crossword puzzle. It was no use. There was the familiar *pooft* of the freezer, the tinkling of cubes against glass. The chimes at midnight. She knew them well.

Mr. Nightcap was calling.

It was all thought out, all fetishized beforehand. If there had been red wine with dinner (and there was always something with dinner), Mr. Nightcap might recommend a nice cognac to finish off with. If beer, then perhaps Master Kyle would prefer a scotch or port for his evening's epilogue. These were the standbys. For the odd night, a different hankering, there was also sherry available, dessert wine, finely aged tequilas, single-batch bourbons, etc. An elixir for every mood. In fact, it was all so finely mapped out, so fastidiously employed and fussed over, that Mr. Nightcap often knew on Friday what Master

Kyle would be drinking as far away as Sunday or even Monday, and with what meal — food being merely the backboard against which the game was played.

Yet his pupil was completely in control. No problems here. Friends praised Kyle's temperance, his newfound moderation. The days of public disgrace were long past. He was a married man now, after all, the old behavior no longer tolerated, no longer desired (mostly). And so Mr. Nightcap administered his medicine to Master Kyle late at night, *every* night, and alone. He had been doing this for so long now that a few drinks before bed were as essential to Kyle's rest, as prerequisite, as sheets on a mattress, as laying one's head upon a pillow.

Invariably, there were the private worries. Kyle wanted to know how long he could expect to live with such habits. His liver was already in arrears from years of abuse — he could feel it on rainy days, that dull soreness — and so he challenged his ghostly attendant with names, with comparisons to the legends.

Richard Burton?

— Died of cancer, sir, asserted Mr. Nightcap. It was the smoking that did him in. Nasty habit, that.

Peter O'Toole?

— Still kicking the last time I checked. Little pale maybe, but otherwise healthy as a horse.

Norman Mailer?

— Heading toward eighty and on canes, but working on a new novel. At eighty, Master Kyle!

Mr. Nightcap had known them all.

The surgeon general has determined that two to three drinks a day can be beneficial to one's health . . . Music to Kyle's ears! When that report was recently issued, he'd rejoiced. It seemed to legitimize his entire way of living, his whole philosophy. On top of everything else, the elixirs were healthy! (I could have told you that, he'd thought.)

His wife was careful to point out that the report condoned two to three drinks a *day*, an amount he more than covered at dinner and occasionally at lunch, while reminding him it said nothing about a midnight session as well.

Then tell her, Mr. Nightcap had replied one night — toasting

Master Kyle with a drink of his own — tell her that you intend to live *twice* as long.

Kyle awoke, fresh and clear. After some scrambled eggs and a little SportsCenter, he went out for his morning coffee and his copies of the *New York Times* (obligatory) and the *Post* (indispensable). Returning home, he found the *Times* was actually juicy today, containing a negative review of a peer's novel. The bad news was delivered with deadly relish, and for a second Kyle experienced a quick surge of exhilaration, which was then quickly extinguished by a much healthier empathy and regret. He, as much as anyone, knew the sting of bad reviews. You told everyone you didn't read them, but you did. And they *hurt*. Kyle was a passing acquaintance of this suddenly besmirched writer, and so he decided he would dash off a quick e-mail to try to confirm for her the rationalizations that she would now be spending the greater part of the morning trying to devise: that such opinions were fleeting and temporal, of no lasting importance; that the world of book reviewing — of all things literary, everywhere — was indeed upside down. (If the review had been a good one, his message would have been a congratulations on being hailed in the final bastion of reliable literary authority.)

Before he sent his e-mail, though, he backtracked through the *Arts* section and discovered a lengthy meditation on the state of contemporary writing, an overview that posited yet another comeback of literature. On the top of the page were twelve or so photographs of authors the *Times* was hailing as the writing elite, those of the older generation who were still carrying the torch, and then some of the younger writers who were "reinventing" the form. Try as he might, Kyle could not find his likeness among the photographs. Nor, after a second and third reading, could he locate his name anywhere in the text. Among the twenty-five writers included were a few of the fathers, of course — Roth, Bellow — along with his old nemesis, Devon Schiff, who in recent interviews had stated that there was still a tiny piece of glass from a champagne flute lodged in his face where Kyle Clayton had hit him nearly four years ago. Kyle doubted it, but what did that matter now? Who cared? Devon Schiff was *in;* he was *out.* It wasn't simply fashion either. Nearly all the writers listed were excellent, Kyle admitted, and so the conclusions he drew from this discouraged him: respectable now, married, semisober, his book sales neither brisk nor fashionably meager — and worst of all, pleasantly, if cursorily, reviewed — he was simply slipping off the radar, no longer in the first tier of writers. Something, he decided, must be done.

Time, he thought, to get ahold of the Pixie. Sic her on their ass.

Ms. Birquet was not available, or so he was told when he phoned. Kyle was pissed. What, he thought, she wasn't wearing her phone retainer? No doubt Patience's assistant had a hierarchy of names that were to be put through: writers, publishers, family members, lovers, etc. Yet another list Kyle Clayton was not on. Small fish, big pond.

He was beginning to miss Larry Wabzug. By the time Kyle had decided to break from his erstwhile agent, both the man's mind and his methods had seemed antiquated. Lately, though, leaving him felt like a big mistake. Kyle had gone for the Big Money, and Patience had delivered — sort of. But then Kyle had got the feeling she was utterly dispassionate about his writing — didn't get it, didn't particularly like it. Larry, meanwhile, had marveled at his work. Larry always picked up the phone.

And who knows, maybe his old friend could have got just as much as Patience had for his new book. Maybe Larry Wabzug could have got more. Maybe it shouldn't have mattered either way.

All doubts were dissolved a short time later when Kyle, still smarting over the *Times* article and unable to concentrate, got a mysterious call.

"Mango and peaches," announced a voice without introduction, "thinly sliced."

"Excuse me?"

"Ripened avocado, Kyle. Syrup from a fruit cup, my face shimmering like a glazed doughnut."

With this last image, Kyle finally caught on. This was a familiar frolic of the agent's, the one where she tortured the newly married man with her latest sexual conquests.

He was talking pussy with the Pixie.

"Who is it now?" Kyle asked unhappily.

"The hostess."

He racked his brain for possible candidates.

"From lunch the other day. You know."

Kyle sat up at his desk. "*Hostess?* You don't mean the one —"

"From City, yeah. The one you couldn't take your eyes off of. I banged her."

"You what?"

"Yeah, got her number on the way out. We went on a date last Friday." Patience giggled. "Banged her."

"What are you talking about? You're . . . You can't . . ."

"Oh, I banged her," she said.

Suspending her boast for the moment, she went on to explain another bit of good news: the Muslim piece, the chunk from Kyle's novel, had been bought by none other than *NYC* magazine to the tune of $5,000. He could expect it to run in four to six weeks.

Kyle's heart surged. *NYC!* If there was a more prestigious place to have a story published, he couldn't imagine it. Still the most literary magazine in the country. Hadn't all of the fathers published there?

Was she something, Patience wanted to know, or was she something?

After a moment or two, though, Kyle looked down at the *Times* article, at the faces of the lauded writers, and his elation ebbed. Doubt began to nudge at him. He was publishing in *NYC* magazine, wonderful, but then it wasn't exactly "The Snows of Kilimanjaro" we had here. Who was he kidding? What we had here was a moderately humorous rendering of his conversion to Islam. Something to peruse on the beach when the sun got too strong. Something for a quick chuckle, perhaps. Nothing that anybody would really notice.

"Thanks, Patience," Kyle said into the phone, but then realized she was already long gone.

Magnificent Failures

"Oh, no," said Helena as her niece held up another piece of junk. "Oh, dear."

Three weeks had gone by, but The Room had proved stubborn. Erin had barely made a dent. Not that Helena had been helping much. Mostly she'd stayed hidden in some back bedroom, huddled up with the morning's newspaper. Occasionally she would emerge in a stylish blouse and scarf (for what? Erin would wonder, for where?) peering in The Room with cryptic aversion. "What's that?" she would ask, referring to some item Erin happened to be digging out at the moment, and then her niece would have to hold it up for inspection while Helena rolled her eyes, in woe over some sad memory twenty years past. Only to disappear once again.

This time it was a bathing suit, a maroon one-piece. Helena stood in the doorway, groaning at the sight of it.

"I wore that at Jones Beach, years and years ago. Do you remember those days at all?" She didn't wait for an answer. "It was quite a nice place, back then. The family would all go together."

Wishing to be agreeable, Erin offered some quaint remembrances.

"Yes, and the clam chowder on the boardwalk," Helena added, quite enlivened now. "I never knew anything could taste so good. And the paddle tennis we used to play. Such wonderful memories!"

What she wouldn't say now was how disintegrated everything had become, how disparate it was now. Some of the older generation had passed on, while Erin's own parents had moved to a gated community in Willimantic, Connecticut (*Romantic Willimantic!* read the brochure). And then all her aunts and uncles and older cousins whom she had worshiped so unquestioningly back then — and who, yes, would certainly become famous actors and musicians and writers — had done their creative thing and had moved on, retreating back to suburbs only slightly more exalted than those they'd come from.

Now all that remained of the Wyatts' ambition was Helena, last in the long line of family dreamers. What would happen to them? Erin often wondered. Would she herself, without so much as an agent, suddenly break in as an actress in her early thirties, when others her age were already viewed as relics? Had Helena, the reclusive dilettante, somehow discovered God among the stacks of *New York Times* in a disintegrating apartment on Manhattan's Upper East Side?

The Actress. The Book. The *Room*. Sometimes Erin was quite sure that being a Wyatt was synonymous with being a fool.

Ever since Erin had started plucking around among the ruins of The Room these past weeks, her aunt had begun to seem more tired, more fragile. Along with this subtle deterioration also came a litany of criticisms of Erin's life, a territory into which her aunt had never before traversed. She was not pursuing her acting hard enough, Helena contended. She liked pleasure too much: vacations, meals out, nice clothes, men. She'd given her niece $3,000 for Christmas last year, and what had she done with it? More acting lessons? A jaunt to L.A. for auditions during pilot season? A few weeks off from her job to appear in a low-paying show downtown, if for nothing else than exposure?

No, she goes shopping in SoHo, a pair of boots here, a handbag there. Dinners at Balthazar with men she has asked out (she pays, she scores!). *Brideshead Revisited* on VHS.

"Helena," her niece would argue, "I'm a member of the Actor's Studio, okay? I've studied with Uta Hagen . . ."

"So?"

"So, I don't need any more acting lessons! Nobody out there is more trained than I am. It doesn't even matter anyway."

"What doesn't matter?" Helena seemed baffled.

"Training. In fact, if you want to know the truth, I believe the ability to act is actually a *dis*advantage to finding a paying job in movies and television. I'm convinced of it."

"You don't really believe that."

"It's all about a *look*, Helena. I'm telling you, that's all it is."

Helena pursed her lips, barely satisfied with this. She herself had enjoyed some minor success as an actress years ago, having shared the stage with Robert Duvall and Gene Hackman before they'd segued into film. Though this was only in summer stock — and most of the other actors she'd worked with hadn't segued anywhere — Helena somehow held this experience over her niece as granting her ultimate wisdom on the acting life. No matter that it was more than forty years ago now, and everything, absolutely *everything,* about that world had changed.

What her aunt didn't know about the trajectory of a contemporary actress could fill twenty Rooms, Erin thought.

"And so," the niece continued, "as for some more guerrilla theater down on the Lower East Side in an abandoned synagogue where nobody gets paid and no goddamned agents or producers ever show up anyway, well, I didn't need that last year, and I certainly don't need it now. I've done that to death." Feeling herself thoroughly wound up now, she reached into her bag for a rare cigarette. "I didn't know that there was a responsibility attached to this money that you've given me, Helena. I really appreciate it, believe me. It's been a great blessing. But if there are strings, then I don't think you should do it anymore."

This show of pride momentarily mollified her aunt; but it was a tricky game, Erin knew, since she didn't really know if she was prepared to back up her words. In fact, it was precisely these sudden infusions of cash that had made life bearable over the last few years, when her aunt had begun unloading some of her roughly million-dollar estate — the idea being that Helena could at least see some of the fruits of her generosity, rather than Erin, and any other beneficiaries, living it up after she was gone. Anything $10,000 and under was tax exempt, and Helena had been dispensing amounts like these to her niece every Christmas for the past few years. It was a nice padding to the approximately $40,000 she netted working part-time at City, and Erin loved the idea that she could go to a great restaurant, or head down to Miami for a weekend when the weather turned bitter, no questions asked. The extra cash had really made a difference, made her feel like a real person, with a real life. What the hell else was money for anyway?

Still, the niece knew that Helena's accusations carried with them the pith of truth. Erin was ready to admit that lately she was not pushing hard enough for her career. She was, for instance, e-mailed the daily "breakdowns," the complete list of current auditions going on in New York. It was illegal, the lists sold by unscrupulous interns from the major casting agencies, but every hungry actor paid for these reports as a major shortcut to landing a job. Why wasn't she utilizing this, crashing auditions or deluging producers and casting directors with headshots and résumés? Why wasn't she networking more, or updating her performance reel, which was much more important these days than auditioning?

She was getting lazy, and she knew it. She was wearing down, moving half-assed toward her dream. She was becoming a Wyatt.

And now, if The Room was taking a toll on Helena, it was also getting to Erin. What was most eerie was how everything was layered, like the rings of a tree or the gradations in an ancient stone, each stratum revealing another year. Every layer Erin mined, she could date: the style of clothes, the gimmicky Christmas gifts never opened, the pictures in the shoeboxes. The first three feet had revealed things from the early nineties and late eighties: a blouse with Chinese lettering, a Rubik's Cube, a skinny tie someone had given Dick and that he (wisely) had refused to wear. Now she was coming across items from the mid- to late seventies, the dust worse and the yeasty smell of the old clothes more acute. In a sooty box of books she found *Yoga Made Simple; The Joy of Sex* (oh, Helena!); *Rich Man, Poor Man;* something by Erica Jong. There was a wooden tennis racket, a giftsize bottle of Jean Naté, a canvas PBS handbag from a donation drive. The clothes were frilly and beaded, orange pantsuits flaring out at the bottom, the jewelry all jangly and loose-fitting with large "mystical" stones.

Here were the dishes she'd bought for the parties never hosted. Here the suitcases, tags still attached, for the places she'd never gone. The boxes of photos pronouncing *Here is a life!* when in fact most of the pictures were from family holidays, which had always been Helena's primary social interaction. And through the newspapers, the endless piles of *Times,* she had what passed for her daily experience.

We're not closers: this was Erin's conclusion. Generation after generation, no Wyatt had ever fully realized his or her dream, had ever brought home the prize, so to speak, and with each day spent in The Room the reality of this worked itself into her head a little more, seeped deeper into her pores. Cell memory, DNA tracking, nature and nurture, *destiny* — call it what you will, she thought. I'm doomed like the rest of them. There was only one thing that could save us all, Erin knew, one hope that could redeem the life her aunt had pushed aside, that could justify the family and its fallen dreams. The Book. The raison d'être, the excuse for everything. So far, there was no sign of it.

In The Room it was already the mid-seventies. It was getting a little late.

The Father

As Time hurled Itself toward that radiant and anxious year of 1999, the holy month of Ramadan, which calls for a month of daylight fasting, was observed with much inconsistency in the Clayton household.

Strange, but of all the earthly elixirs that tempted the Great Kurban during these days, it was coffee that proved most irresistible. Kyle was pretty sure that his entire imagination resided inside that magical black bean, and without it his creativity languished — thus coffee was sneaked with regularity. Then there were the holiday lunches with publishing friends, of course, looking to ring up their expense accounts before the new year. Who was Kyle Clayton to thwart such fiscal urgencies? Business was business after all, and he so hated to be rude.

Still, Ayla was rather touched, watching her husband at least try to deny himself things. She herself cheated on occasion — she was so ravenous after a morning at the gym, for example. Last year, their first Ramadan together, Kyle had all but ignored the holiday, though afterward she was surprised to hear him say that he'd regretted it.

Ramadan, as it turned out, impressed him. Of all the religious rituals in Kyle's experience, after a number of Catholic and Jewish girlfriends and their attendant holidays (one year suffering through no less than Kwanza), only Ramadan invoked a vision both spiritually demanding and morally practical. A month of fasting, plus 5 percent of one's yearly earnings for the poor. Your money where your mouth is, so to speak.

In fact, since he'd been married, there were times when Kyle had been secretly rooting for Islam to take hold in his life: as an antidote to all he'd found wanting in the lax Presbyterianism of his youth, for all that in his very modern, so-called sophisticated New York life, sometimes bored him to death. Intellectually, too, Kyle found Islam an exciting and useful gambit. If it was scorn he was looking for, well then, what better way to find it than to become an American Muslim? What could be more unlikely or outrageous for Kyle Clayton? Had he not seen the odd looks friends and acquaintances had tried to mask when he told them of his conversion, the overanxious acceptance or barely buried revulsion they choked down as liberal Northeasterners? *A Muslim, well, isn't that fascinating* . . . He even found himself defending his new faith at bars and the occasional dinner party, the arguments igniting along the table like wildfire. He hadn't been this passionate about an issue since his early twenties, before he'd realized he knew nothing and never would. Now, suddenly, after voluminous research, he was articulating Palestinian grievances with lawyerlike precision, rectifying the infinite misnomers about the Koran and the entire Muslim nation. A WASPy mullah with beer breath, that was Kyle Clayton. On the cocktail circuit, at least, he went to the mat for Islam.

But for all the contrarian posturing, Kyle knew he would never become a true Muslim, would not go to mosque, or pray, or even believe in God, for that matter. Would never *become* anything at all — except, perhaps, a husband, and this was still suspect. It was just not Kyle's nature to join. On principle, he eschewed all academies, literary movements, and schools of thought. He was averse to anything incorporating terms such as *guild, institute, alliance,* or *foundation.* And his least favorite word in the English language was most certainly *committee.*

As a would-be Muslim, Kyle couldn't even manage Step One:

accepting Muhammad as his prophet. He found Muhammad a magnificent though deeply troubling figure. A man of epic paradoxes.
Muhammad, the enemy of greed but also the savvy merchant who at
twenty-five marries Khadija, the forty-year-old widow of immense
fortune. Muhammad, the Prince of Peace with his two coats of mail
and double-pointed sword, the Dhu'l-Faqar, or "Cleaver of Verte-
brae," so fiercely brandished in battle. Muhammad, the sentimental-
ist who weeps openly at the bloodshed at Uhud, but who personally
helps dig the graves in the marketplace at Yathrib before the massacre
of the Jews. The Warrior Prophet! Another term Kyle could never
cozy up to. His attitude was that Islam had as much to answer for as
the next religion, and since this particular faith had fallen into his lap,
so to speak, had thrust itself upon him for his inspection, he would
hold it as accountable as anything else.

Xanax, thought Ayla, parking the car up along the curb in front of her
father's house in Fair Lawn, New Jersey, should be as plentiful as
aspirin. Pull in to a deli and they should be hanging near the counter
on the pinched wire frames, affordable two-packs in varying degrees
of strength, right alongside the pain relievers and cold medicines. She
thought this because her own prescription had recently lapsed, and
she had failed, for the first time in years, to bullshit her therapist into
another batch of two-milligram beauties.

She thought this because Kyle Clayton was coming with her again
to her father's for Bairam.

For Turks, Bairam was the name of the three-day feast that com-
memorated the end of Ramadan, arguably the most important of Muslim holidays. The year before, their first as a married couple, Ayla had
informed Kyle that their attendance at this event was absolutely
mandatory, beyond negotiation. When still he'd balked, Ayla reminded
him that she had just endured Thanksgiving at the WASP's Nest — his
cousin Kent's house in Winston, New Jersey — complete with argyle
sweaters, noontime Bloody Marys you could see through, and a roaring fireplace the size of her first New York City apartment. He was
damn well going to Bairam.

At the time, Kyle had yet to meet the father. Murat was his name,
and he so greatly disapproved of his daughter's union to the Great Kurban that he had not attended the wedding at the mosque in Paterson,

nor the secular ceremony in New York City. For the father, Kyle's Christian birth was just the beginning of the young man's shortcomings. Murat was of the Cherkes, one of the many Russian tribes inhabiting the farming villages of western Turkey. The Cherkes were steeped in tribalism, and among their many conservative tenets was to forbid their daughters from marrying outside the village. Even if Kyle Clayton had been born in Istanbul, for example, a devout and prosperous Muslim, able to recite the Koran (make that the Qur'an) from memory and fart the Turkish national anthem on cue — he still could not have married Ayla. Ayla was to marry a *Cherkes,* though how she was supposed to have met a Cherkes goat farmer in the contemporary sprawl of Fair Lawn, New Jersey, or later below Houston Street in downtown Manhattan, no one was able to say.

Her father could be volatile, and of course her husband's thirst for conflict spoke for itself. In fact, she wasn't even sure that Kyle was welcome at this event (there had been no formal invitation), but she was determined not to let her father's stubbornness prevent her from seeing her family on such an important holiday.

It was a gloomy afternoon in December. They had arrived late and were forced to park down the street. As Ayla and her new husband walked toward her father's house — practically the only house in all of Fair Lawn, Kyle had noticed, without holiday decorations — Ayla offered him some last-minute pointers.

"Just remember that whatever happens, my father is not your typical Turk," she began. "He's from a tiny village, very conservative, very uneducated. He doesn't know how to be open like us. You know the Cherkes? Everything in their world is based on respect. Respect, respect, respect. That's all he lives for, all he knows."

She lit a quick cigarette to calm herself; Kyle noticed her hand shaking.

"Relax, it'll be fine," he said, rubbing the back of her neck reassuringly. He couldn't understand what all the fuss was about. His girlfriends' fathers had *always* disapproved of Kyle Clayton. This was familiar territory. "Who knows, maybe your father will even like me. I'm sort of due in that department. You might be surprised."

"No," she replied with a sharp pull of her cigarette. "He won't. He's a dick."

Her eyes were averted as they approached the house, but when they turned on the driveway and began walking up, she was forced to look. There it was, she thought. How the sight of it affected her! After a decade of therapy, Ayla knew she still hadn't put her father behind her — though at least there was some perspective now. He was a bully; it really wasn't much more complicated than that. You could summon arguments about *cultural differences* and *lack of educational advantages* until you were blue in the face, but in the end Murat had decided to push around a wife and two daughters like a schoolyard thug, and without so much as a glimmer of mitigating affection. He was, Ayla and her therapist had concluded, responsible.

And now here came Kyle Clayton, the reaction, the antibody to the disease. American, overeducated, atheistic to the core — a gob of spit in her father's beard — about to stroll into their living room as he did everywhere else: like he owned the joint.

"I'm just hoping he ignores you," she added, stubbing out the butt underfoot. "This is my dream scenario."

Spilling out the door was a receiving line of guests. Ayla and her husband queued up on the rear, paying respects to various aunts, uncles, and cousins, many of whom Kyle had met at the wedding. Murat, he understood, was greeting people at the door. Here was the first tradition of Bairam, Ayla explained to him: the young were required to visit the old, the patriarch receiving the guests as they entered his home.

Kyle got out of line and stood on his toes. Ayla had mentioned that Murat was a building contractor by profession (though semi-retired now), and this fact certainly corresponded with what Kyle saw of him. Mount Murat, mused the son-in-law, for what he saw standing at the door was an intimidating rock pile of a man, a solid mass of fifty-five-year-old granite. He seemed both towering and solidly grounded at the same time, and what little hair he had on the top of his head he made up for with the sort of thick black beard that Kyle associated with religious zealotry.

After a long and frigid delay, the line finally delivered them to the entrance. Murat was standing at the top of the steps, hovering in the doorjamb, and Kyle's height left the two men standing face to face . . . yet the father did not cast his eyes on the son-in-law. Ten seconds he waited, then twenty, until Kyle was relieved to notice Ayla stepping in front of him (the guinea pig, he thought, the cannon fodder, *You got me into this!*). He watched her as she moved tentatively toward the threshold, curious to note the tone of her approach; polite but cold, Kyle had guessed — nobody could hold a grudge like Ayla! But then, watching her in profile, he was simultaneously surprised and appalled to see her face adopt a look of apology, and then, head bowed, she took her father's hand to her lips.

Why, Ayla? Kyle intoned soundlessly. Was this not the man who'd made your childhood a living hell, had blown off your *wedding* of all things? Why the hell are you looking so sheepish?

Head still bowed, Ayla brought her father's hand from her lips to her forehead. Then she whispered something in Turkish that Kyle couldn't follow, but whose inflection was clearly obsequious. Murat nodded, obviously pleased by this show of respect, and his eyes followed her as she moved away into the living room.

Up stepped Kyle.

He'd almost forgotten about this business of the hand-kissing. Though, in fairness, he had been warned. It *must* be done, Ayla had told him. Her father demanded it, and Kyle would never be welcomed into the family without it. As for Kyle, he found the ritual repellent, especially the formality of bringing the hand to the forehead. Even when they'd practiced at home, Kyle was more than happy to kiss and fondle Ayla's long, slender fingers, but he could not, for whatever reason, bring that hand to his brow.

Then he'd reminded himself of what he'd promised Ayla during those difficult weeks before the wedding, that if they were going to do this, if they were really going to get married (which was actually *his* idea and had taken some persuading), then Kyle would have to be open to new things, would have to take pains to try to adopt some of the traditions of her culture, odd or unpleasant as some of them might seem. And to this he had agreed. On this he had given his word.

Yet, now, standing before Murat, he continued to observe the man's contented smile as it followed Ayla, and that old switch turned on inside him, triggering that familiar rush, the sudden flush of anger that led him to irrational acts of defiance, to idealistic foolishness in the face of power. And so here he went again, for though his wife had told him very little about her childhood, had only hinted at incidents, he could pretty much guess the details, and he realized suddenly that he'd been waiting for this all along, was secretly gunning for a show-down.

Murat had certainly helped push things along. What had he done but start things out with yet another tiny cruelty? He had made his daughter bow down to him, when it was *he,* in fact, who should have apologized, *he* who should've been bowing and kissing *her* hand. It's true, Kyle thought now, getting a good close-up of Murat, the face was cruel. Beneath that beard he saw all the flabby-jowled stubbornness of eastern European despots. Think Milosevic, he thought, going too far now but loving it. Think Ceauşescu! That coarse village ignorance that never seemed to manifest itself as doubt, as one might hope, but always in narrow-minded conviction, in the pathetic, insatiable need for tribute from that blithering idiot known as Respect.

And so, stepping up, the son-in-law decided that he would kiss Marat's hand — and yes, put it solemnly to his forehead — if, and only if, the old man would kiss Kyle's dimpled white ass first.

But once again, Ayla's foresight won the day: the new husband was to be ignored. The old man never met Kyle's eyes, never reached for the outstretched hand (the Great Kurban deciding to offer only an ordinary American handshake). Instead he looked past the son-in-law as if he weren't there, and when Murat began talking over the young man's shoulder to the next in line, Kyle had to accept that his own intended slight had been trumped. It was time to move on.

Round one, he thought, to the old man.

He found Ayla waiting nervously for him in the living room.

"Well?" she asked.

"Yup, you're right," Kyle snapped. "He's a dick."

A short time later, the family, numbering around thirty, piled into the large living room. A quintessentially American clan, Kyle thought, with Game Boys, bowls of soggy potato chips, and overly assertive perfume. There was much laughter, of course, interspersed with sharp reprimands to roughhousing children. In fact, except for the language, a mélange of Turkish and English (though Murat had yet to utter a word of the latter), only the music was truly different. From the stereo emanated a famous Arabic singer whom Kyle actually recognized — it was the music they put on at his favorite bar to signal last call. This association brought on an immediate psychosomatic longing for a drink. Where, he thought, was Mr. Nightcap when you needed him? Thus far he'd only been offered tea, and after a brief reconnaissance of the surroundings, this didn't seem likely to change. Suddenly the music was lowered.

"You know, I have to say something," called out the heavily accented voice. It was Murat, roosted on a plaid Barcalounger on the far side of the room. Though the man's English was awkward, that he had slipped into that language at all gave the words a heavy import. "About Ayla, okay . . . If she want to marry dez guy, dez is nothing I can do about it. But I don't have to like it, okay?"

He was addressing not Kyle but the women, huddled in a nest near him on one of the plastic-covered couches. Obviously they'd made some appeal to him earlier, had applied a sly but forceful pressure, such as only women can. They'd wanted Murat to make alms with his son-in-law. This was his response.

"Dez guy doesn't even come to me to ask me if he can marry my daughter; then he wants to know why I say nothing to him."

Kyle felt his ire begin to rise. For the record, Kyle didn't particularly want to know why the father hadn't said anything to him. There was enough malice levied toward Kyle Clayton back in New York City; as for Fair Lawn, New Jersey, silence was golden. True, he had not approached the old man for permission to marry his daughter, but then this had been Ayla's decision. Her father would flatly refuse to give his blessing anyway, she had explained, and would only use the occasion to humiliate him.

"He give me no respect, okay?" Murat continued. "So why should I give him?"

"Respect," Kyle announced suddenly — and as he did, he saw Ayla out of the corner of his eye, already trying to warn him off whatever he was about to say — "respect is something that is *earned*. It is not something to be expected."

With an audible sigh, Ayla's eyes rolled back into her head, seemingly never to return. As for Murat, he appeared not to fully grasp the reply of his smarty-pants son-in-law, but knew enough to comprehend that he was being rebuffed. His response was to nod and sit forward in his chair, taking a deep, resonant breath, as if to gather himself for a comeback.

Ayla tried to head him off. "Baba, please, give him a break." Again, her voice had that unctuous tone that her husband so disliked, and the name *Baba,* for some reason, further grated on him. This was the Turkish version of *Dad,* or *Pop,* he knew, but did her father really deserve such an intimate title? "He converted to Islam so he could be a part of the family," Ayla continued. "He became a Muslim for you. For *you,* Baba. He's Kurban now."

"Kur*ban,*" the father mocked. His grin had a teeth-baring irony that was shocking in its intent to wound. "What kind of man is dez, changes religion like nothing? Like changing a pair of socks to dez guy. Whatever smoothest for life, right?" For the first time now, he looked over at his son-in-law. "Today Muslim, tomorrow Hindu. Friday, a Jew maybe, who knows . . . Kur*ban.* Ha ha ha."

Kyle crossed his arms in front of him, face flush with humiliation. What hurt the most was this notion that he was a man without conviction, that his beliefs flittered toward the winds of convenience. A man utterly without character. You cocksucker, Kyle thought. After all the hell I went through to become a Muslim, maybe the most difficult day of my life, and here you're *laughing at me?* It's true what Ayla said, I did it for you! *You,* you big cocksucker, with your seventh-century values and your second-grade education!

But he said nothing.

Murat's last comments had cleared the room, and now everyone found someplace to rush to, some task in which to bury their attention. Kyle found Ayla in the hall, commiserating with her younger sister, Elsa, over what had just happened. Remarkably, their conclusion was that all things considered, it had gone pretty well. The son-in-law had got off cheap.

"All right, listen," Kyle said, approaching them. Try as he might, he could not control the shaking in his voice. "I just — thought I would let you know . . . I think it's only fair — to warn you both . . . I'm going to go back out there right now to punch your Ali Baba right in his fucking face."

Ayla barely heard the threat, focusing instead on her husband's chin, which was quivering now, spasming in anger and mortification. She had never seen this before and was absolutely stunned. Was this really her husband, Kyle Clayton, centerpiece of scorn, prey to a thousand *Page Six* dropkicks? Was this the same man who'd begrudgingly agreed to accompany her to a Turkish restaurant in Astoria she'd heard about, glum and complaining all the way, until a woman two tables over began haranguing him over dinner ("I hate you, you know that," she'd said, her mouth nearly frothing with disgust. "I really, really hate you. You give writers a bad name. You're the worst. You're *scum*.") and then had positively *glowed* the rest of the evening, thrilled to have inspired such depth of feeling?

Was this really her Kyle, the King of Confrontation, fighting back tears because Daddy didn't like him?

"Right — in the face," he said, voice still quavering, "fat fucking face."

Of course, he didn't mean a word of it. He was the melodramatic friend, calling to let you know he was about to stick his head in the oven again — and this time you *better* not come over and try to stop him. He wanted to be held back, talked out of it. For Kyle was secretly beginning to suspect what everyone else in that room already knew — that Mount Murat could *kick* his dimpled white ass.

That had been last year, and what Ayla had thought was so amazing about it all was how much of the rest of the day they were able to salvage. Though she had offered to leave immediately after her father's insult, Kyle had insisted they stay through dinner. He was all right, he'd told her, no big deal. He'd pulled himself together and seemed resolved that Ayla should spend some time with her sister and, most especially, her mother, whom she rarely got to see. That Kyle would do this for her, given how clearly her father had upset him, filled her with a new respect and love for him, and reminded her all over again of the surprising bursts of generosity of which her husband was sometimes capable.

Could the good vibes carry over to this year? It seemed almost too much to hope for. But the holiday, for the most part, passed smoothly. The preliminary greetings and hand-kissings were circumvented when an icy rain began to fall just as Ayla and Kyle were arriving, and so the long queue that had formed was allowed to enter en masse. Husband and wife slipped in without any formalities. It seemed to set a pleasant tone for the day.

Tea in the living room was a friendly, convivial affair, with no speeches or public denouncements of the son-in-law. Murat coughed and quietly sipped his tea; he had a terrible cold as it turned out, and this left him somewhat subdued. Kyle, meantime, busied himself with that Switzerland of family life, the children, who engaged him in a WWF–type wrestling match safely nestled back in the den.

By dessert the family had broken off into intimate groupings: Ayla with her aunt and uncle (whose good-natured personalities, incidentally, bore no resemblance to their tyrannical brother's) and Kyle with her mother, Fema, with whom he got along strikingly well. We're home free now, Ayla thought to herself; the kitchen clock was showing it to be nearly 8:00 P.M., and so in just a few minutes they would get up, exaggerate the traffic that awaited them, and say their good-byes. Back to New York! A Bairam without incident! *Allah huakbar!*

"Kur*ban!*" her father suddenly exclaimed from down the end of the long table. He and Kyle had intentionally sat apart and would have passed the day without so much as a hello if not for this little parley.

Ayla held her breath. The room grew quiet.

"How you do with the Turkish?"

"Excuse me?" Kyle said. "Oh, you mean the food? Absolutely delicious. Can't get enough."

"No, no . . ." The father seemed annoyed. "The *Turk*ish. The words."

"Oh, the language? Mmm, actually, not so great," Kyle admitted. "I'll have to work on that." He smiled amiably and returned his attention to Fema.

"This is because . . ." Murat's voice trailed off as he picked up his handkerchief to cough.

Ayla, who was a few seats closer, sought to intercept. "Baba, please," she urged.

"Because why?" Kyle asked evenly.

Murat drank some water, clearing his throat. "This is because you're not interested."

Once again, Ayla held her breath, though she was enraged at her father. Five minutes to go, she thought. *Five* minutes.

The son-in-law smiled. "No, actually I am interested," he replied, sweet as can be. "From what I can hear, it's quite a nice language. Right now, though, I'm busy finishing up a new book. Once that's done, I was thinking of taking some lessons."

There was a confused silence. Slowly the family members began to exchange looks, seeking out their closest kin, as if to confirm the unreality of what they'd just heard.

"Lessons?" the mother whispered.

"Lessons?" proclaimed an uncle in Turkish.

"*Turk*ish lessons?" shouted Ayla's sister.

"Well, of course," Kyle answered. "I really want to *immerse* myself, you know. It's the only way. Ayla's been trying to teach me some things here and there, but it's not the same."

Murat's house was again without Christmas decorations, though now the rooms seemed to spontaneously illumine. In the blink of an eye, with a few well-chosen sentences, Kyle had *done* it. He had won them over! The faces at the table glowed with delight. Kurban was going to learn Turkish! Of course it was all bullshit, Ayla knew. Her husband was about as likely to pick up their native tongue as he was one of the African click languages, but it almost didn't matter. What mattered was that he cared enough to lie (yes, she thought, you split such moral hairs when married to Kyle Clayton), and instead of engaging her father in his petty little war, he'd told them all exactly what they'd wanted to hear: that after a lifetime as Turks struggling with the language and culture of this country, of feeling frustrated and on the outside of everything, an American was going to take the time to learn *their* language for a change, meet *the Turks* halfway. Somehow Kyle had sensed this, Ayla thought, and it had been a brilliant, brilliant move.

Best of all for Ayla was seeing her father stifled. There was such talk and excitement about this glorious new development that the momentum of Murat's point was thoroughly diffused. No one seemed to remember what the old man had said, or indeed, that he had been talking at all.

Round two, Kyle thought, to the son-in-law.

But then Murat coughed into a handkerchief, and when Kyle looked over at him the old man caught his eye. There was an intimation from Murat then, a little smirk as if to say, *Clever little bastard, aren't you? Okay, your time will come.*

It was all far from over.

Donny Boy

"I don't want to go," complained Susan Westly.

"We have to go."

"We don't *have* to do anything, Don."

"There are responsibilities."

With Don Westly, of course, there always were.

He knew what they said about him. That he had come in on the coattails of Lonny Tumin. That his friend had been the ambitious one and taken him along for the ride. Everything was because of L. T.

It had always been this way. Even in the old days, back in Orange, New Jersey, where they were both outcasts in their own neighborhood and Lonny had looked out for him. It was Meecham Street, an Irish-Catholic enclave, and here were the Tumins, Jewish all the way, the black sheep. Two blocks over were the Westlys, half Jewish, half WASP, which turned out to be even worse. When the kids in the neighborhood discovered Don's father was a "Brit," they terrorized him to no end, some kind of payback for the struggle back in the "home country." When they grew bored of this angle, they reminded themselves that Don was a Jew.

Pure terror, ever since he could remember. Then he met Lonny.

They didn't meet until high school. On the first day of their freshman year, that very morning, Tumin announced himself. He was small for his age but fierce even then. Five minutes before the bell, everyone huddled in small groups in front of the school, smoking, the boys hissing expletives at girls, acting tough, and Tumin literally marches off the bus right up to a group of seven or eight Irish boys and demands a fight. *You,* he says, pointing to the biggest one. Don hears this and, along with the rest of the school, runs over to watch the Jew get his ass kicked.

The boy Tumin picked was two years older, a junior, and nearly six feet tall. He looked as if he could tear Tumin to bits, but Lonny already had his jacket off and was calmly rolling up his sleeves. Remarkably, the bigger kid didn't move. Don could see what he was thinking; it was what everyone was thinking: *Whoa, who the fuck's THIS guy?* It was Don's first taste of the genius of Lonny Tumin. The sense of initiative, the *audacity.* As a Jew in public school, Tumin knew he was going to get his ass handed to him anyway, so, his thinking went, you might as well take it to them, get it over with. If they didn't fight, then great, you showed you weren't scared and convinced them you had a reason not to be. If they called your bluff and whupped your ass, well, at least you got it out of the way and scored a few points for nerve.

By now there was a huge half-moon of students surrounding Lonny and his opponent. They wanted blood, of course. They wanted limbs bent back at absurd angles and clumps of hair on the dewy morning grass. They wanted to see the Jew get pummeled.

Then everyone looked on in astonishment as the older boy began to vacillate.

"*No?*" Tumin said, looking disappointed. His voice was booming, playing to the crowd. Even as a teenager, it commanded attention.

"It's too early," mumbled the Irish boy. "Maybe later."

"*Too early,*" Tumin said mockingly. "Well, pardon me." He turned to the next biggest kid in the crowd, a heavy boy, but solid and equally tough-looking. "How about you?" he said, but this boy made no reply at all. Tumin made a big show of frustration. "*Any-body . . .* ," he pleaded. "Please. I'm in the mood."

I'm in the mood. Genius, Don had thought. No one had ever heard anything like that in their lives. It had the power of an advertising jingle. *This Lonny Tumin, this crazy Jewish kid, he's in the mood!* Nobody fought Tumin that morning, and thus a legend was born.

About a month later, Don Westly was taking some abuse in the locker room at the end of gym class. Someone had him in a headlock, while others behind him kicked at his rump as if at a phlegmatic donkey. Two more still stood near Don's locker, tearing his books to ribbons. As usual, Don took it all with a minimum of resistance. This was nearly a daily occurrence, after all, and Don had always been of mild temperament. Basically he had learned to curl up like a turtle and wait until they got bored.

Tumin, meanwhile, was just coming in for the next period and was trying to ignore the situation. This kind of thing went on all the time, and anyway, Lonny Tumin wasn't the police. But then he heard one of the Irish kids say, "Half-breed." Looking over at the choking, pale-faced victim, Tumin knew right away what this meant — knew at least what *one* of the halves must be — and so this time he decided to act. Without prelude, and using one of the benches as a springboard, Tumin suddenly dove on the back of the boy who had Don's head, freeing his future friend from the grip. As they stumbled apart, Tumin found himself facing an attacker nearly six inches taller than him — but what he lacked in height, Lonny made up for with ferocity. Toe to toe, he suddenly spat in his opponent's face, an act that was as astonishing as it was blinding, and then came in kicking and flailing away, yelling wildly at the top of his lungs. Again, nobody had ever seen anything quite like this before. Don knew he should run but was too stunned to move, was spellbound by the actions of his maniacal protector. He heard some of the other boys talking of jumping in, but then someone recognized Tumin. *He's in the mood!* In just a few seconds, Lonny had already overcome the boy and had him under one of the benches, banging his head into the stanchions while at the same time kneeing the boy in his kidneys, scratching his face, pulling his hair, tearing at his earlobes, fighting dirty as he would all his life. Underneath Tumin's grip, the poor bully wailed in pain and terror.

Finally the gym coach arrived and dragged Tumin off the boy. It was like being freed from a wild animal. When he stood, the Irish kid's nose trickled blood where Tumin had bitten him.

Later, in the principal's office, Lonny, Don, and the unfortunate bully stood waiting, hair ruffled, their shirts in shreds. Don's attacker moaned and softly sobbed, the blood now seeping through the handkerchief he held to his face.

Tumin leaned over and told him in a whisper that if he thought this was painful, what was he going to do when they gave him the tetanus shot? Long needle right in the nose. *That,* he said, was really going to hurt. Then he turned to Don.

"What's your name?"

He was told.

"Donny Boy," Tumin said, shaking his hand. "You a Jew?"

Westly shrugged, not knowing what to say. His home life was mostly secular, but then he knew a savior when he saw one.

"Yeah," he said. "I guess."

Tumin seemed pleased. He turned back to the other boy. Blood was running down his wrist.

"We're Jews, by the way," he told him. "You'll be leaving us alone now."

It was the same with girls. By the middle of the school year, he and Don had become fast friends, and naturally, girls became an obsession. By anyone's account, Lonny Tumin was not a good-looking young man. Failing eyesight forced him into thick glasses by the age of sixteen, and this was topped off with a fairly severe case of acne that blew up on his face later that year.

It was a simple fact even Tumin himself couldn't escape. "Phew," he would say, catching his reflection in the hall's mirrored trophy cabinet, "I sure am one ugly son of a bitch." Don would laugh, unraveled by the naked honesty of the observation, but then Tumin seemed to take his looks in stride. "Doesn't matter, though," he said assuredly. "If you're a girl it matters. But not a guy. With us it's all about balls."

Biggest balls wins, Lonny would say. That was his motto. Another mantra you never forgot.

As it turned out, he was right about this too. Don watched as Lonny's ultraconfidence began to pay off with a number of impressive miniconquests, and he'd be damned if Tumin didn't lose his virginity at the beginning of his sophomore year to a very attractive brunette in their history class, one that Don himself had his eye on.

Despite the obvious clarity of Lonny's wisdom, Don had always been quite shy about meeting the opposite sex. He could speak up well enough once he was introduced, but he could not, for the life of him, initiate contact with a young lady. This is where Tumin came in. On Saturday night they would ride up and down Central Avenue in Tumin's car (Lonny already making good money working summers as a gopher on the commodities exchange). All Don had to say was "Look at that one," and Lonny was over there in a shot, zits and all, pulling up and introducing the both of them. He seemed to enjoy impressing Don; it was as if the whole thing was just too easy for him, and he'd really preferred seeing his friend happy.

More often than not, though, Don would have to pick from his friend's "leftovers," since Tumin seemed to be able to win over the best girls on sheer will alone. But for someone as shy as Don, these introductions were like a gift from the heavens.

Before you knew it, they were at the same college. Don had gone to the University of Delaware to study history but was having trouble meeting women, was lonely as sin, and so decided to join Tumin at Hofstra, where Lonny knew everybody and was cleaning up with the girls. Once ensconced, Don changed his major to business, just like Tumin. After college, Lonny became a star at the Bellum and Finch brokerage house, a midrange firm downtown. In two years he had single-handedly raised Bellum's annual gross by 33 percent, and so Don followed him there too. Tumin showed him everything, even cut him in on deals. Pretty soon the two of them were making more money than Don had ever dreamed of, though Tumin kept telling him, *We've just begun, Donny Boy. Just getting started.*

By 1979, Tumin had moved on to Drexel Burnham Lambert. He had got himself an apartment on Central Park West at an exclusive no-Jews building he'd raised holy hell to get in, and eventually he got Don in there as well. It was the cusp of a new decade, and they were getting rich. Lonny was arranging double dates for them with some of the best-looking girls in New York. Then he got married to his first wife, Elizabeth, and so now it was time for Don to get hitched.

Lonny took care of that too.

In the bedroom, Don watched his wife shake her head in disgust. In spite of her protests, she continued to dress, striding briskly through the walk-in closet, angrily swirling a silk scarf around her neck as she emerged.

"This is ludicrous, and you know it," Susan announced. She shook her hair out and took a slug from a bottle of mineral water atop her dresser. "This is the biggest fucking joke in our lives."

Yes, this was the price one paid to enjoy the good graces of Lonny Tumin. After that day in the principal's office at Orange High School, Don Westly had never admitted to Lonny his family's religious ambivalence. Don's father had been a lapsed Protestant, his mother a dispassionate Jew, and both were flabbergasted when young Don suddenly began showing an interest in the Talmudic faith during his first year of high school. He began asking for rides to the synagogue for certain services and events, for example, and at Christmas that year he'd asked for, and received, a necklace with the Jewish star on it.

In fact, ever since he was fifteen, Don Westly had been playing up what his wife, Susan, called the "Jew thing," and it had been very good to him indeed. But there were, as he'd said, responsibilities. For as long as he could remember, he'd done the Seder with Tumin — the man with whom he'd made financial history and might soon again — at his home. This year could be no different.

"He always tells you what to do," said his wife now. She sat down at her vanity; a Louis-the-something with red velvet and gold tassels whose cost could still inflame Don's ulcer. "You haven't had a thought of your own since you were an adolescent."

"That's ridiculous, Susan."

This Seder thing always put her in a nasty mood. The two-hour-plus drive from Upper Montclair, New Jersey, to Long Island's North Shore was not Susan's idea of a Sunday. Nor was she thrilled with the idea of spending the day in a house full of *real* Jews. She hailed from Columbia, South Carolina, a city where the Confederate flag was still raised above the county courthouse, and where her grandfather had indeed sat in a rocking chair on the front porch, explaining how all Jewish men had long cleft tails they kept hidden in their britches.

After some bad luck as a debutante in Columbia, Susan Belford had decided to head to New York, where there was no limit to the amount of rich men. She had envisioned herself as a less sentimental version of Holly Golightly, though in truth, she had none of the sanguine charm of that literary character. What she did have was a snappy figure, some well-hewn sexual talents, and, after some hard-knock experiences as a southern belle on the make, a shrewd eye for capturing what she wished to possess. In New York it had taken her less than two years to strike gold with Mr. Don Westly. With Don she'd obviously learned to move past her family prejudices, though with his fair hair, WASPy good looks, and, by that time, nearly $5 million in assets, her predilection was not exactly akin to a march on the Capitol. To this day, Don's Jewishness remained her least favorite thing about him. And despite all of his fine qualities, she would never have married him had she not observed that his religiosity tended to flare up only in close proximity to Lonny Tumin.

"Great," she continued now, "so I have to sit and talk to Diane Tumin all day and pretend she's not ten years younger than all the other wives and that we actually have something to *say* to one another."

"Once a year, Susan."

"And watch Lonny read from the cedar —"

"Seder."

"— and put on this big spiritual farce when we all know he's got twenty women set up in safe houses, like some secret agent, all over the tristate area."

Some fucking nerve, Don thought. Didn't she know that Lonny Tumin made her entire life possible? Did she think this all came without a price? Twenty-eight rooms and four-and-a-half acres in Upper Montclair, Palm Beach in the winter. You think you can have Palm Beach in the winter, Miss Columbia, and not get your knees a little dirty?

Tumin was his partner. For whatever reason, the Seder made the guy happy. What the hell was he supposed to do?

"Just for the record, Lonny mostly defers to me in matters of business."

"Oh, please." She sprayed some perfume on her throat that was so concentrated Don pushed his fist up against his nostrils.

"It's true," he said, thrusting the words through his fingers. "I'm like his conscience. He knows how impulsive he is, and so he doesn't make a move without asking me first. That, essentially, is my job. And I'm damned good at it."

He decided to move away from the perfume and by accident caught his wife's reflection in the mirror. She was getting harder, he could see. The afternoon light punctuated the rigid bones underneath the skin, the taut mouth. Were her lips actually getting thinner? he wondered. Was that even possible? As a young woman she'd been so feminine, so bright-eyed and quick to laugh. And much more erotic than anyone would have guessed. He still remembered clearly the first time they'd met, at one of Tumin's parties back in the early 1980s. Don was not a foot through the door when Susan's eyes were on him, zeroing in before he could even remove his coat. The room was lit by a series of ornate candelabra, and it took her just a few minutes to distract Don to a dark corner. With her already histrionic southern accent, amplified now by the champagne, she'd said what an honor it was to meet an actor of his stature, of his talent. *Excuse me?* Don had replied with a laugh. She'd pulled him a little closer, explaining how he didn't have to be coy with her, she'd just seen a film of his on television, *The Great Waldo Pepper*, yes, that was it. She'd just *adored* it, and what *was* Robert Redford doing at a Wall Street party anyhow?

Later, Tumin told him the comment was a line, a ruse to get in his pants — and, more likely, into his wallet. But Don had fallen for it; or at least half of it. All his life, everyone had been telling Don Westly how handsome he was, though no one could ever get him to believe it. Even then, in his thirties, he thought of it as just something people said to one another, a compulsory politeness, and so the words never had much traction with him. But being told he looked like an actor — Redford, no less! — this was something else entirely. It implied charisma and a certain American *cool*, neither of which Don Westly had ever been accused of having. *Quiet dignity* and the dreaded *nice* were the adjectives much more likely to be ascribed to him, though *boring*, he feared, was not far behind. He knew that women often found him dull, and despite his money and pleasant looks, this dullness had recently cost him a number of spectacular girlfriends.

So Susan Belford's comments had hit their mark. By midnight, she'd let him lure her out on to the balcony, where she artfully warmed her hands in his pants pockets as they looked out at the glittering skyline. In the weeks after, while they were dating, Susan never let him forget how much like Redford he really looked — all her girlfriends said so, he was assured — and almost immediately Don had begun to see himself in a different light. Had he lost weight? colleagues inquired at the office. A new haircut? Something about him seemed to have changed. Most of this, he knew, was simply the surge in confidence that comes with the enjoyment of great sex after a long drought (which had been Don's plight at the time), but then he was wearing his sideburns a little bushier and on weekends had taken to wearing a fancy pair of cowboy boots. One day, Tumin asked him if he suddenly thought he was the "fucking Sundance Kid," and Don stormed away, furious that he'd been found out.

By May he and Susan were married.

They'd had their good times. That next mad decade together, when Don had followed Lonny from Bellum and Finch to Drexel Burnham Lambert, and then on to their own company, Triad, had indeed been fun. He and Susan were having an absolute blast being rich; it was like a fever they'd both caught, and they'd passed so many hours contriving how to spend it all and save it and make it grow that they hadn't had time to generate any of the normal animosities. Things were going too well for them, moving too fast for friction.

But by the mid-nineties, thanks in part to Tumin's tech aversion, Triad had started to level off. The Westlys woke up one day to find that not only were they no longer the richest family in Upper Montclair, but that there was actually less money coming *in* than going *out*, a phenomenon that, by the middle nineties, seemed almost an impossibility — what Susan, in one of her bitchy moods, called "a special talent." Despite the criticism, she herself refused to cut back. She'd insisted on trading up on the Palm Beach house, and then there were the paid vacations and new cars every Christmas for her friends and relatives back in South Carolina. Don had tried everything to stop this foolishness, but then suddenly, out of nowhere it seemed, Susan began to exhibit a treacherous guile, a way of asserting power that would make even a Lonny Tumin blush. Don felt blindsided. What had happened? he wanted to know. Overnight his wife had gone from naive southern coquette to manipulative shrew, threatening to divorce him, to take the homes and kids away, the force applied tactfully and with a surgical cut. And there seemed to be no end in sight.

"Lonny doesn't like having you around because you pretend to be Jewish, okay, honey?" Susan continued. "You can forget that once and for all. He likes you for just the opposite reason."

Don murmured wanly; he'd heard this time and time again.

"No, really. What he likes is your whole silver-haired, country-club thing. It's the way you carry yourself. You have this aura of WASP respectability, Don, and you've always been very handsome. Lonny, meanwhile . . . Well, let's face it, Lonny looks like a bug. You're like his better half. He parades you around like a trophy wife. The Jewish thing is just a bonus to him."

"There you go again, Susan. That old Gamecock anti-Semitism."

"You know I think Jews are perfectly nice people, Don . . . ," she replied, as if to commence a long treatise on the matter, only to quickly run out of concrete data. "Oh, and I love this idea that you think you guys are partners. That's a laugh. *Triad.*" As if to cover up the stink of this word, she opened her blouse and ran a deodorant under her arms. "My ass. How about 'Numero Uno'? Now you're talking."

Here was another thing she was bitter about, the fact that the Tumins had twenty times as much money as they did. She seemed to resent that Don was perfectly comfortable in his advisory position (and often cut out of the biggest deals), was pissed that when all was said and done, he'd rather be golfing, or dining with the Hollywood and publishing moguls who frequented City.

Suddenly they could hear the kids running up the stairs. There was Alison, fourteen, and Gregory, eleven. They had an idea, it was announced. Standing in the doorway, Gregory nudged his sister, having determined that Alison was simply irresistible today in her robin's-egg-blue dress. She came up and sat on Daddy's lap, throwing her arm around his shoulder.

"Oh, boy, this is going to be a doozy," Don murmured with a broad smile. Gregory had been right; with Alison's gesture, there was nothing he wasn't prepared to give them. A pony would be here by Monday morning. Ditto a dog. How was it that they'd never asked for a dog? "What's up?" he asked.

"Greg and I have decided that we'll give up our allowance this week if we don't have to go to Lonny's house."

Don grimaced; it was a quick kick to the shins. His daughter and son, ready to give up their beloved allowance — their absurd, overly inflated allowance — just to stay home!

They'd asked for perhaps the one thing in this world he could not give them.

"Oh, *please*," Alison cooed, sensing defeat. "Eunice is here doing the garden, and I promise I'll keep an eye on Greg. Please, please, please!"

"You're going," he answered firmly.

There was a double-barreled moan from daughter and son. Alison immediately took her arm from around her father's neck and retreated back to Greg, who stamped his foot as if to put out an ember on the carpet. They could hear the driver beeping his horn outside.

"You're both going, and that's *it*." Amid further mumbled protestations, Don pointed to the stairs. "Go to the car now and tell the driver we'll be right down . . . *Go*."

Heads hanging limply, the children exited. Don looked over at his wife, waiting for the celebration, for the victorious glint in her eye. *They'd give up their allowance!* Instead, she offered only a smug shrug of the shoulders.

There she is, Don said to himself, take a good look: Susan Belford, of the Columbia Belfords, his dearly beloved. So, she hated him now, did she? Well, so be it, he thought. He did the math in his head, trying to figure out how many years it had been since *he'd* loved her, and then was only mildly shocked to discover it might have been as long as a decade. She would have divorced him long ago, he knew, except that she could never learn to live with half of what they had. Susan had enough trouble with the whole, never mind the half.

"Oh, well, I guess we're going," she said. She reached into the open bowl of Vicodin she kept on her dresser, the one in which she used to keep the Starbursts. Casually, she tossed two in her mouth, chasing them with a slug of mineral water. Then she removed the spherical pill organizer she kept in her handbag and reloaded.

"Ain't it funny," Susan said then, quickly applying her lipstick in the mirror.

"Funny?"

She stood up, still looking at her reflection. "I thought I was marrying Robert Redford. I know you don't believe that, Don, but I really did. And instead I end up with, I don't know . . ." — her eyes darted around, searching for a name — "Jerry Rothstein."

"Who's Jerry Rothstein?"

She didn't answer. The driver beeped again.

"Well, off to the Tumins', I guess," Susan pronounced. She grabbed her pocketbook and then pounded her chest a little to help the pills go down. "Happy, happy, happy."

A Rake's Progress

Sometimes during sex, when Kyle was off on some erotic verbal riff, some devilish spoken-word gem, Ayla would look up, or back, or down at him with a smirk of disbelief, momentarily breaking character, telling him he was absolutely *the* sickest man she had ever met. High praise indeed.

Or sometimes Kyle would see her on the street by accident, Lafayette or lower Broadway, a sudden flash of sharp cheekbone and lithe frame would catch his eye, and investigating further (as always), he would suddenly come face to face with his wife. And the serendipity of the moment would wash over them both, the freshness of context making everything new again and reminding them of just how lucky they were, partners out in the crowded street, in love. A team, and doubly strong now against the mad, mad world.

So tonight, naturally, Kyle Clayton found himself outside the stage door of a ninety-nine-seat theater on the Lower East Side, waiting around like some sad groupie for Erin Wyatt to emerge.

The route here had been circuitous. His wife had been inundated with work at the Web design firm. The jobs were piling up, and you didn't dare turn away any work these days. Who knew how long it would last. Tonight, for example, Ayla had come home at 5:00 for a quick bite to eat and a power nap, then was back at the office on Greene Street by 6:30. Could be an all-nighter, she'd said.

Kyle, seeing the best opportunity in months, put on a good shirt and hightailed it up to City.

A mob scene. He fought his way to a seat at the bar. There he ordered a twenty-dollar hamburger and a glass of red wine, a stalling tactic in the search for the waitress of his dreams.

When after fifteen minutes or so he didn't see her, he held his stem glass under the bar and called Abu over for the lowdown.

"You want to see Miss Erin?"

"Yeah. She upstairs tonight?"

Abu raised an eyebrow. "What you want with her, Kurban?"

"We're old friends."

Kyle was surprised how well the fib went over. Abu's face grew warmer as he nodded. "I know," he said, "we talk about you last time you were here."

Ah, thought Kyle, just as I'd suspected.

"She's not here, though. She has an . . . *action* tonight."

"Huh?" Kyle suddenly felt a spell of nausea. "Action? You mean like a date?"

"No, no," the waiter answered, smiling. He took from his pocket a small flyer, which, Kyle found upon inspection, invited people to the Beaux Arts Theater on Essex Street for a performance of *Shakespeare's Titus Andronicus: The Butchered Version.*

An actress? This was a surprise, Kyle thought. Had his sodden memory forgotten that too, or had he just never cared enough to ask? In any event, he checked his watch: it was just seven-fifteen. Grabbing a cab, he could easily be on the Lower East Side for the eight o'clock show.

"Thank you, Abu," he said. Kyle was about to stick the flyer in his blazer for the address, until a hand sprang to snatch it back.

"No, no," the waiter rebuked, pulling the sheet of paper dearly to his breast. "This one is mine."

Just then, an older woman wearing a choker with pearls the size of Ping-Pong balls tapped Abu firmly on his shoulder.

"Bathroom," she snapped, with no further communication.

"No, *waiter,*" Abu said, pointing to himself. "Bathroom is down the hall to your right."

"Nice," Kyle said when the woman was gone. He gave the Bengali man a discreet low five.

Abu then looked down at his other palm, reading from his precious flyer. "Dirty-two Essex Street," he said. "And Kurban."

"Yes?" he said.

"Be good to my Miss Erin."

The Beaux Arts Theater was all too familiar to Erin Wyatt, and just where the *beaux* came in she'd always wanted to know. Basically it was a large room with metal folding chairs lined along a declivity of tiered flooring, and a ceiling full of loose wires and lighting fixtures that hinted at inspection payoffs. There was a little card-table bar in the lobby, where each night a different cast member would work until show time and then again at intermission. After the performance, another actor cleaned out the toilets and threw away the syringes.

Home sweet home. Erin had done quite a few shows here over the years. It had seemed quite romantic in the beginning. Downtown guerrilla theater! Cultural grenade aimed at Times Square and bourgeois Broadway! Now she'd give a row of teeth for Broadway.

As for the cast and crew of this *Titus,* they were the usual collection of clowns. There was Roden, the Marxist director with his grandiose dreams of a new "progressive" theater that he and he alone would bring to the masses. Silly Julianne, who'd never been on the stage before and was always late for rehearsals — those damned Weehawken buses! — playing Lavinia because no one else had auditioned for it. Motorcycle Johnny, who was actually quite good as Saturninus when he wasn't completely strung out, which turned out to be less than half the time. (His plan to actually shoot up on stage was deemed both ingenious and genuinely progressive by Roden, but the idea was nixed by the "Fascist" theater owner.) And then Titus, as played by the inimitable J. D. Magee, local bartender pushing fifty who had actually done a "deuce" at Rahway State years ago for armed robbery. At their first off-book read for an audience, J. D. was so enraged when he forgot a line that he suddenly turned and put his heavily tattooed forearm through a Sheetrock partition — so now

every cast member was fixed with a permanent grimace when Titus
was on stage, praying for J. D. to make it through his scene without
error.

Not to mention Erin Wyatt as Tamora, Queen of the Goths. *Erin's
credits include:* a Huggies diaper commercial; one line as a nurse on
General Hospital ("Case of amnesia, doctor?"); and countless Beaux
Arts productions, including the "classic" drag version of *Cat on a Hot
Tin Roof,* which included the 250-pound African-American transvestite
Flotilla DeBarge as Maggie the Cat.

In this glorious version of *Titus,* Shakespeare's bloodiest play,
Roden had switched the setting from Imperial Rome to a contemporary butcher shop. The characters all wore butcher's aprons and used
meat cleavers for their ghastly deeds. The production's costliest prop
was the buckets of fake blood Roden had secured by the drumful, the
better to awash each performance in what he called the "dialectical
effluence of ancient white-male bloodlust." In the mimeographed production flyers, however, it was Motorcycle Johnny who was credited
as "chief plasma consultant," he of the great erudition in matters such
as flesh punctures and blood viscosity.

Erin had sworn that she was done with this sort of thing, but
Helena's criticisms had piqued her. Reluctantly she'd bought a copy of
Backstage and noticed the casting call and, unable to think of an
excuse, had gone ahead and auditioned for *Titus.* She wouldn't get it,
of course, she was sure. God forbid! But it would be good to audition
again, to break up the creative inertia that had engulfed her.

Huge mistake, as it turned out. She'd been cast and now couldn't
wait for it to be over, this ten-day run with a band of freaks. Here they
were, just two performances to go, and her half-assed manager was
still a no-show. There hadn't been any reviews yet either, though they
were waiting on someone from the *Village Voice.* And there was certainly no sign of any talent scouts or producers. Erin couldn't help
thinking about all the shifts she'd given away at City, the money it
was costing her to play opposite the likes of J. D. Magee, whose previous experience was limited to the penitentiary stage — Genet, of
course.

On with the show! During the scene in which Lavinia is attacked
by Tamora's sons, the actress Julianne would often become genuinely
terrified — surrounded, as she was, by drug addicts and ex-cons

wielding real meat cleavers — this prompting her to forget her awful English accent and leaving only her rich Bayonneese to fill the air. Tonight, as Lavinia urged her attackers to kill her after being raped, Erin visibly winced as Julianne pronounced, "Tez present *debt* I beg, and one thing *maw.*" J. D. mishandled the blood-filled water pistol attached to the handle of his cleaver while chopping up Tamora and ended up dousing the entire first row, including the theater critic from the *Village Voice,* who had finally appeared. Afterward, when J. D. apologized to Roden, the director seemed resigned: How could an interpretation of *Titus* so ahead of its time ever expect a good review from a Fascist publication like the *Voice* in the first place?

Finally it was over. The audience lent the production a round of applause that seemed born more of relief than gratitude, then quickly filed out. Then the cast grabbed their mops and began the nightly task of swabbing the blood from the stage floor. This completed, Johnny and J. D. stole a few beers from the bar and offered one to Erin; they were going to a bar across the street to get hammered until roughly noon tomorrow, did she want to come? Erin was tempted to explain how she'd rather inject lye into her corneas with one of the bathroom's dirty needles, but instead offered that she was tired. Then she threw on her jean jacket and ran out the side door to find Kyle Clayton waiting for her.

"The hell are *you* doing here?" Erin asked.

Her first thought was that he was banging Julianne — twenty-one and nobody home, that was about Kyle Clayton's speed. Then Erin remembered that he was married.

Then she remembered that his name was Kyle Clayton and so he was probably banging Julianne.

"She'll be out in a minute," she said, lifting her backpack and glancing at the stage door.

"Excuse me?"

"Julianne. She's almost done."

He laughed. "No, no. I'm here to see *you.*"

"Me?"

"Yes, of course."

"What for?"

"Well, I . . ." He looked around.

He was fumbling, somehow surprised by the brusque greeting. What the hell had he expected, she thought, strings and a brass section? The last time they'd met he hadn't even remembered her name.

"A while back . . . I had lunch at City."

"I recall, yes. Congratulations."

"And so I didn't recognize you, Erin Wya*tt*," he said, emphasizing the last consonants with ham-handed sincerity, "and it was very, very rude. I wanted to make it up to you with a beer."

"A beer?"

"Sure, why not?"

Erin laughed a little and took a half-step back on the street, adjusting her pack. She suddenly looked concerned.

"How did you find me?"

"I was at the restaurant tonight, having dinner at the bar," he said. "Abu told me about the show. He seemed very excited for you."

"That's nice." Note to self, she thought: *Kill* Abu next time you see him.

"How about that beer?"

"Oh, I don't think so."

"Why?"

"Well, Kyle, you see, the last time I agreed to have a beer with you we spent the next three weeks in my bed, until you mysteriously disappeared." Right away she saw him reaching for the excuse he'd prepared for this very moment, but she bowled right over him. "Secondly, I understand that you are, at the moment, very married."

"I think you're misunderstanding me."

"Am I?"

"Yes," he replied. "You see, I have this agreement with my wife."

Now Erin was smiling again. My lord, she thought, he didn't think I was going to fall for *that* one. He really did need to be introduced to Julianne.

Kyle continued, "The agreement goes that I'm allowed to have a beer with another human being exactly once a year. This includes the female persuasion. One beer and then go home. My wife's very understanding, very modern in this respect."

Erin tried to conceal a grin. All right, she conceded, that was a little better. She was still convinced this whole thing was some perverse pickup attempt, but at least he was trying to be original. Suddenly she was actually leaning toward going. Wasn't this whole thing just bizarre enough to be interesting?

Besides, her apartment had been a little quiet lately. What were her options? A few SnackWell's and another rerun of *Change of Heart*?

"One beer, huh?"

"That's it."

Erin narrowed her eyes at him. "When was the last time you had one beer?" she asked. "I'm guessing, what, the late seventies?"

Suddenly he looked sheepish. "Yeah, well . . ."

"Yeah, you know, that whole drunken, depraved, slithering-through-the-gutters-at-dawn thing you have down so well."

"Actually, I don't do that anymore."

"Oh, just like that, huh? What happened?"

"Got married," he said. "Got *old*."

"I see. So you're a good boy now."

"Oh, yes, absolutely."

"Amazing turnaround."

"Isn't it?"

"Stunning, really."

Strangely, he began pointing to his head. Erin looked baffled.

"You mean you can't see it?" His eyes were searching above him now, his face deadpan. "The halo," he said.

Erin grinned openly. "Oh, yes," she answered, narrowing her eyes as if finally noticing it. "Except . . . Hmm, *that's* odd."

"What?" Kyle asked.

"Yours seems to be upside down."

They found a dive down the block, some no-frills temple of drinking Kyle remembered from the old days. They got a couple of pints of something amber from the bar and headed to a heavily scarred wooden table in back. It took a few moments for somebody to say something.

"Well, this is weird," Erin offered, lighting a cigarette.

"Is it?"

"Sure. I promised myself I'd never say a civil word to you again."

Kyle was about to apologize once more, but Erin waved her hand.

"Forget it. I'm a big girl. Besides, your days in my life were numbered anyway. Too much chaos, even for me."

"So I've heard."

She blew out some smoke, narrowing her eyes again. "You mean you don't think you were?"

"No, no, I was. I definitely was out of control." He paused. "It's just that there's quite a bit I don't remember from those years."

"Selective memory." She sipped her beer. "I don't blame you."

"No, I mean blackouts."

Erin looked at him with a mixture of suspicion and sympathy.

"No, really," he continued. "There's actually large chunks of time that are completely lost to me. In fact, that's why I didn't recognize you right away."

Erin was wondering if this was some poor attempt at an excuse, some fib so far-out she'd have no choice but to believe it. But then she remembered Kyle on one of his binges. Ludicrous amounts of alcohol. *Baroque* amounts. Actors were not exactly on the public temperance committee, but this was like nothing she'd ever seen before. If blackouts were real, Kyle Clayton would have had them.

"How about that night at the restaurant?" she asked curiously. "Remember our big date?"

He looked at her blankly. "Restaurant?"

Erin sat back with a grin, measuring him. "Well, that's good," she said. "If you're going to forget things, this was the one."

It was supposed to have been their first real date together, she told him; up until then they'd rarely traveled beyond the four posts of her studio bed. Of course, Erin was apprehensive about going out. His reputation preceded him, and even in her apartment he could get pretty wild when he was bombed. But they put on some good clothes and cabbed it up to some swanky place on Park Avenue South that was all the rage. They had a reservation, but the restaurant was mobbed and overbooked, and so they were forced to wait at the bar.

Kyle looked now as if he could see what was coming. "Waiting at the bar, not good," he said. "How long?"

"'Bout an hour."

He nodded solemnly.

Finally they were seated. He was quite charming at first, Erin told

him. He'd had the waitress laughing and then some other writer she'd
never heard of came over and patted him on the back, saying he liked
Kyle's work, that he'd got a bad rap, etc. He bought Kyle a drink, and
then so did another couple who'd recognized him. It was all a big
hoot until about the sixth martini or so, before they'd even had their
appetizer. Despite her warnings, he'd been rocking on the hind legs of
the chair, and so of course he lost his balance and, as she shrieked,
tumbled over backward. *Crack!* This was in the middle of the dining
room, and so now there were piercing screams and people jumping up
from their seats. A manager rushed over, but it was too late for Kyle.
He was down; he was *out.* A pool of what looked like black blood
grew out around him on the floor. Erin had wondered seriously if he
might be dead.

"They splashed some water on your face, but you didn't move. I
could see then you were breathing, but none of the other customers
could. I remember some woman crying hysterically."

Kyle rested his forehead against the rim of his pint glass.

"Then the ambulance comes," she continued. "They bring in a
gurney to wheel you out, and of course now I'm furious. I'm totally
embarrassed, not to mention starving, and I have half a mind to stay
there and eat my meal *and* yours. But of course I stayed with you.
And then . . ." She started to laugh a little. "This is the funny part."

"Great," he said.

"They finally wheel you through the door, and there's all these
people outside waiting to get into the restaurant. They're all looking
down at you in horror; they don't know what to think. Then a blast
of fresh air must've hit you or something, because your eyes suddenly
opened." Now Erin couldn't help it; she started to laugh in earnest.
"And, finally, for some reason — I don't even know how you had the
wherewithal to do it — you suddenly looked up at these people, most
of whom think you're dead, and with your ghostly pallor, you say,
'Kindly eschew the oysters.'"

Kyle let his head drop and covered his eyes, mortified, while Erin
slapped the table and cackled.

"I tell that story all the time," she said.

Kyle looked around and remembered a similar incident from a
few years ago, when he was found outside this very bar lying in the
street. It was a beautiful spring morning apparently (the details were

explained to him later), people on their way to work, children on their way to school, and everyone stepping over him as if he were an old bum. Leaving the bar at dawn, he must have lost his balance and smacked his head on the curb. He woke up in St. Vincent's Hospital a day later to a bad concussion and a $3,500 dental bill. That's when he began rethinking the whole lifestyle, started seriously considering cutting back a bit. But just like all the other times, the thinking was about as far as it ever went, and it seemed in the end that nothing would ever change.

It was shortly after this he'd met Ayla, and the long, sad party that had become his life slowly began to dissolve.

"Now that I think of it," she said, "it was the last time I saw you."

He didn't know what to say. There was another extended silence. Erin lit another cigarette and offered one to Kyle, who declined.

"You know what I do remember?" he remarked after a while. It was time to move away from tales of his past debaucheries. "Your aunt's book. The one about God."

She brought her glass to the table with an extra thud. "I told you about that?" she asked. "Boy, you remember the damnedest things."

"You kidding? A writer never forgets a story like that." He sipped his ale. "How long did you say she's been at it?"

Erin took another puff of her cigarette. "Thirty years," she said ruefully.

"Well, you've got to admire the ambition."

"I'm not sure there's much else to it."

He decided not to follow through on the implication. "Well, tell her to keep going," he said. "That's the secret to writing, you know, grinding it out. The dull repetition, year after year after year . . . Whereas sex, of course, is a completely different animal."

She gave him an eyebrow, the one of theatrical heights, just to let him know she recognized the segue and thought it was lame.

"Why, *marriage* sex isn't any good?" she asked, jabbing back.

He shrugged, trying to slough off the question.

"No, c'mon," Erin continued, "now *this* is an interesting topic." She leaned forward on the table, the idea seeming to stimulate her. "Tell me about marriage sex, Kyle. I'd really like to know. Does it suck? Or maybe it *doesn't* suck, which is a whole other problem."

"No," he said, after a short hesitation. "It's good, actually." Did he dare tell her this? "Sometimes it's even pretty great."

"Really," she said. "So, what am I doing here?"

The directness of this again tied Kyle's tongue.

"I mean, you did invite me here to get in my pants, didn't you, Kyle Clayton?"

Slowly, he raised his eyes to meet hers. "Yes," he said.

"So, what is it then? Things are great at home, but you have to have your *variety,* is that it? You've got to be a *man?*" She said the word *man* as if it were a hideous skin condition. "Your wife's got big tits and you miss the little ones, or she has a small ass and you want a big one now, like mine — which is getting larger by the year, by the way; you probably wouldn't even recognize it. I mean, this is just the way men *are,* right? We're supposed to just accept this."

"No," he said.

"No?"

He reconsidered. "Well, yes, some men are like that."

"Ah, but not you," she said, punctuating this with a drag of her cigarette.

Once again he was tongue-tied. Precious momentum, he knew, was being lost. He needed to regroup, spark a late rally. At the same time, he tried to remind himself the valuable lesson he'd learned over the last ten minutes: that if he was going to let the bullshit fly, it would have to be of a pretty high caliber to get past the likes of Erin Wyatt.

He took a long sip of beer, hoping it might lubricate something. Didn't it always used to?

"Not me," he said. "Not in this particular case."

"Well, what is it then?"

He pushed his hands down on his chair, laughing nervously. "Is this really what we want to be talking about right now?"

"Why not? This is an interesting conversation about complex adult subject matter. And don't think for a minute I don't sympathize."

He looked surprised, hoping for her to continue.

"Oh, I do, Kyle. Absolutely. You think the idea of having sex with the same person for thirty, forty, *fifty* years is any more appealing to women than it is to men? You think your *wife* is looking forward to that same sad old penis staring back at her for decades?" Again, the eyebrow. "It's problematic. I mean, I sympathize with your stab at getting in my pants tonight. I've decided to be flattered. I don't really think you're a scumbag at all."

Now Kyle was completely off-balance. Was this cause for hope, or was she mocking him?

"What is it you miss the most about new women?" she asked. She sipped her beer and then dragged at her cigarette again, trying to feign clinical disinterest. "The adventure of it? Is that it? The mystery of a new person? Yeah, that's part of it, right? What will her apartment look like? you wonder. What will she look like naked? Will she do *this* for me, will she do *that?* Not so much the fucking. Not the *mechanics.* There's knowledge there. That's what you're after, don't you think? And, of course, the ego boost. You're famous, after all — or were. You're used to being told how wonderful you are."

Kyle squirmed a little, wondering if her last little remark might have landed dangerously close to some truth. Yes, the ego had taken quite a beating in the past years, hadn't it? He missed the great attention that had come with his debut, there was no use denying it, and he acknowledged that its trappings had left him with some nasty habits. He thought it practically shameful to see how even as his celebrity had waned, women had let him trade on it for sex so easily. In fact, even more than the drinking, he'd used sex over the years to mollify his growing disappointment in himself.

So what was he to do now? He had disbanded a small harem to marry Ayla, but on those nights when the ghosts of failure came spooking around, and Mr. Nightcap proved no tonic, he hadn't known where to turn. Not until now.

"Touché," he told her, remembering what he thought was her weakness for compliments, "brilliant. So you want to go to bed?"

Erin leaned back, fishing for something in her bag. "Not tonight," she retorted. She stood and threw some money down on the table, enough for both of them, then drained the last of her pint. Kyle felt a wave of disappointment rise through him from his waist.

That, he recalled, is when you know it's not happening. When they put down their own money.

"Why not?"

"One beer, you said, remember?" Erin hoisted the backpack onto her shoulder. "Anyway, thanks for an interesting night. A little strange, but interesting. Better than the play, if you ask me."

She got a few steps before Kyle called out to her.

"You were good, by the way," he said, cashing in his last chip. "I meant to tell you that."

"Thanks," she said. She kept going.

He watched Erin move toward the door, her walk a Levi's sway that made him want to weep. Then he went to the bar to grab a stool and ran into Mr. Nightcap. As they talked, Kyle revealed that Ayla wasn't due home until morning, and so the two of them began to go over old times with a singular enthusiasm.

Mr. Ohka

Of the many cultural curiosities of the era, none was perhaps more pervading than the trend of "Less is more," which inspired business-people to rarefy the presentation of their venture, or even themselves, to the point of absurdity. Take lunch at City, for example, where people ordered in inverse proportion to their ambition and power. *Still water with dandelion greens*. It sounded like something hanging in the Met, but beware the person who ordered such a meal: he / she wanted your money, your business, your job, your wife, your husband, your children, your cock, your cunt, your *soul*. That order had its own voice, saying, in effect, *I'm distracted by nothing but the task at hand. I'm all business, fucker.*

So it was in these days that a trendy shoe store named Shoe arose in Kyle's neighborhood. A bicycle shop named Ride. A Thai restaurant named Rice. (A local handbag purveyor called In the Bag had recently closed, apparently done in by prolixity.)

And so it was with City. Tumin had wanted to call it Food, but that was already taken. Steak? he'd asked. Taken. Eat? Taken. Lunch?

Ditto. *Ditto?* queried Tumin in furious exasperation, but then Barnett sheepishly volunteered that it was the name of a copy shop in his Chelsea neighborhood. Fuck! Tumin had exclaimed, which was in fact an East Village clothier, but nobody was saying a thing.

City it was.

Business might have been a more apt alternative. If New York was the epicenter of the financial universe, and City the restaurant of the moment, was it too much to propose that a great deal of the world's commerce was stoked behind City's doors? Inside the private rooms, for example, it was big-time business nearly *all* of the time. These were the playhouses of the major investment firms, the sandboxes of the rich and powerful, but before they played, they did business. Decisions were made here between the hours of twelve and three in the afternoon, and then again between six and ten at night, that would shake the world by its collar by the following morning. In fact, had Erin Wyatt the least bit of interest in money matters — her own 401(k), for example, or an on-line portfolio, such as Abu maintained to great success — she might have parlayed a modest server's salary into a small fortune. The things she heard in those rooms!

But she was theater trained, obsessed with the graceful parlance of Shakespeare and Tennessee Williams, and so the clunky argot of business talk fell on her ears like a hatchet. So arch, she thought, so *vulgar.* Meaningless euphemisms like *synergy, proactive,* and *methodologies.* The words of nothing-speak, a vain verbal adornment akin to putting salt on your Big Mac. Much like lawyers, these techies and investment übermen had invented a language designed to keep all "others" away, a clandestine patois that would ensure a usefulness, which was clearly slipping now with the advent of home trading and the abundance of financial information available on the Net. Yet even through all the muck, Erin did often overhear remarkable things in those rooms, alarming caveats and insider tips that might have netted her thousands of dollars by the next morning if she'd just go home and open up a damn E*Trade account. And there were plenty of moments, in those almost daily flights of despair, when she promised herself she would.

But then the speaker would launch into one of his or her *A Clockwork Orange* droog monologues, minus the poetry, of course: *The unprecedented execution challenges to Internet invention and YTD performance prioritization rely heavily, of course, on the mainstream global adoption of consumers and businesses, notwithstanding the P/Es and / or EBITDA multiples as the L-sector matures . . .* And so Erin's ears would just shut down, and she'd think, Screw it, I'd rather stay a cranky, impoverished waitress than absorb a syllable of this mechanistic horseshit! — a conclusion that was, of course, a *mendacious growth model,* not to mention a *zero-sum game.*

Erin had to hand it to Tumin on this front; he banned all such techie-speak and all other new-business verbiage from his meetings. If a client began speaking in war terms, for example, "Supreme excellence, it's been said, Lonny, would be breaking the enemy's resistance *without* fighting," Tumin would cut him or her to the quick: "Okay, so somebody gave you a copy of *The Art of War* at a closing dinner, and you actually read a few pages. Congratu-fucking-lations. Now talk to me like a human being." And then Erin would have to gnaw on a knuckle to keep from laughing.

But today Erin wasn't gleaning any yucks from Mr. Tumin. This afternoon she was hearing things (invisible, as ever, the little monkey) that shocked and amazed her.

It was Lonny and the tiny Asian man, speaking in direct, plain language, saying things that blew her mind.

Don Westly followed the slinky Asian hostess up the stairs, trying not to be impressed by the way her shoes' vinyl straps bound the pearly-white ankles. She informed him that Mr. Tumin was in the Humidor Room today, which he knew could only mean one thing: Mr. Ohka was in the house. All important meetings were conducted in the Airplane Room, but then who could blame Mr. Ohka if he preferred to do business somewhere other than among the B-29s headed toward Okinawa?

On the second-floor landing, Don pulled out a roll of bills the size of one of the restaurant's mountainous hamburgers and, for no particular reason, handed the hostess a fifty — a habit that never failed to infuriate his wife. Nearing the Humidor Room, he encountered Leon, the hulking bodyguard known for his garish sartorial sense. Tumin had a rotation of three men he kept for protection, though as far as Don Westly was concerned, Leon was the only one with any pizzazz. Despite Tumin's protests, the man favored loose suits of bright, primary colors — like the rappers and NBA stars that were his heroes — and instead of the ubiquitous .9-millimeter handgun, Leon carried the cannonlike .357 Magnum, à la Dirty Harry. Sunglasses, of course, were a constant. Today it was so dark in the hall that Leon lowered his shades to identify Don.

"Mr. Ohka, I presume?" Don asked, tilting his head toward the door. The blinds were drawn.

Leon held up a hand and shook it. "Hey, I'm not trying to hear any names around here. Know what I'm saying?"

"Smart man."

Don knew a little secret — one of the blinds had a segment broken off the end that left a sizable peephole. He looked in and saw just what he'd expected: Tumin and Mr. Ohka, tête-à-tête, the guest with his back to the windows. But with his sixth sense, Tumin looked up, his eyes flashing anger at his inquisitive partner. Then, before Don could pull away, Mr. Ohka doubled the favor by turning and offering him a barely suppressed sneer.

Feeling somewhat ill-treated, Don turned to the bodyguard. "Seems I'm not invited to the party," he said with a sour smile.

"They barely let the waitress in there," Leon informed him, trying to stifle the man's embarrassment. He knew Don was always good for one large, unnecessary tip, and so the bodyguard wanted him in a good mood. "What they got goin' on in there anyway? Nuclear weapons?"

Don's look of alarm was only half in jest. "Hey, don't give these guys any ideas."

He hit Leon with a wanton fifty, then headed down the hall to the main cigar lounge. The room was delightfully unoccupied now in the late afternoon, and Don seized the opportunity to plop himself into one of the antique club chairs. When Erin appeared, he ordered a beer and then, almost as an afterthought, requested a Cuban cigar from Tumin's special stash. Yes, he thought, why the hell not?

Turning on the TV, he was pleased to find Tiger Woods teeing off at the Kemper Open; he let his eyes study the man's backstroke off the tee while he concerned his mind with the mysterious Mr. Ohka. What did he know of him? They'd met only twice, though Tumin had been doing business with him now for nearly six months. A small man. Bowl haircut and silver horn-rimmed glasses bound tight against an expansive face. Mr. Ohka from Japan, who did not particularly know how to dress and never ordered a drink. He and Tumin were working on a project together, and very, very privately, for the details were obscured even from Don. All he knew was what he had gleaned from Acquisitions: that Triad had just purchased a subpar software company called Monarch, which was to be overhauled and taken public as soon as possible, Tumin's first taste of tech. Mr. Ohka was in charge of rounding up investors. He had associates, "friends" was how Lonny described them, in the places that Triad did not: Tokyo, Hong Kong, Jakarta, Manila, etc. Venture capitalists, all mad for American IPOs. Mr. Ohka "brought people together," knew how to "make the numbers work for us" — meaning, of course, that he'd figured out how to lie more creatively than anyone currently employed at Triad.

Neither Don nor Rob Barnett was privy to these meetings. "What the hell do you two know about software?" Tumin had bellowed when Don and Rob had the temerity to challenge their exclusion. Barnett happened to know a great deal, and either of them could've turned the question back on Tumin, but Don knew it would do no good to remind Tumin of his own ignorance; his boss was obviously putting his fears about tech behind him. What, Tumin had finally concluded, had he known about cola formulas or the gadgetry of vending machines? Of strip malls and restaurants? Buying a software company wasn't about double-clicking or packet switching, or even copyright law, he'd decided; it was about vision, about brains and balls, about *business* — and nobody was going to outdo Lonny Tumin on those fronts. He was going to show these young bastards, once and for all. He would teach them how L. T. did it *old school.*

There was a story that Don sometimes told in discreet company, the one about Tumin meeting Bill Gates. The software mogul was having dinner at City one night, in the Humidor Room; Lonny had heard about it and had decided to stop in and say hello. They'd never met before, but Gates knew who Tumin was, of course, had even been quoted somewhere lamenting that the head of Triad had fallen on hard times. In fact, he'd said publicly that Tumin was one of his heroes of the eighties, a "model of the form." So when Gates learned that his old hero wanted to come up and say hello, naturally he agreed.

Don decided to wait outside but made sure to watch through the glass as the two stepped up to greet each other. Who could miss this? Gates had three guests with him for dinner, and everyone in the room was up on his or her feet, beaming, to witness the historic event. After a few minutes of pleasant chatter, Don noticed Gates's look of apology. Gates took Tumin's hand to shake, clearly intimating his need to return to his dinner. But then something went wrong, the handshake didn't end — Tumin wouldn't let go. Don watched helplessly as Gates tried to get loose of the man, first passively and then more firmly, but Lonny had him in those powerful hands of his, and now the software king began to panic, eyes darting over to his fellow diners (distracted now with their own conversation), then even through the glass to Leon (also oblivious), desperately trying to free his hand. Finally, just as Don was thinking of intervening, Tumin whispered something in Gates's ear and released him.

Tumin emerged from the room with a cheek-splitting grin, though he grew quickly agitated when Don asked him what the hell had just happened.

"I told him the truth, goddamnit, that he'd gotten lucky, and that if he thought L. T. wanted his pity, he was goofier than he looks. I warned him that if he ever tries to strong-arm me, I'll go after him."

The older and more powerful Tumin got, Don realized, the more he seemed frustrated with boundaries, the more he longed for the quick, violent justice of youth. This was Lonny's version of a midlife crisis: he wanted to fight; he wanted to get physical with people who crossed him. The Gates incident and the morning with the golf ranger were proof positive. It was like Orange High School all over again, Don thought. L. T. against the world, and lately Lonny had been very much in the mood. Along with the secrecy of Monarch, all this erratic behavior was making Don Westly very nervous.

Don was in the lounge with his feet up on the ottoman, watching Tiger and puffing away on a Romeo y Julieta Perfecto, when Lonny came striding in.

"That one of my pre-Castros, you cocksucker?" Tumin asked.

Don nodded in the affirmative, pleased his boss was irked and that Mr. Ohka was nowhere in sight. Lonny took the chair next to him.

"Sure, Donny, take it easy. Kick back and whittle a bit, why don't you?"

"Not much else to do," he replied, blowing out some smoke.

"Oh, you want something to do? Good, because I've got something for you." Tumin reached into his briefcase, took out a magazine, and tossed it into Don's lap. "Get me something like this."

It was Jack Welch on the cover of *Business Week*. Don looked back at Tumin, clearly surprised.

"A profile? I thought you were done with journalists."

"Yeah, I mean I hate the bastards, but what am I gonna do? They have their usefulness." He gestured to the magazine. "I'm thinking something like this, or maybe even classier. *Esquire,* that sort of thing. Get some momentum rolling for Monarch. You think we've got a shot at a cover?"

Don nodded without hesitation. There was no reason to think otherwise. No matter how much his partner's success had waned in recent years, he knew the Tumin name still held a certain cachet — the hint of corruption attached to it had always (paradoxically) given Lonny a strange glamour. And the cultural winds were blowing in their direction. CEOs were the new superheroes, supplanting Hollywood stars on magazine covers. Now it was Jack Welch starring as Gene Hackman, Michael Dell as Bruce Willis. Why not Lonny Tumin as, say, James Woods?

Don was thinking *GQ* perhaps. Tumin in pinstripes by Valentino, cigar in hand, airbrush turned on high. Had they put a CEO on their cover? he wondered. If not, there were other options. New magazines were springing up every week.

"There's a lot of early interest in Monarch right now," Tumin said excitedly. "If word gets out that I'm involved in an IPO, that stock opens at eighteen bucks, minimum."

Don figured eighteen was a bit optimistic, but certainly a wave of press would be essential. And he knew nabbing a cover for his boss was a task for which he was perfectly suited. Tumin no longer trusted publicists, and Don's friends from the restaurant — the ones he drank and dined with in the evenings — tended to be people from the world of film and publishing rather than finance. He was sure to find someone who could help.

"Make this happen with one of your buddies," Tumin said. "And

I want to handpick the writer this time so there's no funny business. I'm thinking someone who comes to the restaurant all the time. It's unprecedented, the excitement that goes on in this place on a nightly basis, Donny, don't you think? Someone should capture that. Someone that knows it from the inside."

"How about Dominick Dunne?" his advisor suggested. "He has lunch here at least three times a week."

"That's good, though I was thinking more Halberstam," Tumin countered. "You know, Pulitzer Prize and all that shit."

Halberstam was a nice choice, Don thought. He was an old friend of Tumin's (though nobody could remember exactly why), and it was obvious that the writer got a kick out of Lonny, regarded him as a genuine New York character, the irascible tycoon from another era. The piece would romanticize Tumin in a way that would play to their cause. Also, Halberstam hadn't paid for a meal at City since it opened, so perhaps it was time to reacquaint the old Harvard boy with his Latin — *quid pro quo* for example.

Suddenly there was loud cheering from the television. Tiger Woods had just hit a 300-yard tee shot that rolled gracefully to the front of the green.

Tumin fluttered his lips with contemptuous reverberation. *"Tiger,"* he said distastefully.

"You don't like him?" asked Don, though he knew already. For someone who'd grown up having to constantly defend himself (and Don) with hand-to-hand combat, Tumin was strangely sentimental about his hometown: Lonny had never forgiven "the blacks" for what they'd "done" to Newark and Orange. They'd turned it into a shantytown, he'd asserted, a war zone. And God knows he'd shown no patience for any of the socioeconomic arguments Don had put forth over the years.

"He's smug," Tumin said finally. "Anyhow, check the market."

Don flipped to *MarketWatch*. The NASDAQ was up two hundred and change, the Dow a buck and a half. The Italian cutie was once again grinning away on the Exchange floor, as if this were all her doing.

Another extraordinary day down here . . .

Erin appeared in the lounge. "Iced tea, Mr. Tumin?" she asked.

"Please," he replied, not looking up. Then, when Erin turned to leave, Tumin immediately craned his neck to follow her out. "Damn if I don't keep forgetting what a piece of ass she is," he remarked with crude amazement.

His partner didn't reply. Don flipped the channel back to Tiger, who was pumping his fist in a triumphant uppercut, though his own mind was still set on Monarch.

Tumin's gaze lingered on the doorway where Erin had just passed, as if to track the tail of a comet. "I really oughta do something about that," he said.

Faithless

(From "The Counterfeit Conversion," NYC magazine, May 11, 1999)

All Muslims are mad, of course. Not mad in the sense of angry, though they are certainly that, but daffy mad, glazed-eyed-crazy-stare mad, ipso facto mad . . . or so Clark, in his ignorance, had always believed. Iran and the hostages. Khalid Muhammad and his "white devils." Crude oil and swaddling veils. Belly dancers, whirling dervishes, etc. Mad, he thought. All of them.

So how was it then that at the age of thirty-six, Clark found himself zooming up along the Garden State Parkway in an SUV the size of a Panzer tank, on the way to Chestnut, New York, and his Muslim conversion?

"You son of a bitch."

On the car ride to Saugerties, Ayla unleashed her fury. She'd read "The Counterfeit Conversion" on her lunch hour and had been in a lather ever since.

"You *son* of a bitch."

"What?"

"Fucking bastard."

"It's fiction, Ayla."

She turned to him, and with her hands still on the wheel, angled her head at him threateningly. He was perilously close to getting slugged.

Of course, the story was supposed to have been funny. It was a farce sending the hero, Clark, a hedonistic, atheistic WASP writer ("*Real* stretch," she'd told Kyle, "great imagination") stumbling through his Muslim confirmation. Included in the mayhem were some barely disguised caricatures of Ayla's friends and family: the hopelessly suburban "Shyla," for example, obviously based on her sister, Elsa, "hot cherry" body tulle from Victoria's Secret visible under her burka; or Moadh, the family Imam whose name the writer had not even bothered to substitute, and who may or may not have accidentally placed his hand on Clark's backside during the recitation of the Articles of Faith.

Naturally, her father had got the worst of it. It was apparently not enough revenge for Kyle to describe "Abdul" as the "obese ogre of adolescent tribalism." Not hardly. He'd also had to include the true story of Murat's attempt to prevent Elsa's marriage. Two years ago, after learning that his daughter was engaged to an American man — a cop, ironically enough — her father had stormed into the local police station, demanding to see the man in question and shouting aloud how he was going to kill him. Lucky for Murat, his daughter's fiancé was a pretty understanding fellow, and once everything calmed, all charges were dropped. Kyle had used these details and then some, elaborating on them, heating up the material — and not any of it did Ayla regard as funny.

"You used them," she added now as traffic slowed again on the Henry Hudson Parkway. "My family and the people I've known and loved for years. My *religion*. You served them all up in the name of your supercilious humor."

He sat silent and repentant, though she knew what his answer would be once he summoned the nerve to defend himself — some bullshit about fiction's roots in autobiography and artistic freedom. Yes, well, she'd be ready for him when he got on *that* jag. Ayla didn't believe for a second that every*thing* and every*body* was fair game for writers. She respected writers. She saw how hard Kyle worked, all the worry and stubborn effort it took to produce a book. But this idea that novelists had license to forage for and exploit anything so long as it was "interesting" or "illuminating" drove her to apoplexy. What, because her husband practiced a craft that occasionally reached the level of art (most novels were failures, after all), that gave him the right to turn people she knew into fools?

It was the same with the Salman Rushdie affair. Ayla had been in Istanbul when the fatwa had been decreed. She'd gone back ostensibly for her parents, to indulge their hope of her finding a Cherkes husband (she promised to drop in on the old village), but really to work in the fashion biz, to which her fluent English gave her entrée, and to spend August on the Italian Riviera scouting for German boys. Turkey, probably the most progressive of Muslim countries, was divided on the issue of *The Satanic Verses,* but Ayla found herself defending some of Rushdie's critics. All of her coworkers were liberal, cosmopolitan Turks, lapsed Muslims enthralled with all things Western, and so Ayla, who was almost as fond of being contrary as her future husband, often found herself in virulent arguments.

She conceded that Rushdie had not committed blasphemy. Muhammad himself was not divine, but only a messenger of God, therefore blasphemy against Muhammad was impossible. What he had done was to commit *shatin,* meaning the writer had insulted one of God's messengers. Muslims had a right, even an obligation, to protest. In fact, when conservative students organized an event to burn copies of *The Satanic Verses,* Ayla had zealously participated — an episode she had yet to share with her husband.

Furthermore, though she viewed the fatwa as essentially misguided, Ayla could have little sympathy for Salman. He had gratuitously insulted the honor and dignity of a serious faith. He was a Muslim himself, well versed in the ardent passions of Islam. What had he expected? His *Why me?* stance was ridiculous in her eyes. It was like sticking your hand in a shark's mouth to amuse the crowd, then crying foul when you lost a thumb.

"It's not easy to have faith, Kyle," she said now. "Do you know that? Yours is the easy way, not believing in anything."

"I believe in things."

She laughed. "Like what? Every citizen's right to a dry martini?"

A cheap shot, Ayla admitted to herself; she knew it as soon as she'd said it. Kyle Clayton believed in things and had paid a price for them — even his worst detractors would admit that. He believed in things or else she wouldn't be with him.

"Actually, that's what I was trying to do with 'The Counterfeit Conversion,'" he explained. "Trying to narrow down some of my ideas. Crystallizing my concerns about Islam."

"What concerns?"

"Muhammad, to be precise. I'm troubled by his warrior status."

Oh, that's right, Ayla thought, lest she forget, the story got even better. Forget the satiric lancing of her family, readers of "The Counterfeit Conversion" were also treated to Clark's scrupulous observations about Islam. As the hero researches the religion he is being forced to embrace, he bridles at its tenets:

> *Clark read on. He discovers the Koran's assertion that men have "rank" over women, and that the Koran also includes provisions for a man to beat his wife, an interpretation even the most liberal of Muslim scholars don't deny. "You beat her, but not on the face," an Imam kindly clarifies in* What Muslims Believe. *"You beat her with something that does not leave a mark or injury. The Prophet gave an example: he got two pieces of cloth and put them together, and he said, 'Like this . . .'"*

Kyle's voice was calm as he continued, chastened but determined to make his point. "You see, I keep hearing how Islam is about peace. I hear this from you, from your family, from the Imam on the day of the conversion — but I just don't see it. And I certainly don't see it in the Koran."

"You don't see it in the Koran? The Koran says, 'If you kill one man, you kill the whole of humanity.' What is it that you're seeing?"

"No, Ayla, you're wrong. The Koran says, 'If you kill one man *without good reason*, you kill the whole of humanity.' You haven't read it in a while, have you?"

Ayla was having a hard time keeping her eyes on the road. *Did* the Koran really say that? It was true that she hadn't read the book through for many years, and it infuriated her that this gave Kyle — this atheist, this heathen — an untoward advantage.

"Dissonance," he continued, "this is what you see in the Koran. A call to peace and a call to arms, side by side, sometimes on the same page. Love and hate in the same breath. And I think the problem, as I've said, lies squarely with Mr. Muhammad."

Naturally she'd heard some of these ideas before, in their private conversations, but never as exacting, never as well researched as in "The Counterfeit Conversion": Kyle — no, excuse her, *Clark* — expounding on the paradoxes of the Warrior Prophet; Muhammad preaching peace even as his legendary sword, the Dhu'l-Faqar, drips blood; and then the coup de grâce, the beheading of the six hundred Jews at Medina, sanctioned by Muhammad himself (at the behest of Allah! he proclaims), the subsequent enslavement of the women and children. At the climax of "The Counterfeit Conversion" there is an interior monologue in which Clark, in the midst of the conversion ceremony — even as he is reciting the Articles of Faith to a room full of Muslims — asks himself, in all honesty, if he believes Muhammad to be a hypocrite. And his answer? Ayla remembered the lines precisely:

"Yes," Clark thinks to himself, for he was not one to flinch at even the most awful of truths, "yes, yes, yes . . ."

"All religions have their tragic flaw," continued Kyle now, urging his wife to keep her eyes on the road, "and to me, this is Islam's. You embrace a soldier as your prophet, what do you get? You get Kashmir, you get Algeria, you get Somalia, you get the West Bank, you get the Ottomans, you get . . . I mean, why go on? The point is, you get a sanction for violence."

"Unlike the peace-loving Jews and Christians," Ayla countered. "I seem to remember the Old Testament reading an awful lot like the *Iliad*."

"You don't think I'm saying that Muslims have some special claim on hypocrisy?"

"Well, Kyle, you've always expressed a partiality to Jesus Christ, even if you are an atheist. Not that I'm knocking it — it's the one glimmer of spirituality you have; I'll take what I can get. But c'mon, Christ is your guy because it's familiar to you, it's what you grew up with. Clearly Christians have perpetrated as much violence, if not more so, as anyone else."

Kyle held up a finger. "Ah, but there's a difference," he said. Suddenly excited, as if this were the very crux of the matter, he turned in his seat toward Ayla, his countenance glowing only half from the dashboard light. "You see, if you are a Christian and you intend to harm another human being, *ever,* be it in defense of your religion, your family, even your own person, then you cannot kid yourself that you are doing Christ's bidding. The New Testament — which supersedes the Old Testament for Christians, by the way — is not ambiguous on the question of aggression. There is no room for rationalization. If you are in the military, to take one example, and have ever engaged in battle, then you may not call yourself a Christian by any reasonable standards. Of course, many do, but then they're . . . Well, let's be honest here, they're lying to themselves. On the other hand, if you are a passionate young Muslim man, enraptured by the life of Muhammad, the urge to do battle, to fight for Islam, almost seems compulsory. Muhammad was a soldier for Islam, you tell yourself, therefore *I* will be a soldier for Islam. Terms like *jihad* and *infidel* are pretty elastic when there is the will to do harm. This is where I say the Koran fails its readers. What person who kills doesn't think they have *good reason?*"

"But you forget one thing, Kyle."

"What's that?"

"Historically speaking, there was no other way for Muhammad. He had no choice. Without war, there would have been no Islam."

When she quickly turned to register his reaction, she saw him staring back at her, smiling beatifically. Unconsciously, Ayla realized, and rather succinctly, she had just made his case.

Saturday morning they woke late, managing then to ignore each other most of the day. Kyle raked some leaves left over from the fall and worked on his new novel. Ayla read and napped on the hammock, then hung some curtains for spring, dreaming of the day they could live here without returning to the filthy, chaotic city.

So here was yet another minefield they'd been skipping through together recently: Kyle had been urging them to do away with the second home and the added financial pressures, while Ayla not only wanted to keep their residence in Saugerties but also preferred to live there full-time. Yes, she admitted, money *was* a nagging problem, so why couldn't they give up the Manhattan apartment and go live a simpler life in pastoral Saugerties, New York? Kyle could write there unheeded, while she herself could do some freelance Web design from home. Money would be plentiful. They could finally have that baby they'd been talking about.

But no, Kyle was not ready to leave New York; he'd made that very clear. The city was his inspiration, he'd said. He needed to be a part of it, to keep an eye on things firsthand — while the real reason, she knew, was that he'd miss the restaurants, the parties, the bullshit glamour of being a writer in New York. Not to mention the women, whom he liked to look at on the street and in the shops, sometimes even as she walked with him. The ones that wrote him "fan" e-mails that included their phone number and occasionally even had the gumption to call the apartment. *That's* what he wanted to keep an eye on, Ayla suspected, *that's* what he'd miss — the aura of it-can-happen-at-any-moment sex that ran through the streets of New York during the day like a current, and at night thrashed its tail around like a downed power line.

But there would be no arguing about the house today; today they were still too stunned from last night's jousting to risk such sensitive matters. By late afternoon, in fact, they were experimenting with a kind of truce, actually deciding to go into town together (though still engaging in only the most perfunctory small talk). They stopped at the farmer's market and, as always, the wineshop. Naturally, Ayla thought, biting her tongue. What would Saturday in the country be without a bottle of wine entirely beyond their means? After they arrived home, the usual rituals took shape. Ayla made a fire (the nights were crisp here, even in May), and Kyle went off to the kitchen to prepare yet another lavish dinner. This was how he wound down from a day of writing in the country, with the preparation of three- and four-course extravaganzas. Unfortunately, the appreciation of these meals was mostly lost on his wife. From her parents, Ayla had adopted a certain asceticism, especially toward food, making it all the more ironic that she had married a man like Kyle. The man for whom dinner was a *happening*.

Watching him during these times could be quite entertaining, she

had to admit, the libertine in his lair. First was the music. Rachmani-
noff was a perennial favorite, sounds of the Second Piano Concerto
lilting through the house, or opera if he was making Italian. Music
both bombastic and sentimental, like the man himself. Orchestra
engaged, he moved on to the bar to craft himself one of his exquisite
martinis — the plop of the olive, the rimming of the twist — and only
now could the chopping commence, the smell of minced herbs reaching her in the living room: fresh rosemary, oregano, and lemon-thyme
picked from the garden. And garlic, of course.

"Not too much garlic," Ayla would yell out, already thinking of
Monday morning at the office.

"You don't like garlic, you don't like *life!*" Kyle would bellow
back over the music, the power of his voice buoyed by the gin. As a
weekend guest, you could be blacklisted indefinitely for requesting no
garlic.

Here now the prodigal wedge of cheese would appear, something
expensive he'd sneaked past her at the market, and now of course
he'd have to open the wine to go with the cheese, swirling it in the
glass, smacking his lips in a euphoria of indulgence. A taste of the
wine, then the cheese, then a slice of pear. All of this topped off with a
teaspoonful of whatever butter-laden sauce he happened to be working on and, lest he forget, a final swig of the martini.

"Another *master*piece!" he'd roar out humorously, though more
often than not he was right.

Tonight's menu was Tuscan-style steak, dry-aged and herb en-
crusted, preceded by his pasta puttanesca, his sauces always more
delicious than any from the trattorias of her Italian summers.

From the kitchen, Kyle announced that dinner was ready.

"So," he said, approaching the table, arms bedecked with the
steaming platters. A certain food runner at City, she had learned, had
taught him to carry four plates at a time. It was quite a sight, though
Ayla had promised herself to remain grumpy at least a while longer.

"*So?*" she repeated, taking her seat. "So what?"

The plates were set down with a smooth, waiterly flourish. He'd
outdone himself, as usual. The food looked impossibly gorgeous, the
flesh layered with architectural panache, the colors arranged in careful tableaux. He had even . . . my God, she thought, the plates were

garnished! On a more sporting evening, Ayla might have asked her husband to reassure her he was straight.

"So, what's the resolution on this whole *story* thing?" he asked, sitting down. "Am I still in the doghouse?"

"Well, it's published, isn't it? I'd say it's pretty resolved."

Kyle poured out some more of the wine, suddenly reminded of its necessity.

"In all fairness, Ayla, I think there's plenty that's made up. And I certainly never meant to hurt anyone in your family."

"Except my father."

Kyle, who had been mostly contrite up until now, suddenly looked irritated. He tilted the rim of his wineglass toward her, as if practicing his aim for some future event.

"I *owed* him that one. And you know it."

Ayla was tempted to challenge this, but instead she smirked, hinting at capitulation. She didn't want to fight anymore. She was tired. She'd worked her *ass* off this week, her job was getting crazy, and now she just wanted to eat dinner with the fireplace popping behind her and be in love again.

Let the attrition of marriage strip off a little more, she thought. *I give.*

They clinked glasses in a muted toast. Ayla admitted that some of the story had indeed made her laugh, and he had made some interesting points about Islam. Then, with uncharacteristic spontaneity, Kyle slid his chair over and took her hand to his lips. This gesture, after a whole day and night of bottled-up anger, set her emotions flowing.

"Are we going to make it?" she whispered into his neck.

"What are you talking about?"

"I wonder sometimes."

"Ayla, don't talk like that."

"I can't help it," she said, her voice a little weepy. "I've been having those dreams again."

His hold on her relaxed.

"I'm sorry," she said, "I can't help it."

"Ayla, who is this woman who you think I'm sleeping with?"

"You're *not* sleeping with her, I told you. You *want* to sleep with her."

She watched as Kyle took a deep sip of wine and stared into the candlelight. "What am I supposed to say to that?" he asked.

And now she waited for the joke that would follow, the playful rejoinder he always used to deflate serious matters.

"I mean, who is this girl? Tell me she at least has a nice rack."

In keeping with tonight's armistice, Ayla offered him a polite smile; privately, though, she held to her concerns. She was not a Turkish farm girl for nothing, having learned to trust not only faith but also a few myths and superstitions, and, above all, her instincts. She was convinced this was what these dreams were — an intuition, a feminine warning. Just once and she might have dismissed them, but these visions of Kyle and another woman had been persistent. No, she decided, she was *on* to something.

But what could she do? she wondered. Ultimately, what choice did she have but to trust him? How could you live any other way?

"You didn't eat much tonight," he said to her afterward. They had moved to the couch to watch the fire. "You didn't like it?"

"No, I loved it," she said enthusiastically. "It's just . . ."

"What?"

Their coffees sat on a small table near the hearth. Ayla sipped hers black, while Kyle took his with a shot of brandy, three sugars, and a special Austrian half-and-half immune from pesky pasteurization laws.

"Dinner was almost *too* flavorful," she said, a little embarrassed. "I don't know. Just a little seemed enough."

"Too flavorful?" The notion seemed to confound and even offend him. "That's an oxymoron. That's like *too* happy, or *too* much sex."

"There's no such thing?"

"Hell no," he said without thinking.

Interlude for Allah

Syeed Salaam, or Rick the Doorman, awoke early on a Saturday morning and immediately set about praying to Allah for forgiveness, for he was sincerely worried about the state of his soul.

Inexplicably, so it seemed to Syeed, he had spent yet another night dreaming of the coat.

It was spring, and an especially warm one, but night after night the coat had appeared in his dreams. Its colors and textures were so palpable, so real: snow-white fleece ribbed with darker hair, the weight a surprising heft on his shoulders. Syeed was originally from Saudi Arabia, but in this dream he trundled along an icy steppe in what he imagined as something like northern Russia, leaning headlong into a lashing snow, the coat providing unparalleled warmth and, most shamefully, a bit of glamour. Despite all attempts, he seemed powerless to prevent this vision, though its source was obvious enough. Sometime toward the end of March, a man had come to the restaurant wearing this very same coat, a tall, handsome man, who Syeed noticed was also sporting a robust winter tan. Syeed simply could not rid the image of this man from his mind. He looked so . . . *exquisite,* this man. So happy, so complete. Syeed knew these impressions to be false, of course. There could be no happiness in a place of such *haraam,* and this man could never be truly complete, since he had clearly failed to embrace Allah.

So why then, Syeed asked himself, do I want that coat more than anything else in the world?

Covetousness was certainly new for him, an exception in an otherwise holy life. He worked the door at City twelve shifts a week and lived in a tiny third-floor walk-up in Astoria, Queens. Each month he sent as much money as possible back to his family in Jidda, a port city on the Saudi coast. He read the Koran regularly and prayed five times a day, every day, regardless of mood or health. He lived sparingly, ate no pork or shellfish, and had never taken a drink in his life. In fact, he was a man almost immune to thoughts of unholiness — though sometimes saliva did run thick in his mouth when the smell of frying sausages wafted up from the Demarco family's kitchen below him, and he would occasionally linger at the window when Julie, the St. John's University sophomore in the basement apartment, went for her morning jog.

Syeed was convinced that these sinful thoughts could be blamed directly on his job at City. He should never have gone to work in such a place to begin with, what with the drinking of alcohol and the seemingly endless parade of swine coming from the kitchen. (How someone ate an animal that lived in its own feces was beyond him.) Then there were the customers, many of whom were bankers or players in the stock market, and therefore practitioners of *riba,* strictly forbidden by the Koran. He knew he should quit, thought of it every day, in fact, but then what were the options for an uneducated Middle Easterner in America? He wouldn't make nearly as much money driving a cab, for example, and there were so many people that counted on him back home. There was his immediate family — his wife, Aisha, of course, along with his parents and younger brother, Yusef (a no-good layabout when it came time for work!). Then there was Aisha's family — the two older sisters, both still unmarried, along with her parents *and* grandparents, all of whom Syeed was expected to provide for. He accepted the responsibility without complaint, but the separation from his wife hurt him terribly. He had not seen Aisha for nearly two years now, and even then had only known her for a month before leaving to make his fortune in America. He should never have left Jidda, he thought again now with a heavy heart. He should go home. He would be poor there, but at least he would not be surrounded by such *haraam,* such temptation. In Jidda he would never have to look at a girl in her jogging shorts, for example, nor would he have to see a magnificent fur coat on a handsome man entering a restaurant.

Suddenly thinking of his wife, Syeed retrieved from the kitchen table her most recent letter. Aisha was just nineteen and not very educated. Her Arabic was poorly constructed and her handwriting required great scrutiny to understand, but for Syeed, these pages could not be more cherished if they were from the Koran itself.

Dearest Love,

Thank you again for the big money in January. I am happy to see something good comes from Western holidays which of course are so silly and thoughtless. And yet, if people spend more at these times, leaving tips and such kind of things, then good for us! One day you make biggest money and come home forever. For this I pray every day.

We are all of us very good here. Grandfather too sends his regards and much thanks. As I said last time before, the money you send paid for doctor who is very knowing of kidneys. You saved his life, Syeed! You very big hero in my family's eyes. Bismillah!

When can I see you? I am very much lonely here. As you know, money for grandfather was saving for trip to America. I am glad for him, but sad for me. I want to see you but only have distant memories. When I want to think of you I have now to look at your brother Yusef, to see your face in him which I'm sad for all time. Don't for me worry though. Yusef watches after me and makes me stay home mostly with him and your parents. He says if I am so pretty and his brother's wife he will not have me outside for other men to see. Can you see his love for you in such thoughts? WE ALL MISS YOU SO!

Please make biggest money and come back here soon, or me have come soon. Either way, soon, soon, soon, okay?

LOVE, Aisha

With this, Syeed took his mat from the closet and knelt, the flooring nearly as hard and unforgiving as the sidewalk across from the restaurant. He had the mat turned east, of course, in approximation of where the Holy City might be. In Jidda it was easy to know where Mecca was, he thought resentfully, but here, who really knew for sure? This wasn't a city where people looked east. They tended to look up — at the stock tickers, at the great buildings rising too high — or else right through you. For an Arab in America, everything, *everything,* was compromise.

Below him he could hear his kneecaps crunching even through the prayer mat. Good, he thought, let it hurt. Reading the letter had made him even more ashamed of his visions of the coat. They plagued him even now, even as he knelt before Allah!

Must return to Jidda, Syeed thought. Must find a way to make the "biggest money," as Aisha said. Must come home once and for all. In the meantime, he decided he would get back to becoming a good Muslim. He would pray for this now, in fact, plead for a task, some service he could perform that would set things right with Allah. If only He would tell him what it was, Syeed would do it. He would do whatever Allah asked, without exception.

Knees gnashing against the floor, heart yearning, Syeed prayed.

Team Tumin

From her table along the wall of banquettes, Erin stood and smiled with pride as she watched her aunt stride regally into City restaurant at the height of the lunchtime rush. Though she was probably twenty years older than anyone in the room, a number of heads turned toward Helena as the hostess steered her to Erin's table, the eyes following her not for her beauty, which in truth had long since faded, but for her sense of wizened charisma, that air of mystery she had never quite relinquished. It was an allure you could not fake. Helena was, in fact, a mysterious woman — a mystery to everyone who knew her, and very likely to herself.

In The Room they had reached the late sixties, and her aunt, ever frugal, had picked out a few choice items and was wearing them today to maximum effect: a black-and-gold scarf, beige chiffon blouse, formfitting slacks that flared at the bottom, all topped off with a pair of dark sunglasses, dusted off just this afternoon, which Helena had decided to display even as she strolled through the restaurant's tenebrous dining room. A sharp observer might have noticed a

bit of jealousy in the eyes of a few of the older women who looked at
Helena, wondering how she did so much with so little, and at that
age. The clothes were a quarter of a century old but had a thrift-store
panache usually considered the exclusive domain of the young.

Stephen came over and gallantly pulled out the table, Erin offering her aunt the preferred banquette seat. Helena slipped in with
exaggerated ease, then lowered her sunglasses just enough to take in
the room with a wide-eyed exhilaration.

"Well, this certainly *is* the scene, isn't it?"

"That's what they say," offered Erin, for whom familiarity had
ruined all romance.

"And you work here," Helena added. "What *fun* that must be!"

Erin held back a grimace. On another day, she might have scolded
her aunt for such a comment. Clearly it was the remark of someone
who'd never *had* to work, who had no concept of what it was like to
engage these high-strung soldiers of fortune in their daily eating and
drinking habits. But today Erin decided to grin and bear it. Today,
she'd decided, was Helena's day.

There was no more pretending — her aunt's condition had wors-
ened. The excavation of The Room was causing Helena great
anguish. At night she was mixing Elavil with scotch, claiming it
helped her sleep. Erin would arrive at the apartment and find Helena
in a state of confusion: *No,* her aunt would say, she didn't remember
that they were supposed to meet today. *Yes,* they certainly *should*
work on the room this afternoon. Dick was away on a business trip
and would be back soon. He so hated to see the place a mess.

So Erin was relieved now to see that when Helena took off her
sunglasses her aunt's eyes were clear and bright, and that there
seemed a definite snap to her step. The whole idea of the lunch had
been to get her out of the apartment, to give her an afternoon off from
the trauma of overhauling her life, to have a little fun. Plus, as an
employee of City, Erin was getting 50 percent off.

Stephen was their captain. Ordinarily it was awkward to be
served by people you worked with, but she knew Stephen would
make it easy. They ordered some wine, which Raoul poured ("Did he
just say *swine?*" Helena whispered), and then her aunt momentarily
dismounted from her high horse to tell her a story about the old La
Côte Basque.

"I think it was around 1968, the last time Dick and I were there. We used to have lunch there every Friday when he was in town, and invariably we used to run into Truman Capote."

"You knew him?" Erin asked, quite surprised.

"No — well, not really. But that was the funny thing, you see, he thought he knew *me*. Quite a few people used to say I looked like Lee Radziwill."

"You still do."

"Well, thank you, darling. I suppose there is a certain passing resemblance." Helena was suddenly lit with pride. "Anyhow, Truman took it to the extreme. Of course, he was drinking quite a bit in those days, and so whenever I walked in he would immediately leap up from his chair and accost me in the middle of the dining room. 'Lee, how are you?'" After a sip of wine, Helena summoned the nerve for an imitation. "'*Lee, you* MUTHT *come and thit with us,*' and so on."

"My God," Erin said, delighted. "What did you do?"

"Well, of course I tried to tell him that he was making a big mistake, but then I could see that he was drunk and was getting insulted by my denying to be Lee Radziwill. He thought it was Lee trying to get rid of him. So what could I do? I played along. I'd offer a few polite words, apologize for not being able to join him, and watch him skulk back to his table. Then, one day, none of his friends had shown up at all. He was there completely alone, and so he ended up spending the entire afternoon at our table, with Dick and me, drinking bottle after bottle of our wine. He practically begged us to come back to his apartment with him, to continue the party."

"And you had to pretend to be Lee Radziwill the whole time?"

"Isn't that ludicrous!" Helena tittered. "Luckily I knew just enough about this woman to wing it. I'd say, 'We're going out to the house in East Hampton this weekend, Tru. If we weren't so full up, I'd ask you to join us.' Things like this. The old acting skills really came in handy." Helena smiled in fond remembrance, then lowered her eyes as her tone became more somber. "Naturally there was some guilt, but in the end I like to think we were being kind. It would have been much worse to send him back to his lonely little table, believing I was trying to avoid him. Don't you think?"

Coming to take the order, Stephen flirted mightily with Helena, which had her blushing like a debutante (and for which Erin now owed him *big* time). Abu brought the bread, bowing to Helena and turning on all his exaggerated Bengali charm, though this was meant to impress Erin as much as her guest. She could tell that his crush was getting worse lately, and when she stood to greet him, she made sure to make her hug both as brief and sisterly as possible.

Just then, a world-famous actress was seated two tables away. Suddenly the air in the dining room seemed thinner.

"Oh, God," Erin chirped petulantly, turning away her eyes.

"My, she's stunning," Helena remarked. The aunt had put her sunglasses back on, pulling them down now just enough to see. "A little short, though, don't you think?"

"They all are. You should see the men; they're like midgets."

"Really, darling," her aunt continued, now boldly surveying the actress from head to toe, "you're positively statuesque compared to her."

For Erin, it was little solace. Prettier, taller, more talented — it didn't matter. What mattered was that this woman arrived here today like a queen, the room already at her feet, while for Erin it was merely a fluke that she wasn't serving her lunch. This actress was unusual in that her career was both successful and dignified. She appeared in interesting films *and* on the stage, while at the same time making more money than anyone would be able to spend in twenty lifetimes. She had precisely the sort of life that Erin had been dreaming about on a daily basis since she was twelve, and so naturally she despised her.

"Don't look at her," Erin hissed.

Helena had pulled her sunglasses down completely now, observing the actress much less discreetly than before. "Why not?"

"Don't give her the satisfaction."

Helena laughed. "Why, I think she's terrific. Don't tell me you don't like her?"

Like her! Erin thought disdainfully, but then she found her own gaze drifting back toward the movie star. There absolutely *was* some sort of magic that followed her, it seemed. The woman had a presence so intense that it was almost as if she weren't real at all, as if she had stepped off the screen and into City restaurant like some ghostly hologram.

This dynamism clouded Erin's mood all the more, and now a perilous question was begged: Had this woman been born with an irresistible mystique and therefore had no other possible trajectory but to become a world-famous actress? Or was she just a very pretty, hardworking girl who had got a few breaks and now only appeared to have this allure, simply because she was in the movies? Erin could hardly think of a more alarming notion, this idea that some people had *IT* and some people didn't, and that whatever *IT* was, it was something no one of any consequence had yet accused her of possessing.

"Why don't you go introduce yourself, tell her how you're an actress too?"

"Oh my God," Erin said with a laugh. "Are you *insane?*" She turned in her seat now, flipping her legs to the other side so as to face the bar. "Can't you see that just the sight of someone like this drives me crazy?"

"If it drives you so crazy, why don't you do something about it?"

"Like what?"

"Make a *move.*"

"Oh, here we go . . ."

"New York is not helping you, Erin darling. You've done New York."

"I'm *not* moving to L.A.," she told her aunt firmly. "I've already told you that."

Erin was getting ready to leave the table for a moment, a little trip to the ladies' room to cool down, when she saw Lonny Tumin enter from the foyer. As usual, he regarded his customers skeptically, coming too close to tables, sizing them up — then scowling when they invariably disappointed him.

Somehow overlooking the actress, he headed right over to Erin and her aunt.

"What's this?" Tumin demanded as he approached. Erin knew that his irascible voice always made him sound as if he were upset with you, even if it were the very opposite, but she couldn't help feeling guilty about letting him see her on the other side of the table. Why hadn't anyone warned her he was having lunch today? Would she be expected to go wait on him now?

"Oh, hi, Mr. Tumin. Just having . . . a little bite." Erin stood up, pulling nervously at the shoulder strap of her dress. She introduced him to her aunt.

He dispatched Helena with an efficient smile, then quickly returned to Erin, whom he looked up and down with an unembarrassed hunger. "You look fantastic."

Erin realized that he had never before seen her out of uniform. "Sorry," she said, "nobody told me you were coming today, so, you know . . ."

"Nonsense," he remarked, sneaking another glimpse at her legs. "I tell you what, for my favorite waitress, lunch is on me. How 'bout that? And Irene . . ."

"Erin."

"Remind me to speak with you about something." Tumin's hand rested on her shoulder as his eyes fixed on her. "I think we need to talk."

She smiled, though secretly she was perplexed. What could Lonny Tumin possibly have to say to her, except to bring him another iced tea, and quick?

"Fine, sure," she replied.

Tumin nodded a quick farewell to Helena, then stopped after just a single step. "You," he said, bobbing his finger at the mysterious woman. "You look familiar."

"Do I?" replied Helena, looking around. She seemed quite pleased.

"What did you say your name was again? Aren't you. . . ?"

Erin was shaking her head vigorously, but to no avail — Helena was already smiling.

"Why yes, that's me," she said. She looked around surreptitiously. "Let's not make a scene of it, though, shall we?"

In the Airplane Room, the bombers were poised for battle. On one side of the table sat Rob Barnett, Don Westly, and the lawyer, Ivic Rennert — the latter tottering, as always, on his wide-bottomed chair. On the other side sat the mild-mannered golf course ranger, whose name, ironically, turned out to be Jim White. Next to him was his lawyer, Dana Wallace. Notes were spread about the table, along with bottles of mineral water and some glasses. Although there was some quiet chatter among the teams, neither side talked to the other. After months of purposeful, anxiety-inducing delay, the course ranger and his lawyer had finally agreed to meet with Tumin and his crew.

When Lonny walked in, he ignored everyone and marched right up to Jim White to shake his hand.

"How do you do?" he asked.

"Been better," White managed to reply, limply returning the handshake. He did not stand to greet him, and so Tumin bent over the man, hand resting on the back of his chair.

"Tell you what," the mogul began in a lower though somehow more aggressive tone of voice. "I wondered if you and I could have five minutes alone. You know, just one on one, before we start."

Dana Wallace, leaning over to eavesdrop, smiled knowingly. He was well aware of what kind of move this was. Tumin had exactly a zero percent chance of talking to his client alone and knew it, but he wanted to set things off on a confrontational note. It was the old evil eye, a quick little reminder of just what a steely pair of balls they were up against.

As for Lonny, he was secretly nervous, for on his way in he had got a good look at the lawyer named Wallace, and he knew they were in trouble.

First off, he was black, a little tidbit that Ivic Rennert had failed to mention and that now infuriated Tumin since it was clearly so significant. The race card was out on the table, faceup. Ace of spades, if you will. Tumin also thought Wallace was exceedingly well dressed and had exactly the kind of sharp, elegant manner that went over well with liberal jurors.

The third tidbit was a detail Ivic *had* mentioned, though it was no less daunting for having known it was coming. Tumin had never felt comfortable around homosexuals. Triad practiced a de facto "no gays" policy, but it was impossible to enforce this at City. With both gay staff and customers, Tumin's faux pas abounded; he would try too hard to show that he was "hip" to it, which he wasn't, and end up being insulting in an attempt to buddy up. Then, disgusted with having ingratiated himself, he would go too far the *other* way, suddenly becoming defiant in his right to an opinion, to dislike any group of people he so chose. Wasn't that, he told himself, the American way?

"Excuse us, Mr. Tumin," said Dana Wallace now in a voice that was not effeminate at all, as Ivic had dramatized, but actually quite the baritone for a thin man, "I think it's discomforting enough for my client to have to be in the same room with you at all, never mind alone. I think that possibility was erased during a certain incident that transpired a few months ago on the Stonyhill golf course."

"Transpired?" Tumin announced, feigning surprise. "I don't remember anything *transpiring* on any golf course. Unless you're referring to the fact that I shoot a round with the president from time to time."

"I was not, Mr. Tumin."

"How about you, Donny, you remember anything *transpiring?*" Tumin went over and stood behind Don Westly, putting his hands on his adviser's shoulders. "Donny Boy here always golfs with me. If there was any incident at Stonyhill, I'm sure he would remember it."

As usual, Tumin was using Don as his rock, his wall of integrity to hide behind. But as Westly looked out at White and his lawyer, his solid, uncorrupted features remained impassive. Everyone waited for Don to say something. This recalcitrance was just about to make things uncomfortable when Jim White suddenly rose halfway up out of his chair.

"You did too!" he suddenly blurted out, pointing at Tumin. "You *grabbed* me. You — cain't do that, mister! You — cain't!" His quavering voice reflected the long-bottled-up hurt of an ordinarily mild man. "You don't grab a man and call him them kinda names."

"All right, now, Jimmy, *all right,*" urged Dana Wallace. It was his turn now. He stood up and rested his hands on his client's shoulders, gently guiding him back to his seat. Wallace then treated Tumin and his crew to a purposeful glint as he stood behind him, his own memo now clearly intimated: *See what we have here, boys? Got myself a simple, dignified, hardworking black man pushed around and called a nigger by one of the world's richest white men. And you gonna paaaaaaaaaaaaay.*

"Well, Mr. Tumin," the lawyer said, "obviously Jim here's got a different story to tell. Question is, do we settle the matter between ourselves, or do we involve the courts? And by extension, of course," he added, "that would unfortunately include the media." He made a show of fiddling with his notes, but really he wanted that last word to hang in the air for a moment or two, have Team Tumin visualize Jim White, Mr. Black Everyman, telling his story to, say, Lesley Stahl on *60 Minutes.* "Mr. White here is a very private individual, Mr. Tumin, but when it comes to matters like racial intolerance, he recognizes a social responsibility when —"

Tumin smothered the last words with a laugh. "Spare us, Mr. Wallace. We all know why you're both here. In your fancy suit."

The opposing lawyer's eyes quickly flashed up. Wallace had a reputation for being unflappable, but the implication seemed to have inflamed him. "You question my motivation, Mr. Tumin?"

Don shifted a bit in his seat.

"No, no, you're doing this for your *people*," Tumin said. "We all know that already."

Ivic looked over at Don, and the two of them winced in unison. Paradoxically, Wallace seemed to grow calmer. He returned to his seat.

"Why don't we return to the business at hand," Wallace remarked coolly.

"Excellent," Tumin replied with a quick clap of his hands. Finally he came out from behind Don Westly and sat down. "In fact, why don't you just go right ahead and give me those numbers? Tell me what it's going to take to make you two go away. The digits, as I like to say, Mr. Wallace. Just the digits."

Again Wallace smiled, and now Tumin crossed his arms in front of his chest defensively. This was the second time, Tumin thought. What the fuck was this guy *smiling* at?

"I appreciate your bluntness," Wallace explained, "but I think I speak both for myself and Mr. White here when I say that it's not in our nature to simply blurt out sums of money during these sorts of negotiations."

Ivic nodded, as if this sounded right to him, but then Tumin let loose a disgusted snort, and Don had to set a hand on his arm to quell him.

"Let's try this," Wallace suggested. "Why don't I write a number down, leave it in an envelope, and you can consider it after we're gone. I don't hear from you by the end of the day, I'll assume we'll be seeing each other in court."

Everyone grew quiet again as Dana Wallace, obviously prepared for such a moment, opened his briefcase and immediately pulled out an envelope and an appropriately sized piece of paper. Using the case as a shield, he pulled a pen from his pocket and leaned down to begin writing.

After a moment, he looked up with another congenial smile. "Out of ink. Can you believe it?"

"Allow me," Ivic said, ever the southern gentleman. He pulled a gleaming platinum pen from his breast pocket, then, straining his girth forward in his wheezing chair, handed it to Wallace.

"Louisiana, am I right?" Wallace asked him.

"Excuse me?" Ivic replied.

"Your accent? Louisiana, correct?"

Ivic suddenly offered an expansive grin. "Baton Rouge," he said proudly.

"Ah, yes," replied Wallace, nodding slyly to himself. "Good ol' Ba-*ton* Rouge."

Ivic grinned again, pleased with the mere utterance of the home he so dearly missed. Soon though, his face began to twitch with an almost indiscernible discomfort.

"Actually," he said, "it's pronounced *Baton*." He began his familiar heavy breathing again. Apparently these last few sentences had begun to tire him. "You know, like . . . *battle,*" he said. "Baton."

"Not to me," Wallace replied. He kept his eyes down on the paper, hesitating as if he were still making up his mind what to write. "Nope, for me it will always be good ol' Ba-*ton* Rouge. Ever and always."

Ivic shifted around in his seat like a baby too old for his high chair; he was getting uncharacteristically agitated. "Actually, no," he replied, more firmly now. "Excuse me to be such a . . . *stickler* on this matter, Mr. Wallace, but it's my hometown, you understand. And so it *is,* certainly, *Baton.* Just plain *Baton.*"

"I prefer a different pronunciation, Mr. Rennert."

"Who gives a fuck!" exclaimed Tumin, writhing in anticipation of Wallace's penmanship.

"It's my *home,* Lanny," Ivic said plaintively. "Baton Rouge. And if Mr. Wallace here had ever . . . *been* there, perhaps he'd know —"

"Oh, I've been there," said Dana Wallace, prompting surprised looks. "Oh, yes, Ba-*ton* Rouge. What was it now, '82, '83? Yeah, I've been there. Never forget a place like that."

Instead of writing, Wallace began to tap the pen absently, the thoughtful orator.

"I'd just passed the bar. So a friend and I, a *male* friend, Mr.

Tumin," he said, looking over at Lonny, whose face had suddenly stiffened, "decided to go to Mardi Gras. To celebrate."

Don's lips pursed appreciatively as Wallace went to work.

"We're thinking New Orleans, right? Jazz and good food. Crazy times. Only we never got there, Mr. Rennert. Never made it. Got pulled over in Baton Rouge." This time Wallace utilized the traditional pronunciation. "Fifty-eight in a fifty-five-mile-per-hour zone. Two black boys, one maybe with a certain extra height in the heels of his shoes, shirt tied around his waist, maybe a certain way of walking — no, not me, Mr. Tumin, don't look at me like that. My friend. And he had a mouth on him too. He wasn't used to southern cops, and sure, maybe he starts talking out of line, being a little fresh, and the next thing we know they're hauling us down to the woods along the Mississippi. That's when the nightsticks came out, Mr. Rennert. Ba-*tons*, they called them down there. 'Congratulations,' they said, 'you boys done earned yourselves the ba-*tons*.' Me, I just got a few whacks on the head. But my buddy? They used those sticks on him with crea*tivity*."

Any thoughts of challenging this were squelched. Wallace pushed his chair forward and turned his head to highlight a mark on his scalp, a gap just above his right eye where the hair no longer grew. Frowning with anger, he finally scribbled something on the paper, then gruffly stuffed it in the envelope.

"And that, Mr. Rennert," he said, though as he pushed the envelope across the table it came to rest in front of Lonny Tumin, "is why I prefer Ba-*ton* Rouge. If you don't mind." He looked over at Tumin now. "In my fancy suit."

Wallace snapped shut his briefcase, then he and Jim White promptly exited the Airplane Room.

"He serious?" Rob Barnett asked after a few moments. The envelope sat unopened on the table. Even Tumin didn't dare reach for it. "Was he pulling our leg?"

"Doesn't matter," replied Don Westly.

Minutes later, Tumin's men were still wallowing in an impossible silence until Lonny finally bent down for the envelope. As he tore it open, two pieces of paper fell to the floor.

Tumin picked up one, Don Westly the other.

"What's it say?" Ivic asked Don, who was closer.

"It's an affidavit," the other began. He was reading as he spoke. "It's the other golfer . . . Yeah, they found him . . . He corroborates Jim White's story."

"Shit," Barnett said.

Tumin, meanwhile, was staring at the other piece of paper.

"Lonny?" asked Rob tentatively.

The cheeks on Tumin's face were sunken, his eyes wide with incredulity. Having finally had enough, he flipped the piece of paper in the air, watching it float and bank on the currents of the air circulators until it sailed down under the table and disappeared. Then he stood up and headed toward the door.

"Lanny?" Ivic hoisted himself forward, chair squawking as he tried in vain to reach the paper. "*Lanny,* what does it . . . *say?*"

"I told you," said Tumin, glaring back icily at them from the door. "I told you we should've killed this motherfucker."

Ignored

In the evenings, Kyle read his contemporaries.

There was no end to the new writers, it seemed. Each year brought a fresh onslaught of talent, and though Kyle did his best to dismiss them, the mere appearance of these upstarts managed to fill him with a great anxiety. Like all young writers, they were trying to destroy him, Kyle and all the generations previous. Render them dispensable. Wasn't it every month some young thing was declared to be the new Kyle Clayton — as if the old Kyle had disappeared, or was suddenly superfluous? Even worse were the book blurbs or critical declarations he sometimes noticed, in which a new writer was said to show the "promise of a young Kyle Clayton." For Kyle, this was a triple insult. Meaning:

A. he was no longer young,
B. he was no longer good, and
C. at his best, all he had ever shown was promise.

What was most distressing was how very good much of the new work was. Kyle would hear through friends or an editor about some novel that was all the rage, something he just *had* to read, and so he would, opening the binding with the spirit of an assassin: *Okay, who the fuck's* this *guy think he is?* And he'd be damned if more often than not the work impressed him, and therefore *de*pressed him. What the hell was going on anyway? Here the country was supposed to be a poor gaggle of yahoos, a hopeless procession of illiterate bobble heads, and yet every year there was a veritable tidal wave of new books and writers: bright, exuberant, inventive, photogenic, *hateful* little bastards with huge advances and, presumably, voluminous readership.

Where did they come from? Why didn't they go away? Hadn't they heard the whole thing was impossible?

And every year they got younger. When, at twenty-five, Kyle had struck gold with *Charmed Life,* it had seemed a precocious debut. These days a twenty-five-year-old writer was no big deal, sort of middle-aged in fact, at least when compared to these new wunderkinds. Now you had college freshmen outlining their first novel, sophomores researching agents and publishers. Hadn't a high school kid published a novel just this year? *American High* or some such thing? What was next, *The Pre-K Nocturnes*? Things sure had changed since Kyle was first starting out, back when a writer still had some time. Then you could at least count on the majority of your competition getting bogged down in the ubiquitous M.F.A. program, only to wallow a few more years in some mind-numbing job as they dug out of their student loans.

Kyle had skipped all that and so had got a bit of a head start. Still, he knew he'd taken a step back with his last book. *New York Daze* was basically a novella, a slim, polite memoir recalling his early years in the city. It had some of the clearest, most evocative writing he'd ever done, but what did that matter? Who wanted quaint stories of Kyle Clayton selling his books back to the Strand for beer money, or the wacky landlady with mob ties? Who cared for carefully crafted prose on the fertile promise of moving to New York in your twenty-first year, scared out of your wits you wouldn't be good enough, that the city would chew you up and spit you back to whatever dreary little burg you'd hailed from — only to finally triumph?

What they'd wanted, of course, was the dirt. The drinking and debaucheries. The thoughtless punches thrown and the cocktail marathons and the bathroom-stall sex and, of course, some sense of the insane glory of becoming a literary sensation overnight: *How much money did you make, Kyle? How many girls did you fuck* (celebrity names preferred)? *How many drugs did you do? New York Daze* almost pretended as if none of this had ever happened.

Oddly enough, the reviews had been kind. It was just the sort of soft, gentle book the folks from *USA Today* and *Newsweek* lavished superlatives on. But the buying public had stayed away. In the end, Kyle couldn't blame them. It wasn't really a memoir at all; it was fiction, and not very interesting fiction at that. He'd airbrushed his early twenties into something like the first 100 pages of *Sophie's Choice,* when everybody knew it had really been much closer to *The Ginger Man.* Perhaps unconsciously, Kyle had been trying to rewrite his own history, repudiating his past with Eastern Bloc–style disinformation. The public had smelled a rat and had turned up their noses. Good for them, he thought. He'd have to be sharper next time.

The problem now was money. Based upon a mere 100 pages, Patience had secured him $200,000 for his next book. To outsiders this would surely seem a generous, even princely, sum. Practically speaking, though, the figure was quite gruesome. Right off the top came 15 percent for agent fees, for example, then nearly a third more for taxes. That left roughly $120,000. Still good, not exactly a food-stamp case, but then one had to remember to divide that number by *four,* the number of years it was going to take him to write the book. This left you with a far humbler $30,000 a year. In her first year in Web design, Ayla had made more than twice that. So did just about everyone else.

And the two incomes were just not enough. Ninety grand in Manhattan with a second house upstate — never mind a husband who couldn't take a meal without a glass of wine and thought foie gras was one of the five basic food groups. Good luck. Then add the fact that they wanted to have a child and that the rest of the country was (effortlessly, it seemed) getting filthy stinking rich right under their very noses, were basically running through the streets with Hefty bags full of cash, and you had for some tense nights in the Claytons' bedroom just before sleep — what with the incessant fretting about money, babies, and beat-up old cars on their last legs.

It was perhaps with no small amount of serendipity then that

Kyle, reflecting that morning on these very anxieties, received the following phone call.

"*Tits* this chick had. Nipples like scooter pies."

Pussy with the Pixie, he thought.

"Down yonder, you ask? Seventh heaven, though some serious foliage to get through, I cannot tell a lie. We're talking Bush Gardens here. We're talking fully flossed for the month. But, oh, what a payoff at the edge of the glen!"

"Let me guess, you banged her."

"Jealous?"

"You know," Kyle said, deciding to shoot back, "you'd think you'd be a little more supportive of this new stable environment I've set up for myself. It's supposed to be good for creativity."

"You mean marriage? Oh, yes, that's true, Kyle. You'll be quite fecund now that there's nothing else to do. Lot of extra time on your hands, so to speak."

"Thank you, Patience."

"Anyway, fuck all that. I think I got a ten-grander for you."

"Ten-grander?"

"Money, you dipsomaniac. *Money.*" She mentioned the name of a major men's magazine. A celebrity profile. "High-paying fluff. There's a couple of writers' names being tossed around for it, but I can probably get you in."

Magazines, thought Kyle. Ouch. He'd promised himself he was through with that sort of thing. It was all so humiliating. You met some inane young film star over a hotel lunch while they promoted their newest celluloid spilth currently pullulating across the country, and at a theater near you. It was advertising copy, penned by publicists sowing a rampant disease. He despised it.

"Magazines, huh?"

"What did you want me to say?"

"That you have piles of cash lying around in your office designated for Kyle Clayton, tax-free and waiting to be picked up by U-Haul. Just because I'm me."

"Well, stop writing about Muslims and maybe we'll talk. In the meantime, it's ten grand for twelve hundred words you write while you Q-tip your ears."

"Ten thousand," he repeated.

He suddenly remembered the last interview he'd done. "Cuddly" new actor at the SoHo Grand, Kyle sub vino and holding on by a thread as he went down the list of questions dreamed up by a junior editor named Nipper.

Hugs, Matt. Love 'em or hate 'em?

There was a pause during which Kyle saw himself in the backyard of his house in Saugerties, swinging by the neck from one of the old scrub oaks.

He told Patience he'd take it.

"Good, but we'll still have to see," she said. "I tell them you're interested, then we keep our fingers crossed."

Something told Kyle that with a little Patience, things would be all right.

"Oh, and Kyle," she added, "there's been some rumblings about the Muslim piece."

He sat forward. "Oh yeah?"

"Islamic Antidefamation League, or some damned thing."

"Serious?" he asked.

"Nah, don't lose sleep. The Muhammad stuff's got them in a little bit of a dither, that's all. *NYC* got a few letters . . . Anyhow, I'm getting another call. Over and out."

As Patience hung up, Kyle slipped into a momentary funk. So, he thought, a few Muslims had their panties in a twirl. Well, at least it was *something*. Otherwise, not much reaction from the *NYC* excerpt. Sort of come and gone, hadn't it? It was not a good sign. He was reminded now of what he considered the hardest part about being a writer: the lack of returns. You broke your ass for what? Three, four, *five* years? Then you edited the fucker for another ten months — and what did you get, finally? A flurry of reviews for a week and a few phone calls. After that, the dolorous silence.

Charmed Life had been a fluke, of course. The reaction had been intense and had trickled over into years of attention. But lately things had grown thin. Now he was like every other half-assed scribbler — you ripped another book out of your guts and threw it into the abyss, along with the thousands of other titles, the overwhelming mass that made the whole thing seem pointless and, on bad days, like a sort of pollution.

It was only when he called Ayla to tell her the good news that he'd realized he had no idea of what or whom the piece might be about.

Outrageous Fortune

The summer of '99 moved swiftly along, flourishing in all its prosperous glory. In the Hamptons, summer rentals were full, some houses fetching as much as $500,000 for the season, though many vacationers, their laptops set out on the pool deck, were too busy making twice that in an afternoon to enjoy much of the weather or sweet corn. In Boston, students from MIT skipped the Cape for jobs at Internet startups, earning their complete four-year tuition in a single summer, many deciding not to go back to school at all. In the Silicon Valley, tract homes on less than a quarter-acre went for $1.5 million.

All across the country, cocaine sales were up.

On Park Avenue, nervous gaggles of Shih Tzus and Yorkshire terriers were once again the rage, while in certain other neighborhoods — just a few blocks north in Washington Heights, for example, or in West New York — there was no discernible change at all.

In Europe, from Lisbon to Brussels, financiers whispered about the new arrogance of the American businessman. *Look what we've done now!* seemed to be the attitude. A swagger and self-congratulations.

None of the Europeans who complained of this stopped doing business with Americans.

Back in the United States, the market forecasters were optimistic beyond all discretion. The NASDAQ was just getting started, they announced, and would increase steadily for the next seven to ten years. Dow 20,000 was inevitable, 30,000 not out of the question. It was pretty clear to everyone that the good times would never end.

Everyone except Lonny Tumin.

August meant East Hampton for Tumin, the compound on Further Lane. Time to unwind for a few weeks, to heal from the slings and arrows of maintaining an outrageous fortune. And, this particular summer, to cool off from the humiliations of the golf course ranger and his slick-ass lawyer.

The number Dana Wallace had inscribed on the paper inside that envelope had seemed ludicrous, a pipe dream blown out of his ass for kicks. But Tumin had paid it. Kicking and screaming, and on Don Westly's advice, he'd paid it, and then gone on a binge of Tums washed down with copious amounts of rationalization. Everything was more expensive these days, wasn't it? he told himself. Real estate, women, even simple good taste. Everything had another zero tacked on the end — while never stopping to think how the whole thing was just bad judgment, and could have easily been avoided.

He lay now in the hammock in the backyard, sipping his iced tea, trying in vain to relax. The missing money continued to vex him, and the country life was no help. Trees, fresh air, sunshine — this had never been of any interest to Lonny Tumin. His preferred environ was definitely urban in composition. Put him in a tower of corrugated steel (at the top), with windows (opaque from the outside), then add a herd of scurrying minions hell-bent on making him richer than he already was, and Lonny Tumin was happy. This country shit was for the birds, man.

Ditto the ocean. A mere football field away was the Atlantic, always palpable with its cool breezes and mists that swept over the property like a briny perfume. But these charms were also wasted on Tumin. Water views were commonplace to him. Didn't their home on the North Shore already overlook the Sound? Wasn't there a bay view in Palm Beach? Come to think of it, Lonny Tumin had had it up to *here* with water. Three homes on the Atlantic, plus swimming pools. Why they'd had to add this monstrosity just recently was beyond him, but Diane had been stuck on the place. Do we really need more water? he'd asked her. I can't even fuckin' swim. I'm from *Newark,* for Chrisakes. But then hell, Tumin thought, she *was* worth it.

As if on cue, he heard the cool slither of the patio doors, and Diane Tumin emerged in her bathing suit.

Get a load of that, would you? Tumin told himself, peeping over his iced tea like the pool boy. Now I see how she does it, how I let her bleed my assets like air from a farting balloon. Still the best-looking woman anyone had ever laid eyes on. Mid-thirties and firm all the way down, blond hair shining like the tail of a horse. Naturally, he knew what people thought when they saw them together. He could see the surprise in their eyes when he and his wife strolled into a room, the barely contained guffaws. *Oh, you've* got *to be kidding . . .* Lonny a good three inches shorter than her and skin like a pepperoni pizza. It was beauty and the beast all the way — Tumin would tell you that himself. But go ahead and titter, you snide bastards, he'd always wanted to say. I'm married to the piece of ass of the century, and you're not.

What he couldn't abide though, was the moral smugness, the pathetic conceits they held about his wife's attraction to him — this idea that because her love was based on money it was somehow more shallow than, say, if it had been based on looks. Oh, I see, Tumin had thought, sandblast my cheeks and give me an abdomen like a reptile and suddenly it all made sense. Suddenly *then* we're not so superficial! No, it was a simple matter of aesthetics, he knew, of practicality. In fact, a woman who went for money was actually much wiser, had a more sophisticated perspective of the world. For what fool didn't know that marriage was the enemy of attraction? Passion wanes, my friend, and kindly hold the sanctimony. Basically, it came down to this: Did you want a pretty *thing,* which you'd be bored of in a few short years, or pretty *things* that would never stop coming?

Surprisingly, Diane and he still had their moments in bed, even after ten years together. Their sex life had reached a sort of barter phase. In dreary February, for example, Diane would announce she was bringing two girlfriends with her to St. Bart's, with Lonny footing the bill. Oh, really? her husband would counter, well, then that'll cost you "five" — by which he meant five encounters, *however* and *whenever* he wanted them. Diane would counter with an offer of three, throwing in a parking-lot blowjob as the kicker (his favorite, her least). Then, approximately two weeks later — after countless drafts, last-second proposals, and various incentive clauses — a deal would be finally struck.

It was an arrangement in which both managed to find a surprising amount of excitement. All her life Diane had been bred to be the good girl (that illusion of purity she might parlay into a fortune — bull's-eye on that!), and she was damned sick of it. In fact, her long ruse of chastity had only made sleaze that much more enticing. Lonny, meanwhile, businessman to the core, was only able to become aroused if sex involved some sort of financial transaction. Straight sex with a woman who actually found you attractive? Maybe when you're *fifteen*, he'd say. Now I'd rather take a nap. Lust could only be found in a certain kind of coercion, a situation in which a woman (not necessarily Diane) was obliged to do something for him that ordinarily she would not. In this way, he used his own unattractiveness to turn himself on, to heighten his sense of leveraged power. His ugliness, paradoxically, was the eros.

Even now, as Diane wandered to the edge of the diving board in her bikini and beach clogs, waving girlishly, Tumin thought of taking her to the pool house and exacting yet another installment on the Further Lane tab, a sexual mortgage that would leave her prostrate deep into the new millennium. But then Tumin heard the sound of the Sikorsky, the blades cleaving the near sky to evaporating ribbons, and Ramon, the elegant Cuban servant, came out to announce the arrival of one Mr. Donald Westly.

"Putting on a little weight, are we?" Tumin ventured.

They were under the great chestnut tree at a small café-style table. In the mushroom cap of leaves and branches above them, some birds chirped assiduously, salutations to their beneficent landlord.

"What can I say?" Don told him. "Gettin' old." He looked down at himself with a wry smile and patted his slight paunch. Then he alerted Ramon, who stood waiting for a drink order, that he'd like a beer.

"Dinners with your Hollywood friends," Tumin guessed. "Doesn't look good on you." He did something with his eyes to Ramon, and the Cuban headed back to the house.

"Why, are you thinking of asking me out on a date, Lonny?" Don took off his jacket and laid it on the back of his chair.

"You depressed?" Tumin asked.

"Excuse me?"

"Are you depressed?"

Don laughed a little. "No. About what?"

"I don't know . . . How about your wife?"

Don sat more erect in his chair. "What's that supposed to mean?"

"Susan's on your ass, isn't she?" Tumin grinned knowingly and grabbed a carrot from a plate of raw vegetables. "Want me to talk to her?"

"Talk to . . . No. Hell no."

"She and I are old friends." The boss crunched his carrot loudly. "Maybe I can help."

Irritating as this line of questioning was, Don's overriding sensation was more of incredulity. It was testimony to the acute instincts of Lonny Tumin that he'd known there were problems in the Westly marriage. Monumental problems, in fact; after a week of heavy infighting, Susan had taken to sleeping in the guest room during the evenings, joining Don in their bed at dawn to keep up appearances for the kids. She had announced that she could no longer stand to look at her husband.

While Don pretended the feeling was mutual, he actually found the whole episode quite earth-shattering, if not thoroughly humiliating. Susan told him she'd had a sudden "realization" that her husband was a failure, nothing more than Tumin's whipping boy — the Mascot Man, she called him — and that despite their elevated financial status she could neither love nor respect such a man. None of this being anything Don could share with his boss.

"All right, I'll tell you what, Lonny, since we're being frank here, I don't appreciate being left out of Monarch. I don't think it's right. I don't think it's fair."

"Can't be helped," Tumin said flatly.

Across the wide lawns, Ramon came striding with a tray of sandwiches and drinks. Don noticed that the beer he'd ordered had not come. In its place, the Cuban had brought him an iced tea.

"Ramon."

"Yes," the man answered, setting down the glasses.

Don held up the iced tea. "This is not what I ordered, Ramon."

"We're all out of beer," replied the Cuban without a hitch. He flashed his eyes to Lonny and then offered a tight bow. "Enjoy your lunch."

Don looked over at Tumin. "Ra*mon*," he called out.

The server turned back after a few steps.

"Sir?"

There was a long pause; Ramon waited. Don could see Tumin looking on with interest.

"Ah, fuck it," he murmured.

"Sir?"

"Nothing," Don called out, waving his hand.

Ramon headed back to the house.

"Look, I want in on the Ohka deal," he told Tumin now, with what seemed like exaggerated force. "I'm serious; I'm tired of this shit."

His boss seemed to register some surprise. "Tired?" he said. "Of what? Getting rich and having very little to do?"

"*Yes*. Exactly. I'm bored, Lonny. I'm fucking bored to death."

Despite the obvious conviction of Don's words, Tumin seemed unmoved. "Sorry, but you've never been that creative, Don. Not your forte. Of course, that can be limiting. I think you've done very well for yourself, considering."

"Considering what?"

Tumin put an elbow on the café table and leaned forward. "All right, you want to talk turkey, Donny? Fine, let's talk turkey. How many years have we been working together? Twenty, twenty-five? Now, I want you to name one project you've come to me with in all those years . . ." When Don began to stir, Lonny rapped his knuckles on the table for emphasis. "No, listen to me, I want you to tell me — right here, right now — the name of one business, one investment, one fucking *lead* you've come to me with that made us money."

Some of the steam suddenly seemed to leak from Don Westly. He slackened in his chair.

"I do the deals, Donny. Me, okay? I find them, I put them together, so I take home the big prize. You're given a damned fine

piece, considering." Slightly worked up, his boss took an obstreper-
ous bite from the grilled vegetable sandwich that had been placed in
front of him. "You have your strengths, Don," he said, talking
around the food. "Know what they are and what they're worth."

Feeling another growing mortification, Don looked down into the
deep plush of the lawn, trying to distract himself. The grass, he
noticed, was green to the point of macabre. There were large swatches
that appeared to be purple. He recalled how it was fertilized so much
that guests were discouraged from walking in bare feet.

"Anyway, how we doing on the publicity end?" Tumin's voice
now had the tone of someone determined to move on. This was an
old business style of his: he'd rough you up to get his way, then
quickly go about rebuilding your confidence. "I get the cover of this
piece of shit or what?"

Don's voice was a little flat. "Profile's confirmed, though I think
we missed the cover."

"*What?* I thought this publisher's a buddy of yours."

"Their covers are set a year ahead," he said, lying. "We could
wait, but I think timing is imperative." As it turned out, both he and
Lonny had underestimated how far his boss's star power had fallen.
Don had cashed in a favor and still they couldn't bag the cover. Nevertheless, the publication was both new and prestigious, and wouldn't
hurt Monarch one bit. "Oh, yeah, Halberstam's out, by the way."

"Out?" Tumin seemed to swallow his bit of sandwich prema-
turely, washing it down hurriedly with some iced tea.

"He's writing another baseball book," Don added.

"*So?* That fuck eats in my restaurant for free."

"We can't *make* him do it, Lonny. He sends his apologies."

"Apologies, hey, that's sweet. I'll remember that the next time he
comes in for dinner and it's check time." Tumin gritted his teeth.
"How about Dunne?"

Don shook his head. "He's contracted to another magazine. It's
binding. He's no good to us."

"*Binding,*" Tumin grumbled under his breath. "*I'll show him
binding.*" He took another bite, chewing harshly again. Don watched
the tendons in Tumin's jaw push against the pitted cheeks.

"In any case, I was thinking we could use somebody younger,"
Don ventured. "You're introducing an Internet stock here, a software

company. The whole tech culture's about youth, Lonny, love it or hate it."

"Hate it."

"Well, fine, but that's not that important, is it? What's important is getting somebody who reflects a fresh attitude. A writer who might have actually been on the Internet a few times. You get someone young to do it, somebody contemporary, hip —"

"Hip," Tumin said scoffingly. "I hate that word, *hip*. Hip is shit."

"Fresh, hip, whatever, Lonny. You want young energy on this. Trust me."

Tumin brooded on this for a few moments, then Don offered a list of young writers the publicist had recommended. One of them, Don had discovered, was a regular at City.

His name was Kyle Clayton.

"Never heard of him," Tumin said.

"Mid-thirties, so he's not too young. He's known for a certain New York perspective that might be interesting."

"What's he written?"

Don's voice was tentative. "*Charming Wife*? Something like that."

Tumin shook his head, agitated now. "Never heard of that either," he said, as if he would have.

"You don't need to have heard of him, Lonny. That's not the point."

"What's the point?"

"The point is that everybody under forty years old *has* heard of him, and many of them are the same people we want to hear about *you*."

Tumin pushed his sandwich away and wiped his hands on a napkin. Don had worked with him long enough to know that the tilt of his head now meant he finally thought Don was beginning to make sense. "He's been to my restaurant?"

"Many times, apparently."

Tumin pursed his lips and nodded. It was as close as he ever got to signaling satisfaction.

He said he'd think about it.

In the meantime, lunch moved toward its conclusion. Don wanted to be rid of his boss as soon as possible. This was supposed to be his big vacation, twelve days in August, but somehow Tumin always found a way to abridge your holiday. Don had received a message late last night about today's meeting, and so he'd had to cancel his morning of golf. If he could be back in the Sikorsky in the next fifteen minutes or so, he thought, there might still be time for a round.

Ramon returned to clear the lunch. It occurred to Don how he might now demand the beer that the Cuban had so rudely denied him — not drink it but have it brought to him, to prove a point. There was plenty of beer in Tumin's house, of course, cases and cases, just as there was plenty of everything, for every possible occasion.

But before he could speak, Don decided that waiting for another beverage would just prolong the afternoon with Tumin. Consulting his watch, he felt pretty sure that if he left now he could be on the first tee by four-thirty.

He thanked Ramon for the delicious lunch.

Taxi

From time to time Erin would receive pornographic, though highly felicitous, e-mails.

> All I'm saying is, I'd like to stick my tongue — with which, incidentally, I can tie a captain's knot with a cherry stem — into that crevice where the fleshy underside of your breast meets the silky and, may I add, taut section of your upper abdomen, and then . . .

She had no idea how he'd got her e-mail address, but then such things were simple enough to find these days. The sender, of course, was Kyle Clayton.

> All I'm saying is, a crotchless latex bodysuit and high heels are perfect for this movie I've been telling you about, to be shot on digital starring the one and only Erin Wyatt (just my lower body will be shown), and in which your physicality will be on full display as you dangle from one of the many love harnesses that hang from my bedroom ceiling . . .

Erin never answered these messages, but she knew it must be a symptom of something when she realized that she wasn't deleting them from her mailbox, and that sometimes she even reread them before breaking out the Conair back massager for a "session." Though this self-arousal was generally a cheerless activity, it was preferable to, say, waking up in Bay Ridge in the bed of the restaurant's new sous chef after too many Cosmopolitans — something that had happened twice already this month.

She'd been going out quite a bit this summer. Another symptom, she'd surmised. Two or three nights a week after work, Erin found herself at the Blue Stripe, one of the downtown bistros that served food until 4:00 A.M., hanging with the "guys" from City. Though the players changed from night to night, there was that hardcore nucleus one could always count on: Stephen, on the fritz with his boyfriend and so out on the prowl; Abu, who came to sip Sprite and stare at his Miss Erin; and finally Urlich, the would-be painter / avant-garde filmmaker who came to spew his bile of self-loathing on the only people who'd listen.

In every restaurant in which Erin had ever worked there was an Urlich. He was small and stern, with horn-rimmed glasses and an ambiguous accent, possibly Germanic, possibly Dutch. A painter in his downtime, he thought he would parlay his inevitable fame into avant-garde filmmaking, though things never did quite work out. He was forty-two now, and these disappointments were the driving force in his life.

He had a cheap-seats subscription to the Metropolitan Opera, and liked to boo. All the popular singers got booed by Urlich when they came out for their ovation. His most recent victim was Jessye Norman.

"Why would you boo her?" Stephen was asking now.

It was just the four of them tonight. The table was enveloped in inert aureoles of cigarette smoke, overflowing with bulging ashtrays, smudged-up martini glasses, and the grisly remains of steak *frites*.

"Why not?" Urlich said disgustedly. "She's terrible. I *loathe* her. Ever seen her?"

"No," Stephen admitted, sipping his drink.

"Well, to see her is to *loathe* her. To hear her is to contract a disease."

Erin was almost ashamed to admit that she enjoyed Urlich's company. His bitterness knew no bounds and gave a vicarious voice to her own. Conversely, as a waiter, his pursuit of excellence was truly inspiring. Technically he was the best server she'd ever seen, and she had never met anyone so unflappable at a table. "Never let the customer feel intelligent," he'd once told her. "Always keep the control. Turn your mistakes into virtues."

And so he did. Recently word had come down that a certain dinner reservation was actually a reviewer from a major newspaper, and so Urlich was chosen to wait on the table. Everything was perfection until the appetizers were cleared and the food runners cheerfully delivered the wrong food to the reviewer's table — four entrées that had been meant for the table next to them.

"Excuse me, excuse me, *waiter!*" The reviewer himself had his napkin out and was waving it above his head, calling out across the restaurant. Urlich went scuttling across the floor in a way that was speedy, yet betrayed no panic.

How is he going to get out of this one? Erin wondered, swiftly positioning herself within earshot.

"This is not what we ordered," said the reviewer upon the waiter's arrival.

"Mmm?" Urlich replied. He surveyed the food, his look suggesting this was an obvious and rather silly point to bring to his attention. "Well, of course, sir. I just wanted you to see what you were missing out on."

The four diners looked at one another, somewhat confused.

Urlich's voice did not waver in confidence. "You must agree that this is very attractive food."

The silence continued, their faces growing ever more confounded.

"But we didn't order it," said a woman finally.

"Well, that is no fault of *mine,* now is it, madame?" Urlich gave them a rare smile, then quickly removed all four plates, skillfully layering them along his arm. "I guess you've seen enough," he said, feigning mild insult. "*Your* entrées will be out momentarily."

The review had been a great success.

There were many such funny moments with Urlich, but then there was also an air of tragedy about him. Every once in a while Erin would run into him on the street — they lived not far from each other — and she was always startled to see how different he looked. On the floor of City, on a busy Saturday night, Urlich was a fire-cracker, brusque and furiously organized, totally in his element. Out-side the restaurant, though, he seemed diminished. In the harsh light of afternoon, in his slightly tattered jacket and wool skullcap, a corona of failure seemed to hang over him. Although he told her absolutely nothing about himself, she felt she knew his life well. Her image of him on a Sunday morning, for instance, devastated her: Urlich in his rent-controlled tenement apartment (the one he would die in, she felt sure), smoked whitefish on a bagel and a scowl fixed on the *Arts and Leisure* section. His work shirts hung on the shower cur-tain rod, the rooms reeking of bleach. And alone, of course. Always alone.

Where would he be in ten years? Twenty? It wounded her to think of it.

Underscoring this pathos, of course, was Erin's recognition that her own life might be on a similar trajectory. Realistically, she figured she had one last shot. She was thirty; there was still some small, infin-itesimal chance. Lately she had been trying to keep hope alive with daily affirmations, remembrances of good notices she'd received, people who had singled her out as special. Yes, it was worth one final push, she'd decided. But where? *How?*

In hindsight, she'd actually enjoyed her run in *Titus*. It had reminded her how much she loved acting, even in such a pathetic pro-duction. But it had done nothing for her so-called career. In fact, she was pretty sure now that it had hurt her. Her manager hadn't shown up to any of her performances, and after *Titus* had ended, he'd stopped sending her out on auditions altogether, her phone calls going unreturned. Only months later had Erin finally grasped what had happened: her manager had regarded her participation in such a low-down project as a defeat, evidence of a career in permanent retro-grade. *Titus* had pronounced her DOA as an actress, and now she had fallen into a vicious cycle of needing to stay out late every night to drown her sense of failure, then finding herself too comatose the next day to do anything about it. To bed at 5:00 A.M., up at 2:00 P.M. Shower and work, day after day after day. She'd never been more of a waitress in her life.

The equalizer to all this, she felt, was her aunt. Though she would never admit it, Erin understood that Helena was ailing, now more than ever, and though she absolutely did *not* want anything to happen to her beloved aunt, the simple fact was that the end was encroaching. When she did pass, Erin Wyatt would no longer be a waitress. In fact, she might not ever have to work again. She took some solace in that, unlike her unfortunate workmates, she had a rather humongous safety net waiting for her.

"You see any movies lately, Abu?" Erin asked now, and Abu's face lit up like the moon. All night he'd been waiting for her to say something to him.

"No, I'm not liking most of them, Miss Erin. Veddy bad, I think, these American movies."

"Hear, hear," chimed Urlich, who was getting good and drunk now, and whose private disappointment was starting to bare its teeth. "Loathsome pieces of dung." He raised his glass to toast Abu, though the Muslim did not dare to abut his beverage with alcohol.

"Too much violence," Abu continued, and then, possibly for Erin's benefit, he added, "especially against the women."

The music segued from Latin Restaurant White Noise (known this year as the Buena Vista Social Club, previously the Gypsy Kings) to Billie Holiday, and now Urlich began making his food-poisoned face again.

"Oh, no *way*, Urlich," Erin groaned. "Don't tell me you don't like Billie Holiday. Nobody's too cool for Billie Holiday, do you hear me?"

"You're kidding, right?" the waiter replied. "Billie-please-take-a-Holiday. Lady Bay? Oh, my heavens."

"Who do you listen to?" Stephen challenged.

Urlich mentioned a fado singer from the late nineteenth century who'd died before she was twenty. There was a single recording, he'd said, unfortunately out of print. Four — no, make it three — precious songs, a little staticky, but if you turned up the volume and had a forty-band equalizer, it was Arcadia for the ears.

She let Abu follow her out onto Sullivan Street. This was how these wasteful nights usually ended — Erin a little drunk and trying to flag down a cab for her faithful colleague. Abu was quite dark in complexion, and it was disconcerting to see how hard it was to find him a taxi, especially since the majority of drivers were from his own country, and in one comical instance, was actually a not-so-distant relative.

In truth, Abu didn't mind these long waits for a willing cab. This was as intimate as it got between him and Miss Erin, and to him, every minute was Paradise.

"I didn't know you worked in Japan," Erin said to him. She had one foot off the curb, hand poised half-mast on the empty street. She was buzzed and very tired and didn't want to talk, but knew Abu would be crushed by her silence. "Syeed told me you worked over there for a while."

"Five years," he said. It obviously pleased him to know that Erin had been chatting about him with others. "French restaurant in Tokyo."

"Good money?" she asked.

"Oh, yes."

"And you liked the city?" A lighted cab headed across Spring; Erin whistled, but the car disappeared. "Tokyo, I mean?"

"Sure, oh, yes. Much more than New York."

She seemed surprised. "Really? Why more than New York?"

Smiling mischievously, Abu gestured that he wanted to say something in her ear. Towering above him, Erin leaned down to listen.

"No black ones," he whispered.

She immediately straightened up, hoping to see some irony on his face, some sense that he was kidding, but he was clearly not. Erin was suddenly filled with a sinking feeling; she adored Abu, of course, but the comment threatened to burst her high opinion of him, not to mention its revealing a rather skewed sense of logic. Had he looked in the mirror lately? Erin wanted to know. Didn't he see this was the same brand of idiocy that made it necessary for her to find him a cab every night? That an attitude like this was held by such a reasonable, good-natured person as Abu — and that he'd assumed she'd feel the same way, suspecting it was something they could share — troubled her deeply.

"Miss Erin, I love you," he suddenly announced.

She ignored this, hoping he didn't have the nerve to repeat it.

"Miss Erin? Did you hear me? I love you."

She kept her eyes on the street. Though a single car had yet to pass them, her arm was still outstretched. "No, you don't," she said finally.

"I do, very much."

She turned to him. "Look, Abu. You know that I am incredibly fond of you. I am. You're probably my favorite person at the restaurant, but —"

"I want you to be my wife."

"What?" Erin let loose a muted guffaw, and Abu looked crestfallen. As she struggled to cover up her mirth, a wave of empathy came over her. What was she doing? she thought. Hadn't she too stood out on Manhattan streets in the early morning, saying desperate things? "Abu, c'mon," she said evenly. "That's not realistic, and you know it."

"This is what I want."

"You're *married*."

"I am also a Muslim. I can do this. I bring you back to my country; you can be my second wife."

It was actually good that this was happening, she thought. Now they could end this once and for all, go back to being friends. Erin put her hands on her hips and looked him square in the eye. "And what about me, Abu? What about what *I* want?"

"I open soon a business with my brother back in Bangladesh. I take care of you. Your days as a waitress are no more."

"But that's not what I want, Abu. I don't want to go to Bangladesh, and I certainly don't want to be someone's second wife. I would never do that. I want my *own* man — when, you know, the time comes."

Abu looked down thoughtfully at the sidewalk. Erin could tell he'd never really considered this possibility. No doubt that in Bangladesh, a thirty-year-old working woman would marry him in an instant.

Then her godsend arrived — a cab with its light on sneaked up alongside them. Though it was fully stopped and sitting just a few feet away, Erin waved her hand furiously.

"Tell him no," Abu said plaintively. "I get next one."

"No, you're taking this one," she said. She put a hand on the middle of his back and guided him to the curb. "It's late. I'm sure your wife is going crazy waiting for you."

With little resistance, he allowed her to move him toward the back of the car. When he got in instead of Erin, the Jamaican driver barely hid his disappointment.

The taxi pulled away. Standing by herself on the curb, Erin wondered when she'd ever felt so low, so much like shit. This was the fourth night in a row she'd gone out after work, and yet another bout of *frites* and flavored vodka and cigarette smoke had left her queasy. She'd noticed too that the light was beginning to turn blue, and a few birds had begun to sing. She needed to get home; there were shirts to iron before tomorrow's lunch shift.

Walking home along Spring, she began to feel very alone and had the impulse to cry, but she somehow managed to hold it back. Tomorrow was another day.

Mr. Hip

"Is this him?" Tumin said aloud to no one in particular. He was standing under the Sikorsky, his words booming even under the whipping propeller blades. "Is this Mr. Hip?"

They were on the roof of the Triad building, Tumin waiting for them on the helipad. Kyle had been escorted here first by a secretary whom he would have liked to have known better, and then by a strapping blond gentleman named Don Westly, with whom the writer had instantly hit it off. Platonically speaking, Don was his type. He had the dignified, understated handsomeness of a Jeff Bridges, Kyle thought, and reminded him somewhat of his own father. During their walk, he learned that Mr. Westly was the second cog in Triad, though he seemed awfully mellow for a mogul.

But Lonny Tumin was another story. Tumin was what in Kyle's youth they used to call a *pisser*. He stood above them on the slightly raised helipad, hammy actor on his stage, clapping and smiling raffishly. Acerbity dripped from his every pore.

"Well, well, well," he was saying as Kyle and Don approached the small staircase of corrugated steel. Outside the door of the cockpit, a pilot stood in slack attention, waiting for the order. "Mr. Hip is in the *house*. Look at those shades, would you, Donny. Is this dude cool or what?"

Kyle found himself laughing at this antiquated jargon, even as it was meant to mock him. He was indeed wearing sunglasses — just as the publicist had recommended, since the interview was to take place during a helicopter ride around the island of Manhattan at five o'clock in the afternoon. The sun, she'd assured him, sitting at eye level at this hour, would be brutal.

But *hip?* he thought, with mild revulsion. To Kyle the term was an expletive, usually employed by midwestern book reviewers who'd set out to thrash him. He suddenly regretted the old T-shirt he wore under his blazer, which read, "Uncle Tupelo, Barrel Fermented."

"Where's the party, man?" the mogul continued as Kyle and Don took the stairs, still stuck on his theme. "Where's the chicks?"

"You must be Mr. Tumin," the writer shouted as he reached the platform, trying to get his words through the sound-mincing blades. Moving across the helipad, he removed his sunglasses and offered Tumin his hand. For some reason, Kyle was almost surprised when it was accepted. He couldn't help feeling that the billionaire's humor carried with it a tinge of hostility.

"I'm Tumin, you got that right." He looked at his watch. "And you, my hip friend, have got exactly forty-five minutes of my time. What do you think of that?"

Kyle looked to the copter; the cabin door was ajar. Looking inside, he could see a large black man whose sapphire-blue suit suggested he might be the bodyguard.

"I'll take it," he said, forcing a big grin.

As if expecting nothing less, Tumin extended his hand toward the open cabin, entreating the writer to board first. As the pilot grabbed Kyle's elbow, ready to help him up the first rung, Tumin touched his other shoulder to get his attention.

"You okay to fly?" he asked the suddenly pale young man.

"Yeah, sure, I guess." Then, hesitating to take the step, Kyle decided to fess up. "To be honest, it's not my favorite thing in the world. Flying, I mean. I'm sort of scared of heights."

"I know," Tumin replied. He was smiling brightly, distinctly pleased with himself. "That's what we heard. That's why we're doing the interview on the old Sikko." He rapped his knuckles on the belly of the helicopter. "I like to keep writers off-balance, know what I mean?"

Kyle looked back at Don for some support, but the man turned his eyes away, shrugging ever so slightly. *Hey,* the gesture said, *you choose to step into Lonny Tumin's world, this is what you get.*

"C'mon, Brando," Tumin barked, guiding Kyle's arm toward the cabin, "get your ass up there."

Aloft a Manhattan of brass miniatures, Kyle could not prevent his fingers from digging into the spongy leather seating. Paradoxically, everything about the Sikorsky suggested comfort and security: the cabin was a plush eight-seater with a short Japanese-style conference table in the middle, and included a flight attendant who passed out Poland Springs all around. A Vivaldi concerto chirped innocuously from the speakers. No one wore a seat belt except Kyle.

"Hey, Brando," Tumin said again — apparently this was Kyle's name for the day — "check the view."

The panorama, the writer had to admit, was unforgettable. He had lived in New York no less than fifteen years, had visited regularly since he was a boy, and yet what he was seeing outside those portholes was a city both newly wondrous and almost entirely unfamiliar. As they banked out along the East River, what seemed to be a harp-like facsimile of the Brooklyn Bridge, some majestic lyre, passed into view (a little too close for Kyle's taste), and then, over his right shoulder, a gilded, late-afternoon sunlight burnished the buildings of lower Manhattan into side-standing bars of gold bullion. This sight sent a swath of electricity rippling out along his shoulder blades up to the tips of his ears, and for a second he was reminded of that old promise of New York he'd felt so deeply as a young man (before all hell had broken loose), the beckoning luster and grandiosity that challenged you to do your best, that said anything was possible. The idea now chided Kyle — whether or not he had answered that call. Certainly he had done so initially, he felt, with a success both definitive and romantically improbable. But whether or not he had continued to fulfill that pledge was a question that nagged at him continuously, and was especially whetted now by the diorama. Doubt followed him always.

Not so with the man sitting across from him. He could see instantly that Lonny Tumin was not a man prone to philosophical uncertainty, and perhaps with good reason, for who dared challenge his accomplishments? Kyle had read the press packet he'd been sent and was impressed by Tumin's ascendancy. The man had come to New York and *veni, vidi, vici*-ed the joint in ten seconds flat, a triumph that he had sustained over many decades. Whatever his recent problems — and by problems one meant that his wealth had stopped increasing in numerical configurations unfathomable to the common man — whatever destiny Tumin had thought awaited him in the caverns of gold bullion, he must have come damned close to realizing it.

It was only the means, Kyle thought, that could be called into question.

"By the way," Tumin said now, drawing Kyle's attention from the window, "you're not going to fuck me, are you?"

Sensing that the interview had indeed begun, Kyle pressed the Record button on the microcassette and placed it on the table between them. He was both pleased and distressed to notice a few feet away from them that Don and the bodyguard had begun their own conversation. He and Tumin were alone now.

"Um, sorry?"

"You're not going to fuck me, I said."

"You'll have to get me drunk first," Kyle answered, but was disappointed to see the quip go unappreciated. What was it about the very rich, he wondered, that they had no ear for humor?

"Listen to me. The last time I did one of these things I got royally fucked by this . . ." Tumin seemed pained to choke down the word he had in mind. He called back across the cabin. "Donny, what was her name again?"

"Who?"

"Broad from the *Times*. One who called me a 'dinosaur.'"

Kyle could see Don trying to flash a furtive look of warning his boss's way; he was urging restraint, and the writer felt that now he had the key to the mystery of this odd couple: Don Westly was the most expensive baby-sitter in America.

"We're putting that behind us, Lonny, remember? Old news. Forget it."

"Oh, yeah, putting it behind us," replied the billionaire, though with much residual bitterness. Sipping his water, he turned back to the writer. "Anyway, just don't fuck me."

What Kyle found so strange about this caveat was that Tumin's intuition was not so far off. Ordinarily a profile like this was a slam dunk in the subject's favor. A tone would be agreed upon by editor and publicist, a number of "hot points" to be covered, affirming moments, etc. The writer was simply there to fill in the colors.

But in this case, freedom was available to Kyle if he wanted it. *Magazine* was the name of the publication that had commissioned the Tumin profile, and by virtue of its being funded by a large East Coast film company, it was currently the hottest . . . well, *magazine* in the country. By a rather bizarre circumstance, the new editor in chief had turned out to be one of Kyle's oldest friends. Semper Dane was the friend's startling moniker, and Semper — whose legendary contempt for his position, and for magazine publishing in general, only seemed to accelerate his success in that world — explained to Kyle that he had "free rein" with the article. He'd inherited the story from the previous editor anyway, he'd explained, and so why not let Kyle do something wild? If it came out well, Semper could take full credit; if it were a disaster, blame could be dumped squarely on the deposed editor's now ashen pyre. Basically a free pass all around.

"How about we get into some questions?" Kyle asked now.

"Good idea. Why don't you start off by telling me who your heroes are?"

Kyle raised himself a little in his seat, grinning at the man's obvious stab at misdirection. "No, you see, Mr. Tumin, I'm supposed to ask *you* questions. That's how this works."

The older man looked around, simulating injury. "I thought we were having a conversation here."

"Well, yes, we are, but —"

"Okay, so, I want to know who I'm dealing with here, what kind of person you are. I always like to know who a guy calls his heroes."

Kyle's lip crunched under an eyetooth. His watch reported thirty-two minutes left for the interview.

"I don't really have any heroes," he replied. "Not anymore."

Tumin waved his hand, letting loose a sound somewhere between a laugh and a growl. "All right, who *were* your heroes," he said, "back when you had them?"

"I can't imagine any of them would be familiar to you."

"Try me."

"All right," the writer said with a sigh. "Let's see." The longer he jousted with Tumin on this issue, he knew, the longer it would take to get to his questions. "As a boy, Carlton Fisk. Later on, I guess, Mickey Rourke, maybe Paul Westerberg . . ."

"Westerberg," Tumin suddenly replied. "Paul Westerberg, yeah, sure." His voice trailed off for a moment, allowing the writer to succumb privately to a mild heart attack at the recognition. "New hotshot over at Lehman Brothers. Christ, why's everyone wetting themselves over this guy?"

"Actually, he's a musician," Kyle interjected, but the reply had no traction with Tumin. Instead, the mogul was inspired.

"Hey, Donny, what're the chances of getting Paul Westerberg to come over to Triad?" Tumin asked. His better half simply shrugged at this bombastic query, and then Tumin swatted at Kyle's knee. "Can you imagine that, Westerberg coming over to Triad? Lonny Tumin and Paul Westerberg, side by side?"

Kyle's beaming smile was no doubt mistook by the billionaire. "How about you, Mr. Tumin?" he asked then. "Who're *your* heroes?"

"Me? No, don't have any," Tumin announced, the writer looking disappointed. "No, really, I'd tell you if I did. A grown man with a hero isn't living his life, that's what I say. You have to live your life, know what I mean?"

Kyle now took a sip of his water, musing on Tumin's little koan. *Live your life.* Yes, he knew exactly what he meant and thought it wasn't a bad way of articulating it.

"You're living your life, Brando, I can see that."

"Am I?"

"Sure, I can tell just by looking at you. You got piss and vinegar in there." Tumin wriggled a knuckle along the cartilage of one of Kyle's ribs (which would end up being sore for a week after). "That's got you into some trouble in the past, hasn't it? Yeah, I got the word on you, my hip friend."

"I mostly got myself into trouble," Kyle admitted.

"See what I'm saying, though? Look at me, I'm in trouble every other freakin' day — we have that in common. We *live our lives,* man! People resent that. It's the one thing they can't bear."

Kyle found himself softly chuckling at this, mostly because it was preposterous and partly because he felt it was true.

"Don't laugh, Brando. I'm trying to tell you something here. You see, people don't like me very much. Simple fact. *Why?* though, that's the question. They look at me and what do they see besides a butt-ugly bastard?" Kyle laughed. "A man who's *living his life,* that's what. And they hate that because they're not living theirs. Look around" — Tumin gestured to the city below them — "look at that crazy fucking ant farm down there. They hate their lives, all of them, but then whose fault —"

Suddenly the cabin jolted a bit, and Kyle's heart fluttered around his chest like a bingo ball. Great, the engine's blown out, he thought, or maybe they'd enmeshed themselves in the lyres of the great bridge — there would be a jangled, atonal soundtrack to their watery descent.

Tumin simply mumbled "air pocket" and continued on with his theme. "Jealousy, my hip friend, pure and simple. Take Israel, for instance. Perfect analogy . . ."

With this lexical grenade, Kyle saw Don Westly look over again, trying to dissuade his boss with a covert glare. The look did not reach its target.

Kyle looked to make sure his tape recorder was running. It was.

"Why do the Muslims hate the Jews so much? And don't give me this horseshit that it's because the Israelis kill them. Hell, everybody kills Muslims. Hindus kill them, Christians kill them, Milosevic kills them by the tens of thousands. Saddam Hussein kills Muslims, for God's sake! Did you know that? Saddam kills thousands of his own people every year, whereas the Jews kill less than a hundred. But they all hate the Jews. Why? Well, I'll tell you why, because the Jews are *living their lives.*"

"Lonny," Don said.

His boss didn't flinch: "What does the Koran teach you? That Islam is the most perfect expression of what they call the 'great' religions, along with Judaism and Christianity. The best of the three, and yet . . ." It was here Tumin chuckled a bit, in a way that Kyle found unpleasant. "And yet here these poor bastards are starving, living in shantytowns and shootin' slingshots at us, while right next door, right under their fuckin' noses, is a thriving military and economic power-house. I don't get it. How they can continue to look themselves in the mirror and call themselves God's chosen is just beyond me. It's stub-born, is what it is. It's stubborn and it's delusional."

"Lonny."

"Off the record?" Tumin continued, "they're fuckin' nuts. The Muslims, I mean. They really are. They're nuts because they don't educate themselves, first of all, and then they get furious because they're living in squalor. If they want to go back to the fifth fuckin' century or whatever the hell it is, I say, great, be my guest, but don't blame Israel because you —"

"*Lonny.*"

"WHAT?" Tumin exclaimed, spinning aggressively toward Don. "What is it? I'm trying to make an important fuckin' point here."

"He's a Muslim, Lonny."

"Who is?" Tumin's eyes scanned the cabin. "What're you talking about? Who's a Muslim?"

Don raised his chin at Kyle.

"This guy?" Tumin flipped a thumb back toward the writer; he seemed wounded, a man betrayed. "Brando's a *Muslim?*"

Kyle let forth a compunctious grin. He couldn't help but recog-nize the bizarre irony of all this. *Are you a Muslim?* he was being asked. Five minutes ago Kyle would have offered a resounding *no,* but now, strangely, he was reluctant to deny it. What made this espe-cially odd, he knew, was that Tumin had just outlined, in his own crude fashion, some of Kyle's own reservations about Islam. Had even repeated, nearly literatim, the writer's fondly composed opening line, *All Muslims are mad . . .*

But, of course, it was the smugness, Tumin's bullying certitude that had vexed him. Conviction? Yes, thought Kyle. Ardor? Always. But *certainty?* Where? he wanted to know, about what? He tried to remember now that line from the opening pages of the Koran, the one he'd nearly leaped from his chair upon discovering, the one that had sent the hairs on the back of his neck standing at arachnoid attention . . . *This book is not to be doubted.* Shocking, those words.

Far worse, in his opinion, than anything to be found in *Justine,* or *Mein Kampf,* or, heaven knows, *The Satanic Verses.* He'd opened the Koran as a courtesy to his wife, a symbol of his openness, a gesture of love, really — but he'd never got over that line. Never. And his relationship with Islam seemed to have ended before it had begun.

"I'm a Muslim," Kyle was shocked to hear himself say now.

Tumin pulled his elbows back in a posture of stupefaction. "Well, I'll be a wanking walrus!" he exclaimed. "Brando's a Muslim." He turned to Don. "What's this, like the new hip thing now? I thought it was Buddhism. Now it's fuckin' *Islam?*"

"Lonny, for God's sake," Don murmured, though he seemed to think it was too late. His head was lowered, fingers slowly massaging his temples.

"I converted to Islam for my wife," Kyle explained. He was not backpedaling, but thought it was only fair to state the facts. The last thing he wanted was to be perceived as someone who bowed to religious fashion. "She's from Turkey. We couldn't get married until I became a Muslim."

Tumin asked, "So you were what before that?"

"Protestant."

"Right, so really you're a WASP."

"No," Kyle said firmly. Again, he was amazed to hear himself taking this stance. In a milder tone, he added, "No, technically I'm a Muslim."

"All right, all right, *technically.*" Tumin waved his hand again.

"And actually" — Kyle raised his voice so as not to be dismissed — "I have to object to these gross generalizations about my religion, Mr. Tumin. You make no distinction between Palestine and Islam, for example. If you follow your argument —"

"Ronald!" Tumin barked, quickly summoning the flight attendant. "Take her down. We're running late."

Kyle sat stunned as the attendant hurried off to deliver the news.

"Don't get me wrong, I always love to hear another point of view," Tumin said. He slapped the writer's knee again to assuage the disappointment. "Only way to improve your mind, that's what I always say. But it's late, and I have some calls to make before we head down. You guys are still going to dinner, right?" He pulled a cellular out of his jacket as Don nodded toward the writer. "Donny here will fill you in on any other questions you might have. Hell, we didn't even talk about Monarch, did we?"

No, Kyle wanted to say, we didn't. He turned off the recorder and tucked away his notes. Of the thirty or so questions he'd written down, he'd asked exactly none.

The billionaire stood, presumably headed to a more private part of the cabin. He reached down to shake Kyle's hand.

"Salami lick 'em," he said, squeezing firmly, "and all that good shit."

Back at the Triad building, the Sikorsky alighted without further incident. Tumin bolted from the cockpit, bodyguard in tow. He'd try to join them later for dinner, he'd said. Kyle told himself not to hold his breath.

Meanwhile, Don escorted the young man around the corner to City, the two enjoying an easygoing repartee fortified by the balmy fall weather. At the restaurant's canopy, Syeed greeted Mr. Westly with obsequious glee and was rewarded with a lucrative handshake. When Kyle sought to acknowledge their own familiarity, however, the doorman ignored him.

"Rick," he said, "it's me. Kurban."

"You know each other?" asked Don.

"Sure," Kyle replied, and though he kept smiling, Syeed chose to acknowledge neither him nor the writer's outstretched hand. Instead he bowed and opened the heavy door with an oppressive formality.

Slightly embarrassed, Kyle shrugged toward his host. Seeing no point in delay, the two men passed into the restaurant.

Inside the bowels of City, the dining room was already starting to fill. As the hostess guided them through the snarl of tables and roaming guests, Don explained how even during the last week of August, notoriously the worst in the business, the restaurant had been full every night until nearly 1:00 A.M. He spent half his day on the phone now, he said, fielding calls from fleeting acquaintances and pushy celebrities wanting reservations. Pain in the ass, though to him this just emphasized his boss's extraordinary allure, his uncanny ability to reinvent himself. Tumin had left Drexel amid much skepticism, only to form the wildly successful Triad; after that he'd slipped from the spotlight somewhat, but then City had come along. Next up was Monarch.

The lesson, Don said, was never bet against Lonny Tumin.

Kyle thought this opening pitch a little heavy-handed, especially from one as ostensibly graceful as Don Westly. But then his boss had really put him at a disadvantage. That performance back on the helicopter had been one of a kind. It was damage-control time. Kyle didn't want to let him off the hook.

"Yes, I'm dying to hear about Monarch," he said.

As they crossed the dining room, Don made sure to point out Diana Ross, Yankee infielder Chuck Knoblauch, and the ultradiminutive Dominick Dunne — who actually regarded Kyle Clayton as a public menace and had said so in print. Mr. Dunne scowled at him now, in fact, and so Kyle blew him a covert kiss just as the hostess was pulling out a chair for him at Don's usual table.

Awaiting them there was the publisher Semper Dane.

Kyle and he had met five years ago, in San Francisco of all places, finding themselves sitting adjacent to each other at a hotel bar one late afternoon. Striking up a conversation, they discovered they had much in common: both were New York writers giving readings that night at different venues, both bored and dispirited at the end of a long and fruitless book tour. Each of their works was tanking — Semper's slim volume of stories and Kyle's second novel, *Gotham Tragic* — and it was each man's view that San Francisco was indeed a bland little burg, the light beer of cities, and could do with a bit of mischief. By around their eighth margarita or so, it seemed like an awfully good idea to ditch their publicists and have Kyle appear at Barnes & Noble as Semper Dane, reading from his new friend's work, just as Semper would materialize as Kyle Clayton at City Lights, stumbling through a few passages of *Gotham Tragic*. Fuck it, went their way of thinking — no one in this godforsaken city would know who they were anyway. Thus they exchanged books, each going off bibulously to the other's event.

It was the kind of stunt that results in detonated careers and sustained friendships. They returned later that night to regale each other with the hilarity of the evening. ("Why, Kyle, did you decide to name your second book *Gotham Tragic*?" Semper was asked during the question-and-answer portion of his event. "Because I'm gay," he'd answered. "Very, very gay.") And after the laughs had finally subsided, they'd made a pact forged in thumb-pricked blood of extravagant blood-alcohol content, that no matter where their careers ended up, no matter what the circumstance, they would never, *ever,* lose their spirit of devilment and mayhem. Yes, of course, these were just the sorts of promises made to be broken — they knew that all too well. Hadn't everyone they'd ever admired either sold out, rehabbed, or been born again? And so they would *not.* Not them. Promise.

And to the best of their abilities, they had kept their word. While Kyle's calamities rolled famously on, Semper found himself without much enthusiasm to produce a second work of fiction, and so drifted into the world of magazine publishing. There he'd cut a legendary swath of truculence and sedition that was somehow mistaken for passion, the results of which had led to one of the swiftest ascensions in the history of that branch of publishing.

Semper was so fervently superficial it was almost charming, Kyle had always thought. An inveterate name-dropper, he was addicted to celebrities and obsessed with their adornment on the magazines for which he worked. He also loved the pseudofriendships that arose from his position, even as he set about thrashing these celebrities as a matter of course. "Had to go to dinner with that WITCH Juliette Binoche the other night" was a typical Semper Dane locution, which would then be amended with gossip about nose hairs, finger-eating, and body odor, all of it invoked with maximum relish and venality. Not that Kyle himself was above such silly, scabrous banter. It was fun in small doses, and he didn't take Semper's tone of malice too seriously. Knocking the very things he loved was a way for his friend to save face, Kyle knew, to keep his ex-fiction writer's "cred," though he figured it was no coincidence that his old pal had given up *that* pursuit almost at the very moment he realized he would not become instantaneously famous. What, Semper had all but admitted, would have been the point?

Flipping his foppish blond hair, the publisher pulled out his chair and did the half-stand for the new arrivals. Kyle introduced the two strangers, and while Semper affected boredom, Don shook the publisher's hand solicitously. *Magazine* was just six months old but had arrived with much fanfare and attention, and though Don was quite friendly with the money behind the magazine, securing a major profile there for someone like Lonny was a coup indeed.

"So, our Kyle went up in the old heli today, did he?" asked Semper, well aware of his friend's aversion to heights. "How'd it go?"

"No idea, didn't look," he replied. "Far as I'm concerned, we never left the ground."

Semper looked to Don. "Where is Mr. Tumin, anyhow? Will we be joined by the great man himself?"

"He'll try," Don said, eyes refusing to settle in any particular place. Then, in the mode of one determined to finally make a confession, he turned to Kyle. "Look, I'm sorry we had to get into all that religious stuff back there. I'm sure you know Lonny meant no harm."

Bullshit, Kyle thought. "Already forgotten," he said.

"I don't know why he gets on that kick sometimes. I mean, Lonny Tumin, well . . ." Don smiled ruefully. "I love the guy, you know, but he doesn't always see the world in very complex terms. This is common, of course, in people who reach this sort of financial success. Tunnel vision is all."

Kyle nodded politely while stealing a glance at Semper, whose face told him he had some inkling as to what had occurred.

Don continued: "The man truly is a paradox. For example, I think there's no less than fifteen employees here at the restaurant who are Muslim. All well paid and with health insurance, which is something Lonny insists on for all his employees. This is how we judge a man, isn't it? Not by what he says, but by his actions . . . Hello there, Stephen."

The captain had arrived, and Don dispensed with him with equal parts brevity and tact. While Tumin had a reputation for indifference to culinary pleasures, Kyle was pleased to discover that you ate well with Don Westly. He had overheard the whispered orders to the captain (his ears supernaturally attuned to such things); a tasting menu had been arranged, and Raoul was instructed to bring up a few bottles of the "good stuff."

No doubt this was some of the impetus for Kyle's further rush of good feeling toward Don. This, he decided, was truly an agreeable man. The culture dictated there be a degree of contrition to the rich, but Don Westly apologized for none of it, while at the same time conducting himself with the utmost decorum and humility. Please allow him to introduce himself, a man of wealth and taste! The work at Triad was apportioned not unlike the United Kingdom, Kyle could see now, with Lonny as the steely prime minister, making the hard, unpopular decisions, and Don as the royal family, providing the social apparatus and, for those that cared for such things, an aura of glamour.

Now the table's fourth seat appeared to be claimed. Rob Barnett was introduced. Kyle recognized the name from the publicity press packet: this was the soon-to-be third wheel in Triad, the brash new-comer whom Tumin saw as a protégé and eventual successor. As they all stood for the usual greetings, Kyle realized that he remembered the man's face, though could not imagine why, or from where. As for Rob, he showed no interest in meeting the writer's gaze.

Where, Kyle wondered, do I know this son of a bitch from?

After a brief introduction, Don excused himself and took Rob aside. This gave Kyle some time to catch up with his friend.

"How's the magazine world, old buddy?"

"Deplorable as ever," Semper replied, "though finally beginning to be lucrative. What's a girl to do?"

"What's the downside?"

"Downside? Well, let's see, I blow advertisers dawn till dusk, take it in the ass from stockholders over dinner, and then on the weekends go large-mouth bass fishing with Eric Clapton."

"At least there's that."

"No, no, no," he said dismissively, "it's torture, Kyle. It's *work*. Plus, the man's been musically challenged since what, the Johnson administration?"

Kyle murmured in assent. "Anything post 'Bell Bottom Blues' makes my ears bleed."

"Yes, and I've begged him to lay off those *all-star jams,* but to no apparent avail."

"You're still friends, though?"

"Of course," Semper stated, overlooking the paradox. "He played at my wedding, if you remember. I mean, c'mon, man, it's *Eric Clapton.*"

The conversation left Kyle with the usual fond amusement and mild distaste. It was a particularly New York phenomenon, he knew, having good, close friends whom you weren't sure you liked.

"So you gonna drop this Tumin guy on his head or what?"

Kyle shrugged noncommittedly. "Seems almost too predictable, don't you think?"

"Nah, c'mon, you know this guy," Semper replied. "He's a mean-spirited, double-dealing, militant-Zionist, capitalist motherfucker. And yes, so am I, minus the Jewish part, but at least I don't have the audacity to be *ugly* too, on top of it all. I mean, where does this guy get off having the balls to be so ugly in the pages of my magazine?"

Kyle nodded, though his attention was suddenly truant. Over by the bar, Don still had his arm around Rob Barnett and was jawing in the young man's ear; clearly the youngster was getting his ass chewed.

Then, when Rob's eyes flashed up and accidentally caught Kyle's gaze, the writer remembered all at once where he knew Barnett from.

Ordinarily, Tromleys was a friendly, if generic, Irish bar in Midtown. Place for an after-work pint or Monday Night Football on the wide-screen. After 4:00 A.M., however, the doors would lock, though the lights did not come up, and a few carefully chosen whispers would get you into to the haven of the Indefatigables — that is, the die-hard alcoholics, cokeheads, and sexual predators for whom 4:00 A.M. was just not enough, for whom enough was *never* enough. Kyle had been a veritable member, twice a week or more, and he realized now that every leaden memory he could rouse about his nights at Tromleys included Rob Barnett.

They had never spoken, he and Rob, though the man clearly stood out. His prep-school comportment, his fine clothes, suggested a man with responsibilities, one who still functioned despite his nighttime proclivities. At dawn you could be pretty sure that Kyle and the rest of the *pathétiques* of Tromleys would be rolling home to sleep things off until the late afternoon. But Kyle remembered on more than one occasion stumbling in for a final trip to the urinal, only to find him, this Rob Barnett, washing himself in the bathroom sink, combing his hair back with tap water, and finger-brushing his teeth. Next to him was a new shirt wrapped in plastic he'd kept in his briefcase, and a two-hundred-dollar tie folded into his jacket pocket. He was on his way to work.

To find out now that this was the same man destined to become one-third of Triad was almost too much to believe. But it *was* him, Kyle could see now. It was absolutely him.

"C'mon, Clayton, remember our pact," Semper continued, snapping Kyle out of his reverie.

"What pact?"

"Devilry! Mayhem! Catastrophe!" Semper looked sickened by the lack of recognition. "You don't even remember?"

"Oh, c'mon."

"An agreement forged in blood, man!"

Kyle turned to him. "Look, you're a magazine editor named Semper, making what, a hundred and fifty thou a year? And I'm a married guy with a mortgage two points above the prime lending rate. I don't want to blow a chance at other writing gigs. Times have changed, buddy."

Semper took the comment hard, throwing up his hands and returning them to his thighs with a loud slap. "You see? I hate that. I *hate* that attitude."

"What?"

"What we always said, Kyle, what we said a *thousand* times, that the thing we despised more than anything else was these hell-raisers who settled down and renounced their past."

The writer sat up a bit in his chair, obviously piqued by this. "Who said anything about renouncing?" challenged Kyle. "I mean, we still do all right, Semp. You have a terrible reputation to this day."

"You think so?" The publisher's voice lifted a little.

"Hell, yeah, your name's dirt in this town. Nobody in this room would dare hire you to so much as wipe their ass. It's a miracle you got this job."

"It is, isn't it?" he said, smiling. "And, hey, you too, Kyle," he added, suddenly feeling generous. "I mean, I mention your name, and people still shake their heads, spit on the floor, stamp their foot in disgust."

Now it was Kyle's turn to be pleased. "Get out."

"You kidding? I'd say that Kyle Clayton is *still* perceived as somewhere between a hazard and a buffoon. In that general area. No doubt about it."

They patted each other on the shoulder.

"So we're still cool then?" the publisher asked, almost desperately. "We're not just rationalizing?"

"We're not bad," went the reply. "And then, who knows," Kyle continued, "maybe we're not done yet."

The List

All things considered, the meal had gone surprisingly well. Don returned from his scold of Barnett as smooth as ever, as if nothing had happened; though Rob never did join them. Through six courses, Kyle's microcassette spinning once again, Don went on about his boss: the humble beginnings in Orange, New Jersey; how Lonny had introduced him to his beloved wife, Susan; the fact that by the time Don ended up at Drexel, Tumin was like a god, hushing rooms and awing senior partners, until he became too big even for *that* and began Triad. Don told them everything and nothing; Lonny was Moses, Lonny was Henry fucking Ford with a dash of St. Francis of Assisi. His speech would have smashed against the ears like the cloying homily it was, except that it was delivered by Don Westly. He told his tale with ingenuity, with humor, with self-denigration, and all of it peppered with facile compliments: *You're the hottest magazine editor in the country, Semper, so you know what I'm talking about when I say that I think Lonny's understanding of the possibilities in media . . .* Or: *I don't think I have to tell one of the best young writers*

*around that instinct is probably the single greatest secret to success,
and so when Lonny Tumin tells you . . .*

The food sparkled, the wine proved copious and favorably geriatric. Over grappa, Semper assured everyone the story was in place
for March. Business behind them, Don then allowed the conversation
to roam, the discussion turning to Mayor Giuliani, the Mets, and, of
course, the economy, which they all agreed was simply unfathomable.
Finally, a postmeal torpor caught up to them, and Don asked for the
check. As usual, even this simple task was carried out with a certain
aplomb. The bill was signed, Don adorning the check plate with a pile
of hundreds fended from a roll Sinatra would have admired. The gra-
tuity was made hastily, with no care toward amount, its only apparent stipulation being excess. This was not showing off, Kyle observed,
but the manifestation of some sort of careless decency.

Don Westly, both friends agreed when he was gone, was pretty
cool too.

Afterward there was a party Semper needed to get to. Kyle declined
the offer to accompany him and found Erin Wyatt standing at the
upstairs bar. There was no bartender; she was all alone, looking bored
and fairly miserable.

"Well, well," she said as he approached, "if it isn't my pen pal."

She was keeping a barely interested eye on her station, which was
just off to Kyle's left, one of the smaller lounges rimmed with the
usual club chairs, the table occupied by five brokers. On the sixth seat
sat a jeroboam of champagne with a silk tie around its neck in a
Windsor knot. As usual, the blinds were set so that Erin could see in
but they could not see out.

"You boys had a little wine downstairs, I understand."

"One glass with dinner," Kyle retorted, his usual pallor obviously
rosy from drink. "They say it's good for the heart."

"Yeah, well, my sommelier's in a dead sweat from running back
and forth to the wine cellar. Fucking America, he says, never saw anyone drink so much. It was then I knew Kyle Clayton was in the
house."

God she looks great, he thought. She must've gone somewhere
for August; her skin was brown, and somehow she was even taller
than he remembered. To think that he'd had her and could barely

remember a thing was really the best argument he'd ever heard for sobriety.

But Erin also looked more unhappy than when he'd seen her last. She was beginning to get that slightly pinched, acrid-mouthed look of New Yorkers in their thirties for whom disappointment is starting to become a way of life. The disappointments could be anything — sex, money, children, career, *marriage,* anything. But once you got that look, there was no going back. Kyle decided she was about 20 percent there.

Her bitterness, in fact, leaped out immediately. "So, what, you here for the show?" she asked. "Failed artists of the second floor, on view every evening at City! Look, here's one now."

Well, that's hardly fair, Kyle told himself. Who knew how these bundles of good fortune were distributed, why some people brought the food and some people ate it? Not Kyle, that was for sure. Was it his fault that the world of art and entertainment was like a huge funnel in which only a few made it through the tightly constricted neck? It was axiomatic that most would *not* make it, in fact. You knew that going in, unless you were a fool.

"Hey, don't play sad sack with me," Kyle said, trying to keep things light. "I saw the tip Don Westly left for the waiter. I'm thinking of filling out an application myself on the way out."

This forced a reluctant smirk. "Yes, we all love waiting on Don."

"How about Lonny?"

"Who, Tumin?" Erin scoffed. "I think that man honestly believes we should all work for free, just for the pleasure of rubbing up on his greatness. No, it's Don who always makes sure we get tipped when we wait on Tumin's table."

"You guys get insurance, though, right? That's not bad for a restaurant."

"Yeah, we get it," she said, running her fingers through her long hair. "Again, that's Don."

"Not Lonny?"

"You kidding? I heard Don had to fight with him just to have it offered, and even then we pay half . . ." She suddenly flipped her eyes up at him. "Since when do you give a damn about people like Lonny Tumin?" she asked.

Kyle explained about the profile, making sure to include its connection to his dinner with Don Westly — lest Erin see this night as further proof of some romantic creative life from which she was excluded.

"You and Lonny Tumin? How'd you manage that?"

"My agent put it together."

She was looking straight ahead, remembering when she'd waited on them at lunch. "She's good, huh?" Erin asked enviously. "Your agent?"

"Yes, as a matter of fact, she is. She's like a bulldog, though you wouldn't know it to look at her."

"Boy, I'd kill for a bulldog," Erin murmured, almost to herself, her stare of longing suddenly interrupted by a muffled *woo-hoo!* escaping from the nearly soundproof room. Peering in through the blinds, to make sure the walls weren't coming down, she gestured for Kyle to join her.

"What's up?"

"You see that?" she asked in a discouraged voice. He looked in and saw the jeroboam propped up on the seat with its expensive tie. "They're honoring somebody who couldn't be here," she explained, "so they want me to pretend the bottle is a person and serve it food and wine. 'Treat him like a customer,' they tell me. So I have to bend over and go through the motions of taking its order and serving it. Welcome to my life, Kyle Clayton."

He nodded sympathetically, but left it alone. She was in bad way tonight, he could see, and even the most innocent comment risked seeming callous or patronizing.

"Look, I'm sorry for seeming so bitter," she said, sensing his unease. "Things aren't going so well for me on the acting front. Anything but bad news about somebody creative puts me in a foul mood."

"You'll snap out of it."

"No, I'm not so sure I will," she said unflinchingly. "There's a family curse, you know."

"A curse?"

"The Wyatt dreamers. We go back generations."

He remembered The Book. "No sign of the magnum opus, I presume."

As one of the brokers fed the jeroboam a piece of bread, which it rejected to a pile on the floor, Erin looked up at Kyle. "Oh, sure, didn't you hear? Nietzsche's dead, God exists. The world lies stunned . . . No," she said, looking back down into the room. "I'm afraid the book's just the big hoax we always thought it was."

There was some laughter then behind them, and a disheveled couple emerged from the rarely used second-floor men's room. They were still adjusting their clothes, though without embarrassment, as they passed by the bar to return downstairs.

Kyle said, "Maybe you and I should go in there, make sure they didn't break anything."

"We could," she replied with a smirk, reviving her sense of humor, "but then my entrées are about due. You got my e-mails, right?"

Oh, yes, he told her, he'd got her e-mails. Who could forget? A few months into his cybercrusade to get in her pants, Erin had finally begun to reply to his invitations. Very funny and very lurid e-mails she'd sent, mostly of pictures she'd downloaded from the Net. Elephantine phalli, ravenous vaginas, gaping fundaments, and puckered lips, all underscored by Erin's sordid captions. Under one hyperbolized rampart she'd written, *Guy's got nothing on you, K. C.!* And then, under yet another frighteningly outnumbered lass, was the inscription *NO HOLES BARRED!*

Kyle had laughed. It was all very, very funny. *Wasn't* it?

"I thought you were just kidding around."

"I was kidding," she said, her eyes flashing up, "in the same way you were when you sent me your e-mails."

"I wasn't kidding," he said.

Suddenly, from down the hall, came the sound of clattering stainless steel.

"Oh, boy, here he comes," she remarked. Abu appeared around the corner, struggling with a tray on which sat six entrées, the plates in stacks of three and balanced on warming hoods. *"Easy,"* she called out as he approached, "don't let the sauce run over." Leaning back, she whispered to Kyle, "He's not great with big trays. He probably shouldn't be working upstairs, but I don't have the heart to complain."

She and Kyle helped him heave the tray on to the bar.

"Nice job," the writer told him, once things were settled, only to be greeted with the same steely silence and averted gaze that the doorman had offered.

What the *fuck* was going on with the Muslims? he thought.

"Abu, it's Kurban," the waitress reminded him. "What're you doing? Say hello."

Abu handed Erin the dupe ticket but kept his eyes attended to the dark hall opposite them.

"Abu?"

"I have nothing no more to say to Mr. Kur . . . to Kyle."

If the waiter had been trying to hurt his feelings, Kyle was startled to find that he had succeeded. Hearing Abu address him by his American name stung him in a way that he hadn't expected.

Erin, however, needed to move on. She handed two plates to Abu, and off he went.

"Look, I have to get back to work," she told Kyle. The four remaining plates were balanced effortlessly on her arms; he was actually surprised she was letting him see how good she was at this. "See you around."

"Whoa, hold on."

Heading toward the room, she slowed but did not turn around.

"How about tonight, after work?" he asked.

"Can't," she said over her shoulder. "Going out with the crew."

Now he was unsettled to discover that he was mildly jealous. This, he thought, is very, very dangerous.

"How about next week?"

"We'll see," she said.

"No holes barred, right?"

Burdened by the plates, though still graceful, she turned just enough to show him that high, arching eyebrow, which in a better world, he felt, would have been the envy of Hollywood.

Back downtown, Kyle sheepishly entered the small apartment where the only light came from the room they kept as an office.

"Hello?" his wife called out.

He'd been hoping Ayla might still be at work or, better yet, asleep so that he might have a clearer head before having to face her; he needed some time until the buzz of seeing Erin wore off. But here she was, awake, and obviously in the throes of something intense.

"Hey, honey," he replied. His voice, he realized, was a little stiff. He turned on the light and threw his jacket on the couch.

"Kyle, you want to come look at this, please."

In the office, he found Ayla looking rather plain in sweat clothes and eyeglasses, staring at the glowing computer. The monitor radiated a scrim of Arabic lettering. Palms up, she held her hands toward the screen as if it proved everything she'd been trying to say throughout these long years.

"JOL dot com."

"Sorry, sweetie," he said. "Not familiar."

With some vehemence, she said, "Jihad On-line, Kyle. You know what *jihad* is?"

"Of course, but . . ." He saw the look on her face. "What, you're mad at me now? I don't read Arabic, Ayla, I'm sorry."

"Okay, I'll tell you what it says." Returning her eyes to the monitor, she used the mouse to pan slowly down. "Here we have the usual hysterical rhetoric, '*Death to America . . . Death to the infidels . . . blah blah blah . . . America is on our holy lands . . . Israel . . . not going to stand for this . . .*' All right, here we go."

She scrolled down farther to a long list of names, perhaps two hundred or more, some in Arabic, some in English. Many of the latter Kyle recognized. There was Madeleine Albright, George Bush, Bill Clinton, Colin Powell, the three major news anchors, the publishers of the "Zionist" publications the *Washington Post* and the *New York Times,* and then, farther down, a more international roster. Kyle's eyes flitted toward the writers: Naguib Mahfouz, V. S. Naipaul, and ol' reliable Salman Rushdie. Near the bottom — a recent addition, apparently — he saw the name *Kyle Clayton.*

"That's me," he said with innocent excitement.

"Yes, honey, it is you. Only problem is that this is not a list of Nobel Prize candidates." She looked up. "It's a hit list."

Kyle was silent for a moment. "Oh, c'mon."

She scrolled back up and read the caption at the top. "'*It is our contention that Muslims everywhere now face the greatest challenge in our history from the West, and only with the death of the following individuals can we be assured . . .*' Et cetera, et cetera."

Kyle stroked his face and helped himself to a gulp of Ayla's water. He needed to hydrate his brain, clotted as it was from yet another night of too much wine, good food for which he was not paying, and thoughtless lust. He looked down at Ayla, her head bowed and glasses raised, as a large tear fell and pooled in one of the keypads — crying not because her husband was in danger (reason suggested the threat was more formal than anything else) but because the list bespoke another danger, the manifestation of all that was wrong between them.

"I've been on the phone for the last two hours; I couldn't get ahold of you," Ayla said, wiping her eyes.

"I had my phone off during the meeting." He grabbed the box of tissues off the desk and handed it to her.

"The police put me in touch with the FBI."

"Christ, what did they say?"

"There's nothing they can do, apparently. The site is constitution-ally protected. Can you believe it? First Amendment, Kyle. The one you love so much." He decided not to challenge her on this. Wiping her eyes, she continued, "The guy at the FBI played it down. He said to be alert — that was his word, *alert* — but not to make too much of it. He said we're on the FBI's *radar,* which is, you know, oh, so comforting."

Ayla relaxed in her chair and let her head fall back. She'd been exhausted anyway — twelve-, sometimes fifteen-hour days she'd been putting in — and now this. She looked worried, mildly nauseated, and thoroughly fed up with her husband.

Kyle kneeled in front of the monitor, just to make sure his name was there. Confirming this, he discovered its presence simultaneously frightened and excited him.

"How did you find this?"

"Patience sent it to us," she replied. Her voice was depleted now, without intonation. "One of her writers brought it to her attention. She wants you to call her tomorrow."

I'll bet she does, Kyle thought. Yes, Patience would certainly be enjoying this. No doubt her phone was tied up at this very moment while she "accidentally" leaked the story to the *Post,* the *Daily News,* and the *Observer.* Then on to any magazine contacts who would lis-ten. Her stance, of course, would be one of moral outrage; at the same time she would be urging him to title his upcoming novel *The Coun-terfeit Conversion.* Kyle smelled contract renegotiation.

Now, though, he put his hand on his wife's back and tried to lighten the mood. "Jeez, I knew the story could use a little work, but I didn't know they'd try to kill me for it."

His wife glowered. "That's not funny," she said. "You think this is *funny?*"

"A little levity, Ayla."

"You want to be hated? Fine, you got it, buster. Only this time it's not some poor gaggle of New York liberals, let me tell you." She breathed out in frustration. "God, are you ever going to let this *go?*"

"What?"

"This . . . *performance* your life has become."

"It's not a performance. That story was about things I believe in."

"Oh, c'mon," she replied. "You told me how much you miss being famous."

Kyle narrowed his eyes. "I do, I admit it. So what?"

"Well, then you can't tell me that this story isn't a cry for attention. *All Muslims are mad* . . . What're you, fucking insane? You're practically begging for a fatwa, Kyle. You want your old fame back so much you're willing to put yourself in the firing line just so you can feel noticed again."

He hesitated, wondering if this were at all true.

"What, you're not on my side?" he asked.

"Of course I am."

"But?"

"But it's hard, Kyle. It's *hard*. I'm a Muslim woman, remember? I mean it's one thing to have your husband reject Islam — I've been dealing with that. But it's another thing for him to be known publicly as an enemy of your religion! And for what, Kyle? So you can be the hot topic at cocktail parties again? It's pathetic."

Kyle arose from his crouch, his voice now taking on the edge of someone hurt and wanting to hit back. "Well, what is it about Islam that doesn't allow for contradictions? Have you ever asked yourself that? How can you embrace a religion where if you express any skepticism whatsoever, you suddenly end up on a hit list? I can't understand that. Where's the peace, Ayla, in this glorious faith of yours? Where is it? Where's the love?"

The irony did not escape Kyle that in the course of the day he'd woken up a skeptic of Islam, pronounced himself a Muslim just before dinner, and was renouncing it again as a focus of a jihad, just before bed.

Ayla came up off her chair and rested her head on Kyle's shoulder. "I'm really scared," she whispered.

"I know," he said, stroking her hair. "Don't worry, though; even the FBI guy said —"

"No, I don't mean that now," she interjected. She glanced up at him. "Don't you even know what I'm talking about?"

After a pause, he replied solemnly, "Yes, I think so."

"I can't take much more, Kyle. I've started praying for us at night. I know you don't want to hear that, but I have."

He hugged his wife tightly and then held her out by her shoulders so he could look at her; guilt suddenly afflicted him like a virus. "Listen, why don't we go to the house next weekend? We haven't been in a while. It'll be good for us; we can get out of here till we know what's going on . . ." He felt her shoulders stiffen under his hands. "What now?" he asked.

"We're already going," she said. "You don't remember?"

"We are?"

"My family's coming." She had a small ironic smile, highlighting her disappointment. "Elsa's bringing the kids. Everyone's coming up to Saugerties, even my parents. You don't remember?"

"Your parents?" he said.

"Yes."

"Meaning your father too, I guess."

"Yes, Kyle, a father is a parent."

"Great," he mumbled, "Mr. Jihad himself."

She fixed him with her eyes. "We agreed on this a month ago, Kyle. This is old news. You even promised me you'd be on your best behavior. *Promised* me."

He recalled none of this, though it was like Kyle to conveniently forget events that didn't appeal to him. And yes, he would certainly have to be on his best behavior. He would have to let Mr. Jihad come into his house and walk all over him, allow the man to gut him like a fish with insults, stamp down on his face if that was his wont. (And God help me if he's heard about my story, Kyle thought.) All these things, if his marriage was to survive. This weekend, he felt, was everything.

"All right then." He pulled her in one final time, looking down hard into her eyes, which were almost touching his and which betrayed a wariness, a sense of doom Kyle was determined to upset. "I promise," he said.

The City Is Very Hot Now

Though Kyle Clayton's bad name was, in fact, spreading far to the East, albeit slowly, the progenitors of Jihad On-line could be found no farther than the Buyuk Mosque in Astoria, Queens. It was here that the Great Kurban had become the focus of the postprayer discussion group.

The assembly was run by one Khalil Adami, a heavyset man of Syrian / Saudi descent. He wore thick robes in the dead of August, tottered side to side with a cane as his tenuous center of gravity, and had stuck just above a forestal beard a pair of horn-rimmed glasses, as if to suggest reason in the midst of anarchy. With permission from the Imam of Buyuk, Khalil had reorganized the mosque's basement storage area and ran his discussion group there on Friday afternoons after prayer; he pushed the folding chairs and tables up against the walls, spread out Middle Eastern rugs along the floor, and set out tea strong enough to fuel an aircraft carrier. Khalil's cantankerous message was not for everyone, however — his audiences, after an initial voluminousness, had recently dwindled to a mere handful. Among the faithful were Khalil's son, age eleven, who ceaselessly rocked and nodded as his father spoke; two Pakistanis and a Jordanian, quiet, intense men, and the covert publishers of JOL; and Syeed Salaam, part-time City doorman and full-time ascetic.

Syeed's attendance at these meetings had begun the previous spring, just as his isolation seemed to be catching up with him. Friday mornings he walked through his Astoria neighborhood with an aching heart, the occasional dogwoods and blooming window boxes reminding him of the public gardens in Jidda, along with the other Muslim men and their families heading along Steinway Street toward the mosque. Why am I always the one to be alone? he would ask himself. Why *me*, all the time? He was vaguely embarrassed at this solitariness and sometimes imagined that some of his Muslim brothers had begun to look at him strangely. Do they think I have no passion for women? he wondered in horror. If they could only see how beautiful his Aisha was, he thought, how delicate and feminine, they would not look at him as they did now. And anyway, what purpose had they to bring their women so near a holy place? The proximity of these females to the mosque disgusted him, and though his heart still longed for companionship after prayers, he now refused the tea and pastries in the main reception area (that *haraam* of commingling genders!) and found himself retreating instead to the basement and the teachings of Khalil Adami.

He was a man of great learning, Syeed had surmised. Khalil held the entire life of Muhammad on the tip of his tongue, along with the great histories of the Ottomans, the Persians, and the Turks. He was also not afraid to speak of controversial though, in his words, "incontestable" truths, such as the Holocaust — an event entirely improvised by the Jews themselves, of course, to garner sympathy and secure the holy lands that had belonged to Palestine for centuries. There was no end to the creativity of Jewish deception, Khalil affirmed, white cane quaking for punctuation, the tremendous financial support from the West making the possibilities limitless. Everything from the staging of suicide bombings in Gaza and Tel Aviv (Muslims knew better than to kill women and children) to the vicious lie that the Arabs and not the Jews had begun the terrible war of '67.

The message was firm, but consistent; Khalil warned that not just Jews but all infidels were a danger to Islam. The Unbelievers, as

Muhammad had said, were protectors of one another, and unless Muslims protected themselves there would be oppression and mischief. Syeed took special interest in a piece his teacher read from a local newspaper, the article proving that the West was trying to undermine the youth of his country. The paper reported that Saudi teenagers were becoming difficult to control, every night boys and girls running wild through the streets of Riyadh and Jidda with their cars and music and drinking. What was happening to the children of Islam? Saudi citizens were demanding to know. Soon the source of this chaos was revealed: the teenagers admitted they were imitating this behavior from American movies broadcast on satellite TV. They wanted to be like Americans, they said. The infidel was always finding new ways to infiltrate the purity of Islam.

Every week Khalil brought in interesting articles like this. The information was all around them, he said; you don't know how bad things are until you look. Toward the end of the summer, he brought in a magazine published right here in New York, a local and supposedly intellectual sheet. This issue, he said, shaking the magazine above his head, carried the most disturbing literature he had seen in recent times — yet another vicious attack on Islam carried out by Zionist publishers under the bulldozer of free speech.

Folding the magazine on his lap and waving his cane in the air, Khalil read: "'*All Muslims are mad, of course . . .*' The teacher made meaningful eye contact with each of his followers, then read on. '*Not mad in the sense of angry, though they are certainly that, but daffy mad, glazed-eyed-crazy-stare mad . . .*'"

Khalil's son rocked back and forth, nodding in time with the group's angry murmurs.

The teacher continued: "This story goes on to dramatize, in what I suppose is meant to be a humorous tone, the conversion of a young Christian man to Islam in order to please his wife. Only in this funny little story, the hero turns out to be an atheist and lies to the Imam even as he is reciting the Articles of Faith. Then he criticizes Muhammad for being a great warrior and a prophet at the same time."

Syeed thought it was strange when Khalil began to laugh, and then the other men began to follow him in this mirth. Syeed himself did not participate in this. He could find nothing funny in the slandering of Muhammad.

"What makes this whole thing so typical is that this is obviously a Zionist magazine, though they won't call it that." He turned the page and read aloud some of the Jewish names from the masthead. "Published by Jews, paid for by Jews, and they think nobody's paying attention! But I am, my friends, you see? I am keeping my eyes and ears open. I'm listening to everything, reading everything, seeing everything. The writer of this filth, by the way . . ." Now he turned the pages again, coming to the quick biographies of the contributors. "It says here, *Ky-lee Clayton*," as Khalil pronounced it, "*author of such-and-such a book* . . . here it is . . . *is in fact a recent CONVERT to Islam.*"

Khalil shook his head and dropped the magazine at his feet. He looked up at his followers, each of whom was equally morose in his disgust. Then the Pakistani, who had introduced himself to Syeed first as Patik and then more recently as Raja, asked the teacher what a good Muslim does in the face of such an outrage.

"Well, one could certainly see this as apostasy," Khalil asserted, "since the writer dares to call himself a Muslim. Perhaps the answer resides in the Hadith. I think of Muadh ibn Jabal, one of the Companions of the Prophet. If you remember, he was ordered by Muhammad to go to Yemen, to be governor there. Arriving in Yemen, he found a man tied to a tree. He turned to the people and said, 'Why have you done this to this man?' and he was told, 'First he was a Jew, then he was a Muslim. Now he is slandering Islam, and he is no longer a Muslim.' Muadh replied, 'Don't you know the punishment for it?' And he drew his sword and beheaded him."

Patik / Raja sipped his tea to clear the anger from his throat. "*If a man changes his religion and acts against Muslims, then kill him,*" he recited from memory. "That is the complete Hadith."

Suddenly then there was a stunning interjection: Syeed, who had not yet contributed to any of the meetings during these months, raised his hand. "But let us remember now," he began, shyly but with passion, "the Hadith is not the Koran."

Syeed sat back, pleased with himself. He thought this an important point. The Koran was the direct word of Muhammad, and therefore superior to the Hadith, which was simply interpretations of the Prophet's sayings. He'd read the Hadith and knew it well, but he did not trust it. The Koran was everything.

Also, he knew that Ky-lee Clayton was no less than Kurban, the lax Muslim writer who frequented City. Because Syeed felt this knowledge placed a certain burden on his shoulders, he wanted this question explored fully by his teacher.

"This is true, Syeed," affirmed Khalil, obviously pleased by his follower's contribution. "We must be careful now. The Hadith, we remember, is hearsay, and the Koran doesn't address the question of apostasy directly. Remember, however, what it *does* say, which is, 'Let there be no compulsion in religion.' So you could argue, on the other hand, that no one has the right to tell anyone else they can or cannot apostatize. Do you see? We must be very careful about this."

"So what is the right answer?" asked Patik / Raja plaintively. His close-set eyes suggested a man not at home with ambiguity. "How are we to react to this?"

"Unfortunately there is no easy answer," Khalil concluded. "The Prophet is not here to tell us himself, so we must use our best judgment. I will tell you from my perspective this Ky-lee makes me very angry. This sort of irreverent skepticism, this fashionable atheism, is damaging and insulting to Islam. But again, as I said, we must be very careful. I think if you become a Muslim and you attack Islam the penalty is death, yes, certainly. But in this case you can argue that the writer never *really* was a Muslim. Even though he converted, he was always, in his heart, an atheist. So, again, remember the Koran: *Lakum dinukum wa liya din.* 'To you your religion and to me mine.' And so, for Ky-lee Clayton, pity him. As for dealing with him or men like him, follow your own hearts."

After prayers, Salaam took the N train to 49th Street, his daily route to work. This time, though, instead of walking south toward City restaurant, he headed west.

At 7th Avenue he walked a few blocks north and came to his destination. Janine's Furs. Here he had found a facsimile of the coat he'd been dreaming of and was powerless not to follow its call. He knew all the details: *Winter Ermine / all white, very rare / used / slight tear in the liner. $5,800.* Across the street from the furrier, he crouched and leaned against the wall. He had been inside Janine's many times to try on the coat. Recently, though, he had been banned from the shop, and now he was forced to stand outside and admire it from afar.

You can't come in every day, the manager told him. Come back when you can buy it.

Okay, Syeed replied, proud in the face of his condescension. Maybe I will.

Still leaning on the wall, he removed from his pocket the most recent letter from Aisha, which he had received just yesterday. He had read it nearly twenty times, and the more he read it the more uneasy he became.

Dearest Love,

Missing you more now than ever! Hearing your voice last week made me so happy and then sad. Mother send you more calling cards so you can ring me soon again okay? Yusef has been fired from his job again and mother is very mad for him. She says he has too much going out at night with the girlfriends who call all the times. When he takes me to market with him all the girls are jealous with me and say Yusef looks like movie star. You think so? Sometimes he looks at me and I cannot hold his eyes because he is prettier than me I think. How I miss your face Syeed!

The city is very hot now and sometimes I am so bored. Did you know that some young girls have been found driving cars? They don't want to stay home, these girls. This is our country now, Syeed. Strange things happening, changes too. Sometimes even I wish I would like to drive one time. Your father says it's too hard for girls, but is he wrong if these other girls drive? When you come home maybe will you let me drive a little? I would like one time to try and see. I think I can do it but I don't know!

Please call call call call. It is so hard not to see you hard hard hard hard. Write write write write write write write!!!!!!

Yours, Aisha

Just as Khalil had said, it was not clear which path one should take with many enemies of Islam. But Syeed felt that whatever was to be done, it was up to him to do it. Syeed had sinned, and so Allah was offering him this test. He would stop Kurban from hurting Islam, to make things right with Allah. Though as yet he did not know how.

Cujo

Monarch Soars as NASDAQ Sets New Record

The Wall Street Journal, October 29, 1999 — Investors eagerly snapped up shares of Monarch Technologies, Inc., on its debut Friday, sending the stock as high as $81.25 before closing at $79, as solid economic data buoyed all the major indices to end the week on another high note.

Monarch's debut came after a report that said sales of single-family homes fell 12.8 percent in September to 811,000 units. The biggest slowdown in almost two years, the trend was felt across the country. Still, optimism is high for Monarch, which was absorbed last January by Triad, Inc. Though Triad's earnings have been modest during the recent economic upswing, the company retains a high profile primarily because of its dynamic CEO and founder, Lonny Tumin. Mr. Tumin has been a controversial figure in the financial world ever since his tenure at the infamous Drexel Burnham Lambert

*brokerage firm in the 1980s, though he was never indicted in the
junk bonds scandal.*

*This is Triad's first foray into the technology sector. Despite Monarch
having reported losses the previous nine quarters, the presence of
Tumin and Triad has created excitement among investors. Triad
recently sold Hefty Burger Food Group to Quaker Oats for $1.1 bil-
lion, just four years after acquiring the company for $300 million. As
a result, Mr. Tumin exercised $17.3 million in a special class of Hefty
Burger Food Group options, pushing his total compensation for
1999 to more than $22 million. Donald Westly, Triad's COO, exer-
cised $7 million in HBFG options. Mr. Westly's compensation for
1999 was $9.1 million. Monarch's recently announced EVP, Robert
J. Barnett, netted $6.1 million in compensation.*

*The Stock Index rose 13.13 today, or 2.39 percent, to 562.72. The
NASDAQ composite jumped 91.22 to a record 2,966.44 and the
Dow-Jones industrial average rose 107.33 to 10,729.86.*

"Wool bouclé," said Susan Westly, scratching her thighs near the
braided edging of her skirt, "ain't what it used to be, let me tell you.
This new stuff itches like a motherfucker."

"Chanel's losing it?" asked Lonny Tumin with interest.

"I'm beginning to wonder."

Still giddy from today's numbers, Tumin playfully slapped his
hand down on his wide desk. "That's it, I'm pulling out my stock.
When it comes to designers, I consider the word of Suzy Westly nothing less than insider information."

"Don't try and butter me up," she replied curtly. "I'm here to get
all over your ass, Lonny, and there'll be no avoiding it."

Mrs. Westly took a sip from the glass she had taken into Tumin's
office. It was Friday, the debut of the Monarch IPO had been a smash-
ing success, and so for the first time anyone could remember there was
champagne in the offices of Triad. Tumin's door was open, and you
could hear the bursts of laughter and clinking of glasses down the hall.

"Do you mind?" she asked.

"Not at all."

She closed the door. When she returned to her seat, she turned her
knees to the side so that Tumin could no longer look up her skirt.

"The Vineyard was good to you this summer," he remarked. "You're brown as a berry."

"And now I'm back. Montclair again, in case you hadn't heard."

Tumin nodded. "Don told me. Yes, the great love nest is intact," he said with some satisfaction. "Good move, Suzy. Very smart."

Keeping her knees together, she looked up at the bubbles in her glass. "Is it?" she asked. "I've had my doubts lately."

"Oh, so you don't like being rich? This is news."

She brought the champagne to her lips to drink, then seemed to reconsider. "No, no, I do, very much," she admitted. "It's just that I don't feel very rich anymore. That's why I decided to drop by, Lonny, on the eve of your great success."

She raised the glass to salute him, and when he looked away for a moment she popped the Vicodin she'd found playing fugitive in the bottom of her bag, washing it down with the champagne.

When nervous, Tumin would sometimes swivel from side to side in his chair, such as a boy might do alone in his father's office. As he did so now, he kept his eyes fixed on Susan, measuring her, trying to calculate the motives behind this sudden pretense. She was here on some stratagem, no doubt about it. He could tell by the steely look in her eye and the vague return of her Carolina accent, the reappearance of which, in his experience, meant bad news all around. He knew firsthand how formidable Susan Westly could be. They'd had their time together, he and Miss Belford, and she'd nearly managed to trick him into marrying her, had devised a brilliant net in which he'd almost been ensnared.

But as with the Drexel scandal, and a thousand other close calls both legal and amorous, Tumin had somehow wriggled free. In his place he'd offered up his partner, who'd conveniently professed a crush on the little belle. It had been a good deal for all. In place of Lonny, Suzy would get the vastly more handsome — and less Jewish by half — Mr. Donald Westly. Not to mention Tumin's promise of financial solvency. So long as she stayed with Don, so long as their secret remained intact, the Westlys would prosper under the good graces of Lonny Tumin.

"What are you feeling then, if not rich?" he asked.

"I don't know, sort of, upper middle class," she said distastefully. Leaning forward, she set the flute down on the edge of his desk.

Tumin smiled. He found the comment amusing. "Maybe you need to reacquaint yourself with your bank account, my darling. All the little zeros at the end? That's a good thing."

"I'll give you an example," she countered. "Ten years ago, the Westlys were the richest family in Upper Montclair; now we're not even the richest on our *block*. Two homes down from me there's a twenty-four-year-old college dropout who made more money last year than Don has made in his lifetime. I know my husband isn't very ambitious, Lonny, but I'd like to know how something like this could happen."

Tumin raised his eyebrows and sipped at his bottle of water. Despite the auspicious news about Monarch, he could not muster a taste for the bubbly.

"What do you mean, how?" he asked, smiling. "You live in a damned nice neighborhood, and the market is stupid right now. It's a joke. What do you want me to say?"

"I want you to tell me why this country is five times richer than it was ten years ago and the Westlys have moved horizontal."

Tumin threw his head back, forcing a laugh. "Because, you dodo bird, the country isn't five times richer than it was ten years ago. It's just numbers, Suzy. It doesn't mean anything."

"Tell that to little Richie Tessel from down the street."

"I would; you bet your ass I would." Tumin stopped swiveling and set his elbows down on his desk, trying to intimate a gravitas. "By this time next year, little Richie will be back in his dorm room, asking to borrow cafeteria money. Mark my words. I don't care if the fucking NASDAQ goes up to two hundred million points; a stock is only worth what you *sell* it for. Ask your husband, he knows all this."

"My husband is a borderline golf bum and all-around lazy sack of shit, Lonny. I don't want to hear about my husband and money."

"How about Hefty Burger? What was your golf bum's take on that? Seven, eight mil?"

"You *announced* seven. It was more like five."

"Oh, come off it, Suzy."

"Richie Tessel made ninety million last year. *Ninety* million. What did you make, Lonny?"

Tumin laughed again and touched his forehead to his desktop before looking up at her. "You just don't get it, do you?"

"No, I don't."

"What is it you want, Suzy? Spit it out."

"I want Monarch."

Tumin pushed his bottom lip down toward his chin, trying to look surprised. Of course, by now he knew things were heading this way. She had a trump card, had held on to it for years — then she'd woken up this morning to the preposterous numbers and knew it was time to play.

Kudos, my dear, he thought, for your patience.

"Look, I'll level with you," he began. "If you think this is some kind of sure bet, you're wrong. Monarch's volatile. It's not for the faint of heart, trust me. And, knowing your hubby, he won't like some of the legal gray zones we're moving in here. I'm actually doing him a favor."

"Oh, God, *please,*" Susan said. She moved to the edge of her seat now, apparently not caring if Tumin had himself another eyeful. "Look, right now, while you're all celebrating a hundred-million-dollar morning, my husband is on the phone back at City trying to smooth talk people who couldn't get a table for tonight. I won't have it, Lonny."

Tumin took a moment to watch the cords on Susan's neck tense like railroad cables. What a shame it was that she'd never gone into finance, he thought admiringly. Triad didn't often hire women, but they really could have used someone like Suzy, this Cujo with the brilliant backside and mind like a Borgia.

"It's what he's good at," Tumin replied finally.

She shook her finger in tight, agitated reverberations. "Nope, sorry, Lonny. I said I'm not having it, and I mean it. I want him *in.*"

He was up now, out of his chair and moving back to the large windows that looked downtown. Even through the closed door they could hear the popping of a balloon and the elated shrieks. "It's too late. The contracts are drawn. There's no way."

"Barnett was cut in, what, three weeks ago?" she said.

"That couldn't be helped," Tumin replied without hesitation, though the comment startled him. While it was made public that Rob had made EVP, not even Don himself knew the young man had been brought in on Monarch. Where the hell was she getting her information from? "Rob started out at the brokerage house underwriting this deal. They demanded his presence. They wanted someone they were familiar with, you know, to shepherd this . . ."

"Lonny, Lonny, Lonny," she said. "Read my lips: I-DON'T-CARE. I only mention Barnett to point out that it can be done. It can be done, and you *will* do this for us."

"Bitch doesn't get it," Tumin was saying, murmuring under his breath. "This dumb dodo bird . . ."

"Call me what you like," she said. "You've called me worse than that, God knows. Just have the contracts redrawn. Don is in on Monarch ASAP, with stock options appropriate for a COO. Not these tiddlywinks you've been flipping our way. And for God's sake, give him something to do so he's not thoroughly humiliated, would you?"

Tumin grimaced and came away from the window. When he returned to his chair, he flopped into it in a kind of limp relief. Well, he thought, what the fuck could you do? Galling as it was, she had him by the nuts, and he knew it. The thing they shared was like a bazooka in Don's mouth, and while Suzy wouldn't think twice about pulling the trigger, Tumin himself would never consider it. Jews didn't do that to Jews, he thought. No way.

"Monarch," Susan repeated.

"Okay, I fuckin' heard you," he said, rubbing his face. "I'm warning you, though, it's going to be a hell of a ride."

"Don will take his chances."

Smoothing her wool skirt, Susan rose from her seat. Meeting adjourned. Tumin stood to see her out, and because she had kicked far too much of his ass this afternoon for him to live with, he came around from behind his desk and put his hand on her behind in a lewd claw, drawing her toward him.

"Tell me, Suzy," he said, breathing on her some of the Caesar salad he'd had for lunch, "how did Don like that worn-out old pussy of yours? You know, after I passed you off to him?"

Looking into his eyes, Susan reached down and flapped the back of her hand against Tumin's crotch, which was in one of its rare flaccid stages. He called out a start and hopped back, immediately releasing her from his grip.

"He liked it just fine," she said, Carolina accent in full flourish, "once he got past the worn-out part."

Wey Tu Yong

In Semper Dane's loft in Chinatown, bad things were afoot — or good things, depending on one's threshold for sexual duplicity and moral decay. Bad / good things, perhaps, thought Kyle Clayton, for the Apollonian and Dionysian lobes of his brain were in the midst of a knock-down-drag-out fight right there in the publisher's living room. On a white L-shaped sectional favored by drug dealers and porn stars, Semper sat ear-to-phone, his feet up on a coffee table hand-carved in the Maldives. Strewn across this cleaved surface were the remnants of Semper's past few nights: barren take-out sushi tins, *Time Out* magazine folded back to the *Nightlife* section, phone numbers with no adjoining names, a platinum cigar cutter, *Facial Cumshots #17* in a Kim's Video box, half-empty bottles of Rolling Rock stinking to high heaven (lipstick marks atop), Jets ticket stubs, a rectangle of Tupperware containing the residue of what might have been cocaine, heroin, or merely Sweet'n Low, a kitchen towel with crusty daubs, and *The Collected Poems of Phillip Larkin*.

The room basically screaming out, "Men with Their Wives Out of Town."

"Freedom," Semper announced. He had the phone scrunched between his chin and shoulder and had just rolled the perfect pin joint in seven seconds flat. "Can you dig it?"

Kyle didn't know if he could. There was no denying a certain exhilaration in his current circumstance: his marriage, it seemed, was abruptly over. Dispatched, terminated, suspended — bid adieu. And so all bets were off now, morally speaking. There was no more *watching it,* no *keeping it in check,* no *grinning and bearing it.* Smiles on street corners would now be returned and followed through, flirtatious sentence fragments engaged and run with, all invitations accepted, thank you very much. Let the savage impulses run where they might, went Kyle's way of thinking, and let us go sliding face first into the great smorgasbord known as New York City after dark!

He strode to the minibar, where Mr. Nightcap poured him a double Havana Club with one cube.

But there was a weight too that seemed to be sitting on his chest, a ball or a fist pressing into his diaphragm, a faint nausea hanging on the edge of everything. He tried to remind himself of the fathers — Mailer, Roth, Bellow, Updike, and Cheever — how they'd handled such separations. With guilt, yes; with regret and a heavy heart, naturally; but with a girl, *always.* It was Kyle's understanding that there was always a girl waiting for such men after a split. Not just *any* girl; there were requirements for such a position. She must be no more than half the writer's age, of course, and have studied English literature at one of the following institutions: Vassar, Barnard, or Radcliffe. For Updike and Cheever, she must be a Jewess; for Mailer, Roth, and Bellow nothing but a shiksa would do. They'd move temporarily into her Village *digs,* with books stacked across the dirty windowsills, and give their lass her first orgasm on the floor mattress while a Mingus bass line played on an old phonograph. Kyle was ready for it all.

But where was Kyle's Radcliffe Jewess? he'd wanted to know. Why was it that even in his single days, he tended to wake up in places like Lefrak City with girls wait-listed at Cross Island Expressway Junior College? What did that say about Kyle Clayton?

He returned to the porn couch with his smuggled rum and tried to get into the spirit of debauchery and mayhem.

"Clayton, what girls you got for us to call?" Semper had his hand over the phone while he continued to let the caller ramble on. "Come on, cough up the *numeros*."

"Girls?" Kyle said. He looked confused. "Don't know any girls anymore."

"What do you mean? What about the ones you screwed around with when you were married? You must still have a few in your stable."

Kyle ran his finger along the rim of his glass and looked away. On the muted television, Lennox Lewis was making human carpaccio with his left jab.

Semper sat forward a bit. "Wait," he said, with a slowly compounding dread, "don't tell me. Don't even tell me you were . . . *monogamous*."

Kyle's eyes flashed up guiltily.

"You mean not even once?"

The writer shook his head, contrite and humiliated.

"Oh my God. What was it, like two, two and a half *years*?"

"I tried, though," Kyle urged. "I really tried. There was this one girl who I almost . . ."

But Semper was too upset, too disappointed to listen anymore. He lit his pin joint and resumed his phone conversation:

"*Yeah, yeah, yeah, no* — you're *the best singer-songwriter out there. No, you are. Of course you are. You KNOW that you are.*" Semper held out the phone for Kyle and whispered, "Sheryl Crow. Just did a story on her."

Kyle nodded languidly.

"What now?" Semper asked him.

"Nothing." He knew he was in deep shit with the cool police and wanted to stay out of further trouble. "Not a huge fan, that's all."

"Me either. So what, man, it's *Sheryl Crow . . . What?*" Semper said back into the phone. "*No, nothing babe, just sitting here with Kyle Clayton, the writer . . . Huh? Fatwa guy, yeah that's him. You heard about that?*"

"It's not a fatwa," Kyle said with annoyance.

"*It's not a fatwa, sweetie. Apparently not. No, I don't know what it is . . .* What is it, Kyle?"

"It's, I don't know — it's nothing," he said sternly. "Don't worry about it."

"*It's nothing, sweetie. No, you can't believe the papers anymore,*

*you're right. What, the first book? Really? That's so smart of you.
You're so fucking smart, do you know that? What, you didn't like it?*
She didn't like *Charmed Life,* Kyle."

"I'm crying."

"*Huh? Too masculine?*" Semper fixed Kyle with a scowl. "*Yeah,
well, I don't think he has that problem anymore.*"

The e-mails his wife had discovered in his laptop were the least of
Kyle's problems. Sure Ayla had blown her top over the invitations for
a ride in his "love harness," had been hopping mad at the "whore's"
replies of downloaded smut. How stupid of him to have flirted on-
line, he thought now. He should have known that, driven to suspicion, his computer-whiz wife could retrieve anything, could reach
back into the outer limits of cyberspace and come out with the entire
Clayton family history. But it was really the father's visit and the subsequent blowout that had sunk Kyle and his marriage.

They'd come so innocently, too, had Ayla's family. Dodge Caravan
up to Saugerties, ferrying mother, father, sister, and her two frisky boys.
The first afternoon was filled with talk of the fatwa, of course — or
whatever was the correct title for Kyle's newest imbroglio. Ayla's
mother had been surprisingly helpful on the matter. She had spoken to
a family friend, a leader in the Muslim community, and he in turn had
made some inquiries about the threats. There were no immediate dan-
gers, she'd been assured, but things were not good. Word of mouth had
spread, there was a growing sentiment, a slow wave of animosity; "The
Counterfeit Conversion" seemed to have pissed off quite a few Muslims. What this meant for Kyle specifically, her friend (who himself had
hated the story) was not prepared to say. The situation could heat up,
or it could defuse. It could be forgotten tomorrow, or it could tense to
the point of peril. It was too early to tell.

As for Mount Murat, Kyle learned that the "The Counterfeit
Conversion" had been read aloud to him by his daughter Elsa (with
significant clarifications in Turkish). Word was he'd accepted it with
a stubborn silence. What this silence meant, nobody could discern,
though naturally the writer was driven to speculation. No doubt
Murat was unfamiliar with fiction, Kyle concluded, and therefore
slow to detect the obvious portraits of himself and others in the tale.
Or maybe he'd simply been indifferent. Would it be the first time

that the work of Kyle Clayton had failed to generate a reader's excitement?

In any case, Murat and company arrived on a chilly afternoon in late October when snow flurries had been promised, and so Kyle stoked the fireplace and retreated to the kitchen to fix dinner. The family sat around the hearth drinking tea the color of pennies, trying to keep Esla's pyromaniacal boys from bringing the fire out into the living room. It was nearly 6:00 P.M. when the FBI called. Kyle's hands were busy stuffing herbs in the cavity of a chicken, so Ayla handled the phone.

No, everything was fine, the agent told her. They were just checking in, wanting to reassure the Claytons that they were still on the Bureau's radar.

"Well, how nice," Ayla had answered ironically. More than Kyle, his wife had been discomforted by the whole situation, angry that the government wasn't doing anything to protect them. It only took one maniac, she'd argued. And her husband's membership on the list certainly wasn't any secret: *Page Six* of the *Post* had leaked the story (Patience denied any involvement), and there had been a short mention in the *Times*, so now their phone had been ringing off the hook. The ACLU had contacted them, for instance, offering praise for the First Amendment and legal help if it came to that. A PEN representative said his organization regarded the list as an outrage and was immediately putting together a committee to discuss Islam and censorship. Patience volunteered her house in Quogue for them to hide in (until Memorial Day), and a Tibetan monk Kyle had met at a book fair called to remind them how peaceful meditation would relieve the stress they were under, and invited them both to come to the monastery in the nearby Catskills as his guest.

Ayla had taken that last call too, and her reply had been that while she had nothing against meditation in a sylvan setting, what they really needed was men with guns — very, very big guns. Any suggestions?

When her mother had finished with her update, Elsa saw an opportunity to get her father involved in the conversation. "Baba," she said, "how do you think the Turkish government would react to something like this? How would they protect a writer like Kyle?"

"Protect him?" he said with derision. "Ha, they kill him." From his chair he gestured toward Kyle in the kitchen, knowing the son-in-law would be listening in. "In my village, dez guy would be dead already, believe me." The tone had nothing in it to suggest Murat thought this a bad thing.

"How about a martini, Baba?" Ayla said after the awkward pause.

Yes, thought Kyle, good idea. As it turned out, even the devout Murat cheated on Allah now and again, and when he did, it was with the regal martini. This was as much a relief to Kyle as it was a surprise; if he was going to have a relationship with the man, any sort at all, the fact that he took a little gin on occasion left them with at least a fighting chance. And though Ayla was the ex-bartender, Kyle himself did the honors on the cocktail. He shook it up cold and handed it off with a proud flourish. The father accepted the beverage with a gracious nod — Elsa and her mother tittering with optimism at the sight — and Kyle retreated again to the kitchen to finish preparing dinner.

He was crouched at the oven a short time later when he felt the sisters at his back.

"What're you doing?" one of them asked.

"Basting my bird," Kyle said with a smirk. "So to speak."

Ayla's voice was devoid of humor. "Um, we have a problem."

"Oh?"

"My father's upset."

He closed the oven and stood up. "What now?" he asked.

"Well . . ." His wife jutted her chin at the countertop, toward the glass of wine he'd been sipping. "You're drinking."

"Yes. Your father and I are enjoying a cocktail. In different rooms, but it's a start. You guys want a glass?"

Both women shook their heads, and then Ayla nudged her sister; it was Elsa's turn now.

"You see, in Cherkes culture," she began, twisting some hair around a finger, "to drink you have to seek permission from the eldest man in the house."

Kyle tossed the baster into the sink and quickly wiped his hands on a paper towel. "What are you trying to say?" he asked Elsa.

The two women looked at each other nervously.

"Are you trying to tell me that I can't have a glass of wine in my own house while your father lays out on my couch drinking the martini I just made him? I hope that isn't what you're trying to say, Elsa, because if it is, then that's stupid."

"*Kyle,*" scolded his wife.

"No, no, you're right, it *is* stupid," Elsa conceded. "But that's the way he is. It's his culture."

Kyle picked up his wine. "Well, this is the way *I* am," he said, taking a sip. He found that his voice was louder than he'd meant it to be. "This is *my* culture . . . No, don't fuckin' shush me," he hissed at Ayla.

Elsa put a hand on his shoulder. "Look, just go ask him," she advised. "Do him the favor. He'll love you for it. And I know he'll say yes."

Ayla thought this a wonderful idea. "Yes, please, Kyle. Just ask him and the whole thing will be over in two seconds."

"I will not."

Again the sisters glanced uneasily at each other.

"I'm not doing it, Ayla. I absolutely will not ask permission to have a drink in my own house. No way."

He looked past the them into the living room. Murat was still sprawled out on the couch, pretending to scold the pyros for trying to throw the *TV Guide* into the fire, but Kyle felt pretty sure the father's ears were tuned exclusively to the kitchen. He also suspected Murat was holding his martini aloft on purpose, to rankle him.

"Then at least put it away," Ayla said. "Have a soda or something, all right? Just for tonight." She took the glass of wine out of his hand and slipped her arm around him. "Please, Kyle. Do this for me. I know you can go one night without a glass of —"

"That's not the *point,*" he said, removing her hand. "Don't you get it? It's not just a glass of wine."

"It *is,*" she exclaimed, then suddenly looked wounded. "You mean you won't give up a measly glass of wine for me?"

"If it is just a glass of wine, then tell him to forget it."

"It's a tradition," Elsa interjected.

"I don't give a fuck if it's martial law, I'm not doing it."

Like a verbal kindling, the momentum of something awful began to build. Elsa amended her cultural argument as Ayla harangued him about his selfishness, dabbing her eyes with a napkin. Then their mother finally looked up from her knitting, inquiring with the tone of a Middle Eastern Stepford wife, "What is going on der in the kitchen?" while behind her the *TV Guide* was now a fireball atop a poker held by four tiny pyro hands, then a campfire on the floor, stamped by tiny pyro feet, the room suddenly a crescendo of scolds and threats.

"OKAY, EVERYBODY SHUT UP!" Kyle suddenly announced, storming in from the kitchen. Moving the pryos back from the flaming fireball, he picked up the magazine with his bare hand and threw it violently back over the hearth, sparks firing back at him, then turned and readied himself for his pronouncement.

"All right, look," he began — the floor underneath him was still smoldering, perhaps appropriately, with sooty debris — "obviously we need to clear the air a little bit here, huh? Yes, I think so. So let me say, right off, that I fully respect other people's cultures, traditions, values, *whatever.* And when I'm in their homes I play by their rules. But in *my* house, I do whatever I want. Okay? Period. Thank you."

He waited, but there was no reply. He was just about to walk back to the kitchen when Murat spoke up.

"Dez is not my culture," he said.

Kyle looked at Ayla. She had managed to catch his eye now with a pleading, desperate look — one last chance — but he ignored her and turned to her father. "And what about *my* culture?" Kyle replied, pointing to his chest. He was just a few feet from the couch, and the physical proximity of the two large men created a palpable tension. "Your culture is more important than my culture? We come from different places, okay, but a man in his own house has to be able to play by his own rules. It's the only thing that makes sense."

"*Your* culture."

Kyle turned to the sisters. "Now what does that mean?"

Murat obliged him. "What is your culture? Drinking? Talking bad about Islam? Dez is culture?"

Ah, Kyle thought, there it was: the father had shown his hand. The story *had* distressed him, that's what this was all about — and he knew exactly what he was doing. It was the very reason Murat had volunteered to come to Saugerties in the first place, had to be. The father had sensed that he and Ayla were vulnerable now, given the current controversy, and he might have even heard rumblings from his wife that Ayla harbored misgivings about her marriage. A grand opportunity would have presented itself to drive a further wedge between his daughter and Kyle.

He would have his Cherkes son-in-law yet.

"Drinking is not my culture," Kyle remarked, taking an unconscious step toward the father. "My culture is having the freedom not to be told by someone what to do in your own house. To hold opinions about religion without the threat of *assassination*."

The Claytons' martini glasses were oversized, and when Murat finished his drink, Kyle could see that the father's tolerance was low enough to already be a little soused. Coupled with those burly shoulders it was a worrisome combination.

"How can you criticize Muhammad? Dez is dumb. Muhammad is the word of God."

"I'm not so sure that it is."

Murat shrugged then, as if to say, *Then you get what you deserve.*

Kyle kept after him: "This is hard for you, I know. Freedom hasn't exactly been the cornerstone of Islamic culture . . ."

"*Kyle,*" shouted his sister-in-law. Ayla, however, knew it was too late; she stood apart, shaking her head in wonderment and disgust.

"Why you have to criticize Islam all the time?" asked Murat. "Why?" He set down his glass and rose slowly from the couch.

"Baba, sit down," said one of the sisters.

They were just a foot apart now, so close that Kyle could smell the warm juniper coming from Murat's nostrils. They wanted to kill each other, of course. It was as natural, as elemental, as the dusting of snow that was beginning to cover the earth outside. Marat thinking, *heathen, daughter-fucker, sinner, American.* Kyle thinking, *tribesman, daughter-beater, philistine, Ottoman ogre.*

The father took another step forward, and the son-in-law did not back off. Kyle remembered now that Murat owned a gun and wondered if he had brought it.

The sisters came up on either side of them; Ayla's mother was holding a pyro under each arm.

Kyle said, "I criticize a *lot* of things. Christianity too, all the time. Religion is flawed."

"No, Islam is not flawed. God is not flawed. It cannot be." Murat let a mean smile cross his lips and looked to Ayla. "And he wants to know why they try to kill him."

And that was it. For Kyle it all came rushing out: the humiliation of his counterfeit conversion; the battles with his Islamic wife; the anxious week of trying to ignore the list, to make a joke out of it — when in fact he was quite frightened and aggrieved to be wanted dead — all of this spilling out at once and at the top of his lungs: "CAN SOMEBODY TELL ME, PLEASE, WHAT'S SO GODDAMNED PRECIOUS ABOUT ISLAM THAT IT CANNOT BE CRITICIZED! I MEAN, WHY DOES THE WORLD HAVE TO WALK ON EGGSHELLS FOR THIS MOTHERFUCKING MUHAMMAD?"

Murat took him first by the throat, and Kyle felt his feet briefly leave the ground. Amid screams, the son-in-law attempted to return the favor but managed only a brief swipe at the man's neck, and Murat shoved him back effortlessly and with great force, moving him onto the hearth and nearly into the fire. Kyle could feel heat on him, licking at his legs, until the sisters beat sonorous blows on their father's back, forcing him to release his grip.

The whole thing had lasted less than five seconds, but the emotional aftermath was not unlike that of a murder. Kyle stood hunched over, coughing, neck mottled with red fingerprints, the rest of the family looking around in stunned disbelief. The sisters appealed to each other to say something, to be the first to try to articulate this incomprehensible event, while the pyros looked too frightened even to cry. Only the mother could manage sounds, rocking and murmuring soothing Arabic prayers.

Murat was the first to speak. "I'm leaving now here," he said, and with these awkward words his wife stood too, knitting needles in hand.

"No, you know what, *I'll* leave," Kyle said. Before Murat and his wife could take a step, the son-in-law was already at the bookshelf, car keys in hand. Passing Ayla on the way to the closet, he still had the heat of his final tirade on his lips when he looked at her and said, "And you're ALL fucking crazy."

She didn't stop him. Everyone remained still as Kyle pulled out his coat, flung open the front door and then the screen with the sound of snapping wood. A rush of freezing wet air entered the house, a few flakes floating in, and a few seconds later the curtains were illumined by car lights. It wasn't until the turning over of the engine that the family granted itself permission to make sounds again, the mother praying more loudly, the pyros now crying softly . . .

And Ayla, the car crunching away on the snowy gravel, whispering almost inaudibly, *"Be careful."*

"Good," Semper said now with great emphasis, though his eyes were flashing distractedly around the room. "You did the right thing. Guy's a madman."

They were in a bar / club on Lafayette Street where the motif was Prague subsumed by the Left Bank. The place was jammed, but Semper knew someone, of course, and so they'd both been escorted immediately to a half-moon booth ordinarily reserved for eight. It was just the sort of environment that Kyle had reveled in for so long, fifteen years and counting, and so he was surprised to find that tonight the patrons held a gargoyle aspect for him: dead-eyed blondes and jelly-haired goons, music-television holograms of the brutally stupid.

It would take some warming up tonight, he reasoned. He was out of practice.

"So wait, it gets better," Kyle said just above the din. "A few minutes later, Ayla starts feeling bad about the whole thing and goes to write me an e-mail in New York, to try and soften the blow. She knows I'm going to the apartment — where else am I going to go, right? — and she's so anxious to get ahold of me she passes the office and sees my laptop glowing and decides to go in and use *my* computer, *my* e-mail."

Semper wagged the pinkie finger on his rocks glass. "Oh, no, you see, you've got to keep them out of the office. I weaned my wife off that long ago. She's not even allowed in my building — hell, she's not allowed in *Mid*town during working hours. Hey, look at that brunette."

Again, Kyle strained to get in the mood. The girl Semper pointed out had an equine quality about her, he found, the feathered mane and extended haunches of a two-legged mare. Perhaps he was too intent on his story to appreciate her. "You see Ayla then — on some whim, some dormant feminine instinct that arises out of who the fuck knows where — she goes searching through my stuff, all my old e-mails."

"Should be illegal," Semper said, eyes still scanning the room. "We oughta push for legislation, pressure our congressmen. People like you and me need to stand up — check out the blonde."

"And of course Ayla finds it all there, everything, even though I double and triple deleted the fuckers. She finds 'em anyway. And so now I'm sunk, Semp, I'm finished. And the worst part is, I didn't even *do* anything."

His friend finally wrested his eyes from the crowd and patted Kyle's shoulder encouragingly. "You're not sunk. You're a free man, Kyle. Free! Christ, I sometimes wish I was."

"I'm not free," the writer rejoined. "I've got Islam on my ass, don't you remember?" Kyle suddenly looked around with wary eyes. "Hell, I don't even know if I should be out in public."

Semper shook his head, taking a good sip of his drink. "Screw 'em," he said. "Look at Rushdie. He's got a *real* fatwa, and he goes out everywhere. You can't go to a party or a restaurant in New York without running into the horny toad. This could actually be great for your social life. Forget it, have a good time."

"I'm too tense." Kyle pulled at his collar.

"You need some action, that's all. Why don't you call this girl, the one you've been e-mailing?"

Yes, why not call? Kyle thought. Good question. Erin would probably be delighted to hear from him now that he was a single man. Or she would suddenly be attached — of course, that's how it usually worked. Either way, he knew he wasn't ready for the waitress of his dreams. She was unique, he decided. With her it could get serious quick, and what he wanted, absolutely *needed,* after years of soul-crushing commitment, was to slosh around in the gutters of perversion and moral turpitude. At least for a while.

"She's working tonight," he fibbed. "She's a waitress; she works late." That's all I need, Kyle thought, let Semper Dane get his dirty paws on her.

The publisher checked his watch. "Well, probably just as well. We got two others meeting us here in a few minutes."

"We do?" Kyle's stomach fluttered with dread and excitement.

"Sure, two beauties. A German, and get this" — he grabbed Kyle tightly by the back of the neck, whispering to him with licentious glee — "a Chi*nese.*"

"They sound like menus."

"They are, Kyle, they are, and they *deliver.*"

The girls arrived ten minutes later dressed like cast members from the musical *Cabaret*, Kyle discreetly murmuring his approval to Semper. Under the table he was positively tumescent when, after the blonde slid in next to Semper, the Asian girl came in on his side and immediately kissed him on the cheek. Semper got out the corporate card and ordered Russian vodka and some wildly overpriced caviar, though Kyle was thinking, Why bother? It hardly seemed necessary with such forceful inevitability already hanging in the air.

This was a go, or his name wasn't Kyle Clayton.

"I'm Kyle," he told the dark-eyed waif, already brushing herself up against him. The newness of young, fragrant limbs so close to him was positively intoxicating, and he suddenly wondered why, why, *why* he'd waited this long for such an encounter. It had been nothing short of cruel to deny himself such basic pleasures. Monogamy, he decided, should be grounds for divorce.

"Wey," she said close to his ear, her tender voice barely high enough to supersede the thumping music.

"Way," he repeated stupidly. He was out of the youthful jargon loop and thought this was some comment on the bar or crowd that he was expected to regurgitate on cue. Then she took his hand in greeting, and he realized it was, in fact, her name.

"Wey Tu Yong," she elaborated, and with a nearly indistinguishable Chinese accent.

Semper introduced him to his girl.

"How do you do?" Kyle asked the Fräulein. She smiled absently.

"They don't speak a whole lot of English," Semper murmured.

"I'm getting that."

"The German girl speaks Chinese — she's a language student, I think — but not much English. And your girl's just plain hopeless. There'll be no niggling small talk tonight, Kyle. Don't you just love it!"

The caviar was wheeled out on a cart of polished silver, the vodka served with frosted shot glasses. Kyle immediately reached out for a drink.

"How old are these girls?"

"Relax," Semper implored. He stuffed a tablespoon of caviar in Kyle's mouth, playfully rubbing his cheeks to get him to swallow. Then the publisher threw out his arm, the gesture meant to invoke everything — the room, the girls, Kyle's newfound freedom in general. "The buffet, my friend, is open."

Bulgarian for the Vulgarians

Residing near the fire stairs on City's second floor was the pastry kitchen. The pastry chef herself utilized the space only until about noon, and after this it became something of a clubhouse for the waiters — its applications various but almost entirely illicit in nature. Though the staff was forbidden to smoke in the building, for example, the ceiling of this room had a suspiciously egg-yolked hue. It was also the place where, in a pinch, Raoul might take an empty bottle of '82 Pomerol and replace it with a Bulgarian red of unspecified vintage, cork expertly reinserted. The bus tubs for dirty plates stood outside this room as well, and after clearing a large banquet party certain waiters would descend on the leftovers like buzzards, the kitchen transformed into a mini dining room, or the "Bus Tub Café," as it had been dubbed. ("Holy shit," Urlich remarked one night, looking in the space crammed with masticating waiters, "you need a fucking reservation to get in this place.") It was the room where Hostess A had been conducting her affair with Manager B for six months running, and where Famous Actor Guy had wandered in dead drunk, only to later swear that the pool of urine discovered next to the freezer was not his.

It was also a great place to let off steam when an unruly customer had damaged your spirit or upset your dignity, where the *cocksucking-motherfucking-two-balled bitch* could be properly execrated without fear of being fired. It was also a good place for the waitstaff to let loose a few private tears when need be — a need that arose more often than anyone might expect, as it did now, with Erin Wyatt using a milk crate as a seat and a chocolate-soiled chef's apron for her eyes.

"What going on here?" asked Abu, who'd been looking for her. Though Erin's misery during the lunch shift was all but hidden by the deft actress, Abu was a hypersensitive audience. If there was a crack in the performance, he would find it.

"Nothing. Leave me alone."

"Please, Miss Erin."

When she looked up from her apron, her eyes were swollen. "Look, I told you, we're just friends."

"Yes, Miss Erin, but friends must tell things to each other. You should talk about this hurt to Abu."

Of course, this was mostly true, it was good to talk it out, but then how could she confide what had taken place this morning? How could anyone admit that such a thing had happened? Forever, it seemed, Lonny Tumin had been telling Erin he'd wanted to speak to her, though he'd never followed through, and Erin saw no reason to remind him. But then during last night's dinner shift, a manager had passed on the message that Tumin wanted to meet with her. Was the following morning convenient? They would have breakfast together and discuss some "options" for her in the company.

Erin had taken the bait. Her aunt's illness, it had been discovered, was terminal (liver cancer), and the pain and disbelief of this had suddenly made it impossible, not to mention distasteful, for her to think about wills or estates, or how her aunt's death might affect her future as a waitress. If anything, it made her more frightened about her life, more insecure, and this feeling of being unmoored had manifested itself suddenly as an impulse toward safety. She would keep working no matter what, Erin decided, and so she figured she should make her job at City as comfortable as possible. Tumin liked her; why not let him stick her in some cushy job if it made him feel good? Hadn't the banquet director just quit? Now *there* was a sweet gig! Hundred thou a year, plus benefits. Erin would tell him she'd work three days for seventy-five, then take the rest of the week for her acting.

That night on the way home she borrowed some career-wear from a girlfriend who worked at Condé Nasty, and was at City the next morning by eight sharp.

The cleaning people let her in. Leon the bodyguard met her in the lobby and escorted her into the main dining room, the sight of which startled her at this hour. She had never seen the room so naked, so much in a shambles. The chandeliers had been lowered for dusting, the linen stripped from the tables. The chairs also had been flipped up, showing you their backsides, and now dollops of gum stared at her from every direction. Erin likened the room to a gorgeous call girl who, in the harsh light of morning, you realize has lied about her age.

They found Tumin sitting at a booth, work papers spread out in front of him. He took off his reading glasses and folded them into his breast pocket.

"Ellen, you look terrific."

"Erin," she corrected him.

"Have a seat."

What was most remarkable about the whole thing, she remembered now, was how direct he was, how matter of fact. Over French toast, Tumin made his presentation — a prospectus, really, laid out with strict budgetary guidelines and shrewd preparedness. He began in broad, ambiguous strokes, so it took a few minutes for her to realize he wasn't talking about banquet manager at all.

Her days as a waitress would be effectively over, he explained. She was an actress? Terrific. In fact, that goal would now be easier to pursue. Her rent would be taken care of, as would her wardrobe. She would be given $50,000 a year in spending money. She could go out whenever she wanted to, do whatever she pleased. The only thing she couldn't do was have a serious boyfriend, or, quite obviously, get married.

Erin stared down at her breakfast, feeling as if she'd been punched in the gut.

I know, I know, Tumin had said, it was heavy stuff. A lot to lay on someone at eight o'clock in the morning. But an interesting opportunity, was it not? Could she deny that such a prospect made one think? Remember Serena, the hostess that used to work weekends? She'd taken the opportunity, he'd said. For two years she'd taken it, until she finished school. Now she was a second-grade teacher. Interesting opportunity, he repeated. You should ask Serena if she had any complaints.

He would rarely make more than two visits a week, Tumin assured her, and some weeks he would not come at all.

She would never have to appear with him in public. Never.

Erin drew into herself, receding into a sort of shock. Her lips retracted as she watched the syrup congeal on her plate. She had never in her life been raped, thank heavens, but she wondered now if she wasn't experiencing some of the same feelings of debasement. So *this* is how he regards me, Erin thought — a whore to be propositioned? And what made it worse, the thing that in looking back she could not fathom or accept, was that she'd found herself nodding to him, as if actually considering the proposal. Well, what should she have done? she wondered. How *did* one react to such an offer? She told herself she might have screamed at him, or slapped his face. At the very least she should have walked out. Anything, *anything* but what she had done. *She had nodded!*

Nevertheless, when he finally reached across the table and took her hand, she'd lurched back with a start and trilled in a short burst of fright.

"Easy," said Lonny Tumin, a touch of annoyance in his voice. "No reason to get excited, right? That's a good girl."

She noticed Leon peeking around the corner, but the boss waved him off. Breakfast untouched, Tumin stood up, stuffing the papers into his valise.

"You don't have to decide now," he said. She did not look up at him. "Just think about it, Helen, that's all I ask. We'll be in touch."

Abu brought her a glass of water as she pulled herself together. On a prep table near them sat twelve tarte Tatins, cooling on wax paper. He got a bread plate and a spoon and scooped some vanilla ice cream from a tub in the freezer, then served it to her with one of the tarts.

"Go on," he said. "They won't miss it."

At first Erin shook her head, then quickly scolded herself for being such a chickenshit. She hadn't touched her French toast and was starving, so when she finally decided to have the dessert she dug in ravenously.

"I believe Kurban did this to you, these tears."

"No," she said, talking over a mouthful. "Kyle had nothing to do with it."

"He's bad man I think now."

She looked up. "What'd he ever do to you?"

"Nothing to me. Kurban write bad thing against Islam. Syeed tell me."

She stood, wiping some crumbs off the front of her jacket. "You mean the story they're talking about?" Erin wondered why she hadn't heard from Kyle recently; then she saw in the paper how he was in hot water again, this time with Islam. Kicking things up a notch, she thought.

"He say bad things against Islam, Miss Erin. Against Muhammad. Bad things."

"Like what?"

Abu was uncertain as he looked at her. "I did not read this story, Miss Erin, but Syeed tell me . . ."

"Ahhh," she said, smiling knowingly.

"No, he tell me. It's about a man who pretends to be a Muslim, then makes fun with our religion."

"Read the story, Abu." She hadn't read it either, but Erin was pretty sure that whatever sin Kyle had committed, it was probably a big misunderstanding on Syeed's part. From what she knew of his work, Kyle was primarily a comic novelist — not a perspective that would go over well with the humorless doorman. "Mr. Kurban is a lot of things, Abu, and not all of them good, but I don't think he's malicious. I'm sure it's just a big mistake. Read it and then you tell me."

The waiter frowned, unimpressed with such logic. Erin reminded herself that with Abu watching her so closely, he'd probably sensed something between her and Kyle, and so it would hardly be easy to convince him of the writer's virtue. Hell, it was hard to convince *herself* of the writer's virtue, but it was also ridiculous to judge him on hearsay.

"In fact, if you want to know, Mr. Kurban is going to help me get back at this man who hurt me."

"He is?"

"Yes," she said, then reconsidered. "Or, well, I'm going to try and persuade him to."

The King and I

In the auditorium of the Montclair Kimberly Academy, with its musty arts-and-crafts smell, Don Westly stood in the darkness, trying to stifle his own foolish blubbering.

The windows and halls were strewn with Christmas and Hanukkah decorations, and so it was time again for the middle school's winter musical production. Funny, Don thought, but he did not remember the *The King and I* being an emotionally affecting experience when he'd seen it years ago on Broadway. He did not remember the constriction in his throat as the school's musical director cued those first notes on his piano, nor did he recall that when the players scurried out on stage they did so like a procession of nymphs. And he certainly did not remember removing himself from his seat so as to outrun the hurricane of emotions that were chasing him.

I whistle a happy tune, doo doo doot-doot doot doot doo . . . His daughter, Alison, was playing Anna, and she could not have been more luminous than when she came skipping out on stage in her long silk dress patterned in Thai-styled florals, wearing velvet slippers, and, despite a mild flare-up of acne, her hair pulled back and bunned with chopsticks. The parents in the audience were predominantly transplanted New Yorkers, couples who'd nearly waited too long to have children, and under the heavy perfume and Hermès scarves and faces pulled tight as a snare drum there was the fetid air of fatigue, the resignation of those about to enter life's third act in suburban consolation. So there, the women thought with their silent, yielding sighs, is what I will never be again, this little seraph of beauty and innocence. So there, thought the men in the sulk they hid as a murmur, is what I will never again possess.

Naturally, it affected Don much more than the others. After the first few notes of her solo, he'd raised himself from his seat, Susan clucking her tongue as he pressed by her and compelled the rest of the row to stand as he brushed past. Moving briskly down the aisle, he found a spot in the standing-room section, a dark corner where he coughed, chuffed, and sniffled his way through her number, holding on for dear life.

She was fifteen, and he regarded her performance — this coquette of purity and guilelessness — as a rebuke to everything he currently stood for. He was now the very same scotch-swilling, unhappily married, crudely compromised cliché he'd swore he'd never become. A fallen man. Was Susan to blame for everything? Reason told him that was too easy, though instinct convinced him it wasn't a bad start. Ironically, he remembered that it was Alison herself who had brought him and his wife together. By 1984 Don Westly was still on the fence about marrying Susan Belford, though nobody could figure out why, least of all Don. He was pushing forty and sick to death of dating. Susan and he had been together for many months now, happily cruising along, and she had introduced him to tricks in bed that had caused him to nearly black out from pleasure. And yet, he couldn't bring himself to pull the nuptial trigger. Something, some stubborn impulse, was telling him to hold off.

Strangely, it was Tumin who had seemed most affected when Suzy announced she was pregnant. *"Do the right thing,"* he'd growled to Don after learning the news. This same Lonny Tumin — who was currently trying, in his words, to "divest" himself from his first marriage, and who'd managed to elude no less than three paternity claims — suddenly it was *he* who was putting the screws to Don to marry. The pressure was palpable: Tumin was tearing it up at Drexel but was already talking of forming his own company, had been kicking around some preliminary ideas with Don outside the office. If Don was going to be a part of it, Tumin informed him, then he *must* set things right with Suzy. Who wanted a partner with a reputation for bearing children out of wedlock? (Unlike Tumin's complications, you had to know Susan Belford would make a public stink.) Reputations, in this business, Tumin said, were no small matter. *Marry her, Don.*

Stranger still was the pregnancy itself, given the precautions he and Susan had taken. She was on the pill — Don had *watched* her take it, even checked her pocketbook from time to time when she left the room, just to make sure she was keeping up. It was a trick Tumin had taught him, along with the "withdrawal" method, which he'd also advised. Neither was 100 percent effective, his friend had reminded him, but together you'd be in pretty good shape.

But then, *"Marry her,"* Tumin had demanded. "It's what a good Jew would do . . . And then we take over the world."

When Alison finished her solo, Don went to bathroom to wash his face.

"Hey, Donny," said a voice behind him.

Lifting his head, he saw Jeb Williams in the mirror's reflection. Jeb was a neighbor, a mildly annoying midlevel broker at Goldman Sachs who forever dreamed of the big time. He was a regular guest at the Upper Montclair Country Club but had been denied membership for his habit of trying to glean insider information from the club's more high-profile members. Don guessed the broker had seen him retreat to the bathroom and had followed him in.

"Your daughter's a vision out there."

"Thanks," Don replied, turning off the faucet.

"Wish my son could sing like that. Lucky for us he's relegated to the chorus."

"Well, you ought to get back out there. I think they're almost up."

When he turned, Don's face and hands were heavily beaded with water. Obsequious as a men's-room attendant, Jeb was ready for him with a coarse paper towel. Don dried himself, the broker still waiting for something, making no move to show why he'd come to the bathroom.

"What's up, Jeb?"

"Nothing . . . Well, I was thinking about recommending Monarch to some of my clients. Maybe even buying some myself. What do you think?"

"It's bloody expensive, that's what I think," Don said, laughing, and Jeb joined him with a little chuckle. To everyone's amazement, Monarch was already trading at just over $79 a share. Beyond the reported quarterly earnings, which were merely decent, it had become what was called a "fashionable buy." Tumin was once again a true-blue billionaire, and the mighty Westlys had regained their title as the richest family in Upper Montclair.

"C'mon, Don. You know what I mean."

"What?"

He enjoyed making Jeb wait, so unctuously expectant.

The broker lifted his eyebrows conspiratorially. "What do you *think?*"

Don finished drying himself and crumpled up the paper towel. "Hell, man, what do I know? Doesn't look like it's going anywhere soon." This wasn't what Jeb was looking for, he knew, but then he had no intentions of discussing the stock; Monarch was making him nervous enough as it was. "Look, we both know we really shouldn't be talking about this."

"Rumors are swirling, Donny, that's the only reason I bring it up."

"Like what?"

"You know . . ." Now he was going to get coy, Don could see, direct the power back to himself. *You're so fucking obvious.*

"Like what, Jeb?"

"Like why is Lonny Tumin's first tech offering being underwritten by some no-name joint out of Jersey City, for one."

Don tossed the balled-up towel toward the trash and missed short.

"And then, what about this accounting firm you guys are going with? Very shaky outfit, Donny. What gives?"

"Wasn't my call," he said, now holding Jeb's gaze. It was a real ball buster, he thought, being interrogated by this pudgy-faced medi-

ocrity, but then Jeb Williams had a big mouth, and so was as dangerous as he was irritating. "I came in late."

"I heard," replied the broker, as if this only amended the point
he'd been trying to make. "Oh, yeah, and now I hear Ohka's
involved. What's the deal there?"

"What's that mean?"

"C'mon, Ohka? Reputation's dubious, to say the least. Now you
got him *and* Tumin together? People are talking, Donny. I don't think
you can blame them."

From out in the hallway they could hear the plaintive notes of the
piano cuing another song. Don suddenly took a step forward and
looked hard into his neighbor's face.

"What're you doing, Jeb?"

"Nothing. What?"

"You on your high horse now? You, of all people?"

Jeb smiled but looked uneasy; Don Westly did *not* get angry. The
broker strained to bring down the tension level.

"Nah, I'm an interested party, that's all. I'm looking for an excuse
to recommend the stock."

Don smiled unpleasantly. "Does Monarch look like it needs an
excuse?"

"No, look, I'm just —"

"You see the numbers, Jeb? Does that look like a stock that needs
your help?"

"Whoa, Donny, c'mon. I'm just trying —"

"Don't, okay?" Don's voice quavered with uncharacteristic anger.
"*Okay?* In fact, I forbid you to buy it. Don't buy it, don't recommend
it. Go fuck yourself, Jeb."

A wave of piano music rushed in as Don opened the door and
headed out toward the auditorium. Standing alone in the bathroom,
shaking a bit, Jeb Williams had already started a list of clients whom
he would tell to immediately drop Monarch.

Party Girls

"I absolutely loathe this sort of thing," Urlich proclaimed. All around him the hungover floor staff yawned and stretched in the disassembled dining room. "An insult is what it is. Absolutely *loathe* it."

In truth, they all loathed it. Mandatory staff meetings on the weekend were a no-no, a fact that City management had learned the hard way. But Diane Tumin and Susan Westly were going to be in Manhattan this Sunday anyhow, in town for some voracious holiday shopping, and could not be dissuaded from calling a meeting on the one day City was closed.

The "girls," as Lonny Tumin referred to them, were becoming unlikely friends, though the runaway success of Monarch certainly had something to do with it. It was a matter of familiarity: how many women could fully understand what it was like to get an influx of tens, or in Diane's case hundreds, of millions of dollars? Who was there to share and commiserate on matters such as these? While this absurd surge of income (on paper, Tumin had reminded everyone) might seem a great boon, it also complicated one's life immeasurably.

What's a girl to do with such inexplicable funds? This was the daunting dilemma shared by Diane Tumin and Susan Westly.

Their visions diverged on where exactly the money would go: Diane was thinking of upgrading their $15 million Palm Beach house to a $75 million estate down the road, while Susan was leaning toward buying the Upper Montclair Country Club for Don and herself, closing it to all but a few friends. But there were two points on which they adamantly agreed: (1) that a significant amount of money should go to charity, therefore circumventing a capital gains holocaust, and (2) that they should throw a millennium bash at City the likes of which no one would ever forget. What better way to commemorate this mad, wonderful decade, they decided, than with a no-expense-spared party at one of the world's great restaurants? Lonny Tumin himself had approved the plan without hesitation, appropriating a million dollars of Triad money for the bash in addition to whatever the girls would include from their copious allowances. The party would promise to be one of the most lavish in history, and, therefore, he reasoned, yet another opportunity to publicize Monarch, to show that L. T. was back, returned to his former glory.

In the meantime, the bored and exhausted floor staff for this great event sat waiting for the organizers with impatience, their ire rising with the steam from their paper coffeecups, which they held aloft like intravenous drips.

"How late are these bitches?" Stephen asked now, Erin showing absolutely no objection to his choice of words.

Hussein consulted one of the facsimile Movados he sold on Canal Street on his days off. "Forty minute," he replied.

"They *bddrring* us here on a-Sunday, then they're an hour-a late," Marco, the captain, complained. "I supposed to go to church a-today with my son."

"Fuck church," Urlich interjected. "Today's a matinee of *The Barber of Seville* at the Met. With Pavarotti, no less."

"You hate Pavarotti," said Stephen, the unwittingly gay straight man.

"Yes, so think of all the booing I could do today. It just kills me that all the idiots will be clapping and cheering and there will be no one to put this mound of duck fat in his place."

Finally the door opened, and Diane and Susan entered the restaurant.

Subdued and melancholy as she'd been lately, Erin couldn't help but take notice of the women's attire, so startlingly similar today to her own: boots, blue jeans, and tight black halter top, all wrapped up in a midlength leather pea coat. This was the requisite vestment of the struggling-actress-living-below-14th-Street, as predictable a uniform, Erin would admit, as a banker's pinstriped suit, or the poet from Avenue C's nosering. But as worn by these ladies, the uniform was more like a costume, a burlesque of cool to be worn in Manhattan only. And though their version of the uniform probably cost a hundred times what Erin had paid rummaging around lower Broadway (and their halters bulging with a supplementation the waitress could neither afford nor desired), it almost softened her mood to see that the wives of billionaires were so eager to look like her and her friends.

It occurred to her that she might pull Diane Tumin aside after the meeting and tell her about her husband, the propositions he'd made; but then it wouldn't be much use, she felt sure. Diane was either bathing neck-deep in that great river in Egypt or else knew all about her husband and didn't care. Either way, it was unlikely that Diane would jeopardize all that she had — especially now — for the squawkings of a bitter waitress. She would have to be more clever in her revenge, Erin decided.

Behind the ladies trailed two assistants — harried, unattractive girls in their early twenties — lugging a busload of shopping bags with the names of designers whose clothes Erin had merely gazed at through plateglass windows. With the bags stacked neatly along the banquette, the assistants were dismissed, and when Diane Tumin took off her jacket and leaned forward to place her pocketbook at her feet, Erin could almost sense a lightheadedness overtake the staff. Her beauty, though overscrubbed and vacant, was striking. No one on the staff, from straight to gay, could take their eyes off her, and it took Susan Westly quite a few seconds to wrest away their attention as she stood to address the room.

"Well, he*llo,* everybody," she began, bringing her hands together in a single clap. Erin wondered suddenly if she and Diane hadn't shared a joint in the limo — you had to be pretty high to assume the bubbly tone would go over with this gorgonized crowd. "First of all, I just wanted to tell you how *excited* Diane and I are that we're going to be working this New Year's Eve with such a *wonderful* group of —"

"How much we gettin' paid?" asked Bill the waiter, ever the arbiter of the bottom line. He was laid out like a corpse on the banquette, eyes fixed on the ceiling.

Susan registered a look of restrained disapproval. She was not used to employees talking out of turn, never mind dozing off during meetings, but then every other waiter in town was already booked for the New Year. She could not afford to alienate the staff. Worst of all, they seemed to know it.

"Well, if you must know this minute," Susan said, "it's five hundred dollars for the waiters and two-fifty for the bussers." She sneaked a conspiratorial glance at Diane, both having already agreed the sum was outrageous, and each blaming Don for insisting upon it.

"Before tax or after?" inquired Hussein.

"Frankly, I don't know," Susan said, clearly pestered, "though I'll try to find out for you . . . But listen, let me tell you about some of the ideas Diane and I have put together here, okay? I know this is work for you guys, but I think it's really going to be a *thrilling* event to be a part of."

She reached into her large bag and took out a few invitations to hand out to the staff. Lasered inside the cards was the inscription: *Party of the New Millennium!*

"Whoa, whoa, whoa," someone called as the invitations were distributed.

"Excuse me?" Susan said, looking for the source.

"Major problemo here."

"And just what is your name, sir?"

"Urlich," went the reply, this simple pronouncement already prompting some on the staff to snigger. "Hey, I don't want to be a party pooper, but the new millennium doesn't actually begin until next year."

Susan narrowed her eyes and looked over at Diane.

"Not true," said Mrs. Tumin from the banquette. Though her honey-toned voice melted hearts, her comment was met with silence. No one on the staff was betting against Urlich.

"Sorry, dear, but it is," he retorted. He wafted his invitation in the air. "Don't tell me these went out to your guests already?"

Warily, the party girls nodded, and then Urlich shook his head gravely.

"Okay, wow, because if I'm one of your friends and I read this card about a millennium party, I'm thinking I have a *year* to get ready."

Two Florida tans suddenly blanched; the party girls were visibly shaken. These were idle women, unused to such large-scale organization and deployment, and though they'd been overcome with excitement during the planning of the event (how they longed to do something grand in their lives, to emulate their husband's epic achievements!), each silently shared some concern about whether they could actually carry it off: everything had been done for them since they could remember.

"Well," Susan said, clearing her throat. "I suppose we might consider sending out some new invites." Once again she looked to Diane, who could only offer a worried shrug. Then her tone grew more firm. "But you know what, let's just cool it with the comments and keep going, okay? I know you all want to help, but I've thrown a lot of parties in my life, believe me, and I'd prefer to just roll through this. So, if you don't mind . . ."

She searched the faces of the staff, finding everyone looking dreamily at Diane.

"Along this wall here will be the band. I presume you've all heard of Barbara Cook?" Susan glanced up, expecting finally to have impressed them — only to discover their gaze having shifted to Urlich, waiting for his verdict on the singer. With a twitch of his finger, the waiter hinted that it would be better if they heard from him later on the matter, and that their patience would be rewarded with vicious invective.

She continued on, talking of gold-dusted balloons and white-truffle martinis, of African tribal drumming exhibitions and ice sculptures twenty feet wide. Despite herself, Erin felt a twinge of sympathy for Susan: she knew this speech was meant to enliven the staff, to whet their appetite for work, but then she also knew that the waiters couldn't have cared less, that all they could think of was what a nuisance this was all going to be. They didn't care for torch singers or ice sculptures; they didn't want to be *entertained*. What they wanted was a quick, problem-free shift and to *get the fuck out of there* as soon as possible, and she knew now they were all envisioning the same sort of nightmare: ice melting on the floor, orders drowned out by a geriatric jazz singer, food runners unable to find real estate on the balloon-strewn tables. A million little snafus the party girls could never anticipate.

When talk turned to the menu, the waiters could no longer hold their tongues.

"The first course," Susan said, "is vichyssoise."

"Vichys*soise*," corrected Urlich, emphasizing the *z* sound at the end.

"What?"

"It's pronounced vichys*soise*."

"This is *crrddddect*," Marco exclaimed. "A-yes."

"Fine," Susan snapped. The gracious tone she'd adopted was now thoroughly abandoned. "Vichys*soise,* whatever . . . The next course is duck confit" — she looked to Urlich for confirmation on accent, which was approved — "which will be French-served."

Groans all around.

"And then the poached salmon, which comes with . . ." There was some grumbling near Marco, and Susan let the menu list slap against her thigh. "Yes, sir?"

"Soddy, so soddy," the captain said. "It's just I think a-salmon always taste a-better *gdddddrreeeled.*"

"*Gddrrreeeeled,*" chimed Hussein and Bill, punctuating this with a wacky high-five they'd invented just last night.

Susan looked back to Diane. *Can you believe this?*

"Sir," she said, her eyes slowly returning to Marco, "I wish I had the foggiest idea what you just said. But I don't. So guess what? I'm moving on."

Now Raoul decided to interject. "What time do we serve the swine?" he asked sternly. His face held a saturnine aspect — eyes narrowed and darting, lips twisted in foul displeasure. Clearly this was a concern he'd been sitting on for some time, and one he could no longer contain.

"The *what?*" asked Susan. She seemed ready to lose it.

"Oh, c'mon," replied Raoul, voice flecked with Gallic sanctimony, "your guests have already had duck confit *and* a grilled fish —"

"*Poach-ed,*" Marco said miserably.

"— and still there is no swine. This is *terrible.*"

Susan said, "Excuse me, but there's not going to be any *swine* at this party."

"Uhn, no swine?" In the back, there were some scattered clucks of laughter.

"No, Raoul, there is no swine being served at this party. We're expecting a number of Jewish people —"

"No, no." Raoul threw his head back in dismay. "De *swine*."

"What? What is that you're saying?"

"De *swine*. De *SWINE* . . . Ah, fucking America!"

The room erupted. Bill and Hussein were now actually punching each other in the upper arm, the hilarity apparently so intense they could only relieve it by inflicting pain.

The only person not joining in the mirth was Syeed, with whom Erin shared an empty booth. In fact, no one had seen the doorman so much as break a smile in two weeks, nor had he deigned to speak to anyone who was not a paying customer. Today, apparently, would be no different, for even as the fun swept across the room, Syeed remained quiet. Or nearly so. He'd been breathing strangely today, Erin noticed, and now she could hear him again, the deep, sonorous respirations bringing to mind nothing so much as a bull in a holding pen.

Abu had intimated that the doorman was having problems with his wife back in Saudi Arabia, and so Erin, no stranger to romantic problems herself, decided it might be time to express a little empathy. With the room still roaring, she leaned over to him and whacked his knee with the back of her hand. "C'mon, try and laugh a little," she said good-naturedly. "Things'll work out."

"EVERY-TING FUNNY," Syeed suddenly exclaimed in a forbidding voice. Immediately the laughter in the room began to dissipate. "EVERY-TING FUNNY IN AMERICA, ALL TIME!"

As discreetly as she could, Erin slid away a few inches from Syeed on the banquette. Then she looked out at the staff sheepishly, as if apologizing for awakening this sleeping giant.

"Excuse me, people," Susan announced, oblivious to the new tension. "Hello, out there. Does anybody mind if we . . . Jesus H. Christ, now where are *you* going?"

Syeed was up and heading toward the door. "I go to pray," he murmured.

Susan turned and slapped her notes down on the nearest table, then flopped back next to Diane on the banquette, signaling surrender.

"Praise Allah!" Raoul suddenly shouted out. "Muhammad is good!" He'd had an uncle who'd died in the Algerian uprising of '54, and so liked to prod the doorman when the chance arose.

When nobody laughed, Syeed turned as he reached the vestibule and cut the sommelier with a venomous stare.

"Maybe you see how good, my friend," he taunted. "Maybe you *all* see."

Going Clapton

In the end, he'd decided she was way too young.

Semper Dane had emerged from his bedroom to find Kyle and the Asian girl on the couch enjoying some scrambled eggs and fatuous morning television.

"What's going on out here?" Though Kyle and the girl had been fully clothed, the publisher strode unabashedly in his boxers and unbound robe, chest lewdly flushed. With his Roman nose, long hair, and paunchy midsection, Semper looked strikingly like a debauched emperor, Kyle had thought.

"Nothing."

"I see that," the publisher had replied with displeasure.

It was true that nothing had gone on during the night, unless you count a mutual foot massage and some soothing words when Wey began to suddenly cry for reasons Kyle could not comprehend. Through broken English and crude sign language, he had been able to determine that she was an illegal alien living with twenty other members of her family in a three-bedroom apartment on Bayard Street.

She and her girlfriend, an exchange student from Düsseldorf, worked at the local Laundromat, where Semper had approached them while dropping off his work shirts.

"Like, dude," Kyle had said mockingly, and with some displeasure of his own, "she's eighteen."

"Hey, she votes," Semper had said. "That's the rule."

The great Dane had continued into the kitchen, shaking his head in consternation, then opened the refrigerator to retrieve a large bottled water — with this, Kyle knew, the emperor would hydrate his concubine, ready her for more exertion.

Outside his bedroom door, he'd stopped. "You know, I think you're going Clapton on me, Kyle. I really do. I shudder to see this Tumin piece you're handing in to me next week."

Nearly a week later, those words were still pursuing Kyle . . . *going Clapton.* He was sitting on the window ledge of his Little Italy apartment, watching the snow go patchy on the streets in the warm sun. *Going Clap* . . . Yes, he needed to rid the expression from his mind, he decided. But even as Mr. Nightcap popped the cap on a bottle of beer and handed it to him, Kyle was ready for an admission: if the phrase had a resonant sting, he'd decided, maybe it was because it had come true. Consider, for example, the newest five thousand words currently residing in his hard drive, the Lonny Tumin profile for *Magazine* that he'd been working on all week. The piece stank to high heaven, no doubt about it. Absolutely rancid. Even with his head stuck out the window onto Mulberry Street, Kyle could smell it. It's what he'd come over here to get away from.

Or no, in fact, the piece didn't stink. Rather, it was cynically proficient, the sort of present-tense ass-kissing schlock that anyone in the magazine world save Semper Dane would have welcomed with wet stains of excitement.

Hugs, Lonny, love 'em or hate 'em?

Bored and depressed, Kyle spent the rest of the afternoon sipping beer and putting the finishing touches on the piece. He'd read it over one more time, he decided, then e-mail it off to Semper with a note of apology, signed *Eric.* Get it out of the apartment before he had to fumigate the place.

In the meantime, there were the threats to consider, payloads of hate to keep him company. They — whomever "they" were — knew where he lived now, and this was unnerving to say the least. Letters had come, long, poorly typed manifestos outlining how Kyle had offended the moral dignity of Islam, then detailing his slow torture and dismemberment at the sender's hands. Just this morning, in fact, he'd received a new wrinkle, an e-mail from JOL itself:

WE KYLL HOLE FAMILY MY CUT BALLS OFF STUFF ON MOUTH SCUM!

Definitely *not* an English major, Kyle thought, but on the other hand, just articulate and passionate enough to ratchet up his sense of general despair — and, yes, by God, *fear.* He was, quite frankly, scared shitless; reluctant to leave his apartment and constantly looking over his shoulder when he was forced to do so. In fact, he'd been wondering lately if perhaps Ayla had been right, that this whole thing was nothing more than a publicity stunt gone bad. Did he really believe in the ideas of the story, the need for them to be published, or had he played fast and loose with sacred beliefs in the name of a fading career? He'd wanted to be noticed again, sure, but now the wrong people were paying attention: he thought it ironic that your everyday Muslim now held the novelist Kyle Clayton at the tip of his tongue, and with some passion, while to the rest of America he was barely a whisper.

It also disturbed Kyle that no other writers had bothered to take up his cause since the threats. Usually this was just the sort of thing writers loved to rally behind, the one provocation that could drag them from their hovels. But no, there had been nary a peep — no public communiqué, no private word of support. In the end, only a few bureaucrats from the PEN organization had followed through with any assistance (though, as always, in their fashion). Their "Islam and Censorship" conference was finally off the ground, scheduled for late January at the 92nd Street Y. It looked to be a huge event, they said, prestigious and well publicized. Would Kyle agree to speak, perhaps even participate as a panelist?

Oh, sure, Kyle had answered, and I'll be sure to wear my bull's-eye T-shirt.

When at dusk the telephone rang, the beer told him it was Ayla. Just calling to let him know how miserable she was without him, how she'd realized what a perfectly wonderful husband he'd really been all along. If he would take her back now they could live exclusively in New York, where she would renounce Islam and hunt down mistresses for him during the day, then take them all into their nuptial bed by night. Anything he wanted, she would promise him. Anything!

"Tell me you haven't finished it, Kyle," said an anxious female voice instead. "Tell me you haven't finished the Tumin piece." The voice, unfortunately, was not his wife's.

"Hello?"

"It's Erin, goddamnit. Now *tell me* you haven't finished it."

"It's finished."

"Shit!" she exclaimed. "Shit, shit, *shit* . . ." He heard her strike a flat surface with a sound that was the hand's equivalent of a belly flop. "So that's it. It's in, it's done. Shit, I can't believe it."

"Actually, I haven't handed it in yet . . . What do you care?"

"You haven't?"

"No."

"Scrap it, Kyle!" she said excitedly. "Dump the whole thing."

"What's the matter with you, Erin? You sound . . . Have you been crying? What's going on?"

"Just shut up and meet me at the Shark Bar on Spring. You know the Shark Bar? Wait, what am I saying? You probably have a cot set up in the back."

"How'd you get my number?"

"Reservation book," she replied. "Just meet me there in a half-hour."

"Why?"

"Because," she said, "I've got some stories to tell you about Lonny Tumin."

Apocalypso

By late December 1999, amid the unusually lavish holiday decorations, still-burgeoning 401(k)s, and the already competitive summer-of-2000 house-rental market, there was looming above everything an imperceptible dread. You knew this not because of what you saw on television (the networks weren't going near it), or what you saw on the street (money had kept the mood too buoyant), but rather because of what you heard, the whispers among your family and friends in moments of intimate confession. A fear you told yourself was ridiculous but that you couldn't laugh off, a foreboding you were loath to admit. *Something might happen.* That was the phrase confessed in those intimate moments. "You've got to be crazy to go to Times Square on New Year's," a friend might say, *"something might happen,"* or "I'm invited to a big party in Miami, do you think *something might happen?"* This was not about Y2K, mere computer glitches and benign blackouts. That, we felt, would be the least of it. And though nobody was articulating what this "something" was, we felt that if it happened, it would it be big.

Urlich, of course, had his own theory. Eschatophobia, he said: *fear of the end of things.*

While the major media kept a brave face, the private arena of cyberspace (the public unconscious, some would say) was reeking of doom. By Christmas a Web site dedicated to Y2K anxiety — the symptoms of which were described as "shortness of breath, chest pains, and an urge to hoard bottled water and automatic weapons" — was receiving a million hits a week. There was a chat room available for positive reinforcement, and a backlist of treatise debunking the various doomsayers, trying to throw some rational light on the supposed modes of destruction. The Rapture, the Prophecy, the Tribulation, not to mention the Apocalypse and his plucky little brother, Armageddon. Then there were the calendar gurus to deal with, those that believed in closed sequences, in neat blocks of human time allotment. Two thousand years is *it,* folks, time's up. You don't have to go home, but you can't stay here. Proof of this, these cynics asserted, could be found in the Mayan Long Count Calendar, was manifest in the Phoenix and Yuga Cycles, in the simple fact that it was the Age of Aquarius.

The angels were cleaning their trumpets, getting ready to blow.

The only good news, it seemed, came from the Resurrectionists, who claimed that Jesus Christ was coming back in September 2001. So there was some time to prepare — if anyone was left to greet him.

Glendenburg, Pennsylvania, was not exactly a Kyle Clayton kind of town. Strip malls, dilapidated barns on sullen woodlands, immense fields out of which arose office complexes with all the nuance of a flashcube, and, most unforgivable of all, very, very bad restaurants. What was it that eastern Pennsylvanians had against privately owned eating establishments, anyway? Kyle had wanted to know. And why, in the T.G.I. Friday's on a highway called Cancer, did the waitress seem ready to make a call in to the local police when he ordered a glass of wine with his lunch instead of the ubiquitous soda? The devil's drink, said her eyes, in the *afternoon?* Kyle had no doubt the common cola was a more virtuous beverage. Surely anything containing potassium benzoate and gum acacia and glyceryl abietate — or for that matter, Red 40 and Yellow 6 — had it all over the fermented grape. But really, doll, the police?

He finished his lunch quickly and headed his Rent-A-Wreck toward Monarch Technologies, Inc.

The Tumin piece was done, completely overhauled. Different tone, to say the least. Semper had given him a three-day extension, with the proviso that the extra time would make the article less Claptonish. Then, armed with Erin's indictment, Kyle went on a two-and-a-half-day Starbucks jag that yielded 8,500 words: a calmly composed, radioactive pile of revelation. Now all he had to do was pull out his laptop somewhere, port, and hit Send. Just as soon as things checked out in ol' Glendenburg, PA.

He had no reason to doubt the veracity of Erin's allegations against Tumin. The points she'd laid out in the Shark Bar seemed precise, congruous, and wholly believable. And yet, the account was so damning, the details so volcanic, that Kyle felt a little fact-checking was in order. On the one-in-a-million chance that these were the fabricated musings of a disgruntled employee, he had to be sure.

He drove along roads that were neither urban nor country, through a faceless sprawl of farmlands anticipating development with a woeful resignation. Rusty tractors, the fields of licentious kudzu. Finally approaching the Monarch property, he encountered a well-manicured island with a brick facade containing the company's logo in cool black lettering. In the distance loomed the building itself, a structure the writer in Kyle longed to see as ominous, something to which he might ascribe evil. But it was hardly evil, he realized, nor could it ever be; nothing this prosaic, this unimaginatively conceived could ever be symbolic of anything save banality. It was another Kodak flashcube, this one done in a futuristic soft white with beehive windows. Adjacent to the property was Monarch Park (WE CARE ABOUT OUR EMPLOYEES!), a bleak little lawn with a softball field and a few picnic benches. Kyle drove the car up the long, winding driveway, and when he came up over a rise and saw the mere handful of cars in the lot built for thousands, he had to concentrate to hold the steering wheel, so hard and bitterly was he laughing.

A few days later Tumin's secretary ushered Don Westly down the hall with a hurried solemnity. Rita was her name, and she looked tousled, uncharacteristically shaken. She'd faithfully served Lonny Tumin for more than twenty years, but if Don were a betting man, he'd say the secretary was about ready to hang it up. As they came within sight of their boss's office and heard the rapid fire of expletives from within, she looked up.

Do you hear? Rita's eyes complained. *Why do we put up with this madness, Don? Why?*

"HIP MOTHERFUCKER!" boomed Tumin's voice, bullying its way through the door's frosted glass. Then came the thud of something thrown or struck.

"Everybody all right?" Don asked her. He'd had a hard time keeping up with her brisk stride and was slightly out of breath.

"We're fine; we know not to go near him when he gets like this. He's ruined that beautiful old desk of his, though. Can you imagine?"

Rita put her hand on the knob, more to dissuade Don from entering the room than to assist him. Belying a bit of trepidation himself, he tugged once at the knot of his tie and gestured to her to let him in.

"Lonny?" he called tentatively through the opened door.

As Rita scurried away, Don took a careful step into the cavernous room. Debris was spread out across the floor, including reams of paper, shattered glass, and, most odd, a smattering of wood chips. Then Don looked up at the desk and saw the cleaved notches dug along the front.

Tumin himself stood off in the far corner. He was looking out the windows, silently seething.

"Psst, over here," urged a voice to Don's left.

There, on the studded leather couch, was Ivic Rennert. He was dutifully somber today, his cane prostrate next to him and a four-iron upright between his legs. Don wondered how he'd managed to wrangle the club from his boss's grasp.

"You fucked up, Donny Boy," Tumin announced suddenly, now moving back toward the desk. Don looked to him and was greeted with a large, angry smile. Lonny's jacket was off, and his sleeves were rolled up, his pits sweaty from his lumberjack routine. "You fuckin' fucked up *big* this time."

Don Westly, ever the dispenser of calm, of casualness, took a seat near the desk and crossed his legs. He could see now the gaping wound in front of him, Tumin's mad violence evinced in the jagged blond wood. He realized the damage was irreversible, and this fact struck him with some dismay. The desk, which had once been President

Taft's, was an ornate, gargantuan beauty and had been the envy of anyone who'd ever laid eyes on it. Now it would mostly likely be hauled away to the dump, never to give pleasure again.

Behind the desk, Tumin picked up a small pile of manuscript pages that had been e-mailed to him by his mole at *Magazine* — some cousin of a friend of a niece. There was great risk, of course, but L. T. had made it entirely worth his while.

"Fucking hip motherfucker," he said. He threw the pages back on the desk and pointed at him. "And *your* bright idea, I might add."

Don smoothly recrossed his legs.

"Have a seat, Lonny," he suggested after a moment. "Try to relax."

Tumin laughed viciously. "Oh, right, sure. Do you know how much fucking *money* this is going to cost us? Do you have any idea? I'm ready to dump the whole company right now."

"We kill the story," Don swiftly asserted. "We kill it before anyone sees a word of it. It doesn't exist. Never did."

Tumin paused for a second, eyes searching the room.

"Told you, Lanny," said the lawyer from Louisiana.

"Shut up, Ivic." He turned back to Don. "All right, *how*, genius? How do we do this?"

As Tumin finally sat down, Don reminded his boss of his relationship with Larry Freeze, the executive whose movie studio funded *Magazine*. A few years ago, this man had come to Don, whom he'd known from City restaurant, asking for a favor: he needed a little over a million dollars to keep a movie afloat that was struggling with financing, would Don help him? Perhaps foolishly, Don had said that he would. The movie, while well reviewed, bombed at the box office, and nearly the entire investment had been lost. Still, Larry Freeze had never forgotten the assistance, and had felt beholden to Don ever since. How did Tumin think he got to be in the pages of *Magazine* in the first place? Charm? His good looks?

"You and your movie friends," Tumin admonished now. He looked over at Ivic. "Million and a half out of pocket to be invited to a premiere party. Everybody else went for free."

Don smiled, shrugging off the slight. Tumin, he knew, was jealous, and he seemed to suspect that Don had enjoyed his foray into the film world a little too much. In fact, at one point, Don Westly *had* privately considered a career change — Larry Freeze practically begging him to come on board. Don thought the work actually suited him better than finance and was excited about a new career, but then Susan had menaced all such ideas from his head.

"Actually," Don said now, "I've already taken the liberty of talking to Larry Freeze. I took care of it on the way here, soon as I got the call from Barnett." Tumin and Ivic seemed surprised. "Nobody there has seen the piece except the chief editor, and Larry's assured me nobody else will."

"Did Rob read it to you?" Ivic asked.

"The piece? No," Don answered. "But I get the idea."

Ivic rolled his eyes and whistled. "It's what in Louisiana we call a *humdinger*."

Tumin didn't hear them. He was swiveling in his chair, glowering at nothing, but Don could tell that he'd started to ease at least some of his boss's anxiety.

"All right, let's say it is already dead, let's say we got it in the womb — that still begs the question," Tumin said. He looked at his two colleagues. "Who the hell is it?"

Don looked puzzled. "Who's who?" he asked.

"The *big mouth*," Tumin snarled, pugnacity quickly returning. "Obviously there's a snitch in our midst. Aren't you the least bit curious, Don, who the hell it might be?"

Don watched his boss's eyes shift briefly over to Ivic, and by their look he knew they'd already been discussing him as a suspect before he'd shown up.

"That an accusation?"

Ivic looked down, chagrined, but Tumin shrugged laconically. "Sure, why not? You're awfully nervous these days."

"You bet your ass I'm nervous."

"Why?"

Don moved forward and propped himself anxiously on his elbows, as if he'd been waiting for this very opportunity. "Why?" he began. "Because we've gotten careless. Because there's a sort of gentlemanly, aw-shucks white-collar fraud that everyone expects from people like us and, you know, won't make too much of if we're caught. And then there's the big, arrogant, gaudy type of fraud, which is exactly what we're all involved in now with this time bomb called Monarch. This reckless *lunacy* you and Ohka have souped up."

"I asked you to stay the fuck out, didn't I?" Tumin said. He looked at Ivic. "You see, I told you he didn't have the balls."

"Yeah, well, how the hell was I supposed to know you were going off the deep end on this?" Don asked him, getting hot. "Really, Lonny, I mean I know we've always pushed the limits around here, and I know that a lot of the time it might've been necessary to stay competitive, but this is just . . . It's *nuts*." Don shook his head, as if still astounded by all that Tumin was doing. "But the fact is, I'm *in*, and I'm not dumb enough to talk to some magazine writer and go to jail when I have . . ." He put a finger up to his lips to stop the surge of emotion. "I love my kids too much to do something stupid like that."

The passion of this reply seemed to make some inroads on Tumin's suspicion, and Don was surprised to see it earn him a long, respectful silence.

When his boss did speak again, it was in the spirit of appeasement. "Nobody's going to jail, Donny. Everybody fudges the books a little."

Don stifled a snicker. *Fudging*, he thought cynically. But then, what was the use? He and Tumin had been over this a hundred times in recent weeks, his boss insisting that Ohka had the whole thing under control, that this subterfuge was exactly his sort of genius. And in any event, the whole episode wasn't going to last much longer. They were just waiting now on the Microsoft verdict, Tumin had explained. Gates would lose, he felt sure, and it would be soon. Confidence would be shattered as it was in '91, and then the whole market would come tumbling down — but not before they'd wiped their hands of Monarch.

And if they did get caught? Well, here was the essential thing, Tumin had said, the thing that Don must never forget: *Americans respect avarice*. It's the one crime they'll always forgive. No, they couldn't relate to the common criminal, the petty thug, but in us they recognize themselves. If we get caught, we deal with it. We pay a hefty-sounding fine that's actually a fraction of our earnings. We start the Tumin Cancer Foundation. We look contrite for a year and live happily ever after.

"Anyway," Tumin continued now, "somebody leaked this thing, and it wasn't Ohka and it wasn't . . ." — he looked at his watch — "where the hell's Barnett now?"

The other two gave their sheepish shrugs, and then Tumin stood up again.

"Here's another fucking problem."

Yes, Don thought gravely, it is. Barnett knew about this, he should be here now, but then he was growing increasingly unreliable lately. Missed meetings, erratic behavior. The problem was clear enough, Don had thought, but for some reason Lonny had refused to see it for what it was. *Jews don't do drugs!* had been his stock reply.

"And this cocksucker of a writer."

"Forget him, Lanny," Ivic urged.

Tumin turned back toward the window, where Don could see him clenching and unclenching his fists.

"Five minutes with this little prick. That's all I want out of life. *Five* minutes."

"Forget him. . . ," Ivic repeated, this time with a chortling wheeze, "let the Muslims take care of him."

Though Ivic had been having a hard time gaining Tumin's attention, his boss's head now turned back over his shoulder, eyes locked on the lawyer. Tumin had not heard about Kyle's religious entanglements, and intent on seeing his boss's mood improve even further, Ivic explained them now in rigorous detail.

When he was done, Tumin — radiant, enthralled — asked him to tell it again.

"You heard about this?" he asked Don, who nodded glumly.

"Big news around town."

The irony of it all seemed suddenly to dawn on Tumin. He smiled in what seemed a bitter amusement. "This kid. . . ," he said, shaking his head, "this *crazy* fucking kid. He's on some sort of suicide kick, isn't he? Hey, how far did you have to go to find somebody like this, Donny? I mean, it takes a certain genius, finding a loser like this."

Don was mute, conceding Tumin the criticism. He could not remember a time when his judgment had been as poor as with Kyle Clayton.

Using a remote on his desk, Tumin flipped on one of the televisions embedded in the wall cabinet to their left. They all waited quietly until the Monarch symbol scrolled by on the bottom of the screen. Seeing that the number was more than satisfactory, Tumin shut it off.

"Well, I tell you, I don't blame these Muslims," he said. "For the first time in my friggin' life, I don't blame them." He tossed the remote back on the desk with a plastic thud. "This kid's into provocation? Good, let him learn some things are unforgivable. I'll tell you, there are two things not to be messed with in this life: the first is God, and the second is my money."

Ivic laughed, thinking it was a joke. Meanwhile, Tumin took one last look at the manuscript pages on his desk.

He read aloud: "*Which would be wonderful, except for one problem. Monarch, for all intents and purposes, does not exist . . .*" He shook his head once more and began to tear the paper into little pieces that added to the floor's debris. "I hope they put a rope around this kid's neck, I honestly do," he said. "We'll see how hip he is then."

Role Reversal

In the late afternoon of New Year's Eve 1999, while others in New York emptied their bank accounts, stocked beeswax candles and bottled water, or hopped on that tsunami of doom prophecy and left the city altogether, Kyle Clayton could be found stripping the launderer's plastic sheath from his tuxedo. He had purchased the garment in more affluent times, but only once had found occasion to wear it. In theory, he disapproved of tuxedos. Here was the uniform of exclusivity, he'd surmised, of pompous self-congratulations. Everything he liked to think he was bucking against.

And yet, Kyle so hated to be left out of anything, so disdained the notion that the great Gotham might carry on some wondrous event that he might not be able to observe and soak up — and later satirize — he'd decided in the end it was better to have one. In case something happened.

Discovering an unwanted crease in the slacks, he retrieved the mini-iron from the closet and set the pants down for renovations.

"Glass of champagne, Master Kyle?"

Standing at the refrigerator was Mr. Nightcap. He had commandeered the bottle of vintage champagne Patience had sent him as a Christmas gift, and presented the label for Kyle's inspection like a sommelier. Though the master of the house had envisioned opening this particular bottle not until, say, an hour from now, the question was essentially rhetorical — it being asked of Kyle Clayton — and thus the cork was popped free.

"Big party?" asked the faithful gentleman. His white hair was slicked back tonight — noble air amending a vassal's countenance — and when he poured the champagne, he did so in that expert way in which, like a desperate convict, the champagne's head makes repeated lunges for the ledge, only to be remitted just as it nears escape.

"They don't get much bigger," Kyle replied, sipping the bubbly. He put his glass on the table beside him and smiled wryly as he began to iron. He could not help himself; he was excited about the evening. He acknowledged, of course, that this excitement would be exacted at a price. Kyle's attendance tonight would be but a footnote to the cavalcade of Lame Fame, but someone, somewhere, would make a note of it, and it would hurt him. Critics and reviewers — even, perhaps, a few of his dwindling band of readers — would get wind of his presence and would experience a surge of . . . What? Censure? Disgust? Dare he say, *sanctimony?* And the orgy of finger-wagging would commence.

Why? though, was a question he'd been asking himself ever since his first novel had appeared. Of all the human trespasses, what was it that was so inexcusable, so repulsive to the common mores as A Writer Having Fun? Especially as it applied to one Kyle Clayton. They wanted their "biting satire," they wanted their "tabs on a generation," but they wanted him to hit his bull's-eye with a blindfold on.

He told himself he didn't give a shit and peered back at the invitation that lay behind him on the counter:

The Triad Corporation and Monarch Technologies, Inc., cordially invite *Kyle Clayton and Guest* to the Party of the Millennium! New Year's Eve 1999 at City Restaurant.

9 P.M. arrival–6 A.M. coffee
A formal occasion

The *and Guest* suddenly had Kyle dipping deeper into his aperitif than might ordinarily be necessary at 5:00 P.M., before what would surely be a long night of celebration. When the long sips did no good, he asked Mr. Nightcap to excuse him and rang Ayla's number in Saugerties.

"Hey, how are you?" she said happily.

Right away the tone rankled him. So poised, so sincere. She absolutely *did* want to know how he was doing and was hoping the answer would be that he was well. Not a good sign, he thought. Definitely a turn for the worse. What he was looking for here were the angry undertones, the indignation, the friction and feud of separated couples who still cared enough to be resentful. They'd been apart nearly two months already; she was there, he was here, what the *fuck* was she so happy about?

"I'm great," Kyle said, barely containing his misery. "Just getting ready for this party tonight."

"Do you really think you should go?"

What, he thought, do we have here? A trace of *jealousy*? He tried not to be encouraged.

"I'm just thinking, you know, about the Muslim thing," she continued. "I know you've gotten some threats . . . I'm worried, Kyle."

"Actually," he said, clearing the disappointment from his throat, "I'll probably be in the safest place in America tonight. City will be crawling with security. They're even sending a car for me."

Stating this last fact, Kyle couldn't help but feel the sudden poignancy of guilt, for he could not deny that his attendance tonight was slightly shameful. In just a few weeks, Tumin's publicist would receive a preview of the profile for *Magazine*'s March issue, and the billionaire would hit the roof. Meantime, Kyle would show up at the man's party in the car he'd sent for him (thank you, Don), eat his food, and most certainly drink a good deal of his liquor. It was borderline indecent.

Of course, he'd also really wanted to be there, and so had marshaled an excuse for himself: If he didn't go, would it not be conspicuous? Kyle Clayton, a no-show at the Party of the Millennium? A sharpy like Don Westly would not overlook such a point, never mind Lonny Tumin. Inquiries would be made. The profile could be blocked. Erin might be in jeopardy.

"Ayla?"

"Yes?"

"Come with me tonight."

There was polite laughter on the other line.

"Really," he urged, "just get in the car right now. You can be here in what, an hour and a half? It doesn't start till after nine."

No, she said sadly, there was no way. Impossible. And now Kyle was left with that same sinking feeling he'd experienced two weeks ago, after their "surprise" encounter. Ayla, who'd begun working from home, was to make a rare appearance in the city, dropping by her office for a morning meeting, and had decided to let Kyle buy her lunch in SoHo. She found him at his best that day, charming and sweet and skillfully flirtatious. The newness of seeing him, coupled with just the right touches of familiarity, proved an intoxicating combination. After a bottle of wine and some cajoling on Kyle's part, Ayla found herself back at the apartment. There, through the long winter afternoon, they engaged in ravenous make-up sex that afterward he had labeled apocalyptic, and she had admitted was pretty darned good.

The problem was that while Kyle had viewed the afternoon as a new beginning, Ayla had thought of it as a momentary lapse. Afterward, in bed, there was an unusual role reversal: he trying to hold her, wanting tenderness and fond reminiscences; she turning away distractedly, burning a quick cigarette, and hopping up to leave. Sorry, she said, it had been a mistake. It must never happen again. For Kyle, it was an awful memory.

"Why not come tonight?" he urged now, still trying to get a lid on his tone of desperation. "I know you hate parties, but believe me, this will be something."

"You know why."

He breathed out deeply. "Ayla, I'm going to say this one last time: I have never, *ever,* slept with anyone else since we've been married. Believe it or not, I never did."

"It's not just that," she said. She sounded suddenly fatigued, not caring to argue with him about this anymore. She sounded, Kyle thought with dread, *resigned.* "It's . . . everything. There's the story, and that terrible incident with my father. I'm not saying it was all your fault, but it happened. There's this huge gulf between us now. I know you see that."

He could hear her shifting around on the couch, her feet clearing a path on the coffee table. He knew the whole room and could visualize everything in it, the carpets, the Turkish knickknacks, their friends' paintings on the walls. What he wouldn't give to be there right now, he thought.

"So, what would it take?" he asked.

"For what?"

"To bring us back."

Ayla laughed nervously. "Kyle, this is what I'm trying to tell you. I'm not sure that we can."

"I know, you've been telling me," he said. "But if we could."

"How can I answer that?"

"Try," he said, quite insistently. "What do you think it would take to get us back?"

"I . . . God, I don't know." After a long pause, she said, "I'm sorry, but I can't think of anything concrete right now. Maybe something . . . *unforeseen*. I really don't know."

"A miracle, in other words," he said.

"Basically."

Kyle, who did not believe in miracles, signaled across the room for more champagne.

"Happy New Year, Kyle," Ayla said after a moment. "I love you." Then she hung up.

Feeling more miserable three glasses later, and now attired in his dusty-smelling tux, Kyle was finally ready to question his actions of this most kinetic year, 1999. Was he wrong for publishing "The Counterfeit Conversion"? he wondered. That's pretty much what everything boiled down to, didn't it? Certainly it had been selfish. Certainly it had been reckless. But had it been *wrong*?

In truth, he didn't know. He had done it partly to draw attention to himself — there was no use denying it. And, of course, to pique Mount Marat. But then he had also been striving for bigger themes in his work, a cause to believe in or rally behind, and felt that he had found it with Islam. More than anything else, he'd written "The Counterfeit Conversion" to finally be taken seriously as a writer.

Of course, it had backfired on him, but amid all the idiot squawkings and polarized opinions swirling around him in recent weeks, there had actually been one glimmer of what Kyle regarded as reason and, dare he say, grace. The Imam had contacted him, the very same one who had married him and Ayla. Naturally, Kyle thought the man had called to harangue him. Who better to be infuriated by "The Counterfeit Conversion" than the Imam himself? And so Kyle had held the phone to his ear like a repentant criminal, exulting in his imminent punishment.

Go ahead, thought Kyle, do your worst. I deserve it.

In his calm, sonorous voice, the Imam made his point. He'd read the story very slowly, he had said, and many times over. He'd discussed it with his constituents at the local mosques, argued about it with students. Twice he'd wept privately while trying to come to terms with it, so sad had it made him, and once, in anger, he had even set his copy aflame with a lighter. He thought the story strained to shock, was shoddily researched in spots, and was occasionally cruel to Ayla's family, to Muslims in general. But in the end, he had said (with Kyle wincing on the other line, waiting like a flagellant for the whip) he'd admired it.

Hm, come again? the writer had said.

That's right, said the Imam, he'd admired it. It had liberated something inside him that he had been struggling with for years, his own *agon*, as he called it, with Muhammad. He thanked Kurban and let him know that many of the Muslims with whom he'd talked agreed with him, that the story had not made them frightened or angry at all, that in fact they'd thought it healthy to have their prophet challenged. Not all, but many. The most stupid, he reminded Kyle, always shout the loudest.

As for himself, the Imam had said, "The Counterfeit Conversion" confirmed all over again his love of Islam. Allah, he was coming to realize, had made Muhammad flawed on purpose, so as to appear more human, to give his followers a choice. The dissonance of the Koran was by design, to separate the true believers from the "others." Kyle had actually done Muslims a favor, said the Imam; he had showed that Muhammad could take a hit and withstand it, and now Islam seemed even more glorious to him than ever.

Before hanging up, the Imam had left the writer with a final conundrum: Had Kurban ever considered the possibility that he just might be more of a Believer than he realized?

Remembering these words now, Kyle drained the last of his champagne and tried to smile. His misery was reaching some sort of apex tonight, he could feel it, and he was all the more bitter for having no one to blame for it but himself. Desperate for some anodyne, and just buzzed enough to try anything, he went into the bedroom and opened the drawer of his nightstand. There he retrieved the white skullcap and prayer mat he had been given on the day of his conversion (thus far untouched), along with his own dogeared translation of the Koran. Returning to the living room, he donned the cap and spread out the mat toward the Lower East Side. Close enough, he decided.

Then, with Mr. Nightcap looking on in astonishment, Kurban knelt to pray.

On his knees, he recalled Ayla's common lament. *You never gave Islam a chance. Never even tried!* Well, maybe I'll surprise her, he thought now. Maybe I can win her back with faith! Opening the Koran at random, his eyes fell upon sura 36. He bent back the binding to hold his place, and straightening his bow tie, which had turned askew, began to read aloud: "You can but admonish such a one as follows the message and fears the (Lord) Most Gracious, unseen: give such a one, therefore, good tidings of Forgiveness and a Reward most . . ." What? he thought, eyes suddenly trailing off. Admonish the one who *follows*? He was reminded suddenly of the Koran's agitating syntax, its opaque missives. Why *admonish* the one who. . . ?

He turned the page. "But those who reject Allah — for them will be the Fire of Hell: no term shall be determined for them, so they should die, nor shall its penalty be lightened . . ." Oh, I remember now, he thought, the old fire-and-brimstone routine. Kyle pushed the book aside. Maybe some other time, he thought. Anyway, all he'd really wanted was to ask Allah a favor. (Isn't this what gods did, he thought, take requests?) Just a little miracle, Allah, if you're up to it. Something nice for me and Ayla.

Suddenly the phone rang, and Kyle sat up with a start. Thinking Allah was indeed swift in His mercy, not to mention wholly magnanimous, he reached for the handset with a triumphant smile.

"Ayla?"

"You die soon," announced an unfamiliar Arab voice. "You not make too much into New Year."

Kyle frowned, thoroughly unimpressed — the letters had been much more creative, he thought, though it probably should have alarmed him that they now had his phone number. Perhaps it was the champagne.

"Nah, I'm not going anywhere," he said, tugging again at his still-errant bow tie. "I'm Kurban, baby."

"Kurban, huh? Good. 'Cause soon you make ultimate sacrifice."

Headquarters of Her Dreams

New Year's Eve was a late call for the waiters, so Erin had plenty of time to stop by her aunt's before heading to the restaurant. She'd wanted to say good-bye. Though the excavation had somewhat dimmed the apartment's mythic aura, she felt it was only right to bid the place a proper adieu.

Opening the door, Erin was slightly unnerved to see that she'd forgotten to leave on a light the last time she was here. The room was black except for a solitary window, which let in a swatch of navy-blue light. All the other blinds were closed, though this seemed nostalgic, true to her aunt's old habits. Helena was no great fan of sunlight, of the out-of-doors. On the windows where the venetian blinds had come down (and she'd been too embarrassed to have someone from the building come up and fix them) there were the sheets of tinfoil. On another a Hefty bag was tacked on with electrical tape.

Erin took off her coat, then went into the kitchen to flick on a light. Her steps echoed as she returned to the empty living room and found a box of books she had packed. Here was something sturdy to sit on while she looked around the place, jogged her memory, and tried to get a good cry in before work. She needed to cry. It had been two days since Helena's passing, and Erin had yet to muster any tears. It was a mystery as to why. She'd felt numb, anesthetized somehow, and she worried that the recent disappointments in her life had turned her callous. Naturally, Erin had tried to comfort herself with the facts: that Helena was through with living and welcomed the end; that she believed in God (The Book! The Book!), and felt He would reunite her with her beloved husband, Dick. Still, Erin found herself hounded by a persistent guilt.

Maybe I'm just distracted, she thought. She'd hated to admit it, but Helena's estate was on her mind, and so here now was the shattering of one of her last conceits: that she cared nothing for money. Yes, the world had gone money mad these past few years, and who could forget how she'd criticized the businesspeople at City with their vulgar, narrow-minded pursuit of cash! *Can't these people talk about anything else!* Erin had always complained. But now that she herself was getting a whiff of the filthy lucre, she admitted that the aroma could be exhilarating — musty and wealdy and inky-erotic. No substitute for the friendship and love of a divinely eccentric aunt, of course (why did this need even to be said?), but then also not without its pleasures.

Erin wriggled to a more comfortable spot atop the carton. How much will it be? she wondered, even now unable to help herself. Could it be as much as a million? And what would she do with it? The possibilities seemed both endless and endlessly exciting. (She remembered suddenly how in her first years in New York she had promised herself that if and when she ever came into money, she would use it to realize her dream project: Shakespeare's *Timon of Athens* as a rock opera, the text intact but with music from her favorite undiscovered rock band of the moment. *Timon of Athens, Georgia,* she would call it, with Timon reimagined as a Dylanesque recluse, and part of the dream was that she would employ all her struggling, talented friends, everyone she'd known whose work she'd admired over the years and had been ignored. There were so many of them, of course. Actors, singers, artists, directors, sound and lighting people, musicians. She would take this money — a hundred thousand or so, she'd imagined the cost — and rent a real Off-Broadway theater. No Beaux Arts nightmare here. And in a bar, perhaps on the Lower East Side somewhere, she had clinked glasses with her fellow strugglers and had sworn, sworn to God, that it was *absolutely* what she would do if she ever came into money . . . Now, quick as it had come, she cast the thought away.) Maybe Mexico for a quick vacation, she mused — she'd always dreamed of a winter tan. When she got back, apartment hunting would be a priority. It was time to get practical, she told herself. A nice one-bedroom somewhere downtown. Nolita was still reasonable, wasn't it? Real estate was always a good bet, and she wasn't getting any younger. It was time to start thinking of the future.

Erin fidgeted, unable to get comfortable. Suddenly the apartment seemed to nag at her, these dirty fiscal thoughts. Though everything was packed, these rooms still held a powerful scent, a musty redolence that summoned up for her another era, another Erin. This place, she remembered now, had given the suburban girl her first glimpses of a different life. A messy and cluttered and perhaps delusional life, but oddly romantic nevertheless. This is where she came on those afternoons, a young girl off the bus from Connecticut, to a city filthy and overwhelming and magical. She would be met by Helena at Port Authority, and off they would go to the theater for the Wednesday afternoon matinee. Twice a month, with the great stink of Times Square in her nose, they walked to the majestic palaces of Broadway. And it was here that the actresses got into Erin's head: Colleen Dewhurst and Rosemary Harris and Elaine Stritch. Or perhaps even more so, the women of the movies, for when they had exhausted all the good theater, they went to see a *film,* as Helena referred to them. Perhaps selfishly, her aunt had no interest in bringing her young niece to see *The Bad News Bears* or *Star Wars,* but instead went to the *cinema* to see the great French and Italian filmmakers of the seventies, along with the emerging American directors (and where Erin was delighted to hear the word *fuck* on a regular basis). Jill Clayburgh in *An Unmarried Woman* was an absolute watershed for her — the independence, the sexuality, those groovy scarves! Erin remembered how the evening after seeing it, over Chinese food back at her aunt's, she'd announced that she was going to be an actress, of both the stage and screen, and what did Helena think of that?

And the reply was the same that night as it would be forever after, that being an actress would take tremendous hard work and persistence, but *yes, my dear, it could be done.*

So, Helena's apartment had been the headquarters of her dreams, though recently Erin had forgotten that, or had made herself forget it. Suddenly now, even though she had an hour left before call at City, she had the irresistible urge to flee. To run and never come back.

On her way out through the lobby, Erin gave the keys to the doorman. Would he please allow the Salvation Army into the apartment when they finally deigned to appear? She wasn't coming back, she said. This was it. Good-bye.

Bill came from around the desk, and as with her aunt, Erin was able to stifle her emotion as she embraced the aging concierge, though in this he was less successful.

"You were *this* tall when I started working here. *This tall.*"

"I'll come visit," she said, quite sincerely, but also knowing it probably would never happen.

He dabbed an eye with his thumb, and then, determined to buck up, said, "You know, dear, I haven't seen you take care of the storage yet."

She blinked, long and deliberately, feeling a sudden heat behind her eyes.

"Storage?"

"You see?" he said, with a sad smile. "People always forget."

Every apartment had a storage space in the basement, Bill informed her. He would have the Salvation Army take those things too, if she wanted, but first they would have to be boxed or bundled up. They would not take loose items, he reminded her, and the building would withhold Helena's hefty security deposit if the storage area was not addressed.

"Storage," she repeated, somewhat dazed.

The concierge pointed out the key on Helena's ring, and she took the fire stairs down two flights to the basement.

The storage area was nothing more than a series of large cages, little prison cells, she thought, lined up along a catacomblike stretch of damp concrete walkway. It was quite dark — some of the loose overhead lights were working, others were not — and by the time she found the cage number that corresponded with Helena's apartment, her heart was thumping.

Looking through the bars, she saw a large chest. It was, blessedly, she thought, the only item in storage. She went to open the cage and discovered the chest was not locked. Pulling up the lid, her hand shaking now, Erin saw below her what her unconscious had already known would be there: an electric typewriter, the stacks of yellowing paper, the manila folders labeled with Magic Marker — *chapter 2, ideas for introduction, random notes . . .*

Erin reached for a bar of the cage; she felt woozy. Steadying herself, she picked up a few pages and began to skim. No, it was not a hallucination, she told herself. This was *it.* On one of the folders she even discovered a working title: "God: An Introduction."

"Incredible," she whispered. Growing braver now, she rolled up the sleeves of her sweater. Crouching down to the chest, she collected the folder entitled "chapter one." She could not wait another second, she told herself. She loosened the rusty metal clamp, resolved to dedicate the next hour, then all of tomorrow — and however many days it took after that — to her aunt's lost work.

Inconceivably, *preposterously,* Erin thought, The Book was alive.

Folly and Sacrosanct

On 46th Street, the line of black cars stretched all the way down to Lexington. Condensation issued from Syeed's mouth, but underneath his coat he was sweating. He was having a hard time keeping up with the flow of people, four hundred guests in under an hour, their very presence sickening him to a fever. Women with arms as thin as a chimp's in immodest clothing, their sparkling jewelry and emphatic perfume. The men striding with high-chinned satisfaction, the vainglory of their dressing table. They were peacocks, astrut with an unmanly narcissism. They feared no god.

His eyes hurt. Behind barricades along each side of the entrance was the phalanx of photographers, firing relentlessly with their blinding bulbs, the television cameras held like bazookas. Men lewdly straddled kneeling women and vice versa as they elbowed one another, calling out to faces eager to be noticed, too contemptuous to reply. Only Tumin himself seemed to pay them any mind. He arrived in his white Rolls, the car Syeed had seen only once before, and as he and Don emerged with their wives, Lonny stopped to speak to one of the television reporters. What a great evening! he exclaimed, saying how excited he was to share the millennium with all his friends in the greatest city on Earth. Behind the photographer's queue was a crowd of onlookers, some of them surprisingly hostile, one of them shouting, "Then why do you live in Oyster Bay?" There was cautious laughter, and Tumin smiled until the camera light was off. Then he immediately took a few brisk steps toward the man, reaching for him, until Don got a hand on his shoulder and redirected him to the door.

"Good evening, Rick," Diane Tumin politely murmured as she approached. It was a deceit for the cameras and journalists, he knew. She'd never spoken to him before in her life.

"No more Rick, only Syeed," went the curt reply.

Diane smiled, oblivious to the comment, and entered the restaurant. Don and his wife came right behind, the man squeezing a hundred-dollar bill into Syeed's palm, and when Lonny brought up the rear, he and the doorman seemed to make a point of not looking at each other.

There was a lull now, and so Syeed took a moment to catch his breath. Standing there, ignored, even loathed by the crowd — a blemish on their photos! — he was revisited by the nearly insane sense of grief that had plagued him for the past week. If anyone had cared to notice, they would see that his lips were moving — he was muttering the lines from his mother's letter, the inconceivable words he'd committed to memory and would never forget no matter how much longer he lived: *Please do not despair, my son. Though he is your brother, Yusef is also a child, just like your silly-doll wife, both with too much idle time on their hands. It is impossible to tell how much has passed between them, but I expect that whatever it is will fade quickly. Naturally, Aisha will be severely punished by the community, though I don't dare tell your father yet, since I'm afraid of what he might . . .*

In relentless pairs, the cars kept pulling up. The next group discharged a young couple Syeed did not recognize, though at whom the photographers screamed with a rabid intensity.

The second car revealed Kyle Clayton.

He emerged from the car holding a clear plastic cup (probably booze, thought Syeed), and a very young Asian woman followed him out and slipped in next to him. Kyle and the girl moved slowly along the red carpet, as if enjoying the attention, and the writer wore an ambiguous smirk that piqued Syeed's curiosity. Was the young man pleased with the scene? he wondered. With himself? Or was he scornful? The doorman's eyes, unfortunately, were given no respite. The popping bulbs only increased as the blasphemous writer approached.

"Enemy of Islam!" someone shouted, and all eyes were then directed to a cluster of onlookers far behind the barricades. These eight or ten men were from the Islamic Defamation League, done up in full-robed regalia and pumping their fists. One held a sign that read COUNTERFEET WRITER!

"Where's the bar, Clayton!" shouted another spectator, this time from the opposite side of the barricades. Though the writer had ignored the Muslims, this rowdy was treated to a grin, and Kyle pointed toward the restaurant in reply to his question.

Gnawing bitterly at a node of skin just below his lower lip, Syeed held the door.

"Hey, Rick, we friends again or what?" Kyle had stopped and put out his hand to shake. "What do you say?"

"No more Rick," the doorman said. Much like the last time, his eyes were looking over the man's shoulder, as if in anticipation of a new guest. As of yet, there was nobody behind him. "Syeed is my name."

Kyle paused, and as he breathed the doorman could smell the fumes of alcohol. "All right, tell you what, Sy*eed,*" he said, leaning in. "Go fuck yourself."

As the writer disappeared into the party, Syeed resolved that his mission was just.

Inside, Kyle found a crowded restaurant utterly transformed, though he was of the opinion that most of the change was not good. What had drawn him to City in the first place was the warm clubbiness of the rooms, and yes, its dark, masculine tones. Tonight there were flocks of candy-colored balloons everywhere, and the mirrors and cherrywood paneling had been covered with some sort of scrim, pink in color and dotted with glittering manifestations of the Monarch butterfly.

He led Wey Tu Yong into the packed dining room.

"Champagne?" a waiter intoned, flutes balanced precariously

upon his tray. His voice did not quite make it over Barbara Cook and her eight-piece band.

"Sorry," Kyle shouted, "didn't catch you."

The waiter's back arched defensively. "Well, that's no fault of *mine,* now is it, sir?" Urlich replied, loud enough now, his eyes gesturing back toward the band.

"Didn't say it was," the writer murmured. With the waiter's intent now clear, Kyle took three glasses off the tray: two for himself and one for his date. Kyle had called Wey at the very last moment, unable to endure the idea of being alone tonight. Though her evening wear included a leather skirt the size of a cocktail napkin and a half-shirt that read "Porno Chick," Kyle was thrilled to have companionship on such late notice.

"Raw bar's straight ahead and to your left," Urlich concluded, his tone somehow making it sound like an accusation. "*Enjoy* your evening."

A devotee of anything *bar,* Kyle led his guest immediately toward that destination, though it soon became clear that this time the presentation would far outdo the procurements. It was a cityscape, he could see, a huge, glistening ice sculpture carved with great intricacy. As he and Wey moved closer, the two looming towers helped them discern the real estate. It was Wall Street.

"Big moany," Wey intoned with some awe. "Oh, *big* moany."

Right you are, thought Kyle. The colossal sculpture sat on a long, narrow table whose short hem betrayed the metal gurney underneath, and also its clever moat to catch the drippings. The roofs of the buildings were scooped out to hold the shellfish, though the Twin Towers were too tall to serve anything and were strictly for show. And what a show! The artistry of the sculpture was truly astonishing, Kyle observed, so detailed that he recognized specific landmarks: the American Express Building (shrimp); the Marriott World Trade Center Hotel (oysters); even the discount clothing store, Century Twenty-one (cocktail sauce). The Twin Towers, though, were clearly the artist's focus and easily his greatest achievement. They stood at least six feet off the gurney, two mammoth pillars of sweating opalescence. There was such care taken with these two great busts that each floor, each window, was chiseled to scale. Though Kyle stopped counting at thirty, he approximated that all 110 floors were represented.

A waiter, barely visible above the Amex building, beckoned the guests to approach, but the crowd seemed too awestruck to eat from such an exhibit. Conversation was all but impossible with Wey, of course, so Kyle concentrated on the verdicts of the proximate guests, all of whom seemed to agree: the sculpture was the tackiest bit of absurdity anyone had ever seen, but also somehow thrilling, and they would have difficulty tonight keeping their eyes off of it.

Just when Kyle thought it was time to go in search of someone to talk to, a voice called out his name from behind. He turned, and looking down he found that its source was his agent, Patience Birquet, still four foot eleven and trembling with her unquenchable intensity. She introduced her girlfriend, a very young Lithuanian named Lara who spoke even less English than Kyle's date, and who was taller than the agent by more than a foot.

"Two-fisted tonight, Kyle, I'm so impressed," Patience said, and when he bent down for a double kiss, Kyle could already see her eyes canvassing his date like a minesweeper. "Who's the porno chick?"

"Wey Tu Yong," the girl replied, overhearing her cue.

"I'll say," murmured Patience, her Lithuanian smoldering as she brought Wey's hand to her lips. "Brushing up on our Nabokov are we, Kyle?" the agent whispered to her writer. "Bravo. Any chance she bats lefty?"

"Hey, go for it," he said with no great enthusiasm.

"Something wrong?"

"I'm fuckin' drunk," he said, pulling at his face. "And generally miserable."

"Well, drunk is more than I can say for us." Seeking no permission, Patience smoothly requisitioned one of Kyle's two champagne glasses. "We've been here, what, three, four minutes already?" she asked of her mute date. "And nobody's even offered us so much as a drink."

I think it's called a *bar*, Kyle wanted to say, but decided there was no point with Patience.

Sipping his purloined drink, she leaned over and nudged his side. "Hey, get ready for some flak tonight."

"Christ, what now?" he asked.

"There's a buzz about you being here. Apparently certain guests don't feel 'safe.'"

"Yeah, well, tough titty."

She waved a hand. "Of course, forget it. Everyone's on edge tonight. Y2K and all that crap . . . You hear about Semper Dane?"

"What?" he replied, instantly spurred from his malaise. "No, don't tell me."

"Yup, fired. Again."

Panic seized him, though Kyle immediately reminded himself to try to keep cool; because of her big mouth, he'd decided not to tell his agent about the revised Tumin piece.

He took a discreet look around the dining room to see if he was being watched.

"Is the profile still running?" he asked, lowering his voice.

Patience shrugged, indifferent to the matter. The fee had been paid, anything else was impertinent. Nor had she sought to inquire why the publisher had been axed.

"Anyway, Semper's supposed to be here tonight. You can ask him yourself." Patience's eyes opened invitingly as a tray of canapés came by, only to wave them away when the waiter confirmed that each did indeed hold a thimbleful of white flour. "What's for dinner, anyway?" she asked Kyle. "I'm fuckin' starved, but I've got a shitload of dietary restrictions."

Kyle feigned distraction, craning his neck to search for Semper — he suddenly had a vision of dinner at Patience's table, the agent hounding the servers and rearranging everyone's menu. They said the world could end tonight, he thought morbidly, and if so he'd be damned if he was going out with a dry salad. "Why, are we sitting together?"

Lara took out their seating card and showed it to the boss.

"Table five?" Patience said hopefully.

"Eleven." Kyle felt jubilant. "What a bummer."

Tumin's words pushed through a stiff jaw. "How the fuck do I know what he's doing here?"

He was standing near the band, chatting up a semicircle of heavy Monarch investors, when Don had come up behind him. Yes, he'd seen him, Lonny replied over his shoulder. No, he didn't know what to do about it. Don didn't regret the interruption. The situation was potentially nuclear, and he thought it best to be preemptive.

He gave Tumin a moment to excuse himself and then led him over to a quiet area by the bar.

"We'll have Leon escort him out," Don suggested. "We'll say he's drunk." But Tumin was already shaking his head.

"Absolutely not."

"Why?"

Don waited while Tumin sipped his iced tea and looked over at the band. "Because," he said, "this kid's a loose cannon. He won't go quietly. We'll have a big mess on our hands. No, forget it, it's not worth it."

He was impressed by Tumin's sudden aptitude for discretion but couldn't help wondering from where it had appeared. Wasn't it just two days ago he was ready to turn Kyle Clayton into a human driving range?

Tumin added, "Look at Suzy, would you? Just look how nervous she is." He directed their gaze over to Don's wife, who was admonishing one of the waiters, the cords of her neck gruesomely inflamed. "Diane too, wherever the hell she is. They'll say we ruined their party. You want to tangle with those two? I sure as hell don't," he said. "Not tonight."

Point taken, concluded Don Westly. He turned back to his boss. "What's the kid doing here, Lonny? How could this happen?"

"I fucked up." He looked straight at Don now, as if to commemorate the moment: it was the first time the boss had ever directly admitted a mistake. "I had Diane put him on the list a month ago, because of the profile. So it was my job to tell her to get rid of him, and I forgot." He opened his hands. "What're you gonna do? The kid's here, we deal with it."

"How do we play it? Do you say hello?"

"I suppose I'll have to say something to him," Tumin answered, then rested his hand on his friend's shoulder. "Don't worry," he said with a grin, "I'll be a good boy."

And I'll take no chances, Don thought. He told himself he would keep an eye on them if Tumin and the writer did meet. He was pretty sure that Kyle Clayton, L. T., and sharp cutlery close at hand were not a great mix.

"The piece is dead, correct?" Tumin asked.

"Larry Freeze has given me his word."

"Good, then let's try to enjoy the evening." He moved his hand up to around Don's neck now. "We paid over a million bucks for this son of a bitch, did you know that?"

Don, who was considered prodigal with money and who loved a good party, was aghast.

"No," he replied.

"We did, thanks to the girls." Tumin tugged at his bow tie. "And I'll be goddamned if I don't get my money's worth."

It was the waste that the staff noticed most, the crass commitment to the squandering of delicacies, not to mention the hosts' apparent conviction that this was somehow part of the show. Three shuckers sent out bushel after bushel of oysters, only to have them returned almost immediately and taken directly to the garbage. Keep them coming, instructed Diane Tumin. She, who did not eat shellfish, said that each oyster had a shelf life of about five minutes, and they were to be replenished as such. Out in the dining room, the waiters circulating '75 Dom Perignon were instructed to return every ten minutes to the bar to exchange their tray of glasses for a fresh one. The elapsed wine, case after rare case, was to be flushed down the sink. And finally, Susan Westly wasn't the least bit concerned that barely a dozen out of the two hundred white-truffle martinis she'd ordered set out under the raw bar had found an enthusiast. Each cocktail, after all, cost only fifty dollars to make (thanks to her heated tussle with the truffle purveyor), and they made such a *great* conversation piece.

The kitchen itself was in chaos. The first course was about to be served, and there were four hundred soup bowls spread across every spare inch of counter space. Erin pressed herself into a neutral corner, trying to summon the courage to ask the chef if there was a vegetarian option to the main course, the question already asked numerous times at one of her tables.

The chef seemed rather overwhelmed at the moment, however, beginning to ladle out the soup. "Don't overlap the edges you fucking MAGGOTS!" he screamed at the dishwashers spreading out the bowls. When next he pulled two examples of the offending chinaware to the floor and let them crash around his feet, Erin decided her question could wait.

Raoul arrived in a huff. Why were they serving the first course when the swine hadn't even been poured, he demanded to know, and just what the fuck kind of country was this anyway, America?

"Veddy disorganized tonight, Miss Erin," Abu whispered, squeezing in next to her.

"It's always a tough night for the chef," she replied. Assuming this was her last New Year's as a waitress, Erin could afford a more generous vision of things, and Abu smiled to see that some of her old lightheartedness had returned. "Mrs. Westly has already come in asking where the food is. The kitchen's under a lot of pres —"

They flinched as two more bowls hit the floor.

Urlich, hovering nearby, turned to them. "One more and it's a Greek wedding."

Immediately the chef spun toward the waiter. "SHUT THE FUCK UP, URLICH, YOU KRAUT BASTARD!" Down went another bowl.

"Told you," Urlich whispered, at risk of his life, "eschatophobia."

Things quieted as Ivic Rennert entered the kitchen. He'd been in and out all night, the rotund lawyer hobbling around on his cane, wheezing, drifting from station to station with a spoon in his hand asking what *this* was, and *oh*, could he have a taste of *that*. You could see the chef was fuming, but there wasn't much one could say since Ivic himself was a minor investor, and it would all get back to Tumin anyway. Like so many others, Erin was concerned for the lawyer's life. Word had it he had just returned from an "eating tour" of Spain, and tonight he seemed barely able to stand upright. Stephen, manning the raw bar, reported that Ivic had already eaten well over a hundred and fifty oysters (spiced with the Louisiana hot sauce he drew from his pocket like a six-shooter), and now, as Ivic took a bowl of soup right out from under the chef's ladling, Erin noted that he'd officially completed a full-course dinner, albeit in reverse, before things had even a chance to begin.

Finally the chef and Raoul got it together. The sommelier and his assistants would pour at Tumin's table first, then work their way clockwise around the room. The waiters and food runners would serve in the same fashion. The chef would give Raoul a three-minute head start to pour his wine. Ready, you froggy motherfucker? *Go.*

Erin, of course, was waiting on the Tumin table, and so ninety seconds later she was heading out the kitchen doors with three bowls of vichyssoise and two members of the Bengali Mafia in tow. As she emerged from the doors, she suddenly shrieked and stopped short; in front of her was a half-naked man, his ebony body decorated with white war paint and a thick length of bone threaded under his nostrils. Erin's heart seized as the man reeled toward her, his muscles scarred by coded branding, and struck his crude tom-tom. The sound was then echoed dozens of times out over the dining room, and so she looked up — the restaurant was overrun! — though finally now she understood: it was the Lions of Africa, the group of tribal drummers hired for the occasion.

Later, she would remember the moment with sardonic delight — thirty painted Africans chanting and striking toms with hammers of human bone, while the mostly white crowd fingered their jewelry and feigned acute, anthropological interest. Now, though, the waitress considered them simply a nuisance, a field of tacklers to evade on a kickoff return. Knowing the chef would never take her back into the kitchen, Erin turned to the Mafia and with a simple nod appealed to their sense of honor. *No turning back now guys, right? Let's do it.*

The convergence of tables was ludicrously tight, and naturally Tumin's guests were farthest from the kitchen. But off the waiters went. *Hut!* the tribesmen shouted in unison, and Erin had a near miss as the drummers burst into an unexpected crow's-hop. She held her breath as soup ran up the lip of a bowl, almost spilling on the floor, but she kept moving. She was determined to get to Tumin's table.

Huh! Hut! the men howled next, and now Erin and her crew had to perform a hop of their own to avoid another abrupt dance step, and when this move sealed off their path to Tumin, they resolved to wait, crouching so as not to obstruct the patrons' view. They were so close now, just another ten feet, they *had* to make it! But then, as Erin made a motion to advance, she found herself unable to move, a tiny but powerful hand holding her in its grip. She looked up to see a pixieish face staring at her, the miniature features somehow familiar.

"Where do you think you're going, missy?" the woman blurted over the pounding drums. "We're starving at this table."

Erin knew the face but not the name. It was Patience.

"And I don't like this garnish," she said, looking into the bowls. "You can lose that on mine."

Recognizing this guest as one of her torturous regulars — and with the unexpected boldness of an employee who knows she is not long for this job — Erin leaned over and spoke into the woman's ear in a slow, menacing whisper: *"Okay, shorty, if you don't let go of my jacket pronto, you're going to lose the tip of your nose between my teeth, and I'll garnish your soup with THAT, got it? Never fuck with a waitress on her last night."*

Feeling no resistance now, Erin came out of her crouch and continued on toward Tumin.

The table was set for eleven, with two seats unoccupied; Rob Barnett was a no-show. Great, she thought, less work for me. The first two soups went to the wives, of course, Susan and Diane. Then, leaning down to place the third bowl in front of Lonny, she heard him say clearly to Don, "Well, if Rob's in trouble, then it threatens the whole goddamned . . ." — voice trailing off as he saw Erin positioned just inches from his face. At first his eyes betrayed his lingering attraction, but then something else seemed to register. He leaned back a few inches, as if to widen his perspective, and as he did his eyes became more alarmed, more aggressively discerning.

He knows, Erin thought — the drumming frenzied now, the dance at its climax. As of that moment, he knew it was her. She lowered her eyes and hurried back to the kitchen.

In the gap between entrées and dessert, there was dancing, table-hopping, and a prodigious sense of unease. It was eleven o'clock. The witching hour was near.

Kyle wished to God he'd never come. On the way to the bathroom, he'd been cornered by a busboy who introduced himself as Hussein. Gaining Kyle's ear, the small man explained that they had something in common: like Kurban, he only pretended to be a Muslim, in his case so that he could crack the Bengali Mafia and work at City. Actually, he was a passionate Hindu. Was the writer familiar with the Nationalist cause, the conflict over Kashmir? They wanted Kurban (a big hero among his friends, he said) to help craft their manifesto — a world-famous writer! — articulating the evils of Islam. And had he, by the way, the great famous man, a spare room at home to shelter certain individuals?

Kyle pretended he couldn't understand him over the band and broke for the toilet.

Things were no better back at his table. The nervous guests kept getting up to leave, secretly regarding Kyle as a time bomb, a walking bull's-eye. The crowning humiliation was the incident during the end of the cocktail hour, when a waiter dropped a tray of wineglasses. There was a resounding, high-pitched crash, and everyone within a twenty-foot radius of Kyle Clayton squealed, covered their heads with their hands, or went down to the floor on bended knee — including his date. When in the following seconds the mistake became obvious, there was an embarrassed rush of laughter, and Kyle was left standing by himself, once more the object of hilarity and ridicule.

He hadn't even had a chance yet to speak to Semper Dane. The publisher (ex?) had skipped the cocktail hour, and then twice during dinner the writer had found the seats at Semper's table empty. Yet he'd been assured by a hostess that the publisher had arrived.

Finally inquiring after Semper with a sleepy couple at the publisher's table, Kyle was directed to the dance floor. Once there, the tall blond man was easy to find, cheek to cheek with a brunette, and so Kyle positioned himself on the edge of the floor and waited for them to finish. Half a song later they were done, and the writer stood in a direct line to intercept.

"Clayton, hey, where you been?"

"Looking for you. Let's talk."

"First meet my wife," Semper said. "Alexandra, this is an old friend. The formerly *in*famous Kyle Clayton. Now rather harmless, if you ask me."

Stepping forward was an attractive young woman with sweet brown eyes and a shy, apologetic manner. Kyle immediately felt sorry for her, and even worse for himself. If he had always rationalized adultery, chipped away at it with his intellect until it was something malleable and relative, then here, he saw finally, was the reason you didn't do it. It had nothing to do with the Ten Commandments or the tyranny of monogamy. Nothing to do with stifling bourgeois mores, or even wedding vows. The reason you didn't do it was so that the person you purported to love wasn't humiliated in times like these, so acquaintances and friends didn't pity them behind their back.

"Pleasure," Kyle said, shaking her hand.

"Same here."

"Give us a minute, would you, honey?" Semper asked, and when she was gone, he immediately asked Kyle, "Did you know Michael Douglas was here?"

"Semper, listen."

"You can totally see that whole sex-addict thing when you're close up. Something depraved in those deep lines, those saggy jowls. Of course, who am I to —"

"*Semper.*" Kyle put his hands on the publisher's shoulders. "Have you been fired?"

"Yes," he said after a moment. "Yes, I have." As Kyle released him, he itched the side of his head with his palm. "Wow, news travels fast. They haven't even announced it. "

"Were you going to tell me?"

"Of course."

"When? Next *month?* I could be in a lot of trouble here tonight, don't you see?" He threw his chin over at Tumin, who was entering the dance floor now, hand in hand with his wife. "Where's the article, Semper? What's happened to it?"

"I took it with me."

"You did? Why?"

He shrugged. "To mess with them on my way out," he said. "I didn't want the new editor to have it. Fuck them, they get the old one, the puff piece. I'll publish the good version wherever I go next. You'll probably get paid all over again."

"You sure no one else saw it?" Kyle asked, but the publisher was already shaking his head.

"I told you, never left my desk."

Kyle nodded, thinking how disappointed Erin would be. As for himself, he was relieved. Another shit storm was probably not what he needed right now.

"Why were you fired, Semp?"

He looked away. "Who knows? My first issue bombed, I know that. I saw the numbers. Phew, *terrible.* But like I said, who knows? Who cares? I get a year's severance, plus I'll have another job in two months. My stock goes up every time I'm fired, did I tell you that?"

"You did," the writer said distractedly. Tumin and his wife had been dancing to "There's a Small Hotel," but now Kyle had lost sight of the couple. Over on his left, Don Westly suddenly appeared. Kyle wondered briefly if he should say hello, then ruled against it.

When he looked back to the dance floor, Tumin was striding directly toward him and Semper.

"Hey, Brando," Tumin called out. He had a man with him, the gentleman following behind with some reluctance. "Get a load of who's here. I thought you might want to say hello."

Who the hell could this be? Kyle wondered. A bodyguard come to take him apart? He still thought it possible that Tumin had seen the article and was all set to thrash him, until the big boss stepped aside to present a slightly chubby-faced banker type. Unlike Lonny, the man wore a jolly girth around his waist, though his face revealed the same intelligent cruelty.

"Hello," Kyle said. *Who the fuck are you?*

"Paul Westerberg, Lehman Brothers," ventured Tumin, "meet Kyle Clayton." Trying to hide the strange look on his face, Kyle shook the man's hand. "This young fella's a big fan of yours, Paul. The biggest."

At the mention of the name, Semper Dane now began a low, demonic giggle, which was in danger of growing into a belly laugh until Kyle discreetly backhanded him in the abdomen.

Don came hovering then, wary and protective, and heightening Kyle's anxiety level once more.

"Pleased to meet me," the publisher said, shaking the Lehman Brother's hand and showing him a loony grin. "Paul Westerberg, wow." Kyle held his breath while Semper got a devilish look in his eye and suddenly started snapping his fingers, pretending to remember something significant. "Hey, Paul, what was that last deal you did? You know, that really big one? What was it, a billion, two billion?"

"Oh, I wish," Westerberg said, with forced humility, "though we never like to say exactly how much." He winked at Tumin, who nodded sympathetically.

"Well, of course not," the publisher quickly rejoined, "and I don't blame you guys. I mean, there's a lot of shady shit that comes with a big deal like that. Mum's the word, naturally."

While Westerberg suddenly looked confused, Tumin's eyes narrowed to a point. Possibly from nerves, possibly because he was drunker than he had been in a long time, Kyle too began laughing now, and this, in turn, spurred Semper back on to his jag.

"Yeah, *lot* of shady shit," the publisher repeated.

"All right, all right . . ." Tumin stuck his arm in front of Westerberg, blocking all further contact. "Fuck you two guys," he said through gritted teeth, leading the man away. "Fucking hip assholes."

11:43. Upstairs, in the large cigar lounge, another dinner. Members of the band sit with the Lions of Africa and a good number of the kitchen staff, eating bowls of spaghetti marinara with leftover shrimp, while Abu engages the Lions' chieftain with pictures of his children. Downstairs there is a dessert lull, and so Erin and Abu have been dispatched to help serve the food and dispense drinks to the help. Through the lattice of the thick wooden blinds, she tries not to look at Lonny Tumin in the next lounge over, pacing and, most uncharacteristically, smoking a cigarette. She knows from the itinerary that Tumin is supposed to give a speech just before midnight, though she can't ever remember him nervous before a public address.

When he catches her glancing in, she curses her stupidity.

A few days ago, she remembers, Tumin and Syeed Salaam had a long meeting just before the dinner shift. Erin had been their server. She'd assumed the doorman would be getting an ass-chewing for his erratic behavior recently, but in fact, from what she could tell, the meeting was quite congenial, even businesslike. For the most part she'd been barred from the room, something that had disturbed as well as surprised her.

"Anything left?" inquires a winded Ivic Rennert. As she turns, the lawyer's leaning against the doorjamb, slightly hunched in exhaustion from the stairs. His breathing sounds like a bellows with a hole in it, though his eyes say the journey was worth it. There are two bowls of pasta left on the bar, and he measures them like a panther espying a gimpy antelope. She hands him a bowl and a fork, but he reaches for the second bowl as well, unloading one into the other. As he heads into the lounge, three Lions of Africa — perhaps reminded of a fearsome encounter with a white elephant back home — nearly leap off the couch to let him sit.

Dousing the spaghetti with his hot sauce, Ivic chides one of the line cooks for the skimpy portions on tonight's menu, the tone amiable but not without a touch of authentic irritation.

11:52 In the dining room, Tumin's got his hands on the band's microphone, daubing beads of sweat from his forehead; L. T., the usually organized, confident speaker, delivers his words with distracted, scattershot imprecision: "And . . . Oh, yes, I'd like to thank Matsu Ohka, Monarch's treasurer, for his help in putting together this remarkable company and . . . Yes, please, give him a hand . . . Mr. Ohka regrets he couldn't be here tonight, but . . ." — Tumin glances at his watch — "uh, and, hey, how about a hand for the artists who put together this ice sculpture, huh? Is this unbelievable, folks, or what? Come on, let's hear it . . ."

Outside, the applause wafts across the street, along with the sounds of horns and kazoos and clanking kitchenware from the apartments on Lexington. Syeed is in midprayer in the dirty alcove, murmuring in Arabic: *Raised high above the ranks, the Lord of the Throne: by His command He sends the spirit to any of His servants He pleases, that it may warn of the Day of Mutual Meeting . . . Warn them of the day that is drawing near, when the Hearts will come right up to the Throats to choke; no intimate friend nor intercessor will the wrongdoers have, who could be listened to . . .*

He rises and, glancing at his watch, lights a cigarette. Around him the streets are mostly empty, though the sounds of the city, a mindless, anticipatory cacophony, swell to a higher amplitude. When he dies, Syeed suddenly wonders, will the fur coat go with him? The coat that was bought with Jewish money, though indirectly, and for the ultimate cause of Islam? The answer, of course, was in the great Book, but there is no time now to consult. The time now is for motion and justice.

After a few quick puffs, he stubs out his cigarette, and caressing it yet again, the heavy weight in his coat, walks toward City.

11:56 Kyle's misery is steadily increasing, not to mention his blood alcohol content, as he and Wey sip their midnight champagne. As the band members scurry back to pick up their instruments, Ms. Cook announces, "Four minutes, people!" The room buzzes, wives and lovers separated for a dance or conversation find each other again, huddling up for the big moment. Kyle feels an apprehension toward midnight verging on the bilious. As people are coming together, he is falling apart, thinking of Ayla and the emptiness that the ringing of the hour will only punctuate. Nothing can save the two of them, he is convinced — there are no miracles — and when the mad celebration starts, he will excuse himself and find a quiet men's-room stall in which to weep.

She has a lover, Kyle is reminded now, at two minutes to the hour. A notion confirmed by at least two reliable sources; they've been spotted on the street, also in a restaurant. Fair is fair, of course, but the phrase still astonishes him . . . *Ayla has a lover.* It is a simple fact he has been able to stuff down in the jack-in-the-box of his mind, but that has escaped now, and when Kyle looks up from the rim of his champagne flute, he sees Erin looking at him, and forgetting his date for the moment, he moves toward her.

In anticipation of the hour, the waitstaff is lined up along the wall near the thawing raw bar, urged to clap like cheerleaders, an action only Urlich performs, and with ironic assiduity. Spotting Kyle now, Erin looks wary. So far they've kept their promise for tonight — not to talk to each other, never to reveal the connection — but Kyle's urge for real human contact, for even the tiniest nugget of affection from someone with whom he has a history, for whom he cares even a little, is suddenly overwhelming. Ayla has a lover, so then he will go to Erin, he tells himself, and he will kiss her at midnight, passionately as he's longed to do these many months — because if he doesn't he will die of grief. Absurdly, though resolutely, he believes this.

"One minute!" says the singer, but just as Kyle shimmies somewhat drunkenly through the tight crowd and arrives a few feet from the waitress — *Erin!* he calls as she looks away — there is a commotion at the ice sculpture. Ivic, still foraging there like an engorged buzzard, has let forth a monumental wheeze, congested and breathless, and yet loud enough to supersede the band. *HARREEMPHHH!* he thunders, and one can see him suddenly digging his fist against his chest, twisting it as if to remove a blade stuck there, and when his other hand reaches back to the Amex Building to support himself, the ice is too slick for purchase. Down, *down!* he goes with an impact that oscillates the impossible girth about his face and neck.

"Thirty seconds!" intones the singer, the announcement amended by paper horns, but on this side of the room there is only Ivic and the gasps of surprise and disconcert, revelers stepping back to avoid, revelers rushing forward to help. Oyster guts and cocktail sauce quaver in Ivic's beard, his lower lip distended in anguish or stroke so that anyone near him is hypnotized by these throes of death and therefore does not see Syeed, formerly Rick, now with his coat off, and the dullest glint of gunmetal at his side.

11:59 "Ten seconds, people. . . ! Nine . . . Eight . . ." It is a luxury so opulent, Syeed thinks — this attention drawn to the dying piglet in the corner — that only Allah himself could have arranged it. There isn't even a reason to hide the gun, and as he fixes himself within ten feet of the blasphemous writer, he has time to assume the two-point stance, raise the weapon steadily, and support the firing wrist with his free hand. It's target practice, duck on a pond, though he waits to make sure that anyone near him now takes notice of the gun and does not obstruct the shot. New screams are suddenly directed at him — good, he thinks, stay away — and the waitress Erin finally notices him and grabs Kyle's sleeve in alarm. The writer holds up his hands, moving back for escape, but behind him there is only the wall, nowhere for him to go, *no intercessor for the wrongdoer . . .* The waitress screams, a bloodcurdling *NO,* and he will take her too, Syeed thinks, if she gets in the way. A sacrifice for Aisha, why not?

And then, as he begins to pull, to feel the resistance of the trigger, a terrible thing begins to happen . . .

Abu, Muslim brother and believer in the Faith, sees the gun pointed at Erin and comes between them with an awful timing — the trigger seeming to lure him into the firing line — and the shot goes through his upraised hand and into his throat. Horrified as Abu drops to the floor (a brother, a fellow Muslim!), Syeed's fury is only emboldened, and now he begins to fire toward the blasphemer indiscriminately, rounds thumping in and around his target until the chamber is empty. Then the bodyguard named Leon steps up and, with a calm inevitability, sends Syeed to his beloved Paradise.

The Book

For Erin, there were the interminable mornings taken up with police inquiries, the fingerprinting and DNA tests and seemingly endless number of videotaped interviews. "Am I a suspect?" Erin asked an investigating officer after a particularly arduous session, and though the question prompted a wry smirk, she was careful to make her testimony consistent, with special fealty to detail and time sequence. Nor did she shrink from the gory minutiae. With her fingernails gouging her leg under the table, she explained how after the first shot two of Abu's fingers bounced off her chest, the bullet lodging in the wall just above her shoulder, and how the killing of Syeed was conducted with an almost premeditated deftness — Leon grabbing Syeed by his hair and tilting the head back, huge Magnum tucked neatly under the doorman's chin and angled skyward to eliminate collateral damage. The grisly egress ballooned out above them like some comic's macabre spit take, soiling everyone in its radius.

Terrible, she'd said, as a detective signaled for a box of tissues. Just hideous and unbelievable and goddamned terrible.

When it was over she'd found Kyle Clayton leaning against the wall, grimacing in pain but letting forth bizarre, intermittent giggles. He was bleeding from what appeared to be two places: the collarbone and the back of the head. Erin attributed his giddy mood to the latter, perhaps having struck his skull against a wall molding after being shot, coupled by his usual state of inebriation. He was daffy and confused, a punch-drunk fighter.

"They didn't get me," he said to her in between fiendish snickers. "Ayla? Ayla? What did I tell you? They didn't get me."

From her knees Erin surveyed the battlefield. Near the Twin Towers — thawed down now to two fanged eyeteeth — various partygoers were wiping blood from their face and hair with paper napkins, while others who hadn't run wept openly or sat in defeated clumps shaking their heads in stupefaction. On the ground under the melting city lay the rotund Ivic, table linen already drawn over his head and chest. Closer still was Abu, who had most likely saved her life, clutching his hand and working his feet along the floor in a helpless bicycle motion. Erin went to him, prostrating herself along his side and looking down into his sweet coal eyes. The photos, which he had always displayed with such pride, were held bloody in his hands. *"The chullren,"* he gurgled, *"the chullren,"* and then, strangely, she saw above her the little book agent, the tiny one who was always driving her mad. She had her miniature arms akimbo, directing the frantic foot traffic and screaming at the captain Stephen to hand her the two linen dinner napkins he was holding to his mouth in shock. Snatching the cloths, she threw herself down on Abu's other flank and showed Erin how to apply firm, even pressure on the neck wound, and then took the other napkin to Kyle. "Shut up, save your strength," she yelled at the still-babbling writer, stuffing up his wound. "Cork it, you blithering moron." And when the EMS arrived, it was this woman, Patience Birquet (she knew now after days of questioning), who amid the chaos and delirium had set them straight. "Look, those two over there," she barked, pointing to Ivic and Syeed, "dead, forget 'em. And this one here, he's a goner too," she added ruthlessly, but not incorrectly, for she was pointing at Abu with the hole in his throat. "So you take care of *this one* first, my boy Kyle here. Got it?" She stood up, beckoning the confused EMS with her bloody hands, her impatience finally of some value. "What're you waiting for? Get your asses down here and take care of my boy."

Erin told this story over and over again, each morning for the next three days — to detectives and federal agents, into tape recorders and video cameras. She told it so many times she started to become numb to the details, aloof to the horror, and so it was probably no surprise that in the afternoons and evenings she spent her time looking for God on East 72nd Street.

She arrived at Helena's that first afternoon with a quiet, almost holy determination, hoping against hope to find something of comfort in the pages of The Book, something miraculous with which she might buttress herself against the terror of New Year's, something that might allay the night shakes and inconsolable crying. She had romped with Death, and though she'd never needed it before, she decided she could do with a little God right about now.

It was the books that had given her hope. On the bottom of the chest, beneath the typewriter and stacks of manuscript paper, were twenty or so ill-used volumes of reference. Well, Erin thought, at least Helena wasn't just riffing off the top of her head, or culling from the *Times*. And then, mercifully, the manuscript was not as long as Erin had originally thought. She found that many of the stacks were just old drafts, saved merely because Helena saved everything. So at least there was the *possibility* of focus, of a honed, concentrated argument. That it was also incomplete — Erin could tell this as she started to assemble the manuscript by chapter, the pages laid out over the cement floor — was a fact that she would not allow to dim her optimism. There were plenty of unfinished masterpieces, she assured herself. And then, why did it have to be a masterpiece at all? Weren't notions like "masterpiece" and "genius" just more classic Wyatt pratfalls? A more realistic hope would be that Helena had simply made a few good points, that she had pushed the Almighty argument forward, if infinitesimally. Wouldn't that be enough?

So it was with a great sadness that with each turned page, Erin watched even these modest expectations go up in smoke. The Book was a failure. An obvious and unmitigated *flop*. True, Erin herself was no philosopher, not the best choice to judge a major theological tract, but then "God: An Introduction" hardly required a doctorate to comprehend. As it turned out, Helena was not totally unskilled as a writer, but the discourse ranged mostly from the hokey and familiar to the tired and merely absurd. Old arguments gussied up and reintroduced as her own, trains of thought stuck at the station, or worse, derailed. Even if her aunt had finished it, Erin couldn't imagine it ever having been published.

And yet, that it existed at all seemed to Erin a sort of triumph. She would be certain to tell the family about The Book, she promised herself, to let those who had scoffed and rolled their eyes at Helena for years know that they had been wrong about her. She had been writing, struggling with a work of great reach, of superhuman difficulty. That she had failed to pull it off seemed almost irrelevant, and Erin thought its existence forced one to reconsider Helena's life, if not the entire Wyatt legacy. The Wyatts dreamed — sometimes with a gusto that was foolhardy — but then they had also *tried*.

How could Erin criticize them? It was more than she could say for herself.

Helena dated her work, and so Erin could see that she had abandoned the project almost ten years ago. Perhaps her aunt felt she had become too old; perhaps she saw the book was simply not coming together; perhaps she knew she was slowly dying. It didn't matter. What was significant was that at a certain point Helena knew she was giving up on The Book, but she'd never discarded it. She'd done this so that Erin would see that her aunt had made an attempt, so that the niece might somehow be inspired by it, even after her death. It was, the waitress saw now, a last desperate call to action.

He climbed out of his muddled fog the way he always did — reaching for the edges of the toilet, the walls of the bathtub, perhaps the towel rack, something he might use to pull himself up. Then he would dust the floor's grit off his cheek, splash a little water on his face, and, after the inevitable apologies, the entreaties of forgiveness, find the quickest route to his bed (cab? hallway?) into which he might dive headlong and sleep off the whole, awful episode.

Kyle Clayton knew fogs.

But this time there was no beveled porcelain in his reach, only what appeared to be steel rails, and the abyss into which he had sunk had taken ten or twenty attempts to ascend. When he finally reached the edge, he stopped, dreading the light that summoned him. What absurd sums of poisons had he taken this time? he wondered. What titanic mishaps awaited him to be fixed? Perhaps it was better to retreat, to remain in the milky darkness and face nothing. Perhaps it was better to play dead.

And then, with one eye incrementally opened, a big toe in the ocean, he saw sitting on the bed and looming above him what looked like a pretty nifty redhead. That she reminded him a bit of Ayla seemed completely impertinent, not to mention gratuitous; all redheads reminded him of Ayla these days.

"Finally," said the redhead, now in a *voice* that sounded like Ayla's, including even the hints of a Russian accent; but then all redheads with Russian accents reminded him of Ayla these days.

"I'm sorry," Kyle said with supreme grogginess, eyelids as heavy as bricks. He was still halfway gone.

"For what?"

"For, you know, what got broke." He tried to gesture with his arm, to assure the speaker that he meant *whatever,* the entire mess left in his wake, but he couldn't move his right shoulder. "I'll pay for it, I swear. I always do."

"Kyle, listen to me. It's Ayla, okay? You're at Mount Sinai hospital. You were shot . . . Kyle? Do you hear me?"

Ayla? The name gave him a jolt of adrenaline that allowed him to open his eyes.

"You were shot. Through the shoulder. Can you hear?"

He smiled, looking at the lips. "Yes."

"You've been asleep for a day and a half. You hit your head and had a concussion. They shot you and your collarbone is broken, but you're going to be all right. Do you understand all this?"

"Yes," he said.

"Then why do you keep smiling?"

"Because . . . *you* . . ." He drifted off again, and when he came to this time he could see that there were tears brimming in her eyes. He tried to reach out with his right hand, but it still wouldn't budge, and looking down he could see that the whole of his arm, from the shoulder to his palm, was lodged in a cast.

"Can you get this off?" His voice seemed muddled again.

"Kyle, you were shot."

"So?"

"*So,*" she repeated, the word stamped with distraught sniffles.

"Hey, I'm fine, doesn't even hurt. No brain, no pain."

"You're on morphine, you dummy," she said. She folded her hands on her lap, and with her eyes fixed out the window — eastward one might assume — she began to mutter in Arabic some prayers that had become familiar to Kyle. He watched her in profile, cursing the fact that she looked more beautiful now than he could ever remember.

"Look," she said when she'd finished, "I have something to tell you, okay? Are you awake? Are you with it?" She was wiggling her fingers near his eyes, examining him closely.

"I'm with it."

She reached over, straddling him with one arm, her face just a few inches from his. Then she paused, taking a very deep breath before speaking.

"Okay, wait, I — know what you're going to say," Kyle interjected, his voice still unsteady.

"You do?"

"Yes," he said, taking a slow breath. "You're going to tell me that there's been a miracle, and now we're going to live happily ever after." He smiled. Then, because there were no miracles — and because he knew he couldn't have her anymore since he'd ruined it — he added sarcastically from the side of his mouth, "Yeah, right."

"I'm pregnant."

He blinked.

"Yes," she said, wiping away two sudden tears, her voice a whisper now. "I'm pregnant."

"Holy shit."

She sat up straight, using his bedsheet to wipe her eyes. "I found out yesterday. My period was late, and I was just sitting here all day, waiting for you to wake up, and so I went downstairs and had the test and —"

"Wow," he said, shaking his head. "*Holy* shit." He was wide awake now. "And you're sure the baby is, you know . . ."

"Yours? *Yes,*" Ayla said. She narrowed her eyes to scare off any further inquiry. "It must have been that day we met for lunch, that afternoon at your apartment," she said.

"You mean the 'big mistake.' "

"Oh, you think I don't have my doubts?" she said, somewhat sharply. She looked out the window again and back to him with some distress. "What're we going to do?"

He sat up the best he could and gripped her shoulder with his good hand. "We're going to *do* this," he said, squeezing her, "that's what we're going to do."

"We are?"

"Yes." He winced, feeling his shoulder now. "We're going to have this baby, and we're going to make it work."

"Can we really, Kyle?"

Unable to speak suddenly, he nodded, squeezing her harder.

She reached and put her hand over his. "I won't do this without you, you know," she told him.

"I wouldn't let you."

Her shoulders began to slacken, as if relieved at his answer, and when she spoke her voice sounded strong again. "If we do this, I want to raise our child as a Muslim, Kyle. Boy or a girl, that's what I want. And I want to raise them in a Muslim house."

"Fine," he answered.

"Really?"

"No problem. We'll do all the holidays, whatever you want. But . . ."

"Uh-oh."

"You have to know, I won't censor myself."

Again, Ayla narrowed her gaze. "Meaning what, exactly?"

"Meaning if our child asks me what I think, about religion, about anything, then I'll tell them."

She paused and then shook her head in slow disbelief. "Boy, you're stubborn, you know that? You take a bullet and you're still a stubborn son of a bitch."

"It's a compromise, Ayla."

"All right, Mr. Compromise," she said, "what about my father?" This stumped him for a moment, so Ayla continued. "I haven't talked to him since that night, but I can't cut him off forever. Not if I want to see my mother. I want our baby to have grandparents, Kyle. Flawed as they are."

There was a glass of water she'd been drinking, and he asked for some of it. She tilted it up to his lips. "I'm willing to try," he replied, taking a careful sip. Perhaps knowing this wasn't entirely convincing, he added, "For a child, I'm willing to try. But your father has to try too, you know." He licked dry his lips, paraphrasing a passage from the Koran, *"If you take a step towards me, I will take ten steps towards you. If you come walking towards me, then I will come running towards you."*

"You remember that?" she asked, surprised and weepily delighted.

Suddenly fatigued again, Kyle replied with a soft smile.

Ayla leaned down, trying to navigate the cast and the morphine drip the best she could. When she kissed his forehead, even this tender contact made his skull throb.

"Who shot me, by the way?" he asked.

"Syeed? He's the doorman apparently."

"Rick, huh?" He nodded knowingly. "That's it, he's not getting a good tip from me next time."

"No next time," she replied. "He's dead. They shot him."

Kyle grimaced, and in his face now there was real remorse — perhaps even contrition. He worked his eyes roughly with the fingers of his free hand.

"Can we cool it now, please?" Ayla asked, her tone desperate. "Can we give it a break, this whole Kyle Clayton adventure? I mean, for heaven's sake."

Eyes closed, Kyle's lips betrayed the beginnings of a smile — which quickly devolved into a wince. Ayla grabbed the morphine applicator and pushed down.

"I suppose," he said, pausing to feel the rush, "that this persona has pretty much exhausted itself, hasn't it?"

"There's no place left to go with it, Kyle. It's enough already."

As she stroked his hair, he felt himself slipping back into the abyss.

"Yes," he said, with a great, drowsy sigh. "It's enough."

The law offices were located in what Erin considered the hinterlands, otherwise known as Manhattan's Upper West Side. Before the reading of the will, she'd decided to have lunch with her Uncle Earl, who was the will's executor, and his daughter, Trudy, who was Erin's age and one of the potential beneficiaries. Earl Wyatt and Erin's father were the only two of Helena's many brothers and sisters not to have pursued a creative ambition, and it was argued that both men's lives were a reaction *against* that of their inventor father. Earl had lived conservatively, especially when it came to money, and if Erin had always thought of her uncle as a bit of a bore, then she also could not deny that it was this very quality that made him a perfect choice for executor.

Though they'd lost touch recently, Erin had once been very close to Trudy and her family, so perhaps this was why their silent lunch made Erin fidget with such uneasiness. Had they nothing to say to one another after all these months? she wondered. Naturally a certain solemnity was in order, given the occasion, and their awareness of Erin's terrible New Year's. But then there was something else, she could tell, weighing down the proceedings. Never mind exploding heads and dying fathers clutching photos of their now bereft children, an elephant had pulled up a seat at their table, and its name was MONEY.

"Million-five," Trudy whispered, unable to contain her excitement as they began the block-and-a-half walk from the café to the law offices. "That's the rumor. Can you believe it? Million-*FIVE*." Trudy was, by all accounts, Helena's second-favorite niece and had been instructed years ago that her attendance today might not be without some purpose. Though she felt it slouched toward the vulgar, Erin couldn't really begrudge her cousin's jubilation. Unlike Trudy, she could afford to be cool, since Erin herself was virtually assured of getting the largest cut of the pie (though a million and a half *was* a pleasant surprise, she conceded privately). Trudy had recently divorced and was now struggling financially with two children; Erin figured she would have crossed her fingers too, along with her toes, if that were her predicament.

When they arrived they were escorted to a room of mahogany and leather that reminded Erin uncomfortably of the lounges she used to work at City. Both Helena's lawyer and her accountant were waiting for them. The preliminaries were brief; the lawyer welcomed them and had a secretary serve water and coffee, while the accountant, clicking away on his soiled and archaic-looking calculator, corroborated for everyone the value of the estate. "One million, six hundred and thirty-seven thousand dollars. Plus change," he'd added with a sly grin. Trudy couldn't stop from bleating a small elated chirp at the number, her eyes grown as large as eggs.

Earl was handed the will for recitation. At least initially, Helena's

last testament was a rather brusquely composed document, Erin discovered. This, too, seemed characteristic. It hinted at her aunt's aversion to fiscal matters of any kind. Oh, Helena loved to tell *you* what
to do with *your* money, but her own finances bored her to tears. It
was an apathy that had reportedly cost her millions; Erin's father had
always asserted that if Helena had been the least bit aggressive with
the money Dick had left her — mutual funds, for example, instead of
conservative, low-yield bonds — the estate would have increased five
or six times over the last few years.

But then the estate sounded pretty good to Erin as it stood, and as
her uncle read the will aloud she found herself staring down at her
water glass as a way to harness her own tremulous excitement, unable
to stifle the thought that a million dollars for herself was not at all out
of the question:

*"I bequeath two percent of the said estate to the Society for
Cancer research, six percent to the Children's Fund of America, five
percent to my nephew Ryan Glazer of Fresno, California . . ."*

And so it went, percentage point by percentage point, Erin doing
the math in her head, adding up the numbers so that even with a
fourth of the estate gone she was telling herself everything was going
to be all right.

*"Thirty percent to my niece Trudy Hudley, of Middletown, New
Jersey,"* — both hands leaping forward to Trudy's mouth, unable to
muzzle a series of *Oh my Gods* — *"and finally . . ."*

Earl, who was obviously elated for his daughter, as well as
relieved, could now allow himself to be happy for Erin. And so he
paused for effect and looked up to smile at her, it being so apparent to
everyone what must follow:

*"my beloved niece Erin Wyatt, of whom I have been so fond for
so long, and on whom I had pinned as many hopes as if she were my
own daughter. We have shared so much, my dear, that you'll have to
try to understand the unusual nature with which I bequeath you the
remainder of this estate."* There was the slightest exhalation from
Trudy, a sound similar to the one that Erin would have made if she
were capable of breath. Trouble had arisen, anybody could see that,
and even Helena's doleful accountant and lawyer looked up from
their paperwork as Earl continued, *"And so, I hereby bequeath the
remaining fifty percent to my niece Erin, to be held in escrow and*

awarded not until her fifty-fifth birthday, with the exception of fifty thousand dollars, which is to be drawn from said percentage and awarded upon my death."

Sitting next to her, Trudy put her hand on her cousin's arm, and there was the sound of the accountant clearing his throat in sympathy. Erin did not look up but simply nodded at the table's edge. It was not a betrayal, she knew, but just the opposite — Helena's eccentric brand of love. Fifty thousand was a number they had spoken of before, the minimum amount Erin said it would take to get to Los Angeles, set up a residence there and immerse herself in a pilot season and then a full summer of auditions. Enough to give her one year, one last shot.

Earl's voice was now a cloudy monotone as he finished out the testament, and Helena the writer was let loose one final time, *"I know, my dear, that as you listen to this you are disappointed, but please try to understand. Of course I am aware of your attitude toward the Wyatts, and especially myself. Your love is unquestioned, but I also know that you believe our* hubris, *as you call it, has damaged you. That we have 'infested' you with a penchant for grand ambition without any notion of how to succeed. Well, as you know, I have always rejected this. I don't believe for a moment that it was ever my father's duty to lay out a red carpet to success, just as it is not mine to lay out to you. I am grateful to him — just as I am hopeful that you will be to me one day — that he gave me the capacity to dream. To dream, my dear, and nothing more. The rest being up to you.*

"How fondly I recall our afternoons together at the theater! Do you remember your excitement, Erin? It was not so long ago — yet lately I wonder. And do you know that throughout all your criticisms over the years, as your bitterness grew and you looked for someplace to cast your blame, there was only one thing that ever really hurt me: you never bothered to ask me why I quit acting. Silly of me to be wounded by this, perhaps, but now I'll tell you the answer, whether you want to hear it or not — it was because of laziness. Simple sloth, my dear. You see, I once loved the nightlife as much as you, and Dick had made our lives so prosperous and comfortable that I suddenly woke one day to find I had left my acting behind. And for what? Restaurants and high times? But there was no getting it back; the moment had passed, and I was so filled with remorse over this deci-

sion it wasn't so many years later that I turned my attention to my book, or The Book, as you call it. Of course this, as you probably know by now, turned out to be my greatest folly. I took on too much, I admit now — I was trying to make up for too much! — and in my desperation I overreached for something that was far, far above my abilities. It was not hubris, my dear. You were always wrong about that. It was despair.

"In any event, you've been asking for guidance from your elders on how to achieve your dreams. Well then, here it is finally, to the best of my abilities. Use the money as you will, my sweet niece. Of course I can no longer influence your spending, and you are certainly a creature of pleasure, as I once was. But then please try to remember the regrets an old woman has suffered. And God bless."

Trudy squeezed her arm as Erin looked up and took a sampling of the faces across from her at the table — the lawyer, the accountant, Uncle Earl — and hanging her head again (and not caring that it would be misunderstood) finally let loose those elusive tears for which she'd been searching so long.

The Unsinkable
Lonny Tumin

They had Barnett. Oh, they had Rob Barnett by the balls.

At 6:00 A.M. on New Year's Day, the notorious after-hours bar Tromleys was raided by police. Inside they found thirty-four patrons with drinks in their hands, a cash bar still in full operation, and in the men's room an EVP by the name of Rob Barnett with three and a half grams of Myanmar heroin, which he intended to snort. "Do you know who I work for?" Barnett asked the police as they cuffed him up against a urinal. "Do you have any *idea,* shitheads?" His bluster turned to uneasiness that morning as his repeated calls to Ivic Rennert's emergency line had failed to be returned. Later, when he was told that Lonny Tumin was also "indisposed," Barnett moved into full panic mode. Was he being cut loose by Triad? he wondered. Had they washed their hands of him? By lunch a state-appointed attorney was telling Barnett that a lengthy jail sentence was not out of the question, given the facts, and so then Rob, out of nowhere, was suddenly telling everyone he was ready to talk. About what? they wanted to know. Just get someone from the SEC in here pronto, he'd replied, and they could probably patch this whole thing up by the end of the week. He was not, repeat *not*, going to jail.

Which, Dana Wallace had to admit, was a nice start. Mr. Wallace, the very same lawyer who'd represented the golf ranger in his out-of-court settlement with Lonny Tumin, had to laugh at the coincidence. He'd been courted by the Securities and Exchange Commission for years, ever since law school, in fact, there being such a dearth of African-Americans among the feds. After collecting the big prize with the Tumin settlement, he thought it might be time for a change. A little public service to ease the conscience. He'd just recently been made another offer, his third by the SEC; with the markets out of control the commission had been expanding, trying to keep up with the volume of complaints, suspicions, indictments. And it was only going to get worse, he was told — or better, depending on how one looked at it. Yes, thought Dana Wallace (who'd always had a nose for action, for the main chance), the SEC might be a very interesting place to work in the coming years.

Of course, after just a few months on the job, Wallace regarded the opportunity to go after Lonny Tumin again as almost too delectable. The SEC considered Tumin one of the big fish who'd got away. In 1989, when Milken and Boesky had finally toppled, it was assumed that Tumin would go with them — but L. T., they'd discovered, was a shrewd man. At Drexel, and then in later years, with Triad, Tumin proved a master at covering his tracks, of inuring himself to indictment. In fact, the commission's interest in Tumin was nearly a decade old when word arrived that he was getting involved with Monarch. That morning, one of the agents at the SEC's New York offices literally rang a bell in the hallways, *Attention, folks! It's official. The shark is circling the chum!* When next they discovered Monarch was being developed with the help of one Matsu Ohka, there were handshakes and discreet high fives. Lonny Tumin had begun his flight toward the sun.

Even now, though, it wasn't a slam dunk. The consensus was that Rob Barnett singing at the top of his lungs still wouldn't be enough to nail the unsinkable Lonny Tumin. Even considering the death of the legendary Ivic Rennert, Tumin's lawyers would have a field day with someone like Barnett. A drug addict! A gutless preppy staring at a long prison term! All Tumin had to do was play dumb: *How the fuck was I supposed to know Monarch was running at 3.5 percent capacity? How the fuck was I supposed to know the accounting firm I hired was crooked? How the fuck was I supposed to know the underwriters were scum? Hey, nobody tells me nothin'. I'm just a dumb kid from Newark.*

That's when Wallace had chimed in with the name Don Westly.

He was pushing hard to be a part of the Tumin case, though ethically, Wallace knew he should probably recuse himself. They'd had a history together, after all. On the other hand, what if nobody had to know about it? Even in a securities indictment scenario, he reasoned, Lonny Tumin would never reveal their history together — fraud being much less damaging to him than the details of his morning with the golf ranger. If he could help take Tumin down, he could earn his chops at the commission in a matter of months. A calculable risk, he decided.

So, if they wanted to get to Lonny Tumin, Wallace told the commission, his righthand man might be vulnerable. Did they know of Don Westly? Impressive fellow, this old friend of Lonny's. A gentleman who transcended any room he was in. Certainly he was the moral center of Triad, such as it was, Wallace suggested. Every time a decision was made, anytime anyone made a move, it was not Lonny Tumin but *Don Westly* who was looked to for approbation. *Did I do the right thing? Did I just fuck up?* It was apparently well known that to his boss, Don was like the wise, glamorous older brother. But then Tumin held an undeniable power over his friend; Don was a man forever in the wings, eclipsed by Lonny's overwhelming presence — though it was said he paced there fitfully.

My hunch, Wallace explained (already knowing by the dazzled faces in the room that he was on the case), is that Don Westly might be ready to break out.

They picked him up on a foggy morning in February. Don was coming out of his house in Upper Montclair, striding across the wide lawns with his two children, Alison and Gregory. As usual, his driver was going to drop the kids off at school and then take Don to New York. Wallace knew that the children would be with him and had thought it was okay. The children, he felt, were the key.

There were two agents, Wallace and a man named Rogers, a white guy with a crew cut who everyone said looked like an astronaut. Rogers's career was floundering at the commission, so when Wallace told him about his history with Tumin — and how it might help them to land a huge collar — Rogers said he saw no conflict of interest and could keep his mouth shut.

As for Don, he recognized his old nemesis right away — the finely boned face, the missing band of hair on the scalp. Making eye contact, Wallace nodded; as a courtesy, Don was being allowed to send his children on to the car without him, and privately. Tell the driver to go on, he told them, Daddy's going to talk to these men for a while. Don watched them silently: Gregory, his newly filled-in frame, the lanky stride — Montclair had itself a quarterback in a few years, he thought. And Alison, poor beautiful Alison with her sudden swath of acne, afflicting even the sides of her neck, he could see now. They needed a new dermatologist, he told himself, a New York doctor; this local yokel wasn't cutting it.

When the car pulled away, the agents approached.

"Dana Wallace, Securities and Exchange," said the black man, and when he flipped his wallet open to reveal his ID, he looked at Don somewhat apologetically, as if embarrassed by the cliché. "How you doin', Don?"

"Government work?" he replied. "I wouldn't have taken you for the pay-cut type."

Wallace put the wallet away and grinned. "My old man," he said. "Always harping about public service. Must've rubbed off."

A fine mist began to fall, and the three of them stood on the sidewalk looking at one another. Wallace didn't think it necessary to explain what they were doing here, just as Don hadn't bothered to pretend by asking. What, they all thought, would have been the point?

Finally Wallace gestured to a black car parked across the street.

"Wanna ride?" he asked.

They ended up driving him to New York, Wallace sitting in the back with Don, making his pitch. Tumin's man was his usual calm self, of course, denying nothing, even looking somewhat impressed at the breadth of the state's information. When they'd reached Midtown and Don still hadn't brought up the idea of making a deal, Wallace pulled out his ace.

"And then there's the matter of the doorman," he said, letting his voice trail off.

"Oh, Triad's responsible for that too, huh?" Don allowed himself a hearty laugh. "Sure, why not throw in Oklahoma City while you're at it?"

Wallace struck his knuckles against the briefcase on his lap. "Some funky stuff here, Don."

"You're grasping, my friend," Tumin's man retorted, shaking his head. He turned to the window. "Go ahead, though, let's see what you got."

Wallace removed the folder from his briefcase. "What we've got, Don," he began, reading, "is a doorman who has a two-hour meeting with Tumin on the morning of the twenty-first of December. We've got a deposit of approximately forty-four thousand dollars American from Syeed Salaam — your doorman, correct? — to his bank on the twenty-seventh. And in the closet of his studio apartment in Astoria we got a fifty-eight-hundred-dollar fur coat purchased on, let's see . . . Bingo. Twenty-eighth of December."

Though Don kept his gaze out the window, Wallace thought he saw the back of his neck grow pale.

"I mean, I know Christmas is busy, Don, but these are some pretty wild numbers for a doorman. I'm wondering why I bothered to go to law school, know what I'm saying?" From the driver's seat, Rogers sniggered in concordance.

Don opened the tinted windows to let in a little air. When he asked them to pull the car over on 41st, Wallace thought he was ready to deal.

The agent was so confident in fact, he closed the folder on Syeed. "Look, truthfully? I don't know if Tumin had anything to do with the target practice on New Year's, okay? And I'm not sure there's going to be any indictments. This is an FBI file, not what we do. But Don, please, look at the stack I have here." He began flipping through the raft of papers in his briefcase, each marked with a sticker at the top. "Price manipulation, stock parking, falsifying records, laddering, not to mention record earnings for a company that barely *exists* . . . I mean it's just shitty, man, from top to bottom, and I'd hate to see you get screwed up in all of it."

Don was still gazing on to the misty streets. "Looking out for me, are you?"

"Look, I know you came in late on Monarch. My hunch is you

probably had a heart attack when you saw all the stuff Tumin was into. But then, what were you going to do? You were in, it was too late . . ."

"Not what happened."

"Well, whatever, the fact is you guys are in trouble, and we can make it better. We can make it better for you, Don, but you have to break away . . . Are you listening to me?" He leaned forward to try to get a look at Don's face. "It's time for you to break from Lonny Tumin."

"I should probably walk from here," Don said. "Lonny's got a lot of eyes." He already had one foot out on the street. Over his shoulder, he said, "Thanks for the ride."

Wallace was undaunted. They worked on Don for more than a month, calling him at home, in his car, even bothering him at his office, updating him on the new allegations and regaling him with the accorded lengths of jail time. But he wouldn't crack. Don was very forthright, very up-front. Again, he denied nothing — he just wasn't willing to talk. "Look, I'm not stupid," he'd said. "I know there's some trouble coming. But you have to understand, I've known this guy since I was a kid."

"Don, hear what I'm saying."

"There's too much between us. No."

"Don, listen. They're talking about making an example."

"Ah, bullshit."

"No, listen to me. I'm telling you what I heard. Tumin's been thumbing his nose at us for a long time."

"I'll take my chances," Don said finally. "Don't call me anymore."

Stymied but determined, Wallace and Rogers went back to the only thing they had: Rob Barnett. They knew Barnett was scared — he was hardly the prison type — and they went at him with everything. Rogers told him the bad news, that the state wasn't ready yet to grant full immunity (a lie). He hadn't given them enough, not nearly enough. They needed more about Tumin, about Monarch. Some dirt on Don Westly. *Anything* about *anybody* they could use.

"Don's not talking?"

"No," Wallace replied, and when this made Barnett look even more worried, he kept going. "Basically, Rob, you're fucked. You're all alone on this, and you have no deal yet. You're looking at a serious drug charge *and* the huge shit storm Monarch's bringing down."

But like the other times, Barnett simply shrugged, and they all settled in for another long stretch of obstinance.

"You like girls, by the way?" Rogers threw out.

"What?" Barnett, who'd got himself a new shiny lawyer, looked over at him. "Now what does he mean by that?"

"I'm asking you a question," Rogers said.

"Of course I like girls. Fuck you."

Rogers and Wallace frowned meaningfully at each other, as if this preference were unfortunate, given the future. But Barnett snickered loudly. He took a sip of water and shook his hand at them.

"Cops always say that." Rob looked to his lawyer for support. "Am I right? Cops always threaten you with that jailhouse shit. It's all a myth anyway."

When his lawyer didn't meet his client's eyes, Barnett leaned back in his chair, using a tissue to wipe his brow.

"Well," Wallace said, with some finality. Making sure to sound disappointed, he stood up and snapped shut his briefcase. "No sense wasting everyone's —"

"You know about Susan and Lonny Tumin?" Barnett suddenly blurted.

His lawyer reached out to grasp his client's shoulder, to prevent him from giving anything away for free. It was no use.

"You know about Lonny and Don's wife?" Barnett added eagerly. "About him and their daughter?"

"Let him talk," Wallace said, trying to pacify the lawyer. "If it's good, we'll deal, you have my word." He turned back to Rob. "Now, what do you mean, Lonny and the daughter? You talking funny stuff here? I don't buy it."

"No, no," Rob said. He shook his head emphatically. "No, Lonny's not like that. I'm talking about . . ." He looked away, taking another sip of water before continuing. "Okay, I've only seen Lonny drunk once in his life, but that night he told me something pretty amazing."

In a better, more just world, Lonny Tumin is driving his Saturn near Kingston, New York, after checking the progress of a new minimall, when along a dark patch of road a deer darts in front of him. Nobody knows why Tumin is driving 85 miles per hour on quaint Route 9. It's early evening, and there are no lamps along the highway, though the Saturn illumines the roadside enough to see that dozens, perhaps hundreds of the animals line the perimeter. Interior development has pushed the deer population out toward the highway, where now, in spring, they come at night to feed on the flora so well maintained by the highway commission, and occasionally to discover a half-eaten Whopper with fries, or a Chalupa wrapper they can lick clean for its spicy saltiness.

So in this better world, Tumin is driving too fast, eager to get back to New York for a late dinner at City. One of the deer looks up, its eyes catching perfectly the car's side beams and reflecting back at Tumin like two flashlights whose batteries are running low. Then, inexplicably, it takes off directly for the car. Under ordinary circumstances, Lonny would have been going slower. He would have been warned about these darting deer by the mall's building foreman, who drives this route every night and has had a close call or two himself. But not old L. T. Lonny, seeing the building site was only a week ahead of schedule, ten days at best, has lashed into the unsuspecting foreman with such bruising ferocity that the man either forgets or consciously decides not to tell Tumin anything about the tricky ride home.

And so in this better world, Lonny Tumin dies.

Swerving the wheel to avoid hitting the deer, he's off the road and then down into a shallow gorge where, after a bumpy, curse-laden prelude, he impacts a tree and dies; but not before a last epiphany, of course. In the millisecond of his remaining life, before his entire body is driven through the windshield, he regrets everything — the cheating; the lies, big and small; the meanness; and, finally, even the blistering greed that made a short, pimply Jewish boy from New Jersey feel oh so much better. He makes his peace with God.

Or maybe not. Maybe Lonny Tumin quickly pulls the wheel to the right to avoid a collision and, rumbling along the gully, clobbers a pair of deer — a doe and then a large buck, two of a family. The buck's girth is so formidable that it actually slows the car's momentum enough for Tumin to pull the car up short of the tree. Maybe he gets out, cursing these pests as the countryside's equivalent to city rats. He doesn't see the doe — it's run off to die in private or been knocked into next week — but the buck is still writhing, its stomach spilling organs like shad roe from a Hefty bag. "You big dummy," Tumin says, confronting the animal and finding its eyes, which look through him yet appear to register his presence. He grabs one of the antlers and holds the thrashing head still. "Didn't your mommy tell you not to play by the side of the road? Huh? You big, stupid dummy." He checks the Saturn; the front is destroyed, the bloody, mashed nose of a journeyman boxer, but Tumin knows he's been lucky. He'll make it back to New York, no problem. He'll even make his dinner, albeit a few minutes late.

Out on Route 9 again, Tumin has the car back up to 85 in no time. Maybe he's shaken up a bit, but he's still smiling, the incident rendering in him new feelings of indestructibility. You bastards, he thinks. You write about me, you investigate me down to the crack of my ass, you even try to turn my friends against me — but I'm not going anywhere. *I'm out of your reach, fuckers.*

Then maybe Tumin takes out the cell phone and calls ahead to City, saying he wants the double lamb chops waiting for him when he arrives at 9:30 so his guests won't have to wait. Medium-well, please. Maybe he thinks too of calling the Kingston Police, telling them there is a buck about four miles outside of town, an animal suffering and needing to be put out of his misery.

And then again, reminding himself of the problems he's having with the authorities lately, maybe he doesn't make the call at all.

Revelations

When Tumin arrived at the Airplane Room, he found Don Westly and Matsu Ohka on opposite sides of the table, both looking down at a sheaf of papers and pretending to work. Thirty million dollars later, Ohka had got over the bomber mural. What he hadn't got over was Don Westly.

After they'd learned Barnett had been picked up on drugs and might be pressured to talk, a paranoia was let loose inside Triad. Privately, Ohka told Tumin that the government would need another turncoat, that Barnett would not be enough. He also told Tumin he suspected that person would be Don Westly.

Tumin wouldn't hear of it. He boldly told the Japanese man that long after he'd forgotten the name Matsu Ohka, Don Westly would be at his side. They were Jews, something he could never understand. Besides, what was Don going to do out on his own? Tumin asked. He couldn't do anything by himself. That's the way I set it up, he said. It's how the whole thing had been constructed, ever since they were kids.

Now, as Tumin found his seat at the head of the table, he uncharacteristically took off his tie and wiped the back of his neck with a dinner napkin. He appeared to be sweating profusely.

"So, what are you guys, just sitting here in silence? Jeez, lighten up." He took a long sip from his water glass. "I ran off the road and hit two deer tonight, okay? I don't want to walk in to a bunch of long faces."

Stephen was their waiter, and he brought in the dinner exactly on time, including Tumin's double lamb chops and requisite iced tea. While Ohka seemed eager to talk, Tumin held up his hand, making him wait until the waiter had left the room.

With Stephen gone, Ohka regaled them with the inside information he'd managed to glean in regard to Microsoft. The decision would be coming in just a few weeks; as they'd suspected, it didn't look good for Gates. If Lonny really thought this would signal the end of the market, it was time to get a target date for dumping stock and a lot of other things, most notably Monarch.

"And why do we want to do that?" asked Don Westly.

Tumin looked around, dumbfounded. Ohka rolled his eyes.

"What kind of a question is this?" his boss asked.

Don looked hurt. "I can't ask a question? Fine . . ." He dug his knife into his steak.

"What have we been talking about for the past year?" Tumin continued. "Microsoft goes, the whole thing's over. We start dumping *now.*" He pointed his fork at Ohka. "More important, we start building Monarch back up. It's time to cut the bitch loose."

Don chewed his steak, asking, "You mean build it back up to a real company? So we can get something for it?"

Tumin's fork careened loudly off the china plate. "What the fuck's this, *Romper Room?* What's going on here?" He looked at Ohka again, then back to Don, suddenly examining his partner's countenance. "Christ, you look like fucking Nosferatu. What the hell's wrong with your face?"

Don had seen his haggard visage in the mirror, so he knew Tumin was right. Though the drugs he was on were effective at numbing him, keeping his rage and anguish at bay, they also sedated him to the extent that he could no longer hold up his face, so that all the horror and heartbreak was manifest for the world to see.

"Little tired today, Lonny. I'll be all right."

Tumin's tone softened, growing more intimate. "Look, I know you're still having problems at home. What can I do? You want me to talk to Suzy for you?"

Don looked up, holding his boss's gaze for just an extra second. "I don't think so," he said. "Thanks, though."

It was hard to contain himself, though he was still struggling to believe what he'd been told just a few days ago. He'd recognized, finally, that it was true, but he really couldn't believe it. Barnett had called him at the office — he wasn't taking calls from Wallace anymore — saying there was something big Don needed to know, something that would change everything. Rob had always been full of shit, but Don detected an urgency in the young man's voice that disturbed him. And besides, he was intrigued. Against his better judgment, he decided to take a meeting with Wallace, Rogers, and Barnett in a suite around the corner at the Waldorf-Astoria. There they'd sat on Laura Ashley couches, chatting inanely. Tea was sent up. *Drink some tea,* Rogers urged when Don requested coffee. Then Wallace asked him one last time, pleading with him, "Don, do a deal with us. *Please,* I'm begging you. Get your lawyer in here and let's get it done."

Don had sipped his tea, smiling, telling them they were wasting their time again. And by the way, he reminded them, Ivic Rennert wasn't the only talented lawyer on the Triad payroll. Don't think the SEC wasn't in for a dogfight.

There was a long pause as Barnett and the two agents looked at each other, eyes flickering as their gazes converged. Then Wallace nodded softly to Barnett, who in a slow, practiced voice, told Don Westly that his beloved daughter, Alison, his only wellspring of hope and love, was not his own.

Don chuckled. Good one, he told them. Nice try. Pretty damned sleazy if you asked him, he said, looking to Wallace, though not a bad go at it.

He sat forward, waiting for them to argue with him, but then nobody did. They stayed silent, as if sitting on a truth they didn't have the heart to defend. This gave Don a moment to consider some of his own doubts that, he realized only now, had been unconsciously festering for years.

"You're a liar," he told Barnett, his ire suddenly rising. "You're a drug addict and a fucking liar."

Barnett lowered his eyes, looking disconsolate. He gazed up at Wallace, as if to say, *Am I done now?* But the agent turned away. And so Barnett continued, telling him about that night they were drunk, what Tumin had admitted to him.

"Horseshit," Don interjected after a moment. "I've seen Lonny drunk — he always says stupid things. Christ, he says stupid things when he's *sober.*"

"Well, yes, he was drunk, Don, but he was also very specific. I got the feeling Lonny really wanted to get this off his chest. He told me he was seeing Susan right up until you got married. She'd been a part of his stable apparently — Tumin's word, Donny, not mine — and she was still there while you and her were dating."

"No," Don said, "no way."

"He was paying her way, buddy, I hate to tell you. Right up until the end. She had an apartment, right? Nice clothes? *How,* Don? Think about it. She didn't have a *job.*"

"Fucking lies."

But Don's whole face had changed now. His eyes were wide and electric, and his skin looked damp though the room was cold as a meat locker.

"That's why Tumin pushed you to get married, Don. You know Lonny, he didn't want anything to do with a baby. But there was an accident. She'd forgotten to take her pill the night before or something. And then, you know, a few weeks later . . ." Barnett looked to Wallace pleadingly, but was shaken off. "Lonny hit the roof, of course, but she was thrilled. This was her ticket! Anyway, he made her a deal. He'd get *you* to marry her, Don. You and Susan were a couple already, and Lonny said that you did whatever he told you to do. Those were his exact words, Don. He said you did *what he told you to do.*"

Don was standing up now. He was leaning over the glass coffee table, thrusting out his index finger, yelling in Barnett's face.

"*Liar, liar!*" he said, though the fury in his voice betrayed him.

Barnett pasted himself to the back of the couch, very afraid. Don was not a small man, and it was Rob's experience that when someone as calm and self-controlled as Don Westly became enraged he was even more dangerous than a man like Tumin. But Barnett also didn't want to go to jail, and so he decided to finish it, to put on the final touches. "Think about it. Alison was born, what, eight months later? Look at the height, Don. She's tiny. And the *skin* problems. That's not you or Suzy and you know it. That's *Lonny*. That's pure Lonny Tumin."

Don let out a strange sound, the primal grunt of the mortally wounded — then suddenly vaulted over the coffee table and made for Barnett. Before he could get very far, though, Wallace wrapped his arms around him and, utilizing an old high-school wrestling move, took Don down hard to the carpet. Barnett lent a hand as Don thrashed and screamed on the rug, making the whinnying shrieks that would haunt them all for weeks to come.

And Don had been pretty much doped up ever since. An hour after Barnett's revelation, when the sedatives he'd been offered had taken hold, Don had managed to call in sick to Triad, telling his secretary he'd suffered food poisoning at lunch. Then they'd laid him down on the hotel bed, propped him up with the channel changer; Don was totally numb, not talking, completely in shock. Rogers thought he saw moments of catatonia and considered calling an ambulance, but by early evening Don seemed to rally. He was able to hold down a small dinner, and after a few cups of coffee, he summoned the strength to call Susan.

Don't wait for him, he told her. Don't expect him home. Ever. He was *gone*. Did she hear him? *Gone*. No, he couldn't talk about it now, but it was over, the bloody nightmare was over. And you know what? he told her. He was relieved.

He'd remained at the Waldorf, taking oral sedatives without coercion, taking them eagerly, and making an effort to go to work. Sometimes he struggled to stay awake at his desk, and he often took half-days, hinting to his secretary of marital problems. At night, over room service in the hotel, he practiced with Wallace and Rogers. He memorized the points he was to cover, the questions he was to ask. Then they went over the code words he could recite if things went horribly wrong.

When he slept, he tried not to dream.

Back in the Airplane Room, they continued to talk about Monarch. How they might bleed it just a little more, how they could squeeze it like an old rag to get every last drop before they "killed" it. Don continued to ask a lot of stupid questions, and Lonny, because he believed his friend was exhausted from his rift with Susan and didn't want them to break up, continued to answer them.

Then Don brought up the name Bill Chapman.

"Chapman?" Tumin asked.

"Big analyst at Morgan, the one who inflates the stock price for us so —"

"I *know* who he is. What about him?"

"Well, I just thought we could go over some of the —"

And then suddenly Ohka was up. He hadn't said a word for nearly ten minutes — had in fact been measuring Don with an increasing intensity — and now, still without a word, he pulled out his chair and was up.

"The fuck's *your* problem now?" Tumin wanted to know; he was getting exasperated. Ohka made some sort of signal he couldn't understand and pointed toward Don's chest, jabbing his pointed finger there. Then he dropped his napkin on his place setting and walked out.

Tumin blinked with confusion; had he hit his head during the car accident without realizing it? he asked himself. His mind, he was slowly realizing, did not have its usual sharpness.

He looked to Don, then to the door Ohka had just exited. When his eyes returned, he found his partner staring back rapaciously, accusingly, which only made Tumin more mad and confused.

"All right, I give. What the fuck's going on?" And then on pure instinct, and even before his brain had processed the logic of the maneuver, he was lunging over the table and reaching into Don's jacket. There he got a grip on his shirt and tore as hard as he could, the buttons spilling like teeth. Don's T-shirt was exposed, and now when he looked, Tumin saw the outline of something pushing against the material from underneath, something that looked like a long worm connected to a pack of cigarettes.

Immediately he reached out for Don's tie. Then Tumin stood up and began pulling it, tightening the tie like a garrote, until Don was up off his feet and choking. Spreading his hand across Don's face, but not letting go of the tie, Tumin slammed his partner's head hard against the bomber mural.

"I'm gonna kill you, you hear me? *I'm gonna fuckin' kill you.*"

Flecks of saliva seethed through Tumin's teeth, misting Don's brow. "Dead," he said, banging Don's skull, though somehow reluctantly, hardly enough to do damage, "dead, dead, dead."

Keeping the tie taut, he took his hand off Don's face to look at him. It was the old schoolyard itch — he wanted resistance, he wanted a fight — and so he was giving Don room to make his move. But all Tumin could feel coming off his old friend was a slackness, a frustrating passivity, and when he saw tears in Don's eyes, he let go of the garrote.

"Alison," Don said in a spare whisper.

Tumin frowned, his shoulders suddenly slouched, and he looked away in a manner that suggested a grudging remorse. "Barnett, huh?" he said, nodding in recognition. "That little cunt." He cupped his hands and shouted at the middle of Don's chest. *"You're an ungrateful little cunt, Barnett. You hear me?"*

"How, Lonny?" Don said. "I mean, my God."

"Ah, shit," Tumin murmured; Don began to weep openly now. His boss took a step toward him then stopped, as if wanting to help but not knowing how. "C'mon, Donny, don't do that."

"How? How could you, Lonny? Of all the things."

"Me? Look at you, all fucking wired up for sound." But even Tumin seemed to blanch at this absurd reasoning. Ashamed and embarrassed, he found Don's chair behind him and dropped into it. "Ah, fuckin' hell," he murmured. "What a night." Finding Don's glass of wine there, he took an uncharacteristic gulp. Smacking his lips distastefully, he said, "So now what happens?"

"You go to jail, Lonny."

"No, *you,* Don. What the hell are you going to do now?"

"I don't know." Tumin's man, who'd pulled himself together a bit, took off his dinner jacket and wiped his face on the hem of his torn shirt. "Frankly, I don't care. I don't have the will for anything now. I have nothing, Lonny. It's all gone."

Tumin looked to protest but, again, decided against it. After a long pause, during which he seemed to take the whole thing into consideration, he said, "I mean, if you really think about it, Donny, what does it really matter? Huh?" He waited until Don looked at him and then gave a histrionic shrug. "Know what I mean? Think about it. What does it *really* matter, underneath it all?"

Don's voice was flat. "What does what matter?"

"With, you know, with Alison. What does it really matter if she's . . . What if she was adopted, for instance? You're not going to love her any less. Am I right? Think of it that way."

Don just looked at Lonny, eyes narrowed in disbelief.

"Anyway, don't think I'm going to jail, pal. Don't make *that* fucking mistake."

"Where do you think you're going, Lonny, the Cayman Islands? Like you said, I'm wired up here like you can't believe. They got it all; you're done."

He waved off Don's words. "No, no jail," he said. He took another long sip of the wine, grimacing to keep it down. "Now, don't get me wrong, I'm gonna pay a whopper of a fuckin' fine. Oh, it's gonna hurt like a bitch, believe me. But nobody's going to jail, Donny. I'm guilty of what? A little avarice? Maybe. But people will understand when they see the facts. I told you, they'll sympathize with me, Don. You'll see."

"What about the kid, the writer?"

"What?"

"Kyle Clayton . . . Did you set that up? *Did* you, Lonny?"

Tumin winced through yet another sip of wine. "Hey, that was Brando's own suicide kick. Don't put that on me," he said, looking down at his accuser's chest.

As for Don, he'd known Tumin forever, and he didn't like the expression he saw now on his old friend's face. Finally, he loosened the tie around his neck.

Tumin went on. "Anyhow, that's why you fucked up, you big dodo. We could've worked this thing out . . . Look, I know, I know, it's heavy what Barnett told you. I'm not completely out of touch. But what, maybe we get mad at each other for a little while, maybe I throw a little more in the kitty for you. Then, eventually, we work it out. Like old friends, Donny. Like *Jews*."

Don laughed disgustedly. He was amazing, he thought. Lonny Tumin was truly amazing.

Throwing down his tie, Don leaned back against the wall to rest. He didn't know what to say to this, had no idea whatsoever. What *could* you say to such a thing? They were quiet for a while, and for some reason Don suddenly thought back to their teenage years, those mornings at the temple where they had learned together about adultery and greed, about *thou shalt not kill* and *thy neighbor's wife*. It was very simple, all of it. There was really no ambiguity there, no gray areas in which to navigate. He thought about those fundamental laws that were the buttress of all the great religions and the things they'd done over the years in the name of business, things their colleagues had done, and how on the weekends they all shook it off and went to the functions at the temple, to the church weddings, and even, on the very rare occasion, to the mosques. Don was ashamed now that he'd ever pretended in the first place. Susan was right, he'd realized; this was the worst thing Lonny Tumin had done to him, this pretending to be a Jew. It was worse even than Alison.

And so Don leaned against the bomber mural, wondering if it was time to go about the business of kicking Tumin's ass. That wouldn't be a problem now; he wasn't afraid of Lonny; this wasn't high school anymore. He had grown into a large, powerful man, while Tumin had leveled off long ago — had, in fact, diminished in middle age — and even with all the sedatives, Don was furious enough to do it. He was in the mood.

People would call it "dignified" when they heard about it, and even the Tumin family rabbi, behind closed doors, would say that Lonny had deserved it.

"We were never Jews," Don replied finally. "Don't ever kid yourself about that. Of all the things we were, Lonny, the one thing we can never say is that we were Jews."

Then, in the spirit of forgiveness he had learned so long ago, the virtue extolled by every faith of which he was aware — yet so rarely obeyed — Don touched his old friend on the shoulder and walked out.

Epilogue

The Great Kurban

The father emerged into the cool night air with little Baris in his arms, the three-month-old boy awakened by the cacophony. Baris and family had but one neighbor, and though ordinarily this other house was unoccupied during all but the summer months, the owner's teenage sons had apparently commandeered it for a weekend of mayhem. Crudely performed guitar rock blared through the barren trees that separated their homes, the pounding drums loud enough to jar his rib cage even at this distance. The father, whose hair for the first time belied a touch of gray, paced the lawn with his sobbing child, cursing rock 'n' roll and the reckless stupidity of youth.

Rotten little bastards, thought Kyle Clayton.

Then the music calmed, and the swaddled Baris — whose name in Turkish meant "peaceful" — was quiet in his father's arms. Together they walked under swaying trees bathed in rich moonlight, and something melancholy in the November air had Kyle marking the recent months. Certainly a landmark year for him, a lucky year. A year of survival. A broken collarbone and a bullet hole through the shoulder, some soreness on rainy days; he'd got off cheap, and he knew it (there never had been a formal fatwa, and by now the threats had all but vanished). Then a marriage that had seemed mortally wounded, but had somehow dragged itself to safety.

More surprising, a career on the upswing. His new novel, still in galleys, had attracted foreign rights and some surprising movie interest. The bullet had softened them; the press had grown sympathetic. Overnight, it seemed, he'd gone from fool to martyr. It was a role he'd welcomed. He was *tired,* so very, very tired of the other.

And finally, a son: restless, quick to laugh, stubborn, prone to fury . . . *irresistible.* Kyle's son.

He was a miracle, no doubt about it, though it had become clear that the Clayton marriage was not as fortunate. Even in pastoral seclusion, it still had its knots and snags. They had decided to give up the New York apartment. This was Kyle's atonement to his wife, his reparation, and it had broken his heart. He had enjoyed the country as a foil to his great Gotham, but on its own it seemed remote and lifeless. At night especially, Kyle missed the sounds of the city seeping into his living room, the horns and voices beckoning, *Come out and play . . .*

If there were a windfall from the new book, Ayla had said, they could buy something in the city, though Kyle was not appeased. It was always a long shot with fiction, and then he was afraid New York wouldn't be the same by the time they got back. Everyone was moving to Brooklyn, it was said, and the markets had already begun to unravel. On a recent trip, the city seemed to have lost some of its verve. The Microsoft verdict and the rumors of fiscal mischief had triggered something in that town, a new caution, an apologetic restraint. A fresh mood had taken over. There was a feeling something might still happen, a punishment looming for a naughty decade, though how or when no one could say.

Perhaps foolishly, he and Erin Wyatt were still in touch. She was in Los Angeles now — there was no chance of intimacy — but something about the experience with Tumin, and then, of course, New Year's, had bonded them. She'd sent him messages via his publisher, complaints about auditions, updates on Abu's widow (to whom she'd given a little money), and details of the nightmares from which she still suffered. Her last message had included a surprising bit of gossip:

City restaurant might be closing its doors. Business was down by more than half, everyone's expense accounts had been cut, and the New Year's tragedy had tainted the vibe. Worst of all, there was nobody behind the scenes to keep things running, nobody who cared. Triad had disbanded; Tumin was holed up on the North Shore, numerous indictments pending, while Rob Barnett had very quietly done three cushy months somewhere in Westchester.

Don Westly was the most unexpected development, having taken an executive position at the film company run by Larry Freeze. Erin was actually thinking of sending her résumé to him at East Coast Films. What the hell, right?

After this last communiqué, Kyle had cashed in a favor with Patience Birquet. The agency she worked for, bicoastal and so renowned as to be rarefied to three simple letters, was by no means limited to writers. Actors, in fact, were its primary focus. Did Patience remember the waitress from City? he'd inquired. Tall, brown hair?

Oh yeah, Patience had said, I wanted to bang her.

Kyle explained how she was a talented actress, struggling in L.A. Like the rest of the universe, she needed an agent. Could she get someone there to look at her? Patience took down Erin's name and said that she would try, and then Kyle reminded her that his own binding contract with the agency expired in a matter of months. It would be a shame if he started looking elsewhere, wouldn't it, what with all the movie interest? In short, he got a little puissant with the Pixie.

Try hard, he told her.

Outside now the neighbors were destroying the silence once more — the drummer's deliberate snare march, the guitar following with a ragged, abrasive riff that had Kyle grimacing with each strum. Ayla could sleep through Armageddon, but his son was easily awakened. When the singer announced then through a distorted mike that he was no less than *"Iroooon Maaann,"* Baris began to cry in earnest, and Daddy figured it was time to stop the madness.

It took a few rounds of increasingly louder pounding, but he was finally greeted at the door by a small crew of venal, beer-swilling illiterates who reminded Kyle precisely of himself at nineteen. Baris was still wailing in his arms, though they looked unimpressed and carried on each of their faces the smug confidence of the pack.

"Hey, could you keep it down a bit, guys? My son's having a hard time with the noise." He laughed offhandedly. "Frankly, I wouldn't mind a bit of sleep myself."

The biggest and dumbest-looking of the bunch marched out a few steps from the group. "*Frankly,* it's like fucking eleven-thirty on a Saturday night!" he said, swigging from his beer. They were all very drunk.

Kyle gestured to his son. "Hey, bud, you want to watch the language?"

"Yeah, c'mon, gramps, give us a break," another admonished. This particular Rhodes scholar held out a can of beer to Kyle. "Like, relax, have a drink for once in your life."

"Pass," replied the father, and was thus rewarded with scornful laughter.

"Yeah, why don't you loosen up," shouted another. "YA OLD FART!"

There was more laughter now, punctuated with shoulder-pounding self-congratulations, and the door swung shut in Kyle's face. Heart thumping, he thought it best to pack it in. There was thirty yards of woods separating the two houses, and when he'd traversed just halfway the music began again. Baris cried softly while Kyle reran the insults through his head.

Gramps! Ya old fart! Eleven-thirty on a Saturday night!

It was sort of humorous, actually. No, in fact, it was quite hilarious. *Have a drink for once in your life.* Yeah, right, he thought. If you only knew. If you little bastards only knew.

Another ten yards and the weight of his son had started to weary him. Kyle bent down in the leaves, resting the sobbing boy on his knee. There was some Maalox on his lips — this boy, this Sultan of Saugerties and his volcanic stomach — and the father kissed it away. Kyle looked up then, searching for the moon. He'd told Ayla he would look over some prayers again tonight (he'd promised to help teach Baris someday), but all he could think of now was the other things he would show his son, the moon and the stars, explain it all to him with the best science at his disposal, antidote to these rickety old faiths. Yet the moon had vanished; his eyes were too blurry to see. He must still be laughing, he thought. Those funny things they'd said.

Gramps! Old fart! Eleven-thirty!

He wiped his eyes. On the deck in back of the house he could see Mr. Nightcap in his smoking jacket, waving him in by flashlight. His plea was desperate, the words reaching Kyle on the wind. *Join me,* he said. *We'll ride to the city tonight, a certain place. Come, Master Kyle!*

Kyle shook his head. *Not tonight,* he called back. *My son. Don't you see?* he asked. *My son . . .*

Suddenly his eyes were wet again, the laughter jerking him in spasm. He wiped his cheek. It really was hysterical, wasn't it? Just hysterical.

Peace and Sacrifice, weeping in the moonlight.